"The author deserves kudos for her vivid conception of what a climate change–ravaged world might look like. In her Colony, humanity not only survives but thrives in a situation that feels both familiar and yet very different — life goes on as the populace clings to a willful ignorance concerning ecological devastation ... Manny is an easy character to root for ... His character is also engagingly complex... This is an engaging tale that is optimistic about the future despite a past full of avoidable suffering. A skillful and enjoyable blend of post-apocalyptic drama and soap opera." - Kirkus Reviews

"This author has a grand imagination, and talent for showing the story ... This is a very powerful read, and even though it is the future, it brings out the humanity in people, and their struggle for survival ... When an author can emote such emotion, and almost bring a reader to tears, then they have written and shown a remarkable story! ... A reader can get lost in the story. Both thrilling and intriguing, all the way to the end. A definite attention grabber, so much I couldn't put it down." - Amy's Bookshelf Reviews

"The dynamic cast and the vivid depictions breathe life into the plot. It felt like I was right there next to every character, helplessly watching the scenes unfold. The subtle tone of the storyline, accompanied by the drama, adventure, and thrills, had me flipping through page after page. By juxtaposing the cast's complex traits and bringing out their emotions, the author strengthens the story's grip on reality." - Readers' Favorite

Read the full reviews on **susanfeltman.com**

# Starlight, Shadows and Tears

## Life Underground: Love, Loss and the Long Road Home

**Susan Greenberg Feltman**

*ANJ Press, Leonia, NJ*

ISBN: 978-1-7371642-3-4

Library of Congress Control Number: fill in number

This book is dedicated to
Allen M. Feltman,
my kind and patient husband,
for always listening to me.

"As human beings, we are vulnerable to confusing the unprecedented with the improbable. In our everyday experience, if something has never happened before, we are generally safe in assuming it is not going to happen in the future, but the exceptions can kill you, and climate change is one of those exceptions." - Al Gore

"The floods, the fires, the tornadoes, the hurricanes, the droughts, the water shortages, the earthquakes....Why did I think it would nonetheless be business as usual? Because we'd been hearing these things for so long, I suppose. You don't believe the sky is falling until a chunk of it falls on you." - Margaret Atwood, "The Testaments"

"We are the first generation to feel the sting of climate change, and we are the last generation that can do something about it." - Jay Inslee

"The question is, are we happy to suppose that our grandchildren may never be able to see an elephant except in a picture book?" - Sir David Attenborough

"The measure of intelligence is the ability to change." - Albert Einstein

"The truth is that we are all responsible. We are the generation that will have to explain and yes, apologize to our children. It is our children who will have to live with soaring temperatures, pounding rainstorms, power outages, rebuilding over and over again. Our complacency has reaped a bitter harvest." - Susan Greenberg Feltman

# PRELUDE

*Starlight, Shadows and Tears* is a work of speculative fiction. It is the second book in the *Starlight and Ashes Trilogy*. The first book, *Never See the Sun Again,* was published in 2021. The third book will be coming soon.

In the year 2085 AD, New York City was in ruins, empty and deserted. A powerful hurricane had destroyed most of the City, water and wind combining to sweep across the narrow island, knocking down everything in its path. The only survivors were the 7,000 souls who sheltered in the subway during the storm. Almost everyone else was swept out to sea.

Days passed, and then weeks. The government, over-whelmed with pleas for help from many cities decimated by decades of climate change, was in no hurry to rebuild a Democratic stronghold. Help never arrived. California burned until most of its inhabitants moved inland. Texas seceded as the Midwest built walls to keep out displaced citizens seeking refuge. When the Colony of New York officially seceded, it was almost an afterthought.

Humans are a clever and tenacious species. It wasn't long before society reorganized itself underground, teachers holding classes next to train platforms, foraging parties going out daily to salvage food from ruined supermarkets. Babies were born. Doctors offered their services to anyone who needed help.

Tunnels in the New York City subway system are up to 50 feet wide, with ceilings as high as 18 feet. There are 840 miles of track and 472 subway platforms. Eventually, all of these tracks were filled in with crushed concrete from ruined skyscrapers, doubling the amount of living space, and the trains were permanently shut down. After several generations, most people could not imagine the tunnels being used for passenger trains. Many did not believe that it had ever been that way.

Over three hundred years went by.

In the year 2364, Malcolm "Manny" Stewart was a detective in the NYPD. After a minefield of a childhood, Manny matured into a street-smart, talented and ambitious young man in his mid-twenties. He married his high school sweetheart, Naztazya, his foster-brother's wife's sister, and they had a son, Zack. Finally, life was good, peaceful and filled with promise.

But Fate is a cruel mistress. A sudden unpredictable turn of events blindsides Manny, rocking him to his core, and in that moment, everything changes.

# Chapter 1.

**M**ANNY WOKE AT 3:00 am to the muffled sound of his pregnant wife crying in the bathroom. Suddenly wide awake, he called out, "Sweetheart, are you alright?" When she did not answer, he tried again, louder. "Naz! Everything OK?"

Alarmed, he got out of bed and knocked on the bathroom door. "Naz, open the door!" he said. He tried the door knob, which was locked. "I'm coming in!" he cried. He drew back and kicked once, hard.

The door crashed open. Naztazya was sobbing, sitting on the floor near the tub. There were splotches of bright red blood on the floor. "Manny," she said, "call Mrs. Braun!"

"Mrs. Braun? The midwife? But, Naz – it's way too soon!" he protested. "How about if you just get back into bed and put your feet up?"

"*Manny! Now!*" she shrieked, hands folded desperately across her middle.

He reached for his padlet, the ubiquitous electronic device that was both cellphone and tablet. Every citizen of the Colony of New York was required to have his or her padlet within arm's reach at all times. Opening up Levitate, the popular hologram app, he quickly hologrammed Renata Braun, the Colony's most experienced midwife.

Mrs. Braun picked up immediately. Long years of service had taught her to wake up instantly from a deep sleep, answering calls from her patients at all hours. "Yes?" she said, not bothering with polite greetings.

"Mrs. Braun, it's Manny Stewart. We need you," he said urgently. "Can you come at once?"

"Yes, Detective, I am on my way," she replied calmly. There was no need to ask for his address; everyone knew where the Stewart mansion was, at the 50th Street stop, the old Rockefeller Center. She hung up, not wasting precious time in conversation.

"She's on her way, Naz," Manny said reassuringly to his wife. "Just try to stay calm. Take slow, deep breaths."

There was a knock at the bedroom door. Not waiting for a response, Anna, Naztazya's sister, came rushing in, tying her bathrobe around her waist. Anna and her husband Julio lived in the same house as Naztazya and Manny, as was common in the Colony.

"What's happening?" Anna demanded. "We could hear you from across the hall." Her eyes swept the bathroom, her sister on the floor in tears, the splotches of blood across the floor.

When Naztazya did not reply, she turned to Manny, who was standing helplessly near his wife's side. "Did you -" she began.

"She's on her way," replied Manny.

"Here, let's get you back into bed," Anna said to her sister. Together with Manny, she helped Naztazya get up from the floor.

Naztazya lay back against the pillows, tears streaming down her face. "Anna," she sobbed, her voice breaking, "I want this baby so much!"

Anna slid into bed next to Naztazya, putting her arm around her younger sister's shoulders.

"You have Zach, right?" she said softly. "There will be other babies. You know this happens sometimes, it's not your fault, it just happens." Anna rubbed Naztazya's shoulder very gently, their heads together, speaking quietly to her to keep her calm.

"I'll go downstairs and let Mrs. Braun in," Manny said, glad for something to do. He left the two sisters alone.

Miscarriages were so common, double the rate they had been before the City had moved underground in the year 2085. Now, in this Year of Our Lady 2366, the average miscarriage rate was 18-34%. Scientists were at a loss for an explanation; it could be something in the constantly-recycled water, they said, or maybe the complete lack of natural sunlight.

Mrs. Braun arrived quickly, but it was already too late. She spent a long time with Naztazya and Anna, while Manny waited downstairs with his foster brother, Julio Suarez.

"Women's stuff," said Julio, firmly leading Manny into the study. "We should let them talk."

"It's going to be hard for her," said Manny, worriedly rubbing his face. What was he supposed to say to her? Manny had not grown up around women; he was an only child. He had married his high school sweetheart and first real girlfriend, the sister of Julio's wife.

Naztazya, who was one of five sisters, had always wanted a large family. Manny, on the other hand, had not been keen on having children at all. In the early days of their marriage, Naz had yearned for a baby, a little bundle to hold and hug, going on and on until finally, he had agreed.

Naz had conceived very quickly and Zachary James Luis Stewart, nicknamed "Buddy," had arrived practically in the blink of an eye, or so it seemed to Manny. Zach was now four years old, healthy and boisterous.

Because of his career as a detective, Manny wasn't home much, and Naz seemed quite content to handle the childcare responsibilities without him. Manny, who was one of the wealthiest men in the Colony, had offered to look for servants to help her, but Naz was adamant; she wanted to raise her child herself. Anna, too, was insistent on raising her daughter Julianna herself. Neither of them wanted their children to grow up feeling entitled to a staff of servants.

Julianna, Zach's cousin, was seven years old. As was common in the Colony, Anna and Naz shared childcare duties, seamlessly filling in for each other whenever necessary. Anna, who had just received a big promotion, mostly worked at home. Naz, a schoolteacher who wanted to have more children soon, had not yet gone back to work.

Naz did not come downstairs for the rest of that day, or the next, or the day after that. Anna and Manny took turns looking in on her as she stayed in bed, not eating or bothering to get dressed, alternately crying or staring blankly at the ceiling. Manny told Zach that Mommy had a cold and that he should not bother her too much until she felt better. Zach accepted this as any four-year-old would, spending his time with his Auntie

Anna and cousin Julie, visiting his mother in the morning and then again at bedtime for a goodnight kiss.

On the fourth day, Manny was at the kitchen counter making breakfast when Naztazya, dressed in fresh clothes and with her hair neatly braided up one side, came into the kitchen. Zach looked up with a smile. "Mommy!" he cried, waving his spoon at her.

"Hey, little guy!" she said. She tousled his hair, bright copper red so exactly like hers, and kissed him on the cheek before sitting down in the chair next to Manny. She looked pale, but composed.

"Good morning," he said, trying to gauge her mood. He flipped slices of toast onto a plate. "There's coffee, if you want."

Anna and Julie came into the kitchen. "Good morning, Auntie Naz," said Julie. "Is your cold all better?"

"Much better, thank you, Julie," said Naz, sipping her coffee.

Manny sat down next to her, holding the plate of toast. "You should have something to eat," he said. She looked better than the day before, he thought, like maybe she had gotten some sleep.

Naztazya dutifully took a bite of toast, chewing it for a long, long time before swallowing. She looked up to see both Anna and Manny watching her. Her eyes filled with tears. "I think I'll just take this back upstairs to my room," she said.

Manny reached out and touched her hand. "Stay," he said gently. "Have a little more toast. Then you can rest while I take Zach out for a walk after breakfast."

"But Manny, it's Thursday! You're not going to work?" she asked. It suddenly occurred to her that he had been home all week. "Did you take time off?"

"It's OK, I had some time coming to me," he replied casually. Everyone knew that Manny never took a day off. As an ambitious young detective, he poured all of his energy into his career, working long hours and coming home late most nights. He often did not see Zach during the week at all, since he went to sleep before Manny got home.

4

As the week went on, Naztazya continued to improve. She and Anna were working on some kind of art project with the children, making streamers and decorations. Julio's parents Lucinda and Luis came over one afternoon for a visit to admire their handiwork. Although she was more quiet than usual, Naztazya seemed active and engaged.

On Friday morning, Manny was in the study sitting at the large desk which had been his father's, trying to catch up on some of the week's work. The children were outside in the tiny yard with Julio playing Mets-N-Yankees, a game that consisted of hitting a ball with a bat and then running as fast as possible around the perimeter of the yard with one of the children either perched up high on his shoulders, or clinging to one of his legs.

As Manny tried to work, Julio lumbered past the study's tall glass windows with Zach on his shoulders, hands firmly twisted in Julio's shoulder-length hair, shrieking with laughter. "Faster, go faster!" Zach cried, as Julio rounded the bases.

Manny grimaced. "Hey, can you keep it down?" he called through the open window. When no one responded, he got up and closed the window, sitting back down at the desk with a sigh. He was determined to focus on a complicated and poorly written report from one of his officers about a recent arrest. It was hard to understand exactly what had taken place, and Manny needed to be clear on the details before returning to the office.

"Manny?" He reluctantly turned away from his report as Naztazya came into the study. "You'll be home tonight, won't you?"

"Of course," Manny replied. "Why?"

"Well, we want to make sure everyone is here," she said. "I put a reminder on your Scheduler, remember?"

Their conversation was interrupted by a loud crash as a ball came soaring through one of the large windows, shattering glass all over the carpet. The ball hit the desk, knocking over Manny's glass of frizzleberry juice, then bounced to the floor and rolled to a stop.

5

Julio's face appeared at the broken window. He surveyed the shattered glass and the fruit juice dripping onto the carpet. "Everybody OK in there?" he asked.

"Fine. Just maybe try a little less enthusiasm next time," suggested Manny drily.

"I'll have someone clean this up," said Julio, pulling out his padlet. While the family did not have live-in help, they often relied on A.I. At Your Service, the company which rented robots and androids. A household robot would be perfect for this job.

Manny mopped up the spilled juice, which fortunately had not damaged any of his papers. *How's a person supposed to work?* he thought sourly. He gathered up his papers and put them away. He looked up expecting to see Naz, but she had gone back to the kitchen.

*I need to get out of here,* he thought, exasperated. *Maybe I'll go out for a walk and find a quiet spot to read.*

Manny picked up his papers, folded up his padlet and went out, inwardly sighing with relief as he clicked the door shut behind him. He dearly loved his family, but sometimes he felt out of synch with so much noise and chaos.

Manny had grown up in an empty, silent house. His father, the Chief of Police, had worked long hours and often hadn't come home until after his young son had eaten dinner and gone to bed. His mother, Lila Rose Stewart, had died when he was seven. Manny had eventually gone to live with his best friend Julio's family, but that was not until he was fifteen.

Manny lived in an exclusive neighborhood beneath what had once been the old Rockefeller Center. At one time it had been an underground shopping area, filled with restaurants and small shops, convenient to the Rockefeller Center 50th Street subway stop. The Stewart mansion, as it was known, was actually two townhouses that had been remodeled to become one huge mansion, an unheard-of thirty-five feet wide. It had a real dining room, a huge kitchen with a table for ten people, a library and study, and five full bedrooms upstairs, plus a long curved wooden staircase in the middle leading from the spacious foyer up to the bedrooms. Such luxury was rare in the Colony.

Manny walked to a tiny nearby park-like area with two stone benches and a few potted evergreens, flanked by a rose trellis on either side. Such little "rest-ups," as they were called, appeared everywhere in the Colony, especially in the trendier, more upscale neighborhoods.

Manny sat down on a stone bench and looked around. It was almost dinnertime, and the area was deserted. *And quiet,* he noted with satisfaction.

Manny's padlet vibrated, lighting up cobalt blue around the edges, denoting a text message of the lowest level of urgency. Annoyed, Manny snapped the volume off, shoving the padlet deep into his backpack. Then he picked up his report and began to read.

# Chapter 2.

**T**HE REPORT WAS long and badly written, bouncing around chronologically as the writer attempted to explain what had happened during an arrest. Manny made a mental note to speak to his boss again about the quality of recruits to the Police Academy. *They should at least be able to write a simple narrative,* he thought.

His padlet lit up again, glowing cobalt blue through the fabric of his backpack, another non-urgent text message. *That's probably Naz,* he thought impatiently. He steadfastly ignored the padlet as he read through the rest of the report.

Finally, Manny finished reading and put his papers away. He looked guiltily at the padlet, which was now pulsing scarlet around the edges, denoting an urgent personal text message requiring an immediate response. He unfolded the padlet, smoothing it out across his knees, and saw to his dismay that he had missed not two, but four text messages from Naz:

Naz: *Hey, where are you? You'll be back in time, won't you?*

Naz: *Manny, where did you go??*

Naz: *If you're going to be late, at least text Zach, would you please?*

Naz: *Everybody's here, Manny! We can't wait any longer. Where are you?!*

Worse than that, his Scheduler showed a tiny orange circle bopping up and down, accusingly denoting a missed scheduled event. Opening up the Scheduler, he saw "b/day 6:30 dinner." Damn. Today was Zach's birthday.

Manny stopped on the way home at the only store which was open late on a Friday evening, a store that sold kitchen goods. *What can I buy a child for a birthday gift?* he thought frantically, looking around at the assorted pots and pans. He quickly chose a big frying pan with a lid, a wooden spoon and a wire whisk. While the clerk gift-wrapped it, Manny thought about what he was going to say when he got home.

As he walked up to the house, Manny could smell the enticing aromas of roasted vegetables, fresh coffee and a newly baked cake. His step quickened. As he waved his hand past the Scentinel sensor pad, allowing it to identify his scent and unlock the door, he could hear the family in the kitchen singing the traditional birthday song to Zach:

"Happy birthday to you,
Peace and happiness to you,
May your life be filled with gladness,
Happy birthday to you!"

"I'm sorry I'm late!" he exclaimed, walking into the kitchen. Dinner plates had been cleared, and a big double-ripple chocolate caramel birthday cake, adorned with five brightly-colored paper flowers, stood in the center of the table. A hand-lettered "Happy Birthday, Zach!!" banner hung from the ceiling, with balloons on the backs of each chair.

"Hey, Bud, happy birthday!" he said a little too heartily. He handed Zach the gift.

Anna, seated next to Zach, helped him pull the gift wrap off the large box. "A pot! And spoons!" exclaimed Zach, looking puzzled.

"That's right, Bud, these are your very own. You and I are going to cook something wonderful for Mommy!" Manny beamed, hoping for the best.

Anna bent over and whispered something in Zach's ear. He turned and said, "Thank you, Daddy!"

Naztazya rose and went over to the counter, bringing a plate of food to the table. "We saved your dinner," she said, handing it to him without looking at him. *She's definitely mad,* he thought, *I'd better apologize after dinner.*

"Have some lemonade, man," said Julio, pushing the pitcher towards him. "Where'd you go?"

"I went for a walk and lost track of the time," said Manny, who did not elaborate further. There was an awkward silence. Lucinda handed a plate to Zach, saying, "Here, let's cut a piece of birthday cake for Daddy."

Upstairs later in their bedroom, Naztazya's anger was on full display. "Why didn't you answer any of my texts?" she demanded. "I didn't know where you were, Manny! What made you go out without telling anyone?"

"I thought I'd be back before you missed me," replied Manny. "I've got work to catch up on, Naz, and I can't hear myself think in the house! Not to mention the broken window, and glass all over my desk."

"I'm sorry about that, Manny, but you nearly missed Zach's birthday," she replied. "And that gift – who buys a frying pan for a five-year-old? You forgot, didn't you?"

Manny hung his head. "I did," he admitted. "I'm not proud of it, Naz. Look, I'm sorry I went out. But he's a child! He won't even remember this in a few weeks."

Naztazya crossed her arms and frowned at him. "I'm not so sure of that, Manny. He's not a baby anymore. Besides, you said you would try to spend more time with him, remember?"

"I'll make it up to him," Manny said. "We can take him to the *History and Culture Museum* tomorrow to see the new children's exhibit, just the three of us. It'll be fun."

But things did not go according to plan. In the middle of the night, Zach had a nightmare and came crying into their room, wanting to sleep in their bed. It took him a long time to settle down, and by the time Zach fell asleep sprawled solidly across the middle of the bed, Naz and Manny were wide awake. It took a long time to get back to sleep.

In the morning, Naz said that she had a headache. Manny saw that she looked tired and pale.

"Are you OK?" he said, putting his arm around her shoulder. "Want to stay home, and I'll take Zach to the museum?"

"That would be nice, Manny, thanks," she replied gratefully.

He put both arms around her, kissing the top of her forehead. "You stay here and rest, Naz," he said, holding her close. "I've got this."

"Manny," she said, "Thank you for being so patient."

"Of course," he replied. He wanted to say more, to tell her that he could feel the sadness in her since her miscarriage, that he wished he could help her to be happy again ... but the words collided in his throat, and he said nothing.

He looked up to see that she was watching him. Somehow, she seemed to sense what he was feeling as she took his hand, giving it a little squeeze. "You go on now," she said, "and I'll see you and Zach later."

Manny gave her a quick hug and a grateful smile, and went off to find Zach, marveling at how lucky he was to have a wife who understood him.

Downstairs in the kitchen, Zach and Julie were eating breakfast with Anna. "Good morning," she said, handing Manny a freshly baked chocolate chip scone. "Is Naz still upstairs?"

"Yeah, she has a headache, so she's going back to sleep," Manny replied. "Zach and I are going to the children's exhibit at the *History and Culture Museum,* just the two of us," he said, nodding encouragingly to Zach. "Want to come along?"

"Sure," Anna replied, "that sounds like fun."

The museum was not far from the 50th Street Stop. Like every other New Yorker, Manny, Anna and the children were used to walking everywhere; there simply was no other way to get around. There were no trains; the tracks had been filled up centuries earlier when workers brought in bucketsful of crushed concrete and other debris gleaned from the buildings above ground that had been damaged by violent storms.

Once the tracks had been filled in and made level with the platforms, the amount of floor space was doubled, and simple homes could be constructed. Over the years, more permanent houses had been built.

Row houses inside the tunnels were built using the back wall of the tunnel as the rear wall, each house facing the same way and packed together tightly. These row houses were the least desirable real estate within the Colony. Homes built on the platforms were the most desirable, wider and more spacious, many with two or even two-and-a-half floors.

"Zach! Julie!" Manny called. "You two stay close now, no running ahead."

Anna laughed. "Good luck with that," she said.

Manny liked Anna, a smart and ambitious young woman who had been Julio's sweetheart since high school. She and Naz had different color hair and eyes, but their mannerisms and facial expressions were very similar. Anna was not quite two years older than Naz.

The Museum was a popular place for families on a Saturday morning, and the line stretched out the door. Manny motioned to his family to follow him, and walked directly to the front of the line.

"Detective! How are you, Sir?" asked the museum guard, stepping aside and holding the door open for them.

Manny nodded to the man, whose father worked for Suarez & Sons, the family business. The guard raised his hand and motioned to the woman behind the ticket counter, who waved them through and into the museum.

Anna stopped at the first large exhibit, an explanation of climate change and global warming. "Cars that burned gasoline contributed gases to the atmosphere that forever changed the planet," she read. The photos showed lines of cars stalled in traffic, entitled "Rush Hour in NYC."

"Look what happened, after years of burning fossil fuels," she said to Julie, pointing to the photograph of the peninsula of Florida, the Island of Bermuda, and the little islands that dotted the coast of the Carolinas, all completely submerged under several feet of seawater. "All of the people who had houses there had to move."

"Daddy, what's this?" asked Zach. Manny, who had been following along behind, stifled a yawn and quickly scanned the next exhibit.

"Weather on the surface got more and more violent, knocking down trees and power lines," Manny summarized. "Look at all of the work they had to do, every time there was a storm!" He pointed to a photo, showing teams of workers on ladders, struggling to restring electrical wires.

"They kept repairing the power lines, over and over," mused Anna. "Each time, the same thing."

"Weren't there wireless connections?" asked Julie.

"Yes," replied Anna, "but it's always cheaper to fix what you have, than install something new."

"And so incredibly short-sighted," added Manny.

They moved on to the next exhibit, entitled "Our Colony Under Threat."

There was a large charcoal drawing of a group of about twenty displaced men, women and children, dressed in rags, knocking on the Colony's locked outer doors, begging to be allowed in. The year was 2195.

"No one knows exactly where they came from," Manny read. "But our brave guards protected the people of New York by shooting and killing the mob before they could force their way inside and spread their foul diseases among our people."

"Did they shoot the children, Daddy?" asked Zach, frowning at the drawing.

"Let's see what else is here," replied Manny smoothly, gently drawing his son away from the story of the desperate, starving band of travelers who had been murdered in cold blood, rather than welcomed with open arms as fellow survivors.

"What's this one?" asked Julie, standing by the stairs. The sign read, "Upstairs: Holocaust Remembrance, No One Under 17."

"No, Julie, not that one!" exclaimed Anna, grabbing her daughter's arm.

"Why not?" asked Julie, drawn like a magnet towards the forbidden area.

"You know what," said Manny, "I'm getting a little hungry. I think I saw a frozen tofu stand outside. Let's go see if they have pretzel cones."

# Chapter 3.

ON MONDAY MORNING, Manny returned to work at the police station. While most people in the Colony worked from home at least some of the time, police officers, doctors, municipal employees, teachers, etc., could not work at home due to the nature of their jobs.

The other detectives greeted him as he came in. Tactfully, no one asked why he had been absent, although everyone knew that something had happened at home.

Manny sat down at his desk, took a deep breath and let it out slowly. He had dearly missed being at work. Unlike at home, here at the office there was discipline and quiet. He knew exactly what was expected of him, and he loved it. Manny looked at the stack of folders on his desk, the collection of little notes that the unit secretary had left for him, the reports that needed to be filed, and smiled to himself.

"Tea, Detective?" asked the unit secretary, an elderly woman with gray-blue hair named Matilda. She had been the unit's secretary for thirty years, a record for this precinct.

"Thanks, I'd love a cup," replied Manny.

"Everything OK at home?" she asked, respectfully looking at the floor.

"Fine," he replied monosyllabically. She nodded and went towards the tiny kitchen area to fix the tea.

David Wu, the detective who shared a two-person desk with Manny, each of them sitting at diagonally opposite corners, looked up from his padlet. "Everything OK?" he asked. "Family and all?"

Manny hesitated. If he was going to confide in anyone, it would be Dave. He had known Dave since their days at the Academy; they had been partners back in the day, when they were street cops. Manny had made Detective first, then Dave, and now here they were together again, sitting next to each other every day.

"It was Naz," he said softly, looking down, pushing a few things around on his desk. "She miscarried."

15

"Wow, I'm sorry," replied Dave. "Is there anything I can do?"

Manny shrugged. "Thanks, but there's nothing anybody can do."

"Just give her time," said Dave. "When Jennie miscarried, it took her days to stop crying."

"I don't really know what to say to her, you know?" said Manny in an undertone, aware that all of the detectives in his unit had mysteriously stopped working and were listening mightily. "What did you say to Jennie?"

"I just kept telling her that I love her," said Dave. "Naztazya will be OK. It's their hormones. They go crazy because one day there's a baby, and then the next day there isn't."

Manny nodded, making a mental note to ask Anna about hormones. He wasn't exactly sure what they were, but maybe as a good husband, he should know. Women, as he had found out since his marriage, were mysteriously very different from men.

Over the next several weeks, life at the Stewart household slowly returned to normal. With the resilience of youth, Naztazya once again resumed all of her household responsibilities. While she was a little more quiet than usual, she at least no longer looked depressed. She hadn't mentioned the miscarriage lately. Oddly, neither had she mentioned wanting to have another baby.

Manny was secretly beginning to hope that she would change her mind about another baby. The nights of broken sleep while dealing with a newborn, endless diaper changes, tedious long afternoons of watching a cranky infant so Naz could have a few hours to herself – if he was honest with himself, then no, he really didn't want any of that. He didn't find it rewarding or satisfying at all. Sometimes he missed the young Naztazya he had married, the carefree, funny, happy woman whom he had had all to himself.

~ ~ ~ ~ ~ ~

Manny resumed working long hours, often returning home after the family had eaten dinner. In addition, as a junior member of the City Council, he attended Council meetings once a month, which sometimes lasted late into the evening.

There were twelve members of the Colony's City Council: the President, eight Council Elders and three junior members. Junior members were really "in training," as his former teacher and Council Elder Sarah Blumberg had explained to him. "They're the alternates of the Council," she had said, "available to fill in if needed."

At the most recent City Council meeting, Manny had listened diligently to the different issues being presented. Shoplifting in the stores, uneven walkways that needed repair, a restaurant with an expired inspection certificate – all of these issues were presented and discussed.

Manny left the meeting as soon as it was over, glad that for once, it was not late. If he hurried, he might actually be able to see Zach before he went to sleep.

Manny was nearly home when suddenly everything around him went dark, an inky deep shade of black utterly devoid of any light. Manny could not see his hand stretched out in front of him. Like everyone else around him who was out on the street at that exact moment, he reached for his padlet and turned on the Flashlight app.

The Flashlight app was designed to illuminate the back of a closet or whatever might be hiding beneath your couch; it was not designed to light up a street. Manny realized immediately that the Flashlight app simply did not extend out far enough.

Walkways throughout the Colony were required to be at least two feet wide, wide enough for one person to walk comfortably. In the wealthier neighborhoods, such as where Manny lived, there were spacious walkways that were wide enough for two or three people at a time, and still plenty of space for homes to be built across the platform from each other. At night, tunnel ceilings were lit by special light panels called

Danish lighting, which only came on when a person came within range.

Manny was dismayed to hear people coming out of their houses into the street. He could hear them, although he could not see them. Amidst a growing chorus of alarmed voices, Manny opened up his padlet's special suite of police apps and turned on Strobe, a powerful Flashlight-like app that could light up an entire area of about 100 feet square.

"What's going on?" cried one woman, holding a shrieking toddler on her hip.

"Florence, Florence, where are you?" shouted a man, walking quickly down the street and right into another citizen, who promptly shoved him away.

"Get away from me, you idiot!" he said.

"Who are you calling an idiot? *You* get out of *my* way!" came the response, followed by the sound of a scuffle and someone falling to the ground. Manny could sense the growing confusion and alarm, and knew it was only a matter of time before someone got hurt.

"Everyone!" he shouted. "This is Detective Stewart! You should all return to your houses! No one should be out on the streets, not until we know what is going on!" But the crowd was growing, with everyone talking at once. No one was listening to Manny.

Turning, Manny ran the rest of the way to his house, quickly opening the front door. "Naz, Anna, where are you?" he called as he ran into the study, yanking open the closet door.

"Daddy!" cried Zach, running towards him. Anna, Julio, Julie and Naz were not far behind, all with padlets out, Flashlight apps on.

"Stay here, inside the house! Don't go outside!" Manny cried, relieved to see that they were safe. "I'm going to try to get some of these people back into their homes before somebody gets hurt."

Julio moved closer to Manny, watching him as he quickly rummaged through the items on the closet shelf, impatiently tossing most of them onto the floor. "You looking for your old man's bullhorn?" he guessed.

"Yeah, do you know where it is?" replied Manny. "I need the baseball bat, too."

"The baseball bat!?" cried Naztazya. "What on earth for?"

"Naz, you stay here! Julio, keep them all inside!" Manny said, as Julio slid the ancient bullhorn, an old-fashioned vintage voice-magnifying megaphone, off the top shelf.

Grabbing the baseball bat from the closet and taking the bullhorn out of Julio's hands, he called out, "I'll be back as soon as I can!"

Running outside, Manny turned on the Strobe app once again, lighting up the street. It was filled with people milling about, wondering what could have caused the power to go off, arguing loudly with their neighbors about what would happen next, and searching for loved ones who had wandered away and gotten lost in the total blackness. Manny raised the bullhorn to his lips and began to speak.

"This is Detective Stewart from the Police Department. I need you all to stop what you are doing and listen." He paused for a moment; the crowd began to quiet down.

"You need to return home and stay inside where you will be safe, until we know more about this power outage," Manny urged. "I'm going to turn my light onto one side of the street first, and then the other side, until everyone has had a chance to find their way back."

"What's going on, Detective?" called one man from the back of the crowd.

"When will the power come back on?" asked a woman.

"Honestly, I don't know. I'm sure there will be an announcement soon. Maybe it's a drill! After all, no one has said it's not a drill," Manny replied reasonably. "Everyone needs to stay calm and return to their houses. We will know more soon."

Manny could feel the mood of the crowd shift, as people calmed down. Bits of conversations floated past him as people began to return to their homes, arms around their loved ones.

"Probably just a drill," said one man.

"I bet that's what they tell us in the morning," agreed another, turning towards his front door.

A police drone flew overhead, surveying the scene. Manny waved his bullhorn at the drone, knowing that it was being monitored back at the station. One wing dipped in answer, as it flew past.

Relieved that he had not had to use the baseball bat to disperse the crowd, Manny returned to his house.

"Uncle Manny!" cried Julie, who was keeping watch by the window. "You're a hero, Uncle Manny!"

"Hi, Sweetheart," said Manny, kissing his niece on top of her head. Exhausted, he sank down onto one of the velvet chairs in the foyer.

"Manny!" cried Naztazya, putting her arms around him. "I'm so glad you're home!"

He kissed her, holding her close. "Me, too! I think they just needed someone to calm them down, let them know that everything is OK," Manny said. "Any word about the cause of the blackout?"

"No," replied Anna, "nothing so far. Do you know anything?"

"No, I'm as much in the dark as you are. No pun intended," he added, as Julie giggled.

"What if the intranet goes down?" asked Naztazya fearfully. "Could that happen, Manny?"

"It *could* happen, Naz, but that doesn't mean that it will," Manny answered, keeping his voice calm and soothing.

He glanced at Anna, who as a supervisor at the Jonathan King Institute for Computer Sciences probably knew more than she was saying. Her padlet beeped once, pulsing neon gold around the edges, denoting an urgent work message. She unfolded her padlet and read quickly.

"They need me at work now," Anna said calmly.

"What? Now?" asked Julio, "Anna, can't it wait? Why do they need you now?"

"It's probably nothing, Julio," said Anna lightly, and Manny recognized by her reassuring tone that she was handling Julio much as he had handled Naz.

"Take Julie, will you?" asked Anna, and Naz nodded. "She can skip her bath tonight. I think it's close enough to bedtime now that maybe everyone should just go to bed. In the morning, most likely things will be back to normal."

Julio and Naz took the children upstairs. Anna turned quickly to go towards her office, down the hall from the kitchen. Manny caught her sleeve as she hurried past him.

"Anna, what's going on? Can you tell me?" he asked in an undertone.

"No, Manny, you know I can't do that," she responded. "Let me go, I have to work."

"I'm just going to find out at the station tomorrow," he persisted.

"Rules are rules, Manny, you'll just have to wait until tomorrow," she said with finality, and he let her go.

Upstairs, it was the darkest shade of black, utterly dark. The children were changing into their pajamas by the light of their padlets. Naz had made a sort of game out of it, pretending it was fun, telling them that the lights would be back on in the morning.

"All set?" Manny said when she finished getting the children into bed, coming into their bedroom and sitting down on the antique velvet chair which had belonged to his mother, Lila Rose.

"All set," she replied. "Wow, it's dark, Manny! Do you know what happened?"

"No, you know as much as I do," he replied.

"It's kind of creepy, don't you think?" she asked fearfully, her face and shoulders illuminated by the padlet's app.

"We shouldn't have both padlets on at the same time," said Manny. *We need to conserve power,* he thought, although he didn't want to alarm her by saying that. "I know, wait a second – I'll be right back!"

Manny made his way downstairs into the kitchen. Opening up the cabinet over the sink, he reached far into the back and found a precious tall white candle and a book of matches.

Candles were illegal in the Colony, due to the risk of accidental fires. Candles could only be found on the black market, a thriving illegal enterprise which was patronized by just about everybody in the Colony. Fine jewelry, expensive fabrics like velvet and silk, hard liquor, buckles and buttons, all could be had for a price.

Many of the best customers for this illegal trade were also investors in the company that transported the illegal goods. Manny's father, the former Chief of Police, had been the single most influential investor and regulator of this illegal trade. Under his guidance, the black market had become wildly profitable.

Many of Patrick Stewart's police colleagues were still big investors in the illegal enterprise. After Patrick's death, Manny had inherited his father's empire. The illegal trade was the backbone of Manny's wealth.

Manny carefully filled a wide, flat bowl with a few inches of water and carried it, along with the precious candle and the book of matches, up the stairs and into his bedroom.

Inside their bedroom, Naztazya was in bed, scanning her padlet for updates. "No news yet," she reported.

"I'm sure we'll know more in the morning," Manny replied, setting the bowl of water down on the night table. Naz watched as he carefully placed the candle in the center of the bowl. He lit the candle and stepped back, admiring the soft flicker of the flame, the way it reflected in the bowl of water onto the ceiling.

"You know, it's sort of romantic," she said with a sigh.

He climbed into bed next to her, putting his arm around her shoulders. "Have I told you lately how beautiful you are?" He kissed her gently, his fingers running through her red curls.

"We need to be very careful with the candle," Naz cautioned. "The last thing we need is a fire!"

"Don't worry, we'll put it out before we fall asleep," said Manny, yawning.

He and Naztazya settled back against the pillows, his arm around her, her head resting on his shoulder, the candle flickering shadows against the wall. Within a few minutes, they were both sound asleep.

# Chapter 4.

**M**ANNY WOKE WITH a start as cold water sloshed onto his neck and face. Zach was standing next to the bed, a guilty expression on his face, holding the bowl in his hands. The candle had fallen on the floor, rolling to a stop a few feet from the bed, its tiny flame still burning. A wisp of gray smoke rose lazily into the air; then a narrow ridge of orange-red appeared and began to slowly snake its way along the carpet towards the door.

"Manny!" screamed Naztazya, pointing. "The candle!"

Jumping up out of bed, Manny grabbed the bowl out of Zach's hands and poured what was left of the water onto the tiny, hungry fire. It sizzled, sending up a little plume of gray smoke. Manny stamped on it with his bare feet, pounding it until the carpet was a sodden mess.

Manny turned to Zach. "What did you do?" he demanded angrily. "Why aren't you in your bed sleeping?"

"But it's morning!" protested Zach. "Look, all the lights are on."

The power was on. That was a welcome development. But Manny's adrenaline was still pumping. "Zachary, what made you touch the candle?"

"I wanted to hold the little light! I'm sorry, Daddy," replied Zach, beginning to cry.

"Candles are not for children!" replied Manny sternly. "They are dangerous. Do you hear me?!"

"Manny. Please. He's sorry," said Naz quietly, her hand on his arm. "He's just a little boy. He didn't know."

"And it's our job to teach him," Manny retorted. "We could have had a fire in here, Naz, it doesn't take long."

She shuddered. There were few things feared more than fire in the Colony. There were no glossy red fire engines or tall rescue ladders. Citizens tried their best with impromptu "bucket brigades," but often it made little difference. The Colony depended mostly on a series of fireproof and waterproof doors installed every 200 yards or so. Once the residents had fled, the doors were slammed shut and everything within was abandoned, left to burn to the ground. It was not a pretty picture.

Manny looked at the clock; it was 4:45 am. He sighed. "Come on, Bud, I'll take you back to your bed."

"I don't wanna go back to bed," whined Zach. "Can't we have pancakes?"

"No, we can't have pancakes," said Manny. "You need to go back to bed."

"Are the lights on all over the house?" asked Naz.

"I'll make sure they're off, Naz. You go back to sleep," said Manny dutifully. Manny and Zach left the bedroom, closing the door behind them.

As soon as they were downstairs, Manny said, "Spartana, lights off," to the house software.

"Lights off: confirmed," replied Spartana, clicking the lights off all over the house. Spartana was outdated and clumsy, but worked just fine. Manny had not bothered to update it after he inherited the house.

"Well, I guess maybe it's time for pancakes after all," Manny said. He was wide awake, and Zach looked for all the world like he was used to getting up at 4:45 am. *Maybe this is his usual wakeup time,* thought Manny, feeling guilty. Naz had always gotten up with Zach, especially on weekends, allowing Manny to sleep late.

He made pancakes, making them the way that his foster mother Lucinda had taught him so many years ago. *It's going to be a long day,* Manny thought ruefully.

Anna came into the kitchen, stretching her arms over her head. "Is there coffee?" she asked, yawning.

"Not yet, wanna make some?" asked Manny as he flipped over a few pancakes. "Have you been up working the whole night?"

"Yeah, the whole night. Why are you up so early?" replied Anna.

Manny nodded towards Zach, who was finishing his pancakes. Anna laughed. "Julie will be up soon, too. I'm so glad the power is back on."

He looked at her curiously, but said nothing. He knew that she would tell him whatever she could about her work, when she was ready.

Anna made coffee and sat down, waiting for it to drip through the filter into the jug. Her eyes were closed for so long that Manny thought she might actually have fallen asleep.

"It was a fluke, a rogue burst of power that wiped out a whole section of servers," she said finally. "At least, that's what we think happened. But the official story is that while doing routine maintenance, replacing an old server with a new one, the new server did not come on line right away. It's been fixed, and everything is fine now."

"I see," said Manny, waiting in case she might say more. Anna got up to fill her coffee cup, and sat back down.

"Whoever invented a way to grow coffee was a genius," said Anna. Coffee and black tea had only recently been coaxed into growing successfully in the large greenhouse complex. The humidity and oxygen levels had to be just right. Anna held the cup in both hands, sipping gratefully. "I'll be interested to see what they tell you at the station today."

"I'll be sure to let you know tonight," he said, disappointed that he had not been able to learn more from her. He put the last of the pancakes on a plate, setting it on the table. "I have to go get ready for work. Can I leave Buddy with you?"

"Go ahead," she said, taking another sip of her coffee. "I've got this."

~ ~ ~ ~ ~ ~

Manny was the first officer in his unit to show up for work, the day after the blackout. The other detectives straggled in by 8:00 am.

At 9:30 am, every padlet in the Colony beeped with an official municipal update. Along with everyone else, Manny opened his padlet to watch the video from the Mayor:

26

"Citizens! Yesterday, we experienced a power outage for the first time in decades. I have been in touch with the Department of Energy. Apparently, they were doing routine maintenance on the servers, and replaced an older server with a new one. The new one did not immediately come online, which caused the power outage. The problem has now been fixed.

"I want to commend all New Yorkers on their outstanding behavior last night. People stayed calm, stayed in their homes, conserved power and acted responsibly, in many cases neighbor helping neighbor to get through this emergency."

There was a low buzz of murmuring throughout the usually quiet office, as people digested the news, some skeptical, others merely glad to be able to get back to work. Manny wondered if that was it, or if the police would be given a more thorough explanation. He didn't have long to wait.

The Chief called a meeting and addressed the assembled officers.

"Last night we had a once-in-a-lifetime emergency," he began, striding to the front of the room. "The official reason has been given out as a server which did not immediately come online. I'm here to give you a further explanation, which stays here among us. Do not discuss this with anyone outside of this office.

"The experts at the Institute are not sure what caused this power outage. The entire Colony from 42nd Street north was blacked out. They are working to determine exactly what happened, and we should have a report soon. I don't have to tell you that we rely completely on our computer system to control the air flow, heat, running water and lighting here in the Colony. Without it, we are a group of people living in tunnels, in total darkness, underneath the ground."

Chief O'Reilly unrolled his padlet, projecting an image onto the wall on one side of the room. As one, every face turned towards the wall.

"Pay attention to the lone officer, the one with the bullhorn," he said. He clicked "play," and Manny was startled to see that they were watching drone footage of his street from the previous night. It began as the drone turned down his street, flying towards the area which he had lit up with his Strobe app. His voice could be heard above the shouts of the crowd as he calmed them, instructing them to go home.

"Can everyone hear the officer?" demanded the Chief sternly. Manny's stomach sank. Had he broken some kind of arcane rule about crowd control? True, he was off duty and had no orders to clear the crowd. But it had been an emergency!

"This officer, the one with the bat and the bullhorn," began the Chief, "he saw that a situation was unfolding. Did he just stand there, waiting for instructions? No! He controlled the crowd by getting their attention, calming them, and helping them return safely to their homes. He showed initiative! This man is a credit to the department."

He turned to Manny. "And with your father's bullhorn, no less!" he exclaimed, breaking into a huge smile. He began to clap. The whole unit broke into applause, turning to face Manny.

Manny stood to acknowledge their applause, giving a little wave of his hand before he quickly sat back down. He was surprised, and gratified – and also dismayed. His father, always his father. Would he have to live the rest of his life in his dead father's shadow?

~ ~ ~ ~ ~ ~

Manny stood in front of the Suarez family's house, nearly hidden in shadow at the far end of the 14th Street Station platform. Pushing aside the flowered curtain, he rang the bell.

"Manny!" exclaimed Lucinda. "How nice to see you! To what do I owe this pleasure?" she asked, putting her arms around him and hugging him. Lucinda had been a mother to Manny, raising him along with her son Julio.

"I was working a case not far from here, so I thought I'd come say hello," he said, kissing her cheek. Knowing that Lucinda was a wonderful cook who enjoyed feeding her family, he asked, "Got anything to eat around here?"

They sat together in the tiny kitchen, where he had done homework as a teenager, where they had shared so many family meals. "How's it going at the office?" asked Lucinda, as they dug into tofu pinwheels braised in soy sauce and mirin, and a tossed marigold salad.

"OK, I guess," said Manny.

"I heard about what you did during the blackout," Lucinda said. "Julio told me. Manny, that was wonderful! How did you remember that you had a bullhorn?"

"My Dad used to talk about it sometimes," he said. "How he used it to address large crowds. He broke up a riot with it once. Or so the story goes."

Lucinda laughed. "Some stories get bigger as the years go by."

"He's a hero, down at the station. People talk about him all the time, like he's some kind of role model," Manny said. Lucinda knew all about Manny's childhood, how Patrick had alternately abused and neglected his son. Lucinda actually had known Patrick Stewart when they were teenagers. She and Patrick had dated briefly when she was still in high school, before Patrick married Lila Rose. Even then, as a young man, Patrick had been forceful and controlling.

"That must be difficult to listen to," she said.

"It is," he admitted. "It's almost like they expect me to be just like him. That's the last thing I want to be!"

"I understand," she said. "But you and I, Manny, we know that he was quite different in his personal life than in his professional life."

Manny nodded. They had discussed this many times.

"You'll make your own way, Manny. They won't always be comparing you to your father," Lucinda said.

They ate in silence for a few moments. "How are things at home?" asked Lucinda, one eyebrow arched.

"Things are good," said Manny. "Oh. You mean …"

"Yes, any news yet?" Lucinda said, her smile growing.

"No," Manny said, looking down at his plate. He took another bite of marigold salad. "This is really good, Lucinda! Can I have some more, please?"

Lucinda handed him the bowl. "Are you going to tell me what's on your mind?" she asked, straight-forward as usual. One thing you could count on with Lucinda, as well as the rest of the Suarez clan - they didn't beat around the potted plant.

Manny cleared his throat. "I've been thinking," he began hesitantly.

"Yes?" she asked gently.

"What if I don't really want another baby," he said carefully, lowering his voice despite being alone in the house with her. "Maybe we are good just the way we are, with one child."

"And Naztazya, she wants another baby?" asked Lucinda.

Manny nodded. "But she hasn't mentioned it lately. After the miscarriage, it was all she talked about for a while, and then ... nothing. So maybe she's changed her mind."

"Manny, you need to talk to her! This is an important decision, something the two of you need to decide together," said Lucinda. "Does she know that you are having second thoughts?"

"No, I haven't said anything yet," Manny replied. "I didn't want to upset her right after the miscarriage, and then I've been waiting, but she hasn't brought it up again."

"She may think that you want another child as much as she does, but that you are giving her space, you know, so she doesn't feel pressured," explained Lucinda. "You need to tell her how you feel."

"You're right," Manny agreed. "I guess I'd better talk to her. And soon!"

Lucinda nodded. "Sooner rather than later, I'd say!"

Manny returned to the office, where no one remarked on his long absence. He was proud of this freedom; he had always been something of a lone wolf, and as long as he continued to close cases and do all of his paperwork, no one questioned his whereabouts when he was out of the office.

*Lucinda is right,* he thought, *we need to talk about whether or not to have another baby.* Resolutely pulling out his padlet, he texted Naztazya:

Manny: *Naz, I'll be home for dinner tonight. There's something I want to talk over with you.*
Naztazya: *Good! I have something to talk to you about, too. See you around 6!*

He wondered briefly what she might have on her mind. *I guess I'll find out when I get home,* he thought. He started working, keeping an eye on the clock.

# Chapter 5.

**W**HEN MANNY ARRIVED home at 6:00 pm, he went into the kitchen, where the children were setting the table for dinner while Anna and Julio were peering into the oven.

"That smells wonderful," he said to Julio. "Sweet potatoes?"

"You have a good nose!" replied Julio. "It's sweet potato pie, one of my mom's recipes."

The Stewarts' kitchen had one of the few private ovens in the Colony. Most people reserved time in a commercial baker's oven, hurrying home with their baked or roasted items before they could cool off. Commercial bakers were usually finished baking the day's bread and cakes by mid-afternoon, leaving the oven free for private citizens to rent.

"Where's Naz?" asked Manny.

"She's upstairs, Manny," replied Anna. "She said to ask you to come up."

Manny dutifully turned and went up the grand staircase to their bedroom. He carefully closed the door behind him, and sat down on the edge of their bed. Naz, who had been standing by the window, sat down next to him, taking his hand.

Manny had been married to Naztazya since he was seventeen years old, but he still marveled at the soft roundness of her, so different from his own athletic, strongly muscled body. He put his hand around the back of her neck, pulled her close and kissed her.

"Hello there," he murmured, their foreheads together. "You wanted to talk to me about something?"

She smoothed his hair back from his brow. "Yes, I do." Her hands were perspiring, which was unusual for Naz. "I have something important to tell you," she announced. "I'm pregnant!"

"Wh-what?" he said, wondering if he had heard right.

"Manny, we're having another baby!" she exclaimed. She laughed, her face alight with joy. "You look so surprised! You didn't guess?"

"Guess? No, I didn't. Naz, are you sure?" he asked, his mind whirling. Maybe she was mistaken, women could misjudge these things. There were no pregnancy tests, as there had been long ago; women relied on their knowledge of their own bodies to gauge what was happening inside of them.

"Manny, you're not happy?" she asked, her smile faltering. "You're frowning!"

"No, no, Naz, don't even think that! It's just that I know how hard it was for you the last time, and I don't want to see you go through that again."

As soon as he said it, he regretted it. A shadow clouded her face, at the mention of her loss. *Get it together,* he told himself sternly, *don't screw this up!*

"It's going to be different, this time," she said firmly. She stood up, letting go of his hand.

He stood up, too, and put his arms around her, burying his face in her neck so she couldn't see his dismay.

"I'm sorry, Naz, I shouldn't have said that. I'm sure it'll be fine," he said contritely. "Remember, your mother had miscarriages, and then she had Marya. And after that, the twins came." Carefully, he rearranged his facial expression to something like joy, and then leaned back, looking into her eyes.

"And yes, you did surprise me!" he said. "Let's go downstairs and tell everyone!"

He knew, of course, that Naz most likely had already told Anna; the two of them had no secrets. And if Anna knew, then probably Julio knew, too. But Manny was determined to play the part of the delighted husband. There would be plenty of time later to reflect upon what he should have said to her, weeks ago. Not that it mattered any more.

Later that night, as they were getting into bed, Naz said sleepily to Manny, "What was it that you wanted to ask me, Manny? Remember, you said you had something you wanted to talk about?"

"Yes," he lied smoothly. "I wanted to ask you which of the spare bedrooms you wanted to use as a nursery. You know, just in case."

33

~ ~ ~ ~ ~ ~

"How long will you be gone today?" Naztazya asked, sitting up in bed, yawning. Several weeks had passed. Today was the day that Manny, Luis and Julio would be seeing their point man in Philadelphia.

Manny was a silent partner in the family enterprise Suarez & Sons, a company whose sole purpose was illegal trade. Usually, it was Julio who went to Philadelphia to supervise picking up a shipment; sometimes Luis went, too. Occasionally, Manny would take a day off from work and all three of them would go.

"We won't be back until late," Manny said, picking his sweatpants off the floor and putting them on. "Joshua has something new he wants to show us, and I haven't been to Philly in a while." Joshua Spellman was their main contact in Philadelphia; he had been Patrick's point man from the beginning of the black market trade.

"Do you have to go?" she asked. "I mean, couldn't just Julio and Luis go?"

"Why?" he asked, surprised. "Are you feeling OK?"

"I'm just worried, that's all," she replied. "It's so far away, and what if something goes wrong?" When Naz had been pregnant with Zach, she had often had bouts of anxiety, as well as unpredictable mood swings. With miscarriages so common, everyone knew that pregnant women should be kept calm whenever possible.

Manny stopped getting dressed and sat down on the bed next to her, taking her hand. "If it will make you feel better, then yes, I can ask them to go without me," he said kindly, and was rewarded with her grateful smile.

"Manny," she said hesitantly, "I need to ask you something." She pushed down the quilt covering her rounded four-months' belly. "Do you think I'm bigger this time than I was with Zach?" she asked worriedly.

34

In truth, she did look bigger, noticeably much thicker and wider around the middle than she had been with Zach at four months. "Not that I can see," he lied.

"Nothing fits me! I feel so gross," she said, her hands crossed over her belly.

"You definitely don't look gross to me, Naz," he said, bending forward to kiss her. "If nothing fits, then maybe you need some new clothes," he suggested. "Why don't I have a few dresses sent to you from *The Lady In Waiting?* I'll surprise you."

"Manny, that's very kind of you," she replied.

"And maybe a visit from Mrs. Braun would make you feel better," he suggested. He was not quite clear on what Mrs. Braun could actually do, but it seemed like the right thing to say.

"Yes, that's a good idea," she agreed. "I'll ask her to come. Maybe she could come over later today."

~ ~ ~ ~ ~ ~

When Manny arrived at the office, Dave looked up from their shared two-person desk, surprised. "I thought you were taking the day off," he said.

"Change in plans," Manny replied. Although everyone knew about the black market, especially in the police department where so many officers were investors in the trade, it was an unspoken rule that at work, no one talked about it. Manny didn't offer any details, and Dave knew better than to ask. The two colleagues settled in for a day of hard work.

At lunchtime, Manny ate a sandwich at his desk, as usual. Then he texted Naz's favorite maternity shop, *The Lady In Waiting*:

Manny: *Please send every dress you have in a ladies Size Lovely over to the house. Thank you.*

Store Manager: *It will be a pleasure, Sir! I'll have these delivered to Mrs. Stewart this afternoon.*

Manny smiled to himself as he thought of Naz opening up a big box containing a kaleidoscope of dresses. *That should cheer her up*, he thought.

~ ~ ~ ~ ~ ~

As soon as Manny came home from work that evening, he could tell something was up. Naztazya, resplendent in a ruffled palest green silk maternity dress, greeted him with a kiss, her green eyes dancing with anticipation.

The dining room table was set with the good china, wine glasses and good silverware. A crystal bowl of blue violets, Naz's favorite flowers, stood in the middle of the table. The children had eaten earlier and had already gone upstairs. Manny glanced at Luis, who frowned at him and shook his head briefly, to show that he had no idea what to make of the fancy table settings. Julio was in the kitchen looking for a corkscrew, to open a bottle of white wine.

Dinner consisted of two scoops of black rice with peas and mushrooms, two honey-glazed blue carrots, and two very curly sea beans. Each plate was beautifully decorated with two edible violets. The bread basket, containing two kinds of rolls, was passed from person to person. Water glasses and wine glasses were filled.

Lucinda picked up her fork to begin, looked down at her plate, and stopped, fork in mid-air. She glanced up sharply at Naztazya, who blushed and looked away. Lucinda smiled to herself, and began to eat.

Luis passed the bread basket, while Julio examined his curly sea beans.

"What did Joshua want?" asked Manny, watching Julio try unsuccessfully to impale a sea bean on his fork.

"Do you remember when you and I went to see Joshua for the first time, just the two of us, without Dad?" asked Julio.

"Yeah, I remember," said Manny. "He tried to sell us those little green things. Pills, right? He said they were from Sch-cago or someplace, said they were selling like hotcakes."

Luis laughed. "Joshua thought he could take advantage of you both, as soon as my back was turned. But you boys were too smart for him."

"What did he want this time?" asked Manny, his mouth full.

"He has something new called Fentneel. He said it makes you really high, that people can't get enough of it. He even offered to give us some for free, to try," Luis replied. "I told him that we aren't interested. Then he tried to put some in my pocket!"

"I'm a police officer. I arrest people who do drugs," Manny protested. "How would it look if I was selling those drugs?"

"Exactly," said Julio. "That's what we told him. The trip was a waste of time." Julio gave up trying to use a fork on the sea beans, and picked up one in his fingers, looking at it curiously.

"I saw Mrs. Braun this morning," said Naztazya, changing the subject.

"What did she have to say?" asked Manny, as he ate the last of his edible violets. "Everything OK?"

"Yes, she said everything is fine," replied Naz.

"See, I told you everything would be alright," said Manny. "Every pregnancy is different, like you always say. You're just carrying a little differently this time."

"Differently?" asked Julio, puzzled, looking from Naztazya to his wife, who nudged him sharply with her foot beneath the table.

"Such a good dinner!" exclaimed Manny. He turned to Naz. "Did you make all of this yourself?"

"We made it together, the two of us," she replied. The two sisters exchanged a brief glance, their expressions unreadable. Manny recognized "the look," as Julio called it, a perfect understanding between them, communicated with a single glance. Honestly, sometimes it was almost as if they were twins, they were so much inside each other's heads.

Dessert was served, two chocolate cookies per person. One was covered with chocolate ganache and topped with drizzleberries, gloriously juicy round berries. The other cookie was dotted with Bloomies, tiny, brightly colored candies that "bloomed" when bitten into.

"My goodness, you've outdone yourselves!" exclaimed Luis, pushing his empty plate away. He crossed his hands over his stomach. "I won't need to eat for a week!"

"It was delicious!" exclaimed Manny. "But I wonder ... there's a theme to tonight's dinner, right?" Naz nodded expectantly, eyes dancing.

"There are two of everything," Manny proceeded cautiously, and again, Naz nodded. "Why are there two of everything?"

Naz's face flushed pink. "Why do you think, Detective?" she asked playfully. "Do you have a working hypothesis?"

Manny's heart sank. *Careful,* he warned himself, *be careful.*

"You tell me," he said, struggling to keep a neutral expression on his face.

"Twins," she said simply, joy lighting up her face.

"Twins," whispered Manny. For a moment, he thought that his heart had stopped; he couldn't breathe. He forced himself to concentrate only on Naztazya and the joy in her face.

"Twins!" he repeated stupidly. He drew a deep breath. "Naz, that's wonderful! That's wonderful! Twins! Did Mrs. Braun tell you?"

"Yes, she heard two heartbeats!" cried Naztazya, tears in her eyes. "We're going to have two babies! Manny, we'll have three children!"

"Three children," repeated Manny, making sure that he was still smiling.

"Look at him, he's stunned!" said Julio, playfully punching Manny in the shoulder. "You'll get used to it, bro, don't worry."

*I guess I'll have to,* thought Manny.

Later, when Luis and Lucinda were getting ready to go home, Manny walked them to the door. He and Luis embraced, and then he turned to Lucinda. As he hugged her, she whispered in his ear, "Well played." He drew back, looking at her. She smiled, affectionately touching his cheek. Neither of them would ever breathe a word about his earlier doubts.

# Chapter 6.

ABOUT A MONTH later, Manny woke at 3:50 am to the sound of rhythmic slapping and thumping, coming from the kitchen. Naz was not in bed; he knew that she had been having trouble sleeping lately. Pulling on a bathrobe, Manny went downstairs, ambient lighting turning each step rose pink in the pre-dawn darkness.

Naz was alone in the kitchen, standing as close to the counter as her growing belly would allow.

"What are you doing?" he asked, coming up behind her to put his arms around her, kissing the back of her neck. "Trouble sleeping?"

"It's so hard to sleep," she sighed. "First this one kicks me, then the other one kicks me!" She laughed tiredly. "I'm making bread," she continued, kneading the dough. "It takes hours to make, so I thought I might as well get started."

"Naz, we can buy bread," he said reasonably. "You should be upstairs in bed, resting."

"No," she replied, "I have to do this." In addition to insomnia, Naz had been experiencing mood swings, ranging from fits of melancholy to bursts of energetic activity, sometimes both in one day. Manny remembered her mood swings from her pregnancy with Zach, so he was not surprised.

"Why?" he asked mildly. "I can have a dozen loaves of bread delivered here in thirty minutes, with one text message."

"You don't understand, Manny!" she cried, turning to face him. He could see that she was upset.

"Come and sit down," he said gently, taking her hand and leading her to the kitchen table, pulling out a chair for her. "What don't I understand?"

"I've been thinking," she said. "What if something happens to you? And I have to raise the babies all by myself? We'll have three children under the age of five. That's a lot of children."

"First of all, nothing's going to happen to me," he stated flatly. "And besides, you're not all by yourself; you've got Julio and Anna, too, and our parents. They would be right there to help you."

"It's not the same, Manny, babies need a father," she insisted. "They need both parents."

"Naz, I'm 26 years old. Strong and healthy," he stated confidently. "Have you been worrying about the delivery?"

"Yes! It's a little scary, giving birth to two humans at once." She laughed. "You probably think I'm crazy for worrying about everything like this."

"I don't think you're crazy, Naz," he replied seriously. "I wish I could help you." He paused, thinking. There must be something he could do.

"Listen, Naz, I have an idea. What if Mrs. Braun were to stay here with us until the babies are born? The two of you seem to get along so well, and she'd be right here if you need her," said Manny. "Would that make you feel less worried?"

"She has so many other patients, Manny!" Naz replied. "I don't know if she'd even want to do that."

"Why don't you ask her?" he said. "Of course, we'll compensate her for whatever she would have earned from the other patients during the time she's here with us."

"OK, I'll ask her! Maybe I'll go see her in person later today," she said.

"Good idea!" he said, leaning over to kiss her cheek. A walk would do her good, and the errand would keep her mind occupied with something productive.

"Naz, why don't we go back upstairs?" he suggested. "Look, it's still dark outside."

"Manny, I don't think I'll be able to go back to sleep," she said. "I'm wide awake now."

He smiled, his fingers caressing her wrist. "Who said anything about sleep?"

~ ~ ~ ~ ~ ~

Later that morning, Manny was sitting at work, reviewing CCvideo footage of an arrest he had made earlier in the week, when his padlet beeped twice, along with the padlets of

40

everyone else in his unit. As he picked it up, he noticed it was pulsing neon gold around the rim, meaning there was an urgent work message.

"Attention! Attention all officers! Fire at the Lexington and 51st Street station! All available manpower report directly to the Fire Marshall at the Lexington and 51st Street station!"

Like everyone else in his unit, Manny had been trained for this type of emergency. He stopped what he was doing, put his padlet in his pocket, and without pausing to speak to anyone or ask questions, took off at a run. Fire was a serious threat, and every minute counted. The scene was less than a mile away.

As Manny ran, he gave a silent prayer of thanks for the fire drills each month that required them to run as fast as they could for two miles in full uniform, while carrying a heavy backpack. Like almost everyone, Manny also ran several times a week to stay in shape. Dave, Manny's friend, ran silently alongside him.

They arrived at the scene out of breath. Victims of the fire were lying on the ground in an area far to one side, being triaged by medical personnel. Citizens were milling about, a few holding bundles, but most with just the clothes on their backs. Clouds of dark gray smoke filled the air, making it impossible to see clearly past the heavy metal fire doors, which were still open. The Fire Marshall was speaking through a loudspeaker.

"All emergency personnel! The fire doors will be closing in one minute! All civilians need to exit now! The doors will be closing in one minute! Follow the sound of my voice and exit now!"

Police and EMT's streamed through the partially open fire doors, some of them carrying or dragging unconscious victims of the fire. A few were carrying children, most of them crying, some ominously quiet. The smoke changed from black to dark gray up near the ceiling, big billowing clouds of choking, gritty smoke. The roar of the flames could not quite mask the sound of screaming coming from far off in the distance, as the heavy metal doors slowly began to swing shut.

41

"Let me through!" shouted Manny. "There are people in there!" An officer guarding the doorway stepped between Manny and the open door.

"Detective!" declared the officer, "you can't go in there! Didn't you hear the Fire Marshall?"

Manny unceremoniously shoved the officer aside. "Get out of my way!" he snarled. "Can't you hear them?" He knew, as did everyone else, that the people inside were about to be burned alive.

Dropping to the floor where it was easier to breathe, Manny crawled through the door and moved slowly forward on his hands and knees. He could hear voices off in the distance shouting for help, but the sound was so muffled by the roaring flames that it was hard to tell where it was coming from. Row houses, each one touching the next, passed the flames from roof to roof. Burning debris was everywhere. Manny could barely see his outstretched hand through the murky, thick smoke, but still he kept moving forward on hands and knees, searching for life.

He crawled into, rather than saw, a toddler sitting on the ground, crying. *At least he's crying*, Manny thought, picking the child up. "Don't worry, little guy, I've got you," he said reassuringly, awkwardly crawling forward like a lopsided crab, holding the child firmly in the crook of one arm.

A few steps more and he bumped into someone lying prone on the ground. A woman, presumably the child's mother, was barely conscious, but still alive. Clutched in her arms was a motionless infant. She grabbed at Manny with a strength born of panic, fingers gripping the side of his shirt, struggling to speak. He could see her bright blue eyes through the smoke, whites showing all the way around, rolling wildly as she searched for his face, imploring him, begging him.

Manny put down the toddler and picked up the infant, unbuttoning his shirt and quickly stuffing the child inside, buttoning the shirt back up, making sure that the child's face was not covered. Then he picked up the woman and tossed her over his shoulder in a classic fireman's hold, stretched out along his back so he could crawl, while keeping the toddler in the crook of one arm.

All around him, smoke was so thick that he could not see. The ground was getting hotter. Moving cautiously one step at a time, he carefully turned around and headed back, hoping that he was going in the right direction. It was almost impossible to move, weighed down with his precious, heavy burden.

"Detective! Detective Stewart!! Come out of there at once!" It was the voice of the Fire Marshall. "Detective! The doors will be closing in thirty seconds. We cannot wait for you! Come out now!!"

Manny tried to shout something in reply, but was overcome with a fit of coughing. Inching forward step by step, he propelled himself towards the sound of the Fire Marshall's voice. Somehow, he managed to bump into the door.

Willing hands reached for him, dragging him out of the way as the huge double fire doors slammed shut, bolts falling into place. Carefully sliding the woman to the floor, Manny stood up with the child still held in the crook of his arm and the infant motionless inside his shirt. He turned to the Fire Marshall, opening his mouth to speak – and collapsed to the floor, unconscious. His last frantic thought as his knees buckled beneath him was to fall sideways, sparing the children from being crushed by his weight.

# Chapter 7.

**A** **LIGHT WAS** shining in his eyes, first one and then the other. Manny blinked, turning his head away. The room slowly swung into focus. He was at the infirmary, with a doctor standing next to his bed.

"Hello, Detective," said the doctor. "Do you know where you are?"

"At the infirmary," he replied. "Am I injured?"

"Nothing broken, no serious burns, but there was some significant smoke inhalation. Let me see you take a deep breath, Manny," she replied.

Manny complied, followed by a prolonged fit of coughing. The doctor nodded.

"That's to be expected, for the next few days. I want you to take it easy, stay calm and rest quietly at home for a few days. Other than that, I think you are good to go. Try to speak slowly and not strain your voice for a day or two. Any questions?"

"No, no questions," Manny replied, relieved. He could hear the low murmur of his fellow police officers in the hallway, but oddly, none of his family was there.

The Chief of Police knocked once and then walked in. "Manny, how do you feel?" he said. "You gave us quite a scare."

"I guess I'm OK," he said, trying not to cough. "I'm just lucky that I found my way back to the door. It was pitch black in there, I couldn't see my hand stretched out in front of me."

"We're glad you made it back, Lieutenant," said the Chief. "We need more men like you, not fewer."

"Lieutenant? You mean Detective, right?" Manny reminded him. The Chief must be trying to test his mental fitness after being unconscious.

"No, I mean Lieutenant. That is, of course, unless you don't want the promotion," he added, his eyes twinkling.

~ ~ ~ ~ ~ ~

Worn out from the events of the day, Manny arrived home exhausted. A bath and some clean clothes would work wonders, he thought. He opened the door and walked in.

"Manny! You're home! Are you OK?" Julio reached out and grasped Manny's shoulder as if to reassure himself that he really was home. "We didn't know you'd been released."

"Not too bad. A little hard to breathe," Manny replied. "I'm supposed to talk softly. Not strain my voice."

"Sounds pretty bad," said Julio, turning to look at Anna, who was standing silently next to him.

"I'm lucky. Nothing broken. Only minor burns," Manny replied. "You should have seen it, Julio! The smoke was so black. I couldn't see anything. Where's Naz?" Manny added, glancing towards the staircase.

No one moved.

Manny, a trained detective, took in Julio's tense, white face and Anna's puffy red eyes, the way she was twisting her handkerchief between her hands, the way she could not quite look at him. Suddenly his knees felt weak. He sank onto the velvet chair in the foyer.

"Where's Naz?" he repeated.

Julio took a little step forward. "It's like this, Manny," he began. Anna grimaced, her mouth contorting as she struggled not to cry. Julio stretched out his hand to steady her.

"This morning, Naz went to see the midwife, to ask her if she would come and live here until the twins are born," Julio said. *He sounds rehearsed,* thought Manny distractedly, his heart thudding like a hummingbird inside his chest.

"She left right after you went to work. She hasn't come back. We can't reach her on her padlet," Julio said. Anna moved closer to Julio, leaning against him, drawing strength from her husband.

"What about Mrs. Braun? Did she see Naz this morning? Did Naz leave before the fire broke out?" Manny asked urgently.

"She's dead," Julio said flatly. "She's among the list of names published as deceased. We keep checking the list for Naz."

"I was right there!" gasped Manny, his voice hoarse. "I rescued a woman and her two children! There were people we couldn't get to. I heard them screaming! But I couldn't carry anyone else. By the time I got them to the door, it was too late to go back."

Manny recalled the disorienting darkness, the heat radiating up from the ground, the putrid gritty black smoke filling up his lungs with each breath, the roar of the fire, the weight of the woman on his back making it all but impossible to move.

"Maybe she was there!" he cried. "Maybe that was her, screaming for help! I should have gone back!!" Manny rose to his feet, his face a mask of anguish. Appalled, the three of them stood in silence.

"Manny, you don't know if that was her," said Julio. "Maybe it wasn't Naz at all. Surely, you'd have recognized the sound of your own wife's voice."

Manny paused, remembering. Had it been her, his beloved wife, in the distance screaming for her life, for the lives of her unborn babies, while Manny was saving a total stranger? It was impossible to tell. There had been so much noise, so much confusion in the darkness. Maybe she wasn't there, maybe she had been rescued by someone else, and was even now lying in a bed in the infirmary. He turned to Anna.

"Maybe she's been rescued by now," he suggested hopefully. "Let's go into the kitchen. We can turn on the news in there."

"It's already on," replied Anna. "We've been watching the list of survivors ever since we heard."

The evening news was being projected from Julio's padlet onto the wall in the kitchen. A database was scrolling, showing the names, addresses and status of every citizen who lived in the affected neighborhood, as well as any visitors to the area, updated continuously as survivors were logged in, or as bodies were scanned for their MedID chips.

Later, as abandoned padlets were collected from the scene, they would be scanned for their "blackbox" readouts, information taken from the indestructible fire-and-waterproof chip inserted into every padlet which would continue emitting an emergency signal until retrieved. Within twenty-four hours, every survivor and casualty would be accounted for.

"There," said Anna in a shaky voice, "look, that's the midwife. You can see, she's dead."

The three sat in horrified disbelief, watching the list scroll on and on. Then suddenly, Anna said, "There! Look! There she is. Naztazya Stewart. Deceased."

Manny saw their shocked white faces, and knew that he must look the same to them. He felt stunned, unable to think. Naztazya, his wife, his childhood love, his gentle kind loving smart beautiful wife! And their babies, the twins soon to be born, now never to be born, all three of them gone in one day. How could that be?

Anna covered her face with her hands and began to wail, the timeless sound of unbearable grief. He looked at Julio, who was looking back at him, wide-eyed, unblinking. Anna's padlet began to beep. A heartbeat later, Julio's and Manny's padlets began to beep.

*It will be our parents,* Manny thought, *they will want to come over.* He picked up his padlet and opened it. "Lucinda," he said, and started to cry.

~ ~ ~ ~ ~ ~

The morning after the fire, the doorbell rang. Manny, still wearing the clothes he had worn the day before, rose to answer the door. Anna, pale and exhausted, stood next to him as he opened the tall double oak doors.

"Dave!" he exclaimed. His friend David Wu was standing at the front steps with another detective from his unit, Naomi Chandler. They were in full dark blue dress uniform, white gloved hands, hats tucked carefully beneath their arms. Together, Dave and Naomi both formally saluted Manny, who stood stone-faced, trying desperately not to break down in front of his colleagues.

"Detective Stewart," began Dave, his voice trembling, "as the next of kin." He stopped, swallowing hard. He had volunteered along with Naomi to perform this formal in-person notification, a courtesy extended only within the police community.

Dave continued, with tears in his eyes. "We regret to inform you of the death of your wife Naztazya Stewart and your unborn babies, in yesterday's fire. There are no personal effects to return to you at this time."

Anna slid soundlessly to the floor in a dead faint.

~ ~ ~ ~ ~ ~

Naztazya was cremated on the morning of the third day after the fire, along with the rest of the victims. Manny, who had been notified of the day and time, sat on the floor in her closet, blinded by tears, his arms wrapped around her scarves and dresses, surrounded by the scent of her perfume.

# *Chapter 8.*

THE FOLLOWING MORNING, the family was seated in the memorial chapel, waiting for the service to begin. Manny, stupefied by grief and sleeplessness, sat motionless in his chair in the front row, staring blankly at nothing. Julio and Anna were next to him, with the children. On either side were Julio's parents and Anna and Naztazya's parents.

Behind them were seated Saratina, Julio's older sister, and her husband Yusef. Luis and Yusef did not get along. A man of strong opinions about politics and the role of women, Yusef kept Saratina close to home, away from her friends and family.

Also in the second row was Amanda Mayts, widow of Dr. James Mayts, who had died of a heart attack the previous year. James was Manny's biological father. When he was single, James had had an affair with a married woman, Lila Rose Stewart. Despite being pregnant with his child, Lila Rose had chosen to remain with her husband, Patrick Stewart, who under the law was legally the father of his wife's child.

Manny learned about his paternity from Patrick when he was a teenager. He rarely saw Amanda; she had not been pleased to learn after so many years that her husband had a teenage son from a previous relationship. Manny was surprised and touched to see her at the memorial service.

Zach fidgeted and squirmed in his chair, standing up and twisting around to survey the back of the room. Lucinda reached over and took his hand.

"Zachie, be a good boy and hold still," she said.

"But Abuela," Zach said urgently, pulling his hand free, "I don't see her! Where is she?"

Something in his son's voice roused Manny from his melancholy. He said, "Where is who, Bud?"

"Mommy!" said Zach, his voice suddenly too loud as the room hushed to silence. "Where's Mommy?" he demanded, shrill and insistent.

"Zach," Manny said heavily, "Mommy isn't here. She died in the fire. Now, please. Sit down and behave."

"But when will she be finished being dead?" Zach asked angrily, stamping his foot. "I want Mommy!"

Lucinda grasped Zach's arm and tried to draw him closer to her, but he pulled away, his little face red with anger.

"You said we're going to say goodbye to Mommy!" he shouted at Manny. "She's not even here!"

Lucinda picked up her grandson and fled from the room.

~ ~ ~ ~ ~ ~

After the memorial service, the house filled quickly with mourners, well-wishers coming to pay their respects. Most came with good intentions, but some were merely curious to see the inside of one of the largest homes in the Colony.

Manny, seated on the sofa in the living room, looked around. "Where's Zach?" he asked Anna.

"Upstairs in his room," she replied. "He's calmed down now. You should talk to him, Manny."

Manny sighed; he struggled up from the sofa and went up the stairs.

Zach's bedroom was down the hall from the master bedroom. Lucinda and Zach were together on his bed; Lucinda was reading to him from her padlet.

Zach was nearly asleep, glassy eyes almost shut, his head resting on his grandmother's knee, her hand gently smoothing his hair, over and over. She looked up, exchanging a glance with Manny, who nodded gratefully and turned away, closing the door behind him.

Downstairs, the caterer opened the front door to let in another group of visitors. Manny could hear the voice of his boss booming from downstairs. It was an honor to have a formal condolence visit from the Chief of Police. Pulling himself together, he walked down the staircase.

Manny respectfully touched his right hand to his left shoulder and bowed as he said, "Health and prosperity to you,

Sir," in the correct formal gesture of greeting from a subordinate to his employer. "Here, let's go into the study."

Chief O'Reilly followed him into the study, where he had met so many times with Patrick over the years, closing the door behind him.

"How are you, Lieutenant?" he asked. "Is there anything I can do for you or your family?"

*Can you bring back my wife?* thought Manny bitterly. "No, thank you, Sir, we have everything under control," he replied respectfully. "We're managing just fine." *Except that my son has no mother.*

"You take all the time off you want, Manny. Whatever you need, just let me know," said the Chief.

Despite the polite words, Manny knew that the Chief had little patience with family life. Just as it had been with Manny's father, Chief O'Reilly's job was his life. He demanded the same commitment from his employees.

"Thank you," he replied. "One week off should be enough to get things in order." *Even six weeks won't be enough,* Manny thought.

The Chief nodded. "I spoke to the woman whose life you saved. She wants me to tell you that she's very grateful."

"Thank you, Sir," said Manny automatically, frowning. He had nearly forgotten about the woman and her children. "And the baby?" he asked. "Did the baby make it?"

"No, it was dead," replied the Chief offhandedly. "It was probably dead when you found it." He nodded sagely towards Manny. "You saved two lives that day, Lieutenant. You should be proud."

*Yes, but I should have saved my wife and children*, thought Manny.

The Chief looked closely at Manny. "I know you're hurting, son, but your father would have been proud of you that day. You gave it your all."

Manny winced at the mention of his father, a man who had ruled the department unforgivingly with an iron fist and who had aggressively abused him throughout most of his childhood.

Patrick Stewart had never been proud of him. "Thank you," he replied.

"When you get back, we can talk about scheduling a ceremony for the announcement of your promotion," said the Chief.

"I don't want a ceremony," responded Manny.

"Always the modest one," chuckled the Chief. "I'll see you soon, Lieutenant," he said. "Don't get up, I'll see myself out."

# Chapter 9.

LUCINDA KNOCKED ON Manny's bedroom door once, twice, with no response. Cautiously, she pushed the bedroom door open.

Manny was sprawled on the velvet lounge chair, padlet open in his hand, ear-kernels in, whispering to himself. Dressed in yesterday's clothes, he was disheveled, bleary-eyed and in need of a bath. Manny was so riveted by the images projected against all four walls that he did not notice Lucinda.

A new 4-D app had been developed by the Meyers-Jouan Institute to replay family videos, making it possible to project them into the room on all four walls so that it appeared that the viewer was part of the video. The app had been taken up quickly by the police department for its potential in recreating crime scenes.

In the days following Naztazya's death, Manny had begun altering one of his family videos. Taking each of Naztazya's words spoken in the video, he carefully separated each word so he could string them together to make new sentences such as, "What do you think is best?" and "How was your day, Manny?"

"So this is what you've been doing," Lucinda said softly. "We've been worried about you, up here by yourself for hours and hours."

"I'm fine," he said irritably, glancing longingly at the image of Naztazya frozen on the wall in front of him. "I just want to be left alone, thanks."

"Manny," she said gently, "this isn't helping. Watching videos of Naz over and over again, imagining that you are talking with her - this isn't healthy. It won't help you move on."

"I don't want to move on," he said flatly, his eyes glassy-red, heavy-lidded.

"You have a son, and he needs you," Lucinda reminded him. "Please, turn off your video and come downstairs with me. Zach is struggling, too, and he needs his father."

"He has plenty of people to look after him," Manny said with a shrug, his eyes straying to Naztazya's image frozen on the wall.

"Manny!" Lucinda said, less gently this time. "Zach is your responsibility. He has lost his mother. He needs to see that he still has a father who cares about him. Now, please. Come downstairs with me."

"OK, OK," Manny replied, annoyed. "I'll spend some time with him soon, I promise." Still holding his padlet, he pointedly looked away from her and clicked "play."

Lucinda moved closer to Manny, taking the padlet out of his hand and folding it shut with a snap. The images disappeared.

"Manny. You need to talk about Naz, about her death. It's no good staying up here all alone, bottling things up inside like this." Manny was noticeably thinner, with dark circles beneath his eyes. "It's Saturday morning. How are you going to go back to work on Monday, feeling like this?"

It wasn't going to be easy, Manny could already see that. "Lucinda, young people shouldn't die," he said, as if his careful reasoning could change things. "There is no sense to it. It's not logical." He tried hard to keep his voice steady, but then gave up, anguish and grief overflowing. "She was only 25! It's so unfair! The babies ... they never even had a chance. How could they all be dead?" His hands twisted together. "Why did she have to die?"

Lucinda sat down on the edge of the bed, facing Manny. "Nobody knows why these things happen," she replied simply, "if there's some reason for it, or no reason at all."

"What was she thinking about in those last minutes? Did she know that she was going to die? Did her hair catch on fire? Did she try to put it out with her hands, but -"

"Manny, stop it!" Lucinda exclaimed. "You don't know how she died. Maybe she fainted, or maybe she breathed in smoke and died before the fire reached her."

"Maybe," said Manny, unconvinced. He slumped forward as if carrying a heavy weight. "I can't sleep. I see it over and over again in my head, I hear the screams. If only I had gone back inside!"

"But you didn't. If you had, you might be dead, too," Lucinda pointed out. "At least Zach has one parent left to care for him. Just be grateful for that."

Manny looked down at the floor, lost in his own private hell. Finally, he said in a half-whisper, as if he was almost afraid to hear his own words, "Lucinda, I don't really know how to raise a child. Naz did all of that."

"Nobody knows how to be a parent until they have children of their own," Lucinda said gently. "It takes patience, and practice. You don't have to be perfect, just consistent and kind. But first, you have to show up."

Manny managed a tentative nod. "OK. I think I can handle that much," he replied. "I'm just not sure about the rest of it."

"Show him that you care about him, take an interest in how he is doing. It doesn't need to be a long, complicated conversation," suggested Lucinda.

"Naz was so good with him," Manny explained. "I thought I'd spend more time with him as he got older." Even to his ears, it sounded more like an excuse than an explanation. "I promised Naz on the day Zach was born that I'd be a better father to him than my father was to me. I just never expected … this."

"Why not come downstairs and have something to eat? Zach is in the kitchen eating lunch," Lucinda replied. "It's time to start returning to our normal routines."

Manny nodded. She was right, he had responsibilities. He couldn't hide from them forever.

"Thank you, Manny," said Lucinda. "And please, be careful that Zach doesn't see or hear you watching your video. He wouldn't understand, and it would be very upsetting to him."

"You're right, of course," said Manny. "I'll be careful."

Lucinda nodded, resting her hand on his shoulder for a moment before leaving the room.

Manny waited until she had closed the door behind her. Then he opened his padlet and turned on the app. Carefully, he fast-forwarded to the part where Naztazya, walking in front of him, turned and said over her shoulder, "What do you think is best?"

Clicking "pause," Manny whispered, "I have to go spend some time with Zach, Naz, but I'll be back later. Wait for me here." He closed the padlet, placing it carefully on the charging panel on the wall behind his bed, and went downstairs.

~ ~ ~ ~ ~ ~

"Hey, Bud, how are you?" asked Manny, self-consciously tousling Zach's hair as he took his seat at the kitchen table. Zach looked up, but did not say anything. Manny glanced over at Lucinda, who nodded encouragingly to him as she sat down.

"Manny," said Julio, "we were hoping you'd come downstairs. You doing OK, bro?"

"Yeah, I'm OK," said Manny, wishing suddenly that he'd showered and changed his clothes before coming downstairs, or at least combed his hair. "How about you? And Anna, how are you?" he asked, realizing that five days had gone by and he had not asked Anna how she was doing after her sister's sudden death. They had been very close all of their lives, but especially since their marriages, living together in the same house, raising their children together.

Anna's eyes were puffy, but her pale face was composed as she said, "I'm fine, Manny. I'm sad, we are all of us feeling sad, but I'm OK." She placed an arm protectively around Julie's shoulders as if to remind Manny that they should filter their conversations when the children were present.

Julio was busy helping himself to another portion of French toast. "Why do they call it 'French' toast?" asked Julie, addressing no one in particular. At seven years old, Julianna was smart as a whip, and curious about everything.

"It was originally created in France," answered Manny, glad to have a neutral subject to discuss.

"Is there still a 'France?'" she asked, chewing thoughtfully, resting her gaze on her uncle. "I mean, are there people there?"

56

"Nobody knows," he answered. "Maybe." There was something unnervingly un-childlike about his niece's gaze, he decided, looking away. She seemed to be taking in his disheveled clothes and three-days-growth of beard, judging him, thinking he looked sloppy and undisciplined. Or maybe that was only what he was thinking about himself. Manny shifted uncomfortably in his chair, his eyes straying longingly towards the staircase leading to his bedroom.

Anna delicately raised one eyebrow, glancing meaningfully at her daughter. Julie ceased asking questions.

Manny took a few more bites of his French toast, his first real meal in days. He listened half-heartedly to the conversation swirling around the table, lost in his own thoughts. Lucinda was wearing a bathrobe and pajamas, he noted with surprise, not street clothes. She must be staying here at the house. How long had she been here? And how had he not noticed?

He stood up abruptly. "I'm going upstairs to shower," he announced.

"Maybe later you and Zach might want to go for a walk," suggested Lucinda. Zach, wide-eyed, looked from his grandmother to his father and back again.

"Maybe," agreed Manny vaguely, pushing his chair away from the table. "We'll see."

Manny showered, shaved and got dressed. These simple acts were comfortingly familiar; he was beginning to feel a bit more like himself. He decided that maybe it was time to look through some of the work which had been piling up all week. He opened up his bedroom door to go downstairs to the study, and there was Zach, sitting at the top of the stairs.

"Hey, Buddy, are you waiting for me?" he asked. Reluctantly, his fragile momentum checked, he sat down next to his son.

"Uh-huh," replied Zach, squirming uncomfortably. This new, suddenly attentive father was strange and unfamiliar.

Manny tried again, carefully modulating his voice to sound friendly and patient. "Why are you sitting here at the top of the stairs?"

"Abuela said to wait for you," he replied. "She said you might want to go for a walk."

"Would you like that?" asked Manny, hoping he would say no.

Zach looked down at his shoes, saying nothing.

Manny searched for a suggestion for some other activity, something they could do indoors that would not take too long. What did his son like to do?

"How about a story, Bud? Do you want me to read to you?" he asked.

"No, that's for bedtime," replied Zach.

"I know," said Manny, "let me show you how I used to get downstairs in a hurry, when I was a little boy."

Intrigued, Zach watched as Manny flung one leg over the banister. "Here, hop on and I'll hold you," he said.

It had been many years since Manny had slid down the wide, polished oak banister of this grand vintage staircase. Most of the houses in the Colony had metal spiral staircases with triangular shaped steps, designed to allow vertical movement within a house without taking up too much space, but the Stewart mansion had no such limitations. When Manny was a child, he often was left home alone. The railing had been both playground and playmate, too tantalizing to resist.

Manny held out his hand, Zach climbed up, and the two of them slid, very cautiously, down to the bottom of the staircase.

"Did you like that?" Manny asked, glad to see that his son was smiling. "Do you want to go again?"

"Yeah, let's go again," said Zach.

The two of them walked back up to the top of the stairs and then climbed onto the banister again.

"Faster this time?" asked Manny.

"Faster," agreed Zach. Off they went, sliding at a good pace.

When they reached the bottom, Zach was laughing. "I wanna go again!" he cried.

"Ok!" replied Manny, and the two of them moved back up to the top of the stairs. They climbed onto the banister, Manny put his arms around his son, and they shoved off. The two of them careened downwards, moving way too fast into the curve at the bottom of the stairs, clumsy and out of control. Manny lost his balance and slipped too far to one side, his legs tangling up between the vertical posts of the railing. Zach screamed as the two of them landed in a heap at the bottom of the stairs.

"Zach! Manny!" cried Anna, running over to them, followed by Julio and Lucinda. Zach stood up, shaken up but unhurt, moving closer to Anna, reaching for her hand.

"Manny, are you OK?" Anna asked.

He groaned, not moving. "I think so," he replied, lying flat on his back. Images of an incident from his childhood flooded his mind.

Eleven years earlier, he and his father had had another one of their fights; Patrick had grabbed Manny's arm, twisting it savagely up behind his back until it dislocated. Manny had staggered backwards, eyes closed, and had fallen down the stairs, landing right where he and Zach had just landed.

Julio and Lucinda looked down at him. He could tell by their faces that they were also remembering the "accident." It was Julio who had found him, lying unconscious at the bottom of the stairs while his father was in the kitchen, passed out drunk in the middle of the morning. It was Julio who had taken him to the infirmary. Later, instead of going home, Manny had gone to live with Julio and his family.

Julio extended his hand, pulling Manny up. Manny grimaced. "It's nothing," he said, "I just hurt my back a little." He stood very still.

"What on earth were you thinking?" demanded Lucinda.

"I was spending time with my son," retorted Manny defensively, "like we talked about."

"I thought you two could go for a walk, maybe to the park or somewhere," replied Lucinda, "not risk breaking your necks. Thank goodness Zach was not hurt, too."

Manny frowned as he limped past her, on his way to the study. "He's fine," he said irritably. "It was just a little excitement, that's all."

# Chapter 10.

**M**ANNY RETURNED TO the precinct house on Monday morning. Everyone came forward one by one to greet him, offering their condolences and congratulating him on his promotion.

As Lieutenant, Manny had an actual office, rather than a detective's cubicle. He walked in and closed the door, sitting down behind the glossy wooden desk, relishing the feeling of being alone for a moment. It was good to be back at work, back in an environment where he knew exactly what was expected of him, where he had some control over things.

Manny's new secretary, Agnes Delgado, tapped discreetly and then opened the door. "Lieutenant?" she said. "Unit meeting in ten minutes?"

Agnes was in her early 30's, an experienced Lieutenant's secretary who had been with the unit for a decade. She was smart, dependable and efficient. She was not a beautiful woman, although she had a lovely hourglass figure. Her raven black hair was worn in the fashionable "broomstick" style, pulled into a ponytail on top of the head and then wound very tightly around and around, forming a tall and narrow "broomstick" shape. Lately, women seemed to be competing with each other to see who could have the tallest "broomstick."

"Sure," he said. "No time like the present. And how about a cup of tea, too?" She nodded, closing the door behind her.

The morning flew by. Several detectives from his unit were getting ready to bring in a group suspected of running a child pornography ring. They had been surveilling them for days. Manny was on his way out the door along with the rest of the unit, when Raimone, the Chief's liaison officer, stopped him at the stairs.

"Lieutenant," he said, without bothering to introduce himself. "Your presence is needed here in the office. Accessible to the Chief. Not running around outside, not unless there is an urgent need. Got it?" He smiled impudently at Manny, pushing a large stack of folders into Manny's chest, forcing him to take a step backwards.

"The Boss wants a single spreadsheet containing all of these by the end of the day tomorrow, OK?" Raimone added, then turned and walked away, not waiting for a response.

Manny glared after Raimone as he retreated, struggling to contain his resentment. Then he glanced through the folders, his heart sinking. It was going to take hours to put together the spreadsheet. But the raid! He'd have to keep an eye on it remotely.

Using his padlet, he projected the unit's CCvideo feed onto the wall opposite the desk. The unit was just arriving, getting into position. He watched enviously in real time as his people got ready.

Manny's padlet beeped. He was surprised to see that there was a text from Anna.

Anna: *Zach has a sore throat and fever. What time will you be home?*
Manny: *I don't know, maybe late.*
Anna: *What would you like me to do?*

Manny stared at the screen in disbelief. Did she not realize he was at work? His unit was in the midst of a raid, for goodness sake.

Manny: *Do whatever you think is best, Anna.*
Anna: *Manny, what do you think is best? You're his father.*

Manny groaned inwardly. There were no miracle drugs, no antibiotics anymore; even a sore throat could be fatal. But he had no idea how to nurse a sick child. Naztazya had been a magician with her herbal remedies and teas. He was quite sure that Anna, too, knew how to nurse a sick child. He suspected that she was trying to make a point about parental responsibility.

He stared at the padlet, mulling over what to say. He could not afford to alienate her, not when he so obviously needed her help. She and Naztazya had handled all of the childcare issues, each caring for both children. But now Naz was gone.

A loud knock at the door startled him. "Yes?" he called, as the door swung open.

Chief O'Reilly strode in.

"Hello, Lieutenant," he said. "Just thought I'd stop by and see how things are going." He sat down in the chair next to Manny's desk. "How's the raid?" he asked, glancing at the CCvideo images projected on the wall.

"Fine so far," responded Manny, "nothing much to report yet." He carefully avoided glancing at the padlet lying on his desk, which was pulsing cobalt blue around its edges, a reminder that he needed to respond to a text.

"That's OK, I can wait," the Chief responded. "Care for a little nip?" He pulled a silver pocket flask from inside his jacket and offered it to Manny.

"No, thank you," he replied.

"Really?" asked the Chief in disbelief. "Your Dad, now there was a man who liked his bourbon. You do drink, don't you, Lieutenant?"

"Occasionally, sure," replied Manny, who seldom drank and never bourbon. His father had been a hard-core alcoholic, often blacking out, downing a fifth of bourbon nearly every day towards the end of his life. As a teenager, Manny had often dragged his incoherent father up the stairs, putting him to bed. The smell of bourbon sickened him.

"Well then here!" insisted the Chief heartily, pushing the flask towards Manny. "A little nip can't hurt."

Manny took a polite sip. Generally, there was a strong culture of drinking in the department. The stress of the job, the long hours ... Manny had grown up around police, he knew what they were like. He had known from the beginning that he would need to fit in, not appear judgmental or different, despite his aversion to alcohol.

On the wall opposite the desk, Manny could see the images of the detectives breaking down the door of the building where the bust was happening in real time. On the desk, his padlet now was pulsing a bright shade of scarlet, a sign that there was an urgent ongoing text exchange requiring his immediate response. He took another sip, bigger this time, and coughed.

"Hah!" exclaimed the Chief. "That needs practice."

The Chief turned, looking at the images on the wall. "Looks like they're in," he said. "Keep me posted." He got up to leave, stopping by the door. "Better answer that text, Lieutenant." Then he was gone.

Manny's padlet glowed accusingly. Basil tea with ... what was it Naz had put in it? Turmeric? Ginseng? Ginger.

Manny: *Tea with basil and ginger. If the fever gets worse, call the doctor.*
Anna: *Got it. Do you want to talk to Zach?*
Manny: *I can't right now, Anna, I'm working! Tell him I'll talk to him later.*

Manny closed up the padlet, not waiting to see if she replied.

He worked for several hours, studying the cases in the folders, designing a spreadsheet, entering the relevant information. He stopped briefly to order a sandwich for dinner, eating it at his desk. Manny was not alone in the office; the staff had gone home, but half of the detectives were still working away at their desks.

*I should call home and talk to Zach,* he thought guiltily. But there was so much work to do.

It was nearly 9:00 pm when he finally arrived home, carrying a large bouquet of flowers for Anna. He found her and Julio together in the library.

"These are for me?" she asked, surprised.

"Yeah. I just wanted to thank you for taking care of Zach today," Manny said. "I appreciate it. I know you are busy, too."

Anna regarded him for a moment, weighing his apology against the disruption to her day. "OK," she said dubiously. "We need to talk, though."

"First, how's Zach?" Manny asked.

"He's asleep now. He looked better after dinner, his fever seemed less," Anna said. "I don't think it's anything serious."

Manny started towards the stairs. "I'll go up and say goodnight to him."

Anna started to protest, but Julio stopped her, saying softly, "Let him go. Zach will go back to sleep."

~ ~ ~ ~ ~ ~

"Hey, Buddy – Auntie Anna says you're not feeling so good," he whispered softly, placing a hand on his sleeping son's warm, sweaty forehead. Zach's eyes fluttered open.

"Tell me, how do you feel?" asked Manny.

"I'm sick," he answered. "Auntie Anna made me tea."

"That's good, tea is good for you," replied Manny. "You go back to sleep now, and I'll see you tomorrow." He leaned over and kissed the top of his son's head, as he had seen Naz do every night at bedtime.

"Mommy does that," he said sleepily, eyes closing.

Manny stood for several moments, watching his little boy. He looked so much like Naztazya, but also like Manny's mother, Lila Rose. *He'll grow up strong and happy,* he vowed silently. *I promise you, Naz.*

Downstairs, Anna and Julio were waiting for him. "Let's go into the study," Julio suggested.

"Today was not ideal, not for any of us," Manny said. "Anna, I know that with your job, you need to be able to concentrate during the day. I'm sorry you had to take care of Zach."

"I got almost nothing done today!" Anna exclaimed. "It was very disruptive. If there's an emergency, then of course, you know you can count on me. But as far as day-to-day childcare, we're going to have to figure something out. I didn't plan on having a child at home at this stage."

65

Julio said, "Anna and I put off having another child because of Anna's promotion. We planned it this way. She needs quiet during the day, so she can concentrate." Anna had been promoted recently to supervisor of a unit of IT experts. She worked primarily from her home office.

"I didn't know that," Manny said. "I've got some ideas about childcare for us, now that ... now that things are different."

"OK, we're listening," said Julio, settling back into his dark brown leather club chair.

"First, we could hire a full-time nanny for the children. Or two nannies, one for days and one for nights," Manny suggested.

"No," said Anna flatly. "I've always said that I want to raise my own children. I don't want strangers living in my house."

Manny nodded; he really hadn't expected her to agree. "I understand that," he said. "But I can't be here to take care of Zach during the day. If I'm in the middle of supervising a raid, like today, then I can't be interrupted."

"You try doing your job with a sick, cranky child standing next to your desk!" retorted Anna, crossing her arms across her chest. "My job is no less demanding than yours, Manny. And he's your son. Not ours."

Julio placed a hand on her arm. "Anna, hear him out," he said quietly.

"What I meant was that all three of us have high-powered jobs that require our full attention," said Manny smoothly. "Not that your job is less important than mine." Mollified, Anna sat back in her armchair.

"If you won't agree to having full-time help here during the day, then we could use a daytime baby-sitter more often," Manny suggested. "It might be a solution until Zach starts school in September." Anna and Julio exchanged glances.

"Or, how about this," Manny continued. "We could rely more often on Lucinda and Luis. The children love them, and I know they enjoy being with their grandchildren."

66

"But it's hard for them to go back and forth from here to 14th Street," Julio pointed out. "They wouldn't be able to get here quickly enough if something sudden came up."

"You're right," said Manny, "that's a problem. What would you think of having them live across the street from us? Just think of how convenient that could be! They'd be right there, if we need them."

Julio looked at Anna, trying to gauge his wife's reaction. "That might work," he said tentatively. "But would they want to move? They've lived in that old house forever."

"They don't have to give up the old house," said Manny. "I could gift them one of the new townhouses, and they can keep the house at 14th Street as long as they want it. They could go back and forth whenever they want."

Manny, who had inherited his father's considerable wealth, owned a large portion of the real estate in the Colony. He had recently purchased a row of townhouses which were being renovated from the ground up, right down the street from the Stewart mansion.

"They'd probably love more time with their grandchildren," said Julio. "They could come over for dinner or to babysit, but still have their privacy."

"You know, that might be our best solution," said Anna thoughtfully. "Let's see what they say."

"I'll hologram them and invite them over for dinner. We can all go together to show them the townhouse," suggested Manny. "It will be a surprise."

As they were leaving the study, Julio took Manny aside and said in a low voice, "Is this OK with you? Or did you really want a full-time nanny to live with us?"

Manny laughed softly. "Don't worry about me, bro," he said. "I got what I wanted."

~ ~ ~ ~ ~ ~

"Manny, what is this?" asked Lucinda curiously, her hand on Zach's shoulder. They were standing in the small square foyer of one of the new townhouses. There was a round stained glass window over the front door, letting in the last of the afternoon light; the floor of the foyer was highly polished white marble, and the ceiling was an astonishing thirteen feet high, two full stories.

"There's a maid's room on the ground floor near the downstairs powder room, and there are two full bedrooms upstairs," said Manny. "The master bedroom has its own bathroom, and there is another one in the hall next to the smaller bedroom." Such luxury was unusual in the Colony.

"It looks good, Manny, very good," said Luis approvingly. "You did a fine job on the floor plan."

"Thank you," said Manny. "I'm glad you like it. Do you think you'd like to live here?"

"What?" asked Lucinda. "Did you say 'live here?'"

Julio put his arm around his mother's shoulders. "We thought you might like to be closer to your grandchildren," he said, kissing her cheek.

"Oh, now I see!" said Lucinda. "It's beautiful, but no, thank you. We love our home. Why, we've been there forever, since before you and your sister were born! I don't want to live anywhere else."

"You wouldn't have to," explained Manny. "You can keep the old house just as it is, and spend as much time there as you want. Think of this as your second home."

Luis asked, "And just how much does this second home cost?"

"Nothing. It will be a gift," replied Manny, "along with all of the furnishings. It would be good for all of us to have you nearby. We could really use your help, both of you. Zach has several weeks before he starts school, and Anna can't have him underfoot while she is working."

"Come and see upstairs, Lucinda!" exclaimed Anna. "The master bedroom is beautiful! And the downstairs little room, Luis! It would make a perfect office for you. No more paying bills in the kitchen."

Luis's eyes lit up. He looked longingly down the hall, ready to explore.

68

Lucinda stopped him with a hand on his arm. He looked at her questioningly.

"Manny," she said, turning to face him. "It's a very nice gesture. And we appreciate that. But we can't accept such an extravagant gift from you. We raised our family there, in the old house. It's filled with memories."

Luis kissed the top of her head. "But now," he said softly, "our family is here. They would be right across the street from us." He looked imploringly into his wife's eyes. After a long moment, she nodded.

Luis turned to Manny, saying, "Thank you, son! We are very grateful."

Manny smiled, glad that his idea had been well received. The old home at the 14th Street station probably wouldn't be used much over the next ten years or so, but later, the children might want to live there, once they graduated from high school. Julianna would be on her own in ten years, followed a few years later by Zach.

There was another reason why Manny wanted to have Luis and Lucinda close by; they were getting older. In another ten years, Luis would be 55, ready to retire. Lucinda, a year younger, had retired from her job as a social worker and therapist years ago.

"Excellent!" he said. "The work here will be done by the end of the month; after that, you can move in whenever you are ready."

Lucinda, still holding onto Luis's arm, turned around to get a better view of the kitchen. "Why don't we have another look in here," she said to him.

# Chapter 11.

**M**ORNING, LIEUTENANT," SAID Raimone, coming into his office early one Monday morning without bothering to knock first. "Have a nice weekend?"

"Hello, Raimone," Manny said, coldly acknowledging the presence of Chief O'Reilly's aide. The man was a nuisance, popping in and out of Manny's office unannounced, arrogant and abrupt. Besides, the scent of his cologne, an unpleasant musky smell, lingered in the air long after Raimone was gone.

"Just thought I'd stop by," Raimone said insolently, settling himself into the chair next to Manny's desk, fastidiously adjusting the crease down each leg of his pleated flannel trousers. "You know, I'm going to be leaving the department in a couple of weeks, to be the new Aide to the Commissioner," he confided, as if he and Manny were the best of friends.

"No, I didn't know that," replied Manny, trying not to stare at Raimone's hair, which was parted and slicked back with some kind of shiny goo.

"That's right," Raimone replied, nodding, "and the Chief is looking for my replacement. He likes you, Manny. You keep your nose clean, and you could be the new Aide to the Chief."

"I don't think so," said Manny.

Raimone brushed an invisible speck of dust from his immaculate jacket lapel. "That's how things work, now that you're one of the big boys," he said with a smirk. "Anyone can get promoted at any time. It depends on what position opens up, and who gets to pick the replacement." He stood up to leave.

"You really think the Chief would want me?" asked Manny doubtfully.

"Oh, I know he does," replied Raimone. "He stops by to talk to you more than he does with anyone else."

That much was true. Manny had noticed how often the Chief stopped by, once or twice each day. From Manny's perspective, the visits with the Chief were uncomfortable. He wished his boss would just pass assignments to him and then leave him alone.

What would it be like, to be Chief O'Reilly's aide? Would it involve real police work, or would he be a highly-paid errand boy, getting coffee for the Chief in the morning, laughing at his jokes, being his always-agreeable companion? Manny's heart sank. He was a detective, had wanted to be a detective since high school.

And yet, to turn down a promotion would be career suicide. He could languish in his position as lieutenant for years, passed over for every new opening.

Lost in thought, Manny was surprised by a familiar sound. He glanced down to see that the purple adapter which plugged into his padlet, allowing him access to restricted work files, was on the floor, bouncing vigorously up and down while pinging loudly. This was the third time it had fallen out.

Adapters were carefully guarded. If one fell out, it made progressively louder noises until it was found. The adapter was obviously defective; he'd have to text the IT guys for a replacement.

Manny leaned over in his desk chair to pick up the adapter, but succeeded only in knocking it just out of his reach, where it continued to bounce up and down, now buzzing loudly. He tried again, bent over nearly double in his chair, barely able to touch the adapter with the tips of his fingers. Just a little farther, one more stretch of the arm should do it.

Manny slipped off the chair head first and fell to the floor, landing with a crash beside the desk. The chair fell over next to him.

Agnes, whose desk was just outside of Manny's office, rushed in. "Lieutenant! Are you OK?" she exclaimed. "What happened?"

"Nothing, I'm fine," Manny replied, embarrassed. He pushed himself onto his hands and knees and tried to stand. A shockingly painful sunburst of pain bloomed across his lower back. Manny's face turned ashen, one hand on the desk, for the moment unable to move.

"Close the door!" he said quietly. To her credit, Agnes did not bombard him with questions; she moved quickly to close the door. Manny stood up slowly at the desk, breathing deeply. Color returned to his face.

"Can you walk?" she asked, as she turned the chair right-side up and pushed it into place behind the desk.

Manny took a tentative step. Dull pain slid down the back of his left leg and into his heel, but he was able to take a few steps to his chair and sit down.

"My Dad has a bad back," she said. "He has pain like that, that comes on so sudden."

"What does he do when it happens?" Manny asked, completely baffled by this new and unwelcome turn of events.

"It depends on how bad it is. Here, let me get you something for the pain," she offered, stooping to pick up the adapter, now shrieking loudly, from the floor.

In the Colony, there were only a few remedies for pain. For a headache or mild injury, marijuana edibles were the favorite choice. For worse pain, like a broken leg, there was always alcohol. Wine was legal and widely available. For the fortunate few, there was hard liquor, illegal and expensive, but plentiful on the black market. For terminally ill patients, there were poppies, potent little red flowers which were carefully harvested by highly trained botanists and made into a tincture, to be administered at the end of a person's life.

Manny nodded, breathing deeply, willing the pain to go away, hoping the Chief would not choose this moment to stroll in for a chat. In a few minutes, Agnes returned with a steaming hot cup of tea.

"Here you are," she offered. "Let me know if I can help with anything else."

"Thanks, Agnes," he said, grateful for her help.

Manny took a sip of the tea. It didn't taste too bad. He took another sip, wondering what she had put in it. Not bourbon, he was sure of that. It was something else, something sweet that burned the back of his throat on the way down. Maybe brandy? He tentatively took a larger sip, feeling his lower back ease and relax. Better. Yes. One more swallow, and then he would get back to work.

When Raimone stopped by Manny's office with some papers twenty minutes later, Manny was leaning back in his chair, eyes closed, mouth open, snoring rather loudly. Raimone thought for a moment, and then pulled out his padlet, snapping a few photos, making sure that they were time-stamped. *Never know when something like this could be useful,* he thought, chuckling to himself.

~ ~ ~ ~ ~ ~

Later that morning, Manny was at his desk working when the Chief walked in. Manny could tell immediately from the Chief's demeanor that something was off. As in his childhood years, the hairs on the back of Manny's neck stood up, a sure sign that something was very wrong.

Instead of sitting down, Chief O'Reilly walked right up to Manny's desk, placed his hands palm down on the desk and leaned towards him. "You were asleep at your desk," he accused. "That will not be tolerated, not by you, not by anyone in my house. Is that clear?" he said.

Manny knew better than to try and explain. Now was not the time to offer excuses. "I'm sorry, Sir. It won't happen again."

"You're damned straight, it won't happen again," he said angrily. "I don't care if you have a morning eye-opener at your desk; most of us do. But I do care if you are unfit for duty!"

"Yes, Sir," he replied respectfully. *Unfit for duty??* Manny was stunned.

"Stand up when I am talking to you, Lieutenant!" the Chief thundered. Manny stood up, and then grimaced as pain sliced down the back of his left leg. His hand gripped the edge of the desk as he leaned forward, gingerly shifting his weight to the other foot.

The Chief's eyes narrowed as he watched Manny struggling to stand up straight. "You're injured, Lieutenant?" he snapped.

"Yes, Sir," replied Manny. Standing carefully at attention, his expression impassive, he shifted his gaze past the Chief's head to a spot on the wall opposite, as he had been taught in the Academy.

"Did you perhaps ... have a little nip or two to dull the pain of this ... injury?" asked the Chief, not unkindly.

"Yes, Sir," replied Manny, still standing at attention.

The Chief considered this new bit of information. He liked Manny, had liked him since he was a boy. He had watched him become one of the best detectives in the unit. But Chief O'Reilly would not tolerate sloppiness or unprofessional conduct. Furious, he was ready to suspend Manny for a couple of weeks if he showed any insubordination. But when confronted, his new Lieutenant had not denied it or whined with excuses; he had taken responsibility and apologized.

*He's always been so conscientious,* thought the Chief. *Maybe it was just a one-off. But I need to be sure he gets the message.*

The Chief walked around the side of Manny's desk, deliberately standing too close to him. "I never thought I'd see the day when I'd have to tell Patrick Stewart's son that he'd better learn to hold his liquor," the Chief growled. "If your father had seen you behind your desk, sound asleep!! He'd have been ashamed of you, boy."

Manny turned and looked squarely at his boss, saying evenly, "With respect, Sir. My relationship with my father is over. And I haven't been a boy in quite some time."

The two men glared at each other. Then Manny returned his stony gaze to the spot on the opposite wall. His face reddened, but he continued to stand motionless at attention, one hand gripping the edge of the desk, the other hand carefully relaxed and open. He could feel the Chief's breath against his cheek.

The Chief took his time. He'd made Manny angry, he could see that, but Manny had not allowed himself to be rattled. He hadn't so much as swallowed hard. The Chief knew all about Patrick's drinking and his explosive temper; he suspected that Patrick had been an abusive, even sadistic, father. *Look at him, solid as a rock, even when provoked,* the Chief thought. *He deserves the warning, but maybe I'll leave it at that.*

"Sit down, Manny," said Chief O'Reilly in a friendlier tone, moving back around to the front of the desk and sitting down in the visitor's chair. "Sorry to have to be so hard on you. Sometimes you have to be hard, to be a good leader. Your old man knew that."

Manny sat down carefully behind his desk. Where was this conversation going? *When in doubt,* he cautioned himself, *say nothing.*

"Did you know," said the Chief casually, "that Raimone is leaving, to be the new Aide to the Commissioner? And that there's a rumor going around that I'm looking for a replacement for him?"

"Yes, Sir, I did hear something about that," confirmed Manny cautiously.

"From Raimone, right?" asked the Chief. Manny nodded.

"That little weasel!" Chief O'Reilly exclaimed. "You're the third person he's told that they are about to be promoted!" He chuckled. "I'm not looking for another aide, Manny. I don't really need someone to get my coffee and run my errands. Raimone likes to stir the pot, so to speak, a real provocateur. I'll be glad to get rid of him."

Manny nodded, afraid to say the wrong thing. The Chief seemed lost in thought.

"He's bullet-proof, you know," the Chief said. "Raimone is related to the Commissioner's wife, a third cousin or something. So he can't be fired, not without making the Commissioner's wife unhappy. Raimone's been bounced all around the department, six months here, a year there, never too long with any one unit. He's not a popular man. He told me that he wants to be Commissioner himself, someday."

"Really?" asked Manny, surprised.

Chief O'Reilly chuckled. "You know how it goes – the Commissioner gets to appoint his replacement, and he can choose whomever he thinks will do the best job. Or, in this case, whomever his wife likes best."

"I just wish he wouldn't wear so much cologne," Manny said. "My office reeks after he's been here."

The Chief burst out laughing. Manny dutifully joined in. A knock on the door surprised them both.

"May I come in?" asked the Commissioner, striding into Manny's office. "You weren't in your office, Joe, but I could hear you from the hall. Almost time for lunch."

"Sorry, I lost track of the time," replied the Chief. "Manny, you remember the Commissioner?"

"Yes, Sir, of course," he replied respectfully, carefully standing up.

"You're Pat's boy, right?" the Commissioner asked, looking at him curiously. "I remember you as a little boy, eavesdropping from the top of the stairs while I talked to your Dad."

"Yes, Sir, that was me," replied Manny, inwardly cringing at yet another reference to his father.

The Commissioner nodded. "Work hard, Lieutenant, and you'll go far," he said, as he said to every member of the police force whenever he had the chance.

After they left, Manny sat down gingerly in his desk chair. Agnes walked in, holding a steaming cup of tea. "I thought you could use this," she said. "Drink it slow, make it last all afternoon. That's what my Dad does."

Manny nodded gratefully, taking the cup from her. "I'm curious, Agnes. What did you put in it?" he asked.

"Just a little brandy," she said. "Will there be anything else?"

"No, that's all for now," he replied, taking a sip. Brandy. Well, a cup of tea with a drop of brandy seemed harmless enough.

# Chapter 12.

**M**ANNY WAS AT work at his desk later in the week, when he heard a discreet knock on his office door. Looking up, he saw Dave Wu.

"Dave, come on in," he said warmly.

"Hey, Manny. I wanted to check with you about switching my shift with one of the other detectives next week," he said.

"Sure, that's fine," Manny said. "Pull up a chair! How have you been? How's Jennie?"

Dave sat down across the desk from Manny. "Fine, fine! How's everything going at your house?"

Manny leaned back in his chair. "It's better, thanks. My folks have moved into a townhouse closer to the house, so we have two more people to help us with childcare."

"How's your little guy doing? Zach, right?" asked Dave.

The two were interrupted when the Chief walked in unannounced, pointed to Manny, and said abruptly, "Lieutenant. In my office. Now." He turned and stalked out.

Manny looked at Dave, grimacing, and then followed Chief O'Reilly into his office.

"Let me give you some advice, Lieutenant," the Chief snapped. "Don't fraternize with the detectives in your unit."

"Sir?" asked Manny, not understanding.

"Don't sit and talk with your friend Dave in your office, while the other detectives are at their desks, working," he explained. "It gives the impression of favoritism."

Manny opened his mouth to protest, then closed it. The Chief was right, of course.

"I know, I know. You were partners, back in the day, and you're used to working side by side with him. That's over now," continued the Chief. "These detectives in your unit, they need a leader, not a friend. When you tell them what to do, it's not a conversation. It's an order. That needs to be clear to everyone. Even Dave."

"Yes, Sir," Manny replied.

"That will be all, Lieutenant," the Chief said, picking up some papers on his desk and beginning to read.

Manny went back to his desk. Through the open door to his office, he could see his unit, each detective working at his or her desk. He got up and closed his office door. The Chief was right; he was no longer one of them.

At lunchtime, Manny went out for lunch by himself. Disconsolate, he bought a sandwich and sat on a wooden bench in a nearby park to eat. He ate quickly, as he always did, but then continued to sit on the park bench long after he was finished, lost in thought.

Raised by the former Chief of Police, Manny had listened all through his childhood to his father's tales of police work, story after story about the different ways a criminal could hide his crimes. He had grown up with a well-developed understanding of detective work, and an uncanny ability to spot someone who was being evasive or deceitful. It was like a game to Manny, something he truly enjoyed.

But now, he no longer was involved in the actual detective work. His job as Lieutenant was administrative. He supervised the detectives, guiding them and helping them whenever necessary, but was no longer involved in the day-to-day work of solving the cases.

Manny's afternoon stretched out in front of him, filled with endless spreadsheets. He walked slowly back to the office.

Later that day, there was a unit meeting to discuss the progress on a particular case they had been working on, an abduction of several women. Manny addressed his detectives:

"These women have been missing for a week now. We need to re-canvass the area and make sure that we haven't missed anything. Go back and knock on doors, ask around to see if anybody's been talking. We're fairly sure they're still in the neighborhood, but with each day that passes, we're less likely to find them. Let's get busy, people." Manny paused, then asked, "Any questions? No? Ok, dismissed."

As the detectives gathered their belongings and moved out, Manny saw the Commissioner standing in the hallway directly across from his office door, listening. As Manny looked up at him, the Commissioner turned and walked into the Chief's office, closing the door behind him.

~ ~ ~ ~ ~ ~

"How was work today, Manny?" asked Anna as she passed the baby zebra potatoes to him.

"Today wasn't so great, actually," replied Manny. "I miss going out with the unit to do actual detective work. The Chief's got me sitting at my desk all day, designing fancy spreadsheets for him."

"But it's a promotion, right?" asked Julio, helping himself to another piece of deep fried tofu with Angry Mustard Sauce, speckled with bits of dark purple jungle pepper, a new hybrid pepper that was very hot.

"Yeah," Manny replied glumly, "but I think I liked it better before I got promoted."

"Are you going to stay in this position?" asked Luis. He and Lucinda were with the family for dinner most nights now, since they had moved into their new townhouse.

"There's no set career path above this," said Manny. "I could be promoted to any number of higher positions, theoretically, but first there would have to be an opening somewhere."

"Maybe something will open up soon," Lucinda suggested. Manny nodded gratefully.

"Tomorrow's Saturday," Manny said to his son. "How would you like to go to the park in the afternoon? Maybe see the new fireflies exhibit?"

The brightly colored fireflies were a happy accident, a by-product of research on sources for artificial light. This newest generation of fireflies were all the rage with the children, multi-colored tiny lanterns sparking here and there in the twilight.

"OK," said Zach. "Yeah, I like fireflies."

"Good," replied Manny, knowing that Zach had no idea what fireflies were. It would be a fun activity for him. Zach could run around the park and chase the fireflies, which were nearly impossible to catch.

Manny turned to Julio. "You and Julie want to come with us?"

"Sure, that would be nice," Julio agreed. Julie nodded, her mouth full.

"Could you do me a favor?" Manny asked his brother. "Have one of the guys deliver a bottle of brandy to the house? Or maybe two bottles, that would be better."

"What?? You drink brandy now?" Julio asked, surprised. "I didn't know you liked it."

"I don't, really," Manny responded. "But Agnes, my secretary, she's been putting it in my tea at work. It really helps with the pain in my back."

"That's still bothering you, huh?" Julio asked. "I thought that was over, after you fell off the banister and landed on your butt."

"Very funny," responded Manny. "No, I reinjured it at work the other day. I was reaching for something, and I sort of slipped off my chair and landed on the floor. I could barely stand up for most of the day."

"Manny, I had no idea!" exclaimed Anna. "You didn't say anything."

"No, there's nothing you can do, so I didn't mention it," Manny replied. "Agnes filed a report with A-Char, though, so now I'm going to have to see a doctor. I sort of wish she hadn't filed the report."

~ ~ ~ ~ ~ ~

At the office, there was good news. Manny's unit had successfully recovered four of the six missing women for whom they had been searching for several days. Manny congratulated his detectives, who had worked diligently. He set up a meeting for later in the morning, to go over next steps.

"Lieutenant, a word?" said the Chief, beckoning to him from the hallway. Manny went into the Chief's office. "Close the door," he said, then motioned Manny into the chair by his desk.

"Your unit did well, recovering those four women! Congratulations," he said.

"Thank you, Sir," Manny replied.

"I want to offer a word of advice, for the meeting later this morning. It's great that four lives have been saved. But there are two more women still missing. When you address your unit, you need to emphasize that it's not time to celebrate. They will interview the recovered victims, of course. But they must also continue to search, including re-interviewing and re-canvassing. They will be resistant, since they've worked this case hard, and had good results. That's where you come in."

"Yes, Sir," Manny replied.

"It's the job of the unit's leader to motivate the detectives. I want to see some of that ... how shall I put this? Some of that fire in the belly that your old man had. It's time to lean on them a little harder, make them see that this case is not closed."

Manny nodded. "Yes, Sir, I see what you mean."

"Good. That will be all, then." The Chief stood up and walked Manny to the door of his office, opening it for him, an unusual act of respect which was not lost on any of the detectives sitting at their desks outside of the Chief's office. The Chief was giving him a subtle endorsement, right before the meeting.

Manny used the time before the meeting to go over the notes and CCvideo of the raid one more time. He projected the CCvideo onto the wall of his office, studying the footage very carefully.

When the detectives were assembled for the meeting, Manny turned to address them.

"Good job, all of you," he said to them. "Those four women are safe at home now because of your perseverance and skilled detective work. You should be proud of yourselves." They nodded, listening.

"But it's not time to celebrate yet," he continued. "As you know, two women are still unaccounted for, and because of that, this case is not closed. Did any of you circle back after the raid, to make sure that nothing was missed? Anyone?"

For a moment, no one spoke. Then one of the detectives replied, "No, Sir, we didn't see any need to. The raid was successful, so we brought the victims to the infirmary, and the perps back to the station."

Manny nodded. All had been done correctly, according to police procedure.

"But did any of you notice this?" he asked, flipping open his padlet and projecting the CCvideo feed onto the wall. He pointed to a worn area near the wall, faint but visible in the carpet alongside a Vertical, the ubiquitous tall, narrow space-saving wooden dresser found in most bedrooms.

"Why would the carpet be worn there?" Manny asked. "Not in front of the Vertical, but here, alongside it?"

The detectives drew closer to the image, as Manny enlarged it for them.

"There's nothing there, Sir," replied one of the detectives, shaking her head. "We searched the room, the dresser drawers, under the bed, in the closets, and all over downstairs for clues."

The other detectives nodded in agreement. They were busy, they had other urgent cases, and this had been a successful raid, with four of six accounted for. They had come back to complete the paperwork, and were ready to move on to newer cases. Manny knew the drill; he'd been a detective for years.

"Did you look behind the Vertical?" asked Manny. He let that thought marinate for a moment, watching his detectives, waiting.

Finally, one of the men said dubiously, "Do you want us to go back and take another look, Sir?"

"Do *I* want you to go back?" demanded Manny icily, his voice rising. "No, Detective, I want *you* to want to go back!" He looked meaningfully at each of them. "How could you leave without searching every square inch of that room? What if they are still there? They would be starving, but they could still be alive."

The detectives exchanged glances. This new, suddenly more aggressive Lieutenant was a surprise. They eyed him warily.

"To me, the carpet seems worn in a place where you wouldn't expect it to be worn," said Manny. "Maybe there's a hidden space, like a closet, behind this wall. I tell you this now: this search is not over, not by a long shot, not until every square inch of that home has been gone over with a fine-toothed comb!"

He glared at his unit. "Now go back there! I want you to stay in contact with me the entire time," he thundered, "and I want to see you on your hands and knees, pulling up the carpet, turning over the mattress, moving the furniture, searching that house like it's your own mother who's missing! Now get going! You are dismissed!"

As Manny concluded the meeting, he happened to glance up towards the doorway, and once again, there was the Commissioner, leaning against the wall across from the Chief's office. Avoiding making eye contact with Manny, the Commissioner moved smoothly into the Chief's office, closing the door.

*What's that all about?* thought Manny. *They're watching me. But why?*

Manny returned to his office. He sat down behind the desk, but felt too restless to concentrate. He looked down at his hands, surprised to see that they were trembling. He clasped them together, then put them in his lap.

*But it's my job to motivate them,* he argued with himself, wrestling with his thoughts. *I have to be strong, be a leader who gets results, like the Chief said.*

Manny looked down at his hands, now clenched into two fists in his lap. *The truth is,* he thought, *I liked it. I liked raising my voice and seeing them jump. Damn, but it felt good!*

He closed his eyes briefly, remembering his father's clenched fists. Manny had been twelve years old when Patrick had first punched him in the face. Unsatisfied with beating his young son with a belt, he had thrown the belt across the room, turned Manny around and punched him in the mouth, hard.

Agnes knocked and walked in, carrying a steaming cup of tea.

Shaking off his reverie, Manny said gratefully, "You have good timing!"

She nodded. "I thought you might like some, after the meeting. How's the back?"

"It comes and goes, but yeah, it's better," Manny said. "Agnes, how much brandy do you put in the tea?"

"About 4 tablespoons," she replied. "Why?"

"I thought it might be a good idea to have tea at night, before bed. I want to make it at home the same way," Manny explained.

"That's a good idea," she replied. "My Dad does that, when his back pain keeps him awake at night."

After Agnes had gone, Manny took a swallow of the tea. Within a minute, his hands had stopped trembling and he felt settled, and calm. *Amazing stuff,* Manny thought, surprised.

The door to the Chief's office opened. Manny, opening up his padlet so he could look busy, listened carefully as the Chief and the Commissioner came out into the hallway. The Commissioner was returning to his office upstairs.

"Like his ghost, I tell you," the Commissioner was saying, chuckling. "Yeah, he'll do. He's the best of the lot."

"Do you want to tell him yourself?" asked the Chief.

"No, you can tell him. There's no hurry. Come on upstairs with me. I've got a new bottle of Scotch that is really something," the Commissioner said. Their voices faded as the two men entered the stairwell and headed up the stairs.

# Chapter 13.

**G**OT YOUR BACKPACK? Your padlet?" asked Manny, casting a parental eye over Zach's readiness for their trip to the park.

"Julie? Got everything?" he continued. Julie nodded.

"OK, then, let's go!" said Manny. "The fireflies are only out for an hour or so, when it's twilight, so we want to get there when it begins."

"What's twilight?" asked Zach, looking up at Manny.

"Twilight is the time between daytime and nighttime," said Manny. "It doesn't last long." He took his son's hand.

"Where do the fireflies go the rest of the day?" asked Zach.

"I'm not sure. Maybe there will be an exhibit at the park where we can read all about it," he replied.

The park was not far from the Stewart mansion. The new exhibit was filled with families of small children. Each of the children had been given a small butterfly net, and was trying to catch the brightly colored fireflies. Predictably, they were not having much success, but they did seem to be having a good time.

Julio and Manny sat down on a bench, idly watching as Zach and Julie chased down one luminescent firefly after another, wildly swinging their nets.

"My, how things have changed," Julio observed. "Look at the two of us with our kids, spending Saturday at the park chasing fireflies."

"Better than some of the stuff we used to get into," said Manny. Julio snorted appreciatively.

"Didn't we once sit right here on this bench, casing these houses?" mused Julio, looking around at the larger, wealthier homes surrounding the small park. "It doesn't seem like all that long ago."

Manny and Julio had not only been the best of friends when they were younger; they also had been experienced and accomplished petty burglars. Julio had introduced Manny to his favorite form of entertainment, which he called his

85

"adventures." The boys became adept at breaking and entering into ground-floor apartments, diving in headfirst through a window, careful never to stay very long.

Julio insisted that they take only a few small items from each house, things that had no distinguishing marks like simple jewelry, the coveted prescription Bubble Bars (a THC product cherished by teenagers), and SillySybin (an expensive mushroom derivative ostensibly used in religious ceremonies). By doing this, Julio explained, the homeowner might think that the items had been misplaced, not stolen, and would not report them missing.

When the two boys stole something valuable like jewelry, Julio would sell it to his "fence," an older schoolmate of Julio. It had been thrilling fun for the two young boys. Eventually, Julio grew out of it as he approached 17, the age of adulthood within the Colony. Manny eventually stopped, too, although it was because his father caught him red-handed at the age of 16.

Manny's padlet beeped, the rim lighting up neon gold for a message from work. He opened it, read the message and folded it shut.

"Crap," he said in consternation.

"What's going on?" asked Julio.

"It's work stuff. The Chief wants to know if I'm working today. He wants me to stop by his office for a chat. In other words, come in now." Manny sighed. "I can't very well tell him that I'm too busy chasing fireflies. Can I leave Zach here with you?"

"Sure, don't worry about it," replied Julio. "We'll have a good time just the three of us." The fireflies were sparking brilliant shades of emerald green, fluorescent yellow and sapphire blue as the light slowly dimmed towards evening. Eager children were chasing them as fast as their little legs would carry them, flailing at them with butterfly nets.

"Thanks, man, I owe you one," said Manny. Actually, he was more than a little relieved to have an excuse to go. The idea of spending an hour or more watching children chase fireflies was boring, especially when there was exciting work to be done at the office.

Manny walked quickly over to the station. Because he often worked on Saturdays, no one was surprised to see him.

"Manny, come in, come in," said the Chief with a smile, motioning Manny to the visitor's chair. He closed the door, then sat down behind his desk.

"I've been talking to the Commissioner about a new project he's working on. He's putting together a Task Force, one which will deal exclusively with cold cases," the Chief said, steepling his fingers as he explained. "This is the hardest kind of detective work, dead-end cases, some of them many years old.

"The Commissioner needs personnel for his new unit. He said explicitly that he'd like everyone in the unit to be involved in the day-to-day detective work, even the brass. In other words, it's a hands-on project."

The Chief paused, giving Manny time to take it all in. "I'd like to recommend you to lead the new Task Force," he said.

"Wow! Yes! That sounds great," said Manny enthusiastically. "I mean, it's not that I don't like working here," he added.

"None of that, now, no need to explain," the Chief said, airily waving away Manny's reassurances. "There's no room for sentimentality in these decisions. You're a talented detective, Manny, but you seem a little lost here, supervising the detectives. I think this would be a good fit for you."

"When does this position open up?" asked Manny.

"Not until the fall," replied the Chief. "I'm asking you to keep this under your hat, for now."

"I understand," Manny said, nodding.

"You can start thinking about the detectives you'd like to take with you," the Chief continued. "For instance, Naomi and Dave close more cases than any of the other detectives in this unit. You will probably want both of them." Manny nodded again.

"You'll need about a dozen detectives in all, but I'd ask you not to take any more than two from this unit. I don't want to have a skeleton crew here, when you're gone!" The Chief laughed at his little joke. Manny dutifully joined in.

"You'll be seeing a lot of the Commissioner, reporting directly to him. One of your duties will be attending Council meetings and letting the Commissioner know what comes up, what the Council members are talking about. He gets the minutes of the meetings, of course, but what I mean are the whispered conversations, the half-suggestions, the ideas that don't make it into the minutes.

"You'll be bumped up from junior member of the Council to Council Elder," the Chief continued. "We can do that now; no need to wait for the fall."

"But how will that work?" asked Manny, puzzled. "There are already eight Council Elders. Is someone leaving?"

The Chief laughed. "Yeah, you could say that. Don't you worry about that."

"You're going to need to appoint a lieutenant to the Task Force," continued the Chief, "someone to oversee the scheduling, the day-to-day operations of the unit, leaving you free to do other work, whatever might come up. In view of the work with the Council and these additional responsibilities, the Commissioner will be promoting you to Captain."

"Captain," repeated Manny. "Thank you, Sir! I won't let you down."

"You're welcome, Manny," said the Chief, smiling. "Congratulations! I think you're going to like working with the Commissioner. Now, there's just one more thing."

Manny leaned forward in his chair.

"You're going to want to pick a lieutenant who is capable, not just at solving cases, but also in managing personnel," admonished the Chief. "It will need to be someone you can trust, someone you know well and have worked with. I am guessing that you will want to choose Dave, since you two used to be partners and have remained friendly."

"Yeah, that sounds right," said Manny, nodding.

"Dave will be a good a lieutenant, solid and dependable," the Chief said, suddenly studying the paperweight at the end of his desk. "But I don't think you'd want to push it any further, after that." He looked meaningfully at Manny. "You get what I'm saying?"

Manny understood. David Wu, a talented and hard-working detective, was never going to rise about the rank of lieutenant, not because he did not deserve it, but because he was of Chinese heritage. Everyone knew that most of the top brass were of Irish descent, along with a few of Scottish descent. Even Manny was mostly of Irish descent. Along with everyone else, Manny knew that this was bigotry, plain and simple. So far, though, it seemed that no one was interested in changing it.

"Yes, Sir, I understand," Manny said, deciding that he would make up his own mind later, if and when the time came.

"Good," said the Chief. "I'm glad we had this little chat. Now how about a little drink, to celebrate?" He pulled open his bottom desk drawer.

"This is for special occasions only," Chief O'Reilly said, as he carefully retrieved a dark amber bottle from the back of the drawer. Manny recognized the best-quality Cognac which his company regularly imported from Joshua Spellman.

The Chief poured two small glasses of the precious Cognac, handing one to Manny. "To the fastest move up the ladder that I've seen in a long time," he said smiling, holding up his glass.

"I'll drink to that," replied Manny, clinking his glass against the Chief's glass. The two men raised their glasses, downing the Cognac in one gulp.

"Thank you for coming in, Manny," the Chief said, standing up to signal the end of their conversation.

"Thank you, Sir," he said, his feet barely touching the floor as he left.

Manny texted Julio as he was leaving the office to see if they were still at the park, but they were already on their way home. *Just as well,* he thought, grateful for the time alone. He walked home slowly, savoring his news.

Manny tossed his jacket onto the chair in the foyer and headed right for the kitchen to make himself a cup of tea, measuring brandy into it. Then he settled down in a leather armchair in the study to relax before dinner.

It had been quite a day. Even though he could not tell his family about his promotion just yet, the knowledge of it spread a warm excitement through him. Captain Stewart. It did have a nice ring to it, he thought, taking a large swallow of his tea. Maybe someday he could rise through the ranks high enough to out-rank his late father. The idea made him smile. He finished his tea.

# Chapter 14.

**M**ANNY STOOD UP behind his desk, pulled on his jacket and went to the door. He called out, "Dave. Naomi. In my office. Now, please."

When they came in, body language carefully correct, eyes watchful, he motioned them to sit down.

"Have a seat, please," he said. *How nice it is to be the one in charge,* he thought, relishing the moment. Agnes returned with a cup of tea; he set it down on his desk, after taking an appreciative sip.

"I have some good news," he said. He explained about the Task Force, described the type of cases they would be working on, warned them of the need for secrecy. Both Dave and Naomi were very excited.

"We'll be reporting to you?" asked Naomi.

"Yes, that's right," Manny confirmed. "And I'll be reporting directly to the Commissioner. I don't have to tell you what that kind of access can mean for your careers."

Dave let out a low whistle. "I'm in!" he said simply.

"Me, too," said Naomi.

"Remember, not a word, not to anyone. That means framily," he cautioned; everyone knew that framily - friends and family - would spread this news like wildfire. They both nodded. Manny stood, to show that the meeting was over.

As Naomi left the office, Manny said, "Dave, a word, please?" Manny motioned him back in, taking a moment to close the door before returning to sit behind his desk. He leaned back in his chair.

"This should be good, don't you think?" Manny said. "Cold cases are tough, but it's always a good feeling to crack a case nobody else can figure out."

"Sounds good to me," said Dave. "Thanks for choosing me."

"I'm going to be bumped up to captain," he said, "which means that somebody has to be promoted to lieutenant." He grinned at his friend and former partner. "What do you think, are you up for the job?"

There was a moment of stunned silence. "Me?!" Dave said. "You know I am! It would be my pleasure." As the news sank in, Dave said solemnly, "Manny, thank you."

He would have said more, but Manny airily waved his hand and said, "None of that, now, none of that! You've earned this promotion. Modesty aside, we both know that you're one of the best detectives here."

"I won't forget this, Manny, I mean it," Dave insisted. "This promotion means the world to me."

"Let's have a little celebration, then, to mark the occasion," Manny said, enjoying the moment. He reached into the bottom drawer of his desk and retrieved two small antique crystal glasses and a bottle of brandy, one of the two that Julio had brought home for him. *I'll have to ask Julio to pick up some more, the next time he's in Philadelphia,* Manny said to himself. *These bottles are a lot smaller than they look.*

~ ~ ~ ~ ~ ~

Manny came home in time for dinner, something he was trying to do more often. He quickly changed into sweatpants and a teeshirt, hanging up his uniform jacket in the airing closet, a cedar closet in the upstairs hallway that had an outer wall which had been perforated with little holes to allow air to circulate from outside.

"Mmmm, something smells good," he said appreciatively, as Anna stirred a pot on the stove. "What's for dinner?"

"Stir fried eggplant, mushrooms and ivory peas with jasmina rice," she replied. "It will be ready in about twenty minutes."

"Sounds good," he said, filling the tea kettle with water. "Just enough time for a cup of tea."

"I didn't know you drank tea in the afternoon," she said. "It doesn't keep you awake at night?"

"No," he replied, "no problem so far. I started putting brandy in it, when my leg was hurting. Agnes, my secretary, she was the one who introduced me to it. She says her father drinks tea with brandy, when his back hurts."

Anna raised an eyebrow. "Did Agnes mention that brandy is addictive?"

"What are you talking about?" scoffed Manny. "It's not like the hard stuff, nowhere near as strong as Scotch or bourbon."

"No," she replied, "you're right, it's not, but it's still alcohol, you know. You should be careful, Manny, or you won't be able to stop."

"I can stop any time I want," protested Manny, stirring his cup of tea. He added some honey. "Look, no brandy," he said, taking a sip.

Anna turned back to the stove. "Let me finish up here," she said, adding a handful of trumpeting mushrooms to the pan, pausing to appreciate their little song as she stirred gently.

Manny took his cup of tea and went into the study, closing the door. He took another sip. *Ugh,* he thought, *tea is ghastly without a little brandy.* He sighed. *But if I go into the kitchen now and get the bottle out of the cabinet, Anna is sure to say something about it. Maybe I'll move the bottle here, to this room, where I can get to it without anybody looking over my shoulder.*

"Dinner!" called Anna. Family members emerged from different parts of the Stewart mansion, including Lucinda and Luis. Manny sat down at the head of the table. The news was still on, projected against the wall; Anna had picked up Lucinda's habit of listening to the news while cooking.

Anna reached for her padlet to close it, but Manny said, "No, wait! Hold on a minute, let's hear this."

" ... just coming into the newsroom, and we have a photo for you, too," the news anchor was saying in a smarmy voice. "Look at this, folks, one of New York's finest – who is this, sleeping on the job?"

There on the wall was a clear image of Manny, asleep at his desk, head back, mouth open, looking for all the world like he had nothing else to do. The name placard on his desk showed plainly for all to see.

There was a stunned silence in the room, as everyone turned to look at Manny. He looked back at them, momentarily speechless.

"Manny? Is this a real photo?" asked Lucinda incredulously.

"Unfortunately, yeah, it is," he said ruefully. "It was not my finest moment. I hurt my back – that was the second time, when I fell off the chair in my office. My secretary made me a cup of tea with brandy in it," he continued, carefully avoiding Anna's inquisitive gaze, "and I drank it too quickly. It made me a little sleepy."

"Who took this picture?" demanded Luis.

"I'm pretty sure I know who it was. The Chief has an aide named Raimone. He's a real piece of work, stirring up mischief, telling outright lies to set people against each other," said Manny. "He seems to think he has a career path at the department. Nobody likes him very much, although there's no getting rid of him. He's related to the Commissioner's wife."

Luis said, "But why would he decide to make this photo public?" He turned to Manny.

"I think it's just an act of malice," Manny said, "there's no other explanation for it. He doesn't like me, and the feeling is mutual. He left the department not long ago, appointed to be the Aide to the Commissioner, so I hope I never need to deal with him again."

Anna snapped off the news. "Well," she said, "you know how this goes. It will be big news for twenty-four hours, and then something else will happen to take people's attention away."

"Let's hope so," murmured Manny. "It's pretty embarrassing." His mind was reeling. It was Raimone, of course; no one else would want to humiliate Manny publicly. But why now, when he was weeks away from a promotion?

Dinner was delicious; Anna was a good cook. Luis and Julio had brought home six bottles of beer, which they had placed on the table. Manny opened one of the dark beers.

"This is really good stuff," he said appreciatively. He drank it down quickly, reaching for another. Lucinda and Anna exchanged glances, but no one said anything.

Dinner over, the children left the table to go upstairs, while the adults lingered in the kitchen.

"How's work, Manny?" asked Lucinda. "You seem maybe a little happier lately?"

He smiled. "Actually, I do have some news. But you all have to be sworn to secrecy. I mean it – this can't get out." He looked meaningfully at each of them.

"The Commissioner is creating a new Task Force, to solve old cases. He's asked me to lead the unit. I'll have a lieutenant and a dozen or so detectives working under me," Manny explained. "The best thing is that I'll be doing actual detective work again, not just supervising detectives."

"That's wonderful, Manny! When will this happen?" asked Luis.

"Not for several weeks; I don't have an exact date. It will be sometime in August," Manny said.

"Did you say that you will have a lieutenant working for you?" asked Lucinda. "Will you be promoted to ... what?"

"Captain. I'll be Captain Stewart," he said proudly.

"Congratulations!" said Julio warmly. "That's great, Manny!"

"Thank you, thank you," he said. It was true; he did feel happier. In the months that had passed since Naz had died, his cloud of grief had gradually lifted enough that he could feel his interest in his career returning, and his focus shifting back to the simple routines of daily life.

Julio and Luis got up to clear the table; Anna stood by the sink, washing dishes. Manny gathered up the recycling and said, "I'll just take this around back."

This was a standing joke in the Colony. Citizens kept their recycling containers "around back," meaning that they were kept at the side of the house, far from the street. Actually, it was not possible to go "around back," as every house in the Colony only had three walls. The back of each home was built flush up against the back wall of the subway tunnel.

Opening up the front door, Manny was carrying the recycling bag towards the side of the house, when he heard a noise coming from the potted evergreen bushes. He stopped, listening.

"S-s-s-t-t-t!" There it was again.

"Who's there?" he demanded, suddenly wishing that he hadn't left his padlet inside.

"It's me!" whispered a voice. The bushes rustled and parted slightly; a face peeked out from between the branches. "Can I come out?"

"Loosey?!" Manny exclaimed. "Is that you?! What on earth are you doing here? And why are you hiding in my bushes?"

"I can't be seen, Manny, trust me. Can we go inside?" he whispered, furtively glancing over his shoulder as he tugged his hat lower.

Loosey, whose real name was Ajay, had been Manny and Julio's fence, when the boys had been teenagers. They sold whatever jewelry and small, non-identifiable items they could steal to Loosey, who always gave them a fair price. Manny had not seen Loosey since he was sixteen.

Loosey had gotten his nickname years earlier, when there had been an infestation of mosquitoes in the Colony. The Council had determined that planting tobacco as a natural insecticide would deter the growing mosquito population, as mosquitoes hate nicotine. The tobacco plants flourished (and the mosquitoes did not), but people began to steal the leaves, drying them at home and rolling them into homemade cigarettes. Soon several enterprising people were making a handsome profit selling them as loose cigarettes, hence the name "Loosey."

"Sure, come in, come in," said Manny, standing aside so Loosey could leave his hiding place. "We'll go into the library. We can talk in there."

# Chapter 15.

JULIO WAS FINISHING up in the kitchen as Manny and Loosey came in through the front door. "Loosey?!" Julio exclaimed. "Is that really you? Hey, how are you?"

The three men moved together into the library. Manny closed the door behind them. "Are you in trouble?" Manny asked quietly.

"No. Well, sort of. I need to talk to you, man," he replied, nervously twisting his hat in his hands.

"OK, here, let's sit down, you can tell us all about it," he said, wondering what could have brought his former colleague to his home. After all, Loosey was a well-known petty criminal, and Manny was a police lieutenant, soon to be a captain.

The library was simply stunning, a room lined from floor to ceiling with book shelves, each filled to overflowing with actual paper books, many of them hundreds of years old. Classics like War and Peace, To Kill a Mockingbird, and Willa & Hesper were carefully lined up behind glass doors on shelf after shelf, along with other antique journals and graphic novels. Loosey craned his neck to look up near the ceiling, then all around him, at the astonishing collection of real books. His eyes settled on a painting hanging on one of the walls.

"Is that ... is that real?" he asked, turning to Manny.

"Yes," replied Manny, not offering any details. Actual oil paintings were very rare. While New York City had been filled with fine museums containing hundreds of beautiful paintings before New Yorkers moved underground in the year 2085 A.D., very few of them were still in circulation. No one was really sure how many works of art had been quietly removed and stored away in the homes of private citizens. Now, so many hundreds of years later, it was doubtful that many of them understood their worth.

Remembering why he was there, Loosey returned his gaze to Manny and Julio.

"There's this guy," he began. "He wants information on you, Manny, he wants it bad. He cornered me yesterday when I was

97

walking home and asked me all sorts of questions about you, what you sold to me when you were ... you know. Back in the day. He knew all about it, knew that you guys used to bring me things to sell." Manny nodded encouragingly but did not speak, letting Loosey talk without interruption. It was an interrogation tactic that detectives often used.

"He's seen tapes, Manny," Loosey whispered, his eyes round with fright. "He says he knows stuff about you, but he needs a corroborating witness. And apparently, he thinks that witness is me. He said if I didn't help him, I'd be sorry."

"He's seen tapes? What does that even mean?" asked Manny. "Did he say what kind of tapes?"

"Tapes of your break-ins, surveillance tapes. He said you're on the tapes, and you are, too, Julio." The hair on the back of Manny's neck started to stand up, as a sinking feeling hit his stomach.

"What do you mean, I'm on the tapes, too?" asked Julio, frowning.

"I dunno, Julio, that's what he said," replied Loosey.

Manny, who had not taken his eyes off Loosey's face, was thinking hard. First, there was the photo just released to the press which showed Manny in a bad light. And shortly afterwards, a mysterious stranger shows up, leaning on Loosey to see if he could dig up dirt on Manny's past.

"Is there anything else you can think of, anything at all? Did he mention a name or a specific item?" asked Manny.

"That's the thing, Manny. He wanted to know if you ever sold me a pair of diamond rings," replied Loosey. "I said no, anything you sold to me was just kid stuff, nothing as valuable as diamond rings. And that's the truth, too."

Manny nodded.

Julio turned to Manny. "What's this mean?" he asked uneasily. "And why now, so many years later? We were under age then."

Seventeen is the legal age when a child becomes a full-fledged adult in the Colony. While a child who gets caught stealing would not face jail time, an adult could be sent to jail.

98

Both Julio and Manny prudently had stopped breaking and entering before the age of seventeen.

"Anything else you can tell me about this person?" asked Manny. "Think! Did he have a tattoo on his forehead, an earring, a pierced nose, anything like that?"

"Yeah, now that you mention it. He wore cologne that smelled to high heaven, even after he left," said Loosey.

Manny stood up. "Loosey. Please don't misunderstand, but I have to ask you to leave now."

"But wait, Manny – what's going on?" said Loosey. "How'd this guy know to come after *me*?"

"Loosey, think this through!" Manny said imploringly. "You came to my house, told me what he said, and I thanked you. That's it. I didn't give you advice, or offer any explanations. And if anyone should ask you in the future, maybe even under oath, you would be truthful to say that I listened, and then asked you to leave."

"OK, I get it," he said, "but what do you want me to do, if he comes back?"

"I don't think he will," replied Manny, "but if he does, you'll let me know, right?"

"Of course," said Loosey, "I'll text you right away."

"*No! Don't do that!* No texts, no holograms, no phone calls, nothing that creates a record of contact between us," said Manny. "Just come here and wait for me, like you did tonight." Manny crossed the room and opened the door. Loosey took one last look around at the library, knowing that he was unlikely ever to see a room like it again.

Julio said, "Here, I'll walk you to the door, Loosey." The two of them went out into the foyer, where Manny could hear them talking in low tones. Manny listened, relieved when the door opened, then closed.

Julio sat down across from Manny. "Who's doing this to you, Manny? Is it the same guy, the one who took the photo?"

Manny replied, "I think so. I'm pretty sure he's behind the photo of me sleeping at my desk. He must have showed it to the Chief, who chewed me out pretty good that day for sleeping on the job. I don't know how else the Chief could have known about it; he wasn't in the office that morning."

"But why would he release the photo to the press?" asked Julio.

"Nobody is supposed to know about my promotion, or about the Task Force, but Raimone is now the Aide to the Commissioner. Maybe he saw some papers or something on the Commissioner's desk ... it really doesn't matter how he found out," Manny replied. "Raimone thinks he has a shot at being Commissioner someday, which is laughable. He's trying to make me look bad in front of the Commissioner. He must see me as competition."

"What are you going to do?" asked Julio, looking worried.

"The first thing I'm going to do is look for those tapes. Personally, I think Raimone's bluffing. We searched all through my Dad's papers and files after he died, and there was nothing like that anywhere," replied Manny.

"What if there really are tapes, Manny? And he starts releasing them, one at a time, to discredit you?" asked Julio. "I'm on those tapes, too! Everyone will know that I used to be a thief."

"Don't worry, this is not going to involve you. He's after me, not you. You're nobody to him," said Manny reassuringly. "There's no legal liability to you now, you know," he added. "The statute of limitations ran out long ago, and it's not like your boss is going to fire you."

Julio laughed. He didn't have a boss. Julio, his father and Manny were equal partners in the family business. "It's not that I'm worried about my job, just my reputation," Julio explained.

The two sat in silence for a few moments, thinking about the conversation with Loosey.

"What I don't understand is how Raimone knew about the rings," said Manny thoughtfully. "I gave those two rings to the desk sergeant when they arrested me. I never saw them after that. My Dad said he was going to return them to Mrs. Al-Sayed, so she wouldn't press charges. I guess it's possible that he never returned them. Maybe he had another way to keep her from pressing charges. He was a tricky bastard; I guess he could have blackmailed her or bought her off."

"Poor Loosey! It must have taken a lot of courage to come here and talk to you, you know, now that you're police and all," Julio said.

Manny sighed, getting up from his chair. "Let me see what I can find out at work," he said. "I'll let you know."

*What am I going to say at work tomorrow,* thought Manny, *now that everyone's seen the photo of me asleep at my desk? What should I say to the Chief?* He ran his hand through his hair, anticipating the reaction of his colleagues, cringing at the idea of facing the Chief in the morning.

# Chapter 16.

**M**ANNY STOPPED OUTSIDE of the precinct station, gathering his thoughts before entering the building. He squared his shoulders, taking a deep breath as he straightened his jacket.

He went directly to his unit, not stopping first at his office as he usually did. The detectives were at their desks working, but not a single one of them looked up when he walked in. He wondered if they were actually working, or just trying to look like it.

"Where's Naomi?" he asked, noting her empty desk. Like the other detectives, Naomi rarely missed a day.

"She's home trying to find a dentist," replied one of the detectives. "She's got a pretty bad toothache, cheek swollen out to here," he added, illustrating with his hand.

"Agnes, could you come here, please?" he called.

When she appeared, he asked, "Could you get in touch with Naomi for me? Tell her to go see Dr. William Greenberg, he's my dentist. Make sure she tells him that I sent her." Agnes nodded, opening her padlet.

In an age when so much medical progress had been lost, when shiny medical facilities and miracle drugs were a thing of the past, Bill Greenberg had inadvertently stumbled across the secret to growing human teeth in his laboratory, and could replace a defective tooth. Dr. Greenberg was greatly in demand, so much so that his practice now only accepted referrals.

Manny sat down on the edge of Naomi's empty desk. "I know that by now, you've all seen the photo of me. It was all over the news last night. I want you to know that I am deeply embarrassed, and thoroughly ashamed of myself. It was inexcusable, falling asleep at my desk – no matter the reason."

There was a ripple of laughter. Somehow, everyone knew that Agnes had been making him brandy-laced tea every day, and that he was not used to drinking. Manny felt the tension in the room ease as all of the detectives turned friendly faces towards him.

"Do you want any help tracking down the person who posted the photo?" asked one of the detectives.

"Thank you, but I think I know who it was," replied Manny. "If I need help, I'll take you up on the offer, though. I screwed up, and I apologize. Believe me, it won't happen again."

Manny wondered if he should apologize to the Chief now, or just wait until the next time he saw him. The problem solved itself when he returned to his office; there was the Chief, sitting in the visitor's chair across from his desk, waiting for him.

"Good morning, Sir," he said hopefully, trying to gauge the Chief's body language.

"Good morning. I'll get right to the point," Chief O'Reilly said. "I saw the photo last night. Hell, everybody in the Colony saw the photo last night. It was released to discredit you, and possibly to embarrass the Commissioner for choosing you to head up the new Task Force. Do you have any idea who may have done this?"

"I think it was Raimone," Manny responded. "You mentioned to me once that he wants to be Commissioner. Maybe he sees me as a threat, and wants to discredit me."

"That's what I was thinking, too," said the Chief. "He's nothing but trouble, Manny, and I'm glad he's gone. Let's hope this is the end of his nonsense."

"I want to apologize to you, Sir," Manny began.

The Chief waved his hand in the air. "That's enough apologizing for one day, Lieutenant," he said. "I can honestly say that most of these detectives have never heard their boss apologize for anything."

"I wanted to clear the air, and let them know that the rules apply to all of us, and that includes me," explained Manny earnestly.

Chief O'Reilly snorted appreciatively, whether with approval or amusement, Manny couldn't tell.

"Don't worry about the photo," said the Chief. "You'll see, something else will be today's news of the day, and nobody will remember this a week from now."

Manny exhaled, relieved that his boss was not furious.

"Is there anything else Raimone knows that he could use to try and discredit you?" asked the Chief. "Are we waiting for the other shoe to drop?"

"Yes, Sir, I think there might be," replied Manny.

The Chief waited, but Manny did not offer anything further. "Do you want to tell me about it?" asked the Chief finally.

"No, Sir, I would rather handle it myself, if it's all the same to you," replied Manny. *After all,* he thought, *if there are no tapes, why tell him about the robberies?*

"That's fine," replied the Chief, "I admire a man who deals with his own problems, and doesn't come whining to the brass about fairness or some other crap like that." He rose, ready to leave. "Just keep me posted, OK?"

"Yes, Sir," replied Manny.

The rest of the day was uneventful. There was the usual ebb and flow of meetings and paperwork, but no further mention of the photo. By the end of the day, most people seemed to have forgotten it.

Manny had to leave the office early in order to attend a City Council meeting. He arrived just as the meeting began, and was momentarily surprised that the first order of business was the announcement of the retirement of Dr. Emily Jaine Ramirez, a Council Elder.

The second order of business was the change in Manny's status to a full-fledged Council Member. No longer one of the junior members, Manny would now be required to attend all of the meetings of the Council, and would be privy to the confidential deliberations of the various members. *This is what the Commissioner wants,* Manny thought, *for me to be his eyes and ears on the Council.*

Manny had been a junior member for a long time, but what he heard in this regular session astonished him. There were problems with the ventilation and water systems; a potential leak in the wall of the tunnel in one of the less-desirable residential areas; a colony of bats living on the ceiling in one of the tunnels, splattering their germ-laden droppings on the ground; a falling birthrate; an increase in the annual number of elder deaths by falls or accidents; and potential gang violence near the Munitions Department, where all of the guns and other weapons of the Colony were carefully stored and monitored.

"Now I see what you all talk about, when the junior members are not around," he said to Sarah Blumberg, after the meeting. Sarah had been his teacher when he was a teenager. Later, she became his tutor during the end of his senior year, after Manny was sidelined with grief for his father, who had been euthanized during an outbreak of disease.

"Yes, the junior members are not privy to the confidential workings of the Council," Sarah replied. "They are like the alternates on a jury, kept in reserve for when they are needed."

"What about Dr. Ramirez, do you think she will mind leaving the Council?" asked Manny. "Will people resent me for having forced her out earlier than she planned?"

"No, that's not a problem," Sarah said reassuringly. "She's had one foot out the door for a few years now. She wants to retire so she can concentrate full time on her writing."

"I think you're going to like being on the Council, Manny," she continued. "You already have a good grasp of how things work. It's interesting that some of the work of the Council is done behind the scenes, in conversations before and after the meetings. And sometimes," she added meaningfully, "the most sensitive issues are not put into writing at all."

Sarah looked at Manny thoughtfully. "Usually, when there's an abrupt change in the Council membership, there's somebody pulling the strings," she said. "But you're a lieutenant, not directly in contact with the Commissioner or the Mayor's office. Unless there's something I don't know?"

Manny reddened under her gaze. Sarah was his friend; he could never lie to her. "One never knows about these things," he replied with his most mysterious smile.

~ ~ ~ ~ ~ ~

"How was your meeting tonight?" asked Luis, as Manny took off his hat and jacket.

"It was OK," Manny replied. "I've got some good news. I'm now a senior member of the Council."

"Someone retired?" asked Luis, surprised.

"Yeah, funny thing about that. Dr. Ramirez suddenly decided that she was ready to retire, and now I'm in," Manny said. They both laughed.

The two men went into the kitchen, where Anna had kept Manny's dinner warm for him. It was late, and the children were upstairs getting ready for bed.

Manny reached into the back of the kitchen cabinet for his bottle of brandy, bringing it with him to the table along with a plate filled with stir fried purple beans over udon.

"You drink brandy, son?" asked Luis, surprised. "When did this start?"

Manny took his time, filling his glass with a generous amount of brandy. "It started when I hurt my back sliding down the banister with Zach. Then I had some after I fell, at work. Agnes, my secretary, she put it into my tea. She said her father has back pain, and that's what he does. I don't really need the tea; the brandy works fine without it." He took a large swallow, setting the glass down near his plate.

"Is your back hurting you now?" asked Luis dubiously, eyeing him with real concern.

"No, not right now," said Manny, "but it has a way of flaring up out of nowhere, so I never know when it's going to come back."

Lucinda had been standing in the doorway, listening to the conversation. She came and sat down at the table with Luis, the two of them relaxing as Manny ate his dinner.

"It's not going to prevent your back pain from coming back," said Lucinda. "It's not a pre-emptive remedy. Alcohol is addictive, you know. Have you tried going a full day without it?"

"No, I haven't," replied Manny, recalling that Anna had asked him the same question. "Really, what's the harm, a little glass of brandy at the end of the day? I have a high-pressure job, I need to relax."

"Manny, I am concerned about this," replied Lucinda. "Think about your father. He also had a high-pressure job, and needed to unwind at the end of the day."

Patrick Stewart had been sloppy drunk most nights in the years leading up to his death; often, Manny had had to drag him up the stairs and put him to bed. In the morning, Patrick would not remember anything he had said or done the previous evening.

"As if I could forget!" replied Manny, irritated. "But that was him. It doesn't have anything to do with me. He wasn't my biological father, so I didn't inherit his alcoholism, if that's what you mean."

"I'm afraid that you're headed down a slope without realizing it," she said gently. "Why don't you do this: don't drink at all tomorrow, and see how you feel. Can you do that for us?"

With an effort, Manny stifled his impatience. How could he say no to them, his foster parents who had taken him in out of the kindness of their hearts, raised him as their own along with Julio, back when he was a scared little boy with an increasingly absent father? Their home had been his only safe haven.

"OK, I'll do that tomorrow," Manny agreed, finishing the glass of brandy. "I'll start in the morning." He reached for the bottle, but Luis pulled it away, firmly placing the stopper back in the top.

"You can have this back when you are ready," Luis said, "but for the next twenty-four hours, it's off limits."

Manny struggled to hide his irritation. "I was just going to put it away," he protested. They were treating him like a child! It was his house, and his brandy; he was certainly old enough to do what he wanted.

Just as he was reassuring himself that he could get another bottle any time he wanted it, an explosion of sound came from upstairs, unmistakably, incredibly, the voice of Naztazya

Stewart saying over and over, "What would *you* like to do, Manny?"

Before anyone could react, Manny heard Zach scream, "*MOMMY!!*" as her voice filled the house. The little boy streaked up the stairs like a rocket, with Manny following close behind him.

# Chapter 17.

JULIE STOOD IN the middle of the master bedroom, holding Manny's padlet in her hands, pointed at the wall. Manny's video, his most precious video of Naz, was projected against the four walls. Zach was squashed flat up against the wall, arms spread wide, his face turned to one side, trying desperately to put his arms around the image of his mother.

"Mommy! Mommy, Mommy!!!" he babbled, tears flowing down his cheeks.

Manny crossed the room and grabbed the padlet out of Julie's hands. "Give me that!" he demanded angrily. "What are you doing in here?"

Anna appeared in the doorway, followed by Julio, Luis and Lucinda. "What's going on in here?" Anna demanded.

Manny crossed the room and gently grasped Zach by the arm. "Zach, it's OK. It's just a photo of Mommy. It's a video, that's all." He tried to draw his son away from the wall.

Raw with grief from losing his beloved mother, Zach wailed inconsolably. Manny stood helplessly next to him, unsure what to do.

"I warned you about this," Lucinda said, taking the padlet out of Manny's hands. "I told you to make sure that Zach did not see it!"

"I know, I know. Lucinda, I was careful!" Manny protested. "This is not my fault!" He turned to his niece.

"Young lady, what do you have to say for yourself?" he asked sternly, taking a step closer to her. Anna drew her breath in sharply, moving to position herself between her daughter and Manny.

"Hold on here, let's all take a breath," said Julio cautiously. He stepped closer to Anna, his eyes on Manny.

"What's your daughter doing in my bedroom, with my padlet?" demanded Manny. He was talking to Anna and Julio, but his eyes never left Julie, whose little face had gone white. "How did you know the password?"

"I guessed it," whispered Julie.

"You guessed it," repeated Manny flatly, his disbelief plain to see. "And how exactly did you do that?"

"Well, it wasn't Mommy's or Daddy's birthdays, or yours, or Auntie Naz's, or mine or Zach's," said Julie. "So I tried the name of Auntie Naz's cat, you know, Cat Mandu, only that didn't work either. Then I thought that maybe you had scrambled it, so I tried DuManCat, and that was it."

Manny stared at her in astonishment. A child had hacked into his police-issue padlet, opened up his very private video and blasted it for all to hear. He looked at Julio, who seemed just as surprised as he was. Anna, though, was looking at her daughter with something that seemed suspiciously like pride.

"OK, my little computer wizard, you come with me," said Anna sternly, with a glance at Manny. "No screen time for you for a week." She took her daughter's arm and quickly bustled her out of the room.

"Don't worry, man, we'll make sure she understands how wrong this is," said Julio to Manny, following his wife and daughter out into the hall.

Zach was still sobbing. He had buried his face in Lucinda's dress, half-hidden behind her. "Zach, come here," he said gently. Zach turned his face away.

"When Mommy died, I was so sad," Manny said softly. "I used to watch this video over and over. But it's only a video. That's all it is." He stood helplessly next to his son, not knowing what to do.

Lucinda sat down and pulled Zach onto her lap, her arms around him, rocking him gently as his sobs slowly subsided.

"Can I sleep in your bed tonight, Abuela?" he said. Since Luis and Lucinda had moved across the street from the Stewart mansion, sleepovers had been a coveted treat.

"Not in Daddy's bed?" Lucinda asked encouragingly.

"No, yours," Zach replied.

"Of course, you can, if Daddy says it's OK," she said, looking up at Manny.

"Zach, don't you want to stay here with me?" he asked his son. "You can sleep in my bed."

Zach turned towards Manny, raised his hand and put his thumb into his mouth, sucking furiously. Manny had not seen his five-year-old son suck his thumb in at least two years. Surprised, he looked at Lucinda, who frowned just slightly. Not now, she seemed to be saying.

Lucinda stood up, holding Zach. She said gently, "OK, little man, off we go!" She turned to Manny, who nodded.

"See you in the morning, Buddy," he said helplessly, as Lucinda carried Zach downstairs.

~ ~ ~ ~ ~ ~

Once Manny was alone in his bedroom, his anger gradually subsided. He felt hollow, so empty without Naztazya, worried about his son and the impact he was having on him. *I'm a terrible father,* he thought. *I make one mistake after another.* Without thinking, he went downstairs to the kitchen for the bottle of brandy. It was not on the kitchen table, nor was it in the cabinet.

Luis. Damn him! Just when he needed to settle his nerves, Luis had to go and take the bottle with him when he left. Manny mulled over his options. He could order a bottle to be delivered to the house, but then Luis would know that he had broken his word. He could choose not to drink, an option which was becoming increasingly unappealing. Or ... his flask!

Most police officers carried a metal pocket flask. One of the detectives in his unit had had an extra one, which he had given to Manny one day when the two of them were in the lunchroom at the same time. Manny had never used the flask, but kept it in his closet along with his uniforms.

Hurrying back up to his bedroom, Manny searched through his closet until he found the flask. He gave it a little shake. There was something in it! He tipped his head back and swallowed all of its contents, not knowing or caring what kind of liquor it was.

The liquor burned his throat on its way down. Manny coughed, spluttering, as he caught his breath. It was bourbon.

The smell of it made Manny gag, as the fumes filled his nose and throat.

*As it turns out,* Manny said to himself several minutes later, *the old man may have been onto something. Bourbon is much stronger than brandy. And that's not necessarily a bad thing, not when you've just screwed up so monumentally.* Manny staggered over to the bed and sat down. Better. Yes, he felt so much better. He closed his eyes and began to snore.

~ ~ ~ ~ ~ ~

Still dressed in his uniform, Manny woke early the following morning to a banging headache and a foul, lingering ugliness in his mouth. Disgusted with himself, he showered and changed, leaving the house before anyone else was up, in order to avoid seeing Lucinda at the breakfast table. She and Zach had not come back yet.

Agnes was at the office when he walked in. She brought him tea laced with brandy, as she now did every morning. "Thank you," he said, resolutely moving the teacup to the side of his desk. No liquor today; he would show them all how easy it is to give up alcohol for twenty-four hours.

He sifted through his messages, noting with disgust that there were two more messages from A-Char, requesting that he set up an appointment with a doctor to look at his back.

"Agnes," he called out to her irritably, "would you please get that woman from A-Char off my back? Whatever it takes. Please!"

"Manny," she replied, coming to stand in the doorway, "she's not going to stop pestering you until you agree to see the doctor."

"OK, OK! I give up. Set up an appointment for me. If she won't do a virtual visit, then have her come here."

"She's doesn't make house calls, Manny," Agnes replied.

"I'm a busy man, Agnes," Manny snapped. "Make it happen."

After lunch, Agnes announced that the doctor had arrived and could see him now, if he was free. Not waiting for his response, the doctor walked right into his office, standing in front of his desk. Agnes tactfully closed the door.

"I know you're a busy man, Lieutenant, so I'll be as brief as possible," she began. "I am Dr. Patel. I understand that you fell here in your office, injuring your back. Did you have a history of back pain before the accident?"

"Yes," he replied, keeping his reply as brief as possible, hoping to discourage further questions.

"Does your back still hurt you now, after your fall?" she asked, continuing to stand in front of his desk. He did not ask her to sit down.

"It does, now and then," he replied, "but it doesn't hurt right now. I never know when something is going to set it off."

"Show me where it hurts, if you don't mind," said Dr. Patel, sitting down uninvited.

Manny stood up, motioning vaguely to the various points where his back and leg were painful.

"Across your lower back and down the back of your leg, into your heel?" she asked. He nodded. "Seems like classic sciatica," she said. Manny nodded again; he already knew that. He wished most sincerely that she would leave.

"Unfortunately, we know what it is, but there's not much we can do for it. How do you manage it, when it acts up?" she asked.

"I don't really know what to do," he responded. "I mean, I put heated towels on it when I'm home, but that isn't a solution that works during the day. Mostly, I drink. A good shot or two of brandy really helps."

"Exactly how much do you drink, Lieutenant?" she asked.

"I've gotten into the habit of drinking a little each day," he replied honestly. "A bit of brandy in the morning, and then again before dinner. Sometimes before bed, too. It keeps the pain away."

"I want to warn you about this," said Dr. Patel. "You can't keep the pain away by drinking. If there is pain, then a small amount of brandy will be helpful. But beware, Lieutenant, it's not a preventative, and it comes with its own set of problems. Alcohol is addictive. So don't drink unless you have pain, OK?"

"OK," replied Manny. He paused, torn between wanting to confide in her and refusing to admit that he might have a problem. Finally, he blurted out, "I've noticed that when I don't drink, I feel awful. How do you stop?"

She blinked. "I see," she said. "Have you tried to stop?"

"No, but I promised my family I'd try," he said.

"It's better to taper off slowly, in my opinion, rather than just stop," she replied. "Start by cutting your drinking by 50%, and taper down from there. Remember, one drink a day is better than three or four, and even better would be to just have a drink once or twice a week, socially. You shouldn't drink every day," she said.

Dr. Patel looked curiously at him. "Manny, don't you recognize me?" she asked.

He studied her face. She had reddish-brown hair streaked with gray, arranged on top in that ridiculous broomstick style that the women all favored now, but ... yes, there did seem to be something familiar about her. "Monica?" he asked hesitantly.

"Yes, Monica Stubbs Patel," she replied. "I used to sit next to you in school, when we were kids. Back then, I had long curly red hair."

Manny blushed. "Yeah, I do remember you. How've you been?"

"Good, Manny, thanks. I was sorry to hear about your wife," she replied. "You have a little boy?"

"Yes, Zach. He's five years old," replied Manny.

There was a pause. Good manners would dictate that Manny should ask whether she was married, had any children, etc. The pause lengthened, becoming awkward.

"Well. I know you're a busy man, so I'll let you get back to work," she said finally. "If you have any further problems with your back, or if you need help with the drinking, let me know.

Of course, anything you say to me is confidential, Lieutenant, so if you need me, just text me."

Manny showed her to the door, glad to be done. *Besides,* he thought with relief, *now I can honestly tell Lucinda and Luis that I have consulted a doctor about my drinking.*

# Chapter 18.

**T**HE OFFICE WAS fairly quiet the rest of the morning, with nothing urgent going on. Manny took advantage of the quiet to look through various police databases to see if he could find anything on file about himself. He searched through several databases, looking for his name, but could not find anything.

*That's not surprising,* he thought, *the old bastard wouldn't have left a written record where just anyone could find it.* More likely, Patrick would have put it somewhere safe where he could pull it out years later to use as a weapon against his son.

Leaning back in his chair, Manny laced his hands together behind his head and tried to think of where else the information might be kept. He couldn't think of anything beyond the places he had checked. He sighed, pushing around some of the papers on his desk, not ready to settle into working, but unable to move forward in his search for the files.

His mind kept going back to the events of the previous evening. Zach seemed to prefer being with Lucinda than with him. Zach seemed to prefer his aunt and uncle to him, as well. Manny's head pounded painfully. Idly, he picked up a paperweight, put it down again. Then he gave the paperweight an impatient little shove towards the edge of his desk, where it clanked into the cup of brandy-laced tea.

The tea was cold now, but that didn't matter. He picked up the cup. But no, he'd promised that he wouldn't drink for twenty-four hours, and he would not break his word. He put the cup down, gently. *I should go spill this out in the sink,* he thought, but he did not get up.

Suddenly, Manny snapped his fingers. Tyler Watkins! Tyler, who had been his father's attorney for years before becoming Manny's attorney when Patrick died, would be sure to know if there were confidential files somewhere, maybe on a laptop or written on paper stored someplace safe.

Manny picked up his padlet and texted Tyler. He was just finishing when Agnes appeared in his doorway. "There's someone to see you," she said.

"Who is it?" Manny asked, hoping it would not take too long. "There aren't any meetings on my schedule."

"It's someone in the holding cell downstairs, asking to speak to you," she replied.

"What?" asked Manny, surprised. "Are you sure he wants to speak to the unit's lieutenant?"

"Yes, he asked for you by name," she said.

"By name," he repeated, his heart sinking. *I've got a bad feeling about this,* Manny thought as he got up and put on his jacket before going downstairs. In spite of himself, Manny could feel his hands shaking. He glanced at the cup of tea sitting on his desk, brimming with liquid courage.

"Agnes," he said as he left his office, "give me five minutes. If I'm not back upstairs by then, I'd like you to come to the holding cell with a cup of tea for me. We'll offer something to the perp, too. Can you do that for me?"

"Sure, Manny, I can do that," she replied. He loved the way she followed orders and did not pester him with questions. He'd have to remember to give her a good review when it was time to do annual evaluations.

Downstairs, the detainee had been moved into a conference room for his interview with the arresting detective. He was sitting with his back to the door, his bare arms firmly bound to the arms of the chair with narrow strips of bamboo. No one struggled against these restraints; they soon found out that the strips of bamboo had razor-sharp edges. They were harmless if the detainee held still, but had a mysterious way of tightening, if the detainee struggled.

There was something familiar about this person, even from the back. Manny went into the room adjacent to the conference room, looking through the one-way mirror so he could see the suspect from the front.

It was Loosey.

His heart sinking, Manny entered the conference room, sitting down at the desk across from Loosey and opening up the folder on the desk. "You asked to see me?" he said, his voice abrupt and emotionless, avoiding eye contact with his former colleague.

"Manny, am I glad to see you!" Loosey said with relief.

"You will address me as Lieutenant Stewart," Manny replied coldly, not looking up. He continued to take his time, reading the information in the folder about Loosey's arrest.

Loosey had been picked up by two detectives who were not from Manny's unit. Manny frowned; he could not recall ever having met Detective Thomas Brady or Detective Harry Potter. Ordinarily, suspects were detained and questioned by the detectives who arrested them; otherwise, they would not get credit for solving their crimes.

"Your name is Ajay Sorrenson, aka Loosey, age 28, unmarried," Manny began, looking up. Behind Loosey, high up on the wall, the blinking green light showed Manny that the interview was being recorded. "Now. Why don't you tell me what happened this morning?"

"Manny. Lieutenant. Please, I really need your help," Loosey began. "These two police came to my house this morning and arrested me. I was sound asleep. They wouldn't tell me nothing, just said that I had to come with them. They handcuffed me and marched me down the street in front of the whole neighborhood!"

"What did they say to you, as they were putting on the handcuffs? They must have given you some explanation," said Manny.

"That's the thing – they hardly said anything. They wouldn't tell me why. Just between you and me, I think it has something to do with – you know," Loosey said, leaning forward in his chair and lowering his voice to a whisper. In spite of himself, Manny could feel icy tendrils of dread stirring inside of him.

He pushed the folder to one side. Glancing up at the blinking green light, he held up two fingers and said, "Las Vegas." The light blinked red, and then went dark.

"What's that?" asked Loosey.

"Las Vegas rules," Manny replied. "Whatever happens here, stays here. In other words, we are off the record, Loosey. Nobody's recording what you say." That much was true, although Manny didn't doubt that it was also being observed from behind the one-way mirror by curious onlookers who wanted to know why a suspect would ask to speak to their lieutenant.

There was a discreet tap on the door, and Agnes came in with his cup of tea on a little tray. "Do you want anything, Loosey?" asked Manny. "Water, coffee, tea?"

Loosey looked down at his arms, bound tightly to his chair, and laughed. "Very funny, Lieutenant. You always did have a sense of humor."

"A glass of water for our guest, please," Manny said to Agnes.

As she left the room, Manny pulled the steaming cup of tea towards him. It was very hot, almost too hot to handle. He picked it up gingerly, taking a deep gulp. *If ever a man needed a little something to steady his nerves,* he thought, *that person is me*. He took another generous gulp, coughing a little as the scalding tea burned his throat.

Loosey was watching him, when he looked up. "First drink of the day, Lieutenant?" he said, with a knowing smirk. Manny scowled, pushing the cup of tea away.

"Let's get one thing straight," he said sternly. "You're in my house now, and you will respect my rank and authority." He looked steadily at Loosey until Loosey looked away.

"Now. What I want to know is, why this morning?" Manny continued. "Off the record. These two detectives, Brady and Potter, how did they know to pick you up and bring you here, of all places?"

"I don't know, man, they told me I had to come with them, and that's about all they said. They didn't give me no choice," insisted Loosey. "They brought me here, handed me over to the desk sergeant, and left. The desk sergeant put me in the holding cell. He said he was going to assign a detective from the unit to my case. That's when I asked to see you."

Agnes opened the door briefly, placing a glass of water next to Manny.

"Agnes, could you have one of the detectives check on something for me, please?" asked Manny. "I want to know about two detectives, Thomas Brady and Harry Potter, what units they are assigned to. They dropped off this suspect here this morning with incomplete paperwork."

"Sure thing, Lieutenant." She nodded and left. Manny turned his attention back to Loosey.

"Did you do something, maybe something illegal, to attract the attention of these two police officers, Loosey?" asked Manny. "Tell me the truth, now. If you don't, this is just going to take longer."

"No, Manny, I didn't do nothing! Or, at least, nothing out of the ordinary," Loosey said. He eyed the glass of water longingly. "I could really use that glass of water," he said.

"Soon," said Manny, taking his time. "I have just a few more questions."

Loosey sank back in his chair. "How about cutting me loose then, how about that?" he asked, looking meaningfully at his restraints, arching one eyebrow.

Manny ignored him. "This is just so odd," he mused. "Why would two detectives drop off a suspect at a unit which is not their own? And another thing, the arrest report is not filled out," said Manny. "The description of your offenses has been left blank. In other words, I have no way of knowing why you were picked up."

Manny retrieved a pair of scissors from a desk drawer and cut through Loosey's restraints. Loosey gratefully stretched his arms, rubbing first one, then the other. He reached for the glass of water. Manny reached it first, pulling it just out of Loosey's reach.

"Loosey, I need you to think. Did these two officers say anything to you, or maybe they said something to each other, that would let you know why they brought you here?" asked Manny.

"No, Manny, I swear, I don't know!" said Loosey. "I ain't never seen them before!" he said indignantly. "They can't just do that, can they?"

"It seems that they just did," Manny pointed out mildly. "This wasn't a mistake. I think this was done deliberately. Somebody is sending me a message, bringing you here and dropping you in my lap," Manny said. "This has more to do with me than with you."

Manny looked thoughtfully at Loosey for a moment. "You said that you think this has something to do with that man who came to you asking questions about me," Manny said. "What made you think that?"

"There was just this one thing that one of them said to me, Detective Potter, right before he left me here," said Loosey. "He said I should think harder, or I'd be in for a world of trouble."

"Think harder? About what?" asked Manny. "What did he mean by that, do you know?"

"I think he meant that ... there's something he wants, Manny. And he thinks I know where they are. From the way he looked at me, kind of mean and threatening-like, I'd say he wants them real bad. And I've got a feeling that if he finds what he's looking for, he's -"

Mindful that there were most likely people listening to this interview from behind the two-way glass, Manny abruptly pushed the glass of water towards Loosey, cutting him off. "I'm sorry you had to be dragged into this, Loosey. You were never under arrest. There won't be any record of your visit here today. I'll see to it myself."

Manny's padlet beeped; there was a text from Agnes. He opened it and read, "No record anywhere of a Detective Thomas Brady or a Detective Harry Potter, not in this precinct, not anywhere else."

*What the hell?* thought Manny. *Who were they, two civilians playing dress-up? And if so, why?*

After making sure that Loosey had left the building, Manny returned to his office. He sat down behind his desk, lost in thought. Someone had gone to great lengths to bring Loosey to his workplace, knowing that Manny would not want his previous relationship with Loosey to become widely known. It could only be Raimone pulling the strings behind the scenes, but even for Raimone, this was beyond the pale. How had he managed to convince two men to dress up as police and pick up a suspect, brazenly walking him into the station as if they were legit? And how did those two civilians, if that is what they were, know how to act, what to say?

Leaning back in his chair, Manny's eye fell upon the cup of tea from earlier that morning. Without thinking, he reached for it and took a large swallow. He had finished half of it before he stopped, remembering that he was not supposed to drink for twenty-four hours. *Well, today is not a good day for that; it will have to wait,* he thought.

Manny gathered up the papers strewn across his desk and began to read through them. He was surprised to see a memo dated this morning from the Commissioner; usually, communications were handled by text or hologram. He read:

Press Release; for immediate release to all media outlets

By order of Com. Daniel J. Malone

Commissioner Daniel J. Malone announces the formation of a new task force, the Task Force for Unsolved Murders and Abductions (cold cases). The Task Force will have a dozen detectives. Lieutenant David Wu will be in charge, under the command of Captain Malcolm (Manny) Stewart, who will report directly to Commissioner Malone. The Task Force, which will be situated on the same floor as the Commissioner's office, is expected to be up and running by September 3rd.

"Did you see it?"

Manny looked up to the see the Chief standing in his doorway. "The press release, did you see it?" the Chief repeated excitedly, grinning. "It'll be in the news tomorrow. This copy is for you, in case you want to hang it on your wall or something." He held a glass bottle in one hand and two glasses in the other.

"Here's to you, Captain. Let's drink to your promotion!"

# Chapter 19.

**M**ANNY WAS VERY late coming home; it was 10:45 pm when he walked in. He was surprised to see Lucinda in the library, an afghan spread across her shoulders, sound asleep in one of the leather armchairs.

"Lucinda," Manny said, gently shaking her shoulder, "Lucinda, wake up!" She opened her eyes.

"It's late, what are you doing here?" he asked. "Is everything OK?"

"Yes, everything is fine," she replied. "Zach is upstairs in his own bed. I thought maybe you and I could have a little talk."

"Can't it wait? I'm tired, it's been a long day," Manny said hopefully. "Why don't you and Luis come over for lunch on Saturday, and we can talk then."

"OK, I guess it can wait. But Manny, school starts soon. We want to make sure that Zach is OK to start school," she said. She sat up, pushing the afghan away, reaching up to pat her graying hair back into place.

"Why wouldn't he be ready to start school?" asked Manny, puzzled.

Lucinda paused, wrinkling her nose. "Manny," she began, "have you been drinking?"

"Yes," he said honestly, holding her eyes with his own. "The press release for the formation of the new Task Force is going be released tomorrow morning. The news was all over the office. People kept stopping by to congratulate me on the promotion. They all drink, Lucinda. You know what it's like at work."

"I understand, Manny," she said hesitantly, "but we agreed that today you would not drink at all, for twenty-four hours. Did you forget?"

"No, I didn't forget," he replied. "It was not a good day for it, that's all. But don't worry," he hurried on, seeing that she was about to protest, "I saw a doctor this morning, Dr. Patel. She came to my office to fill out the report on my workplace injury, you know, when I hurt my back. I talked to her about my drinking, and she gave me some good advice."

"Manny, that's wonderful!" she replied, looking relieved. "We have been a little concerned about the drinking." She looked up at Luis, who had been standing in the doorway, listening to their conversation. "Why don't you come in, Luis?"

"Sorry to be eavesdropping," he said, nodding to Manny. "It will save Lucinda the trouble of repeating the conversation to me later."

"That's fine, I don't mind," replied Manny. "I want everything to be out in the open. I'll be cutting back on my drinking, starting tomorrow."

"Cutting back? What's that look like?" asked Luis.

"The doctor said to taper off, not stop all at once. I will still be able to share a drink at work on special occasions like today, and maybe have a drink some nights when I come home. Or a beer before dinner. You know, socially acceptable drinking, not every day. I'm not going to give it up completely," Manny explained. "But I'm also not going to try and hide it from you."

"Sounds like a good plan," Luis said, glancing at Lucinda. "Are you going to stick to it?"

"We'll see, won't we?" replied Manny. "Actions always speak louder than words."

Turning to Lucinda, Manny deftly changed the subject. He said, "You started to say something when I first woke you, something about Zach not being ready to start school?"

"He's been having some problems ever since the night he saw the video," Lucinda explained. "He has nightmares, and he's been wetting the bed at night, too."

"Your bed? Geez, I'm sorry, Lucinda," exclaimed Manny. "I had no idea."

"That's exactly why I waited for you tonight," she replied pointedly. "You need to spend more time with him. It's true, he has an extended family to care for him, but no one can replace his father. He needs you, Manny."

"Sometimes I think he's better off not spending too much time with me," Manny said exasperatedly. "I seem to screw up everything I do, when it comes to him."

"Now you know that's not true," she replied. "Every parent makes mistakes. You just pick yourself up and move on. Please, Manny?"

"OK, I'll spend some time with him this weekend, I promise, Lucinda," he said, carefully hiding his reluctance.

"Good. Ok, then," she said.

"Shall I walk you two home?" asked Manny, getting up.

"No, we're good, thanks," replied Luis. "You're going to bed now, right? No more drinking?"

"No more drinking. I think I've about had enough for today," Manny said, as he walked them to the door. "Home safe," he said, closing the door behind them.

Manny crossed to the study, eyes searching the room. Yes, it was here! His delivery had arrived, a large sturdy wooden box filled with twelve beautiful bottles of brandy, placed discreetly in his study during the day, when only Anna was at home, too busy with work to wonder what was in the box.

At first, he had thought maybe he should have the brandy delivered to the office. But then he changed his mind. *This is my house,* he thought, *why should I have to hide this? I'll put them away here, in one of the cabinets in the study.* Manny placed the precious glass bottles one at a time in the cabinet where his father had kept his bourbon. Reaching for the last bottle, he hesitated, then placed it inside his jacket out of sight, taking it upstairs to his room.

~ ~ ~ ~ ~ ~

"Zach, come and look at this!" Manny said to his son after work the next day. He pulled a package out of his pocket with a flourish and sat down on the sofa in the front parlor, where Zach was seated on the floor playing with blocks.

"What's that?" asked Zach, curious. He watched as Manny removed a tiny electronic four-legged animal and placed it on its charging pad. "It's called A.I. Doggie," Manny said eagerly. "Look, it's wagging its tail for you!" Manny had purchased the toy, which was not yet on the market, for an exorbitant sum plus a bribe for the company's manager.

Zach came closer to the table. "What's it do?" he asked.

"You can teach it to recognize you," replied Manny. "You can name it, and teach it tricks." They both watched as the little dog walked forward, and then fell off the edge of the table.

"You can set up a perimeter for it, so it doesn't do that," said Manny, frowning. "We'll install the app and figure out how."

Zach watched intently for a moment as the little dog lay motionless on the floor, and then turned back to his blocks. Manny, disappointed and annoyed, sat in silence for a few minutes, watching Zach play with his wooden blocks.

"That's quite a project you have there!" Manny said heartily. "Can I help?" He sat down on the floor near Zach.

"Nah," Zach replied, not looking at Manny. "I don't need any help."

"OK, then, maybe I'll just watch," said Manny. "How high is it going to be?"

Zach turned to look at his father. "I don't know," he said solemnly, "I'm not done yet."

Manny watched as his son intently stacked one block on top of another. Several minutes passed, with neither one saying a word. Finally, bored, Manny got up.

"Looks good, Bud," he said, placing his hand on Zach's shoulder. As he turned to leave, the tip of his shoe barely clipped one corner of the tower of blocks, causing it to crash noisily to the floor.

"You ruined it!" Zach cried angrily. "You made them all fall!"

~ ~ ~ ~ ~ ~

"How was your time with Zach?" asked Lucinda. "Did he like the little toy?" She and Manny were sitting in the library a few days later, enjoying a glass of raspberry-mint cannabis iced tea, as the late afternoon light spilled in through the tall glass windows.

"It didn't go all that well," responded Manny. "He was definitely not impressed. He barely looked at it."

"Maybe when he's a little older," she said gently. "Don't give up. It might take a few tries to get through to him."

"I offered to help him build with his blocks, but he didn't want that either," replied Manny. "Then as I was leaving, I bumped the blocks with my shoe, and the whole thing fell down."

Lucinda chuckled. "Did you stay to help him build it back?" she asked.

"No," said Manny. Actually, that had not occurred to him.

Manny sighed. Outside in the yard, they could hear the children and Julio playing a game. Julio trotted past the window, followed by both gleeful, laughing children. Zach wrapped himself around Julio's leg to slow him down, while Julie was trying to pull him down by climbing onto his back.

"Listen to them outside. They seem to be having such a good time," Manny said wonderingly. "What are they even doing?"

"They're playing, Manny," she said gently. "Why don't you go outside and join them?"

Manny hesitated for a moment, then stood up. "That's a good idea, Lucinda," he said. "Why don't I do that?" He stretched, then resolutely went outside.

"Hey, can I play, too?" he said. Julio turned to him.

"Sure! You take one of the kids, and I'll take the other, and we'll race you!" He extricated himself from the children, who were clinging to him like magnets. "Who wants to ride on my shoulders?" he said, dropping to his knees.

"Me! Me!" exclaimed both children, rushing to see who could be first to climb onto Julio's shoulders. Manny stood by as his son shoved Julie out of the way so he could ride on his Uncle Julio's shoulders.

"OK, Julie, you're with me!" Manny said, also dropping to his knees. Julie looked to her father, who gave her an encouraging nod.

"Up you go!" Manny said, firmly holding his niece's legs against his chest as she settled herself onto his shoulders.

"Let's have a race!" said Julio. "First one to the other side of the yard wins!" And they were off, Julio and Manny running across the yard, slow as molasses with their precious cargo.

"Hang on tight!" said Julio. Zach laughed out loud, wrapping his fists firmly around his uncle's shoulder length hair.

"Faster, Uncle Julio, faster!" cried Zach, leaning forward for momentum.

Julie, on top of Manny's shoulders, was quiet. Manny said, "They're not going to beat us, are they, Julie?"

In response, Julie also shifted her weight slightly, leaning forward. Caught off guard, Manny tried to adjust his posture, but it was too late. He lost his balance and landed with a thud on his stomach, face down on the ground.

"Julie, are you OK?" asked Manny, as soon as he could breathe. She had jumped off immediately when they hit the ground. Manny flipped over onto his back. "Where are you?"

"She's fine," said Julio. "Just a little bump, that's all." He put Zach down and came to kneel near Manny.

"You OK, man?" asked Julio. "You look a little pale."

"I'm fine," said Manny, taking inventory of his legs, arms, hands. He carefully and slowly sat up. Amazingly, his back did not hurt. "Yeah, I'm OK," he said with relief. "You guys go ahead and play; I think I'll go inside now."

As he walked slowly back to the house, he could hear Julio say, "Who thinks he can beat me?" The children jumped up and down, shouting, "Me! Me!"

~ ~ ~ ~ ~ ~

Manny glanced down at his padlet, which showed a text from Tyler Watkins, the attorney. Opening it up, he read the one-word text, "Nothing." Tyler, who had been his father's lawyer before his death, was extremely careful about putting things in writing, even though all of their communications were covered by attorney-client privilege. Manny understood that his text meant that Tyler had researched all of his files and had not found anything having to do with Mrs. al-Sayed or the theft of two diamond rings.

Manny sighed; it was another dead end. There was only one more place to check, he thought, opening up the database on civilian employees of the Police Department. *Let's just see now, Raimone,* he thought, *how do you know about those two diamond rings?*

It didn't take him very long to find out.

Raimone had worked for Private Eyes Surveillance Company around the time when Manny had stolen the rings. Manny had been about to exit the old lady's house with her rings in his pocket, when he had noticed the tiny round surveillance drone bobbing up near the ceiling, glowing blue to show that it was actively filming.

Realizing that the surveillance company's employees were most likely standing around a large screen, gleefully watching him in real time as he carefully committed his theft, he had left Mrs. al-Sayed's house by walking out the front door, not even bothering to close it behind him. Everyone in the Colony knew his father, and most people recognized Manny's face from various news and society pages. Manny had gone to sit on a park bench not far away. The police had detained him shortly afterwards and taken him to the police station, where he had confronted his father, who was livid with rage.

Raimone, thinking that perhaps a video of the Police Chief's underage son committing a crime might someday come in handy, must have created a copy of the surveillance tape for himself.

Manny was pondering what to do with this information, when Naomi and Dave walked past his office door, both carrying boxes filled with files and other things from their desks.

"Moving already?" Manny asked. "You know we don't start until next week, right?"

"We thought we'd get a head-start moving upstairs," replied Dave. "Our replacements will be arriving soon with their own stuff, so we thought we'd clear out some space. We can work from up there just as well as from down here."

"OK, Lieutenant Wu, that sounds fine," Manny said, relishing the moment. He hadn't started packing yet; he made a mental note to have Agnes find some boxes.

"Thanks, Captain!" replied Dave with a grin, as the two of them disappeared into the stairwell.

Agnes appeared in the doorway with his cup of tea. He waved her in.

"Thank you, Agnes. Do you think you could find me some boxes? I need to get started packing," Manny said.

"I'll take care of that for you, Sir," she said formally. Something in her voice caught Manny's attention.

"Everything OK?" he asked. Looking directly at her, he noticed that her face looked strained and pale.

"Yes, everything is fine," she said reluctantly, while Manny watched with a growing sense of unease. Finally, she said, "I think there is something you should see."

# Chapter 20.

**O**PENING UP HER padlet, she tapped open an app and handed the padlet to Manny. It was a recording of a news program that had aired earlier in the day.

The anchorman was playing a clip showing a teenage boy in a hooded sweatshirt, cautiously peeking out from the inside of an armoire in a bedroom. Manny realized with awakening horror that he was looking at himself, ten years earlier. The boy in the video was slowly looking around to make sure that no one was home as he came out from his hiding place, then looking up and discovering that he was on surveillance.

For a moment, Manny felt like he couldn't breathe. He was dimly aware of his padlet beeping, then the sound of several padlets beeping from outside his door, then the sound of people close by in the office speaking together in carefully hushed voices.

The news anchor was saying, "Is this the best the Commissioner could do, choosing Lieutenant Stewart to be Captain of the new Task Force? Don't we have better qualified people, you know, people who aren't thieves?"

Manny handed the padlet back to Agnes, his face averted. "Close the door on your way out," he said. She hesitated, sympathy and concern showing clearly on her face; when he did not say anything further, she turned and left him alone.

Manny pulled the cup of tea closer to him, drinking it down in a few gulps. *Thank goodness for Dutch courage,* he thought. Belatedly, he remembered that he was supposed to be cutting back on his drinking. *That's why I am only having one cup,* he rationalized, *and besides, what they don't know at home won't hurt them.*

It did not take long for the Chief to come in. "Lieutenant," he began, and Manny could tell that he was in trouble. "What the hell, Manny?"

"You saw it?" Manny asked.

"Everybody saw it!" exploded the Chief. "The Commissioner isn't going to be happy about this. It will embarrass him publicly, and you don't ever want to do that."

"I can explain, Sir," Manny began. "When I was a kid, I used to be a petty thief, breaking into houses and stealing little things."

"We know all about that, Manny," said the Chief impatiently. "We knew about it when you were a kid. The Commissioner, too." Manny knew that the Chief and the Commissioner had been very friendly with his father; it seemed that Patrick had talked to his colleagues about his son. "We knew when we hired you that you had a history, but those files are sealed. You were a juvenile when all of that happened."

"I think I know who's behind this," said Manny. "Raimone used to work for the surveillance company that filmed my break-in. I think it must have been Raimone who released this to the media. If I'm right, then he's broken more than one law. For starters, this video was the private property of the surveillance company. We could bring him in right now for questioning."

The Chief sat down heavily in the chair in front of Manny's desk.

"I agree, it's probably Raimone who's behind this," the Chief said quietly. "That little worm, I wish somebody would fire him."

The Chief's padlet beeped. Manny could see the rim pulsing scarlet, sign of an urgent text that requires an immediate response. The Chief read the text, then looked up at Manny.

"That didn't take long," he said ruefully. "The Commissioner says you're to stay here with this unit, until the end of the month."

"Stay here!" cried Manny, dismayed. "But I'm supposed to be upstairs with the Task Force! Dave and Naomi are already moving in!"

"That's on hold for right now," the Chief said. "Let's see how the public reacts to this video. Who knows? Something else

133

may come up to take attention away from it. You'd better hope that's what happens."

After the Chief left, Manny kept the door to his office closed for the rest of the day, leaving the office late, after most of the employees had gone home.

Julio met him at the front door. "Manny, I don't know if you've heard," he began.

"I've heard, believe me, I've heard," he replied wearily. "Did you see it, Julio? You're not on the tape, just me. It was my last job, the one I did alone."

"What are you going to do?" Julio asked worriedly.

"There's nothing I can do, not right now," Manny replied. "I'm fairly certain it's Raimone who's behind releasing the tape, but when I suggested that we bring him in for questioning, the Chief didn't seem to like that idea. And I've been told to stay where I am for the rest of the month, not join the new Task Force when it begins work."

"Not joining the new Task Force?" asked Luis, coming into the foyer. "What happened?"

"I'm in disgrace, because of the release of the tape," Manny explained. "Come with me into the study. I don't know about both of you, but I could use a drink."

Luis and Julio exchanged glances. "Don't worry, it's my first drink of the day," Manny lied smoothly, ignoring his bristling conscience. *Tea isn't a drink,* he rationalized, *it's just tea. And besides, it was hours ago.* "I'm not hiding it from you. You can join me, if you want."

The three men went into the study. Manny poured himself a socially correct small-ish glass of brandy. He offered the bottle to Luis and Julio, who each declined.

"What's next, then, Manny?" asked Luis.

"I don't know. I think it's out of my control, at this point," he said, taking small sips of brandy. Its blessed warmth spread throughout Manny's body, unclenching the knots in his stomach. "I am hoping it blows over quickly."

Anna had her usual news program on in the kitchen, where she had been keeping Manny's dinner warm. As he came into the kitchen, she turned off the show, snapping shut her padlet.

"That bad, huh?" he asked, as he took his dinner plate to the table.

"Did you watch it?" she asked.

"I saw some of it at work," he replied. "That was enough."

"It's been airing on all of the major stations," she said. "It's playing everywhere. Your name is all over the news."

Manny ate his dinner quickly; then he went upstairs to his room. He closed the door and carefully took out his precious bottle of brandy, pouring himself a much larger glassful than the ridiculously small one he had had downstairs. *Now that's a man's drink,* he said to himself, holding the glass up to admire it after savoring his first sip. *After the day I've had, I deserve it.*

Over the next few days, Manny bore his humiliation bravely, holding his head high as he walked through the office, taking calls, working cases, managing his unit. Dave and Naomi were working from upstairs, but the rest of the unit was unchanged. The video was played frequently on the talk shows for the first two days, but that had begun to drop off. Manny waited, biding his time.

A week later, sitting behind his desk, Manny stared at his padlet, willing it to beep. He desperately wanted to be upstairs with the Task Force, to greet the new detectives who had been selected from different departments all over the Colony, to take his rightful place alongside Dave. It was agonizing, knowing that they were together upstairs, getting to know each other, while he was stuck downstairs at his desk.

The Chief knocked on his door, then walked in and closed the door behind him. *Not a good sign,* thought Manny, his heart sinking.

"I'll get right to the point," said the Chief, sitting down across from Manny. "I'm afraid that I've got some bad news for you, Manny. The Commissioner has brought in another

Captain from outside of the precinct to head up the Task Force. You're to stay here with this unit, as Lieutenant."

"But, Sir!" protested Manny. "If not for Raimone leaking the video to the press, everything would have been fine!"

"But he did leak it to the press," said the Chief sternly. "I know it's not fair, Manny. But you make your own fairness, as your father always said."

*Great,* thought Manny bitterly, *throw my father in my face.*

"Manny, I'm going to give you some advice," the Chief said, "and I want you to listen very carefully." He waited, to be sure that Manny was taking him seriously. Manny nodded.

"You could arrest Raimone, and maybe you could prove that he copied the surveillance video back when he was working for the surveillance company, and that he was the one who released the video to the media in order to discredit you. If you do go that route, though, this will stay in the news and you will only continue to embarrass the Commissioner.

"You need to play a long game, Manny. The Commissioner likes you, he still likes you. He's placed you on the Council, and that still stands. Be his best eyes and ears on the Council, Manny. Work hand in glove with him to carry information back and forth, you know, the kind of stuff that can't be written down.

"You're not the first man to suffer a setback in his career. You need to think carefully about what you want, about where you want to be in ten years. The Commissioner has a deputy who is getting on in years. Hell, the Commissioner is no spring chicken himself! Do you really want to embarrass him even further by arresting Raimone? Or do you want to put it behind you, swallow your disappointment like a man and move forward in your career?"

Manny swallowed hard. "I hadn't thought of it in that way, Sir," he said respectfully. He didn't like it, but there was truth in what the Chief was saying to him. He needed to think carefully about his future.

"That's good, Manny, I knew you'd see it my way." He stood up. "There's still plenty to do in this unit, and you have two new detectives, the replacements for Naomi and Dave, to meet with and assign caseloads. Let's get back to work."

# Chapter 21.

SOMEHOW, MANNY MADE it through the day. He assigned Dave and Naomi's old cases to the two new detectives, welcoming them and introducing them to his unit. He went through the motions, doing what needed to be done, but his heart was not in it.

A few days went by. Manny, missing his friend Dave, decided to see if he wanted to have lunch together. *He might need my help settling into his new responsibilities as Lieutenant,* Manny thought. He unrolled his padlet and texted:

Manny: *"Lunch?"*
Dave: *"Not today. The Captain is taking me to lunch. Another time!"*
Manny: *"Sure, no problem."*

Disappointed, Manny sat for a moment. It wasn't just that he missed Dave. He felt shut out. He wondered if he should order a sandwich to be delivered. Maybe he would go out and buy a sandwich. Maybe he would just skip lunch altogether.

"Agnes, how about another cup of tea?" he called. When she brought it to him, he thanked her, waited until she had left his office, and then reached into the bottom drawer of his desk, where he kept his office bottle of brandy. He added an extra helping of brandy to the tea, downing half of it in one greedy gulp, refilling it with a generous hand.

*There,* he thought with satisfaction, *no need for lunch,* as he finished the rest of the tea. It was amazing how drinking could blunt the bitterest of disappointments. *They don't tell you about that,* he said to himself with a little chuckle, *they just tell you that drinking is bad.*

Manny spent the rest of the afternoon contemplating the ruin that had been his week. He pushed various papers around his desk and made a chain out of some paperclips. Finally, he left the office early, before any of his detectives, making sure that his flask was full for the walk home. *At least it's the weekend,* thought Manny, exhausted.

Later, Manny was to recall almost nothing about his walk from the office to his home, although it seemed that his feet knew the way. *I must have been lost in thought,* he assured himself.

~ ~ ~ ~ ~ ~

"Tell us the truth, Manny, how much did you have to drink?" demanded Luis. His angry face was inches away from Manny's, as he sat in his chair in the study. "I thought you promised you were going to cut back?"

"Luis, not now," protested Manny, his speech slurred and indistinct. "The Task Force has a new captain, Dave's the lieutenant, while I'm stuck downstairs with the Chief ..." Manny's eyes fixed on a spot across the room, which was beginning to tilt and rotate, although he was sitting quite still. *How does that work?* he wondered.

Luis put his hand on Manny's shoulder and gave it a hard shake. "Pull yourself together, man! Come on, you should eat something," he said. His eyes were hard and unsympathetic. "Come into the kitchen and have dinner."

"No, I'm not hungry," replied Manny, eyes still watching the room move. "You go on. I'll eat later."

"At least come and sit with us," insisted Luis. "Say hello to Zach. You haven't seen him yet today."

"Manny, Luis, dinner is ready," said Lucinda, coming into the study, wiping her hands on her apron. "Manny! Oh, my goodness, Luis, what's going on?" she exclaimed in dismay. "Is he drunk?"

"Pretty close to it, I'd say," replied Luis. "We need to get some food into him."

"Manny, pull yourself together," she said, frowning, "you don't want Zach to see you like this."

*I don't give a damn if he does,* thought Manny bitterly. *Let him see! Let him see that life is hard, and unfair, and filled with disappointment.*

Manny reluctantly came into the kitchen, sitting down in his chair at the end of the long table. "Daddy!" Zach said, turning to him with a certain wariness on his little face.

"Zach," mumbled Manny, carefully sitting up straight in his chair and hoping that no one would notice the strong smell of alcohol emanating from him.

"Have some of the curried cauliflower casserole, Manny," offered Anna, handing him a dish containing something white with a thickly viscous yellowish sauce over it. Manny gagged, waving the dish away with his hand.

"Maybe later. For now, I'll just have some bread," he gasped. Reaching for the bread, Manny knocked over his water glass with his hand. "Crap!" he said under his breath, mopping up the water with his napkin.

"Crap!" exclaimed Zach, biting off a piece of bread. "Crap, crap, crap!"

Manny pointed his finger at his son. "Zach. Don't say 'crap'!"

Zach froze, eyes round. Julianna, sitting next to him, turned to Anna and said, "Mama, Uncle Manny gets to say 'crap.' Why can't Zach say it?"

Before Anna could arrange her thoughts into a plausible explanation, Manny turned to his niece and growled, "You've got a fresh little mouth on you, young lady!"

"Hey!" exclaimed Anna. "Manny, that was uncalled for! You don't talk that way to my daughter!"

"Maybe you need to teach your daughter some damn manners!" he said too loudly. He'd had a hard day, holding his temper, biting down hard on his disappointment, but here in his own house, he would speak his mind. Frustration sparking into true anger, he pounded his fist once, hard, against the table. Plates and glasses jumped. Wary disapproval showed plainly on every face turned towards him.

"If you'd raised her properly, she wouldn't have gone into my bedroom and taken my tablet, now, would she?" demanded Manny bitterly, his tone sullen and resentful.

Lucinda said, "Now, Manny, I thought we agreed we're past that!"

Julio gripped Anna's forearm, as she bit back an angry retort.

"No, *you* agreed. *I* didn't agree," argued Manny, suddenly disgusted with all of them. "Excuse me, I'm going to go and sit in the study." He rose to leave the table.

Julio rose, too, holding up a hand to stop anyone else from following him. He and Manny left the kitchen, walking through the foyer towards the study.

"What's going on with you, man?" asked Julio. "You're pissed off at everything and everybody."

"Let's see, I lost my promotion and my new unit and my son thinks I'm a monster," responded Manny. "How would you feel?"

"That's not an excuse. You need to apologize to Anna and Julie," Julio insisted, grasping his brother's shoulder.

"Get your hands off me, Julio," Manny said darkly, regarding his brother with narrowed eyes. "And keep your little brat out of my bedroom."

"*What?* What did you just call Julie?" Julio demanded. "What's gotten into you?"

Manny put a hand on Julio's chest and shoved. "Back off," he snarled.

"You're drunk, Manny," Julio said, taking a step backwards.

"So what if I'm drunk," Manny said, with a bitter laugh. He reached forward with both hands and shoved Julio again, harder this time. It felt hugely satisfying to channel his anger through his hands.

"Cut it out, man!" demanded Julio, grabbing him by the shoulders.

Manny drew back his arm and punched Julio in the eye, as hard as he could. Julio roared with surprise, covering his eye with his hand. Then he turned to face Manny, holding up both clenched fists in a classic boxer's stance, and said, "Come on, then! You think you can take me? I'd like to see you try!"

As kids, Julio and Manny had spent hours sparring with each other upstairs in Julio's little bedroom in the house on 14th Street. Luis, who had once been a boxing instructor, had given them real lessons, using boxing gloves and headgear. Both of them were accomplished fighters.

But they had never fought each other bare-fisted.

Julio was a natural athlete, graceful and light on his feet, dancing forward and back, bobbing and weaving, while Manny was more plodding and methodical. Manny had always had an advantage over Julio, not only because he was stronger and had more endurance, but because he had a longer reach.

Manny swung again at Julio, but Julio blocked the punch easily, shoving Manny backwards. Manny stumbled into the stairs, catching his balance and bounding back to circle around Julio, more careful this time, feet moving, looking for an opening.

Manny aimed another punch at Julio, who scornfully leaned to one side as Manny's fist sailed past his ear. The momentum carried Manny forwards and into the wall, the room spinning crazily as he struggled to stay on his feet. Julio stood watching, both arms held loosely at his sides.

Manny reached back to steady himself against the wall, shaking his head to clear it. *If you're fighting angry, you're not in control.* The words came floating back to him; Luis had taught them well. Taking a deep breath, Manny pushed himself off the wall and moved cautiously towards Julio.

Suddenly, Julio's fist crashed into Manny's mouth, taking Manny by surprise. He paused for a moment, blinking, looking down at the blood splattered across his shirt. Julio stepped back, giving Manny an opportunity to end the fight. Enraged, Manny charged, rushing straight at Julio.

Feinting with his right hand, at the last minute Manny's left fist lashed out and smashed into Julio, making a loud cracking sound as it connected with Julio's cheekbone. Julio's eyes rolled up in his head as Manny leaned in and hit Julio just beneath the chin in a vicious uppercut. Julio collapsed backwards without a sound, crumpling to the marble floor.

"Julio! *Julio!*" screamed Lucinda. By now everyone had come into the foyer, including the children. "*Julio! Get up!*"

Julie started to cry, running to her father's side, pulling on his hand. "Daddy, wake up!"

Lucinda turned to Manny, her eyes wild with shock and fury. "What were you thinking?" she demanded. "He is your brother! Don't you know that you could hurt him?!"

*Yeah, I know that,* he thought sourly. *That's what I was trying to do.* And yet somehow, he couldn't quite remember why they had been fighting in the first place.

"Julio, get up, man," he said in an undertone, reaching down a hand to help him up. But Julio did not move.

A tense few moments passed, Julie crying, Anna white-faced and staring malevolently at Manny, Zach half-hidden behind the table in the foyer, Luis on his knees next to his son. Finally, Julio stirred, moaning.

Manny ran up the stairs to his bedroom, as much to escape their accusing eyes as to escape the remorse which was galvanizing in the pit of his stomach. He pulled open his closet door, put on a hooded sweatshirt over his bloodied shirt, then took the bottle of brandy and put it in his waistband, underneath the sweatshirt. On impulse, he also took his detective's badge, slipping the lanyard around his neck, hiding it beneath the sweatshirt. Then he ran down the stairs and out into the night.

143

# *Chapter 22.*

**S**ITTING ON A bench in the park, Manny drew the hood of his sweatshirt over his face. He retrieved the bottle of brandy, took a large swallow, and replaced it beneath the sweatshirt. A moment later, he took it out again. After a few more swallows, he stopped trying to keep it hidden.

Bang bang bang. Something was banging against the park bench. A man's voice was saying, "There's no sleeping here, move along now, move along." Surprised, Manny opened his eyes. He had fallen asleep on the park bench. A police officer holding a Billy club was encouraging him to get up, while looking closely at Manny. He did not seem to recognize him. *Lucky for me,* Manny thought groggily.

Manny carefully stood up and moved away. To his relief, the police officer said nothing further, although he did follow Manny for several minutes before going elsewhere.

Manny wandered aimlessly past The Sauna, the nickname for the electric power plant where electricity was extracted from humid air. A few moments later, he realized that he was in front of the Parts Department, the sprawling facility which was home to absolutely anything that someone might want to discard.

Old toasters, broken dishes, worn out linens and clothing, lopsided tables, well-worn shoes, anything which could be repaired or recycled into something else was dropped off at the Parts Department, where the technicians inside would take these items apart and make new items.

*Hah,* he thought, *perfect!* He stood in front of the building and took off his sweatshirt, then the NYPD Lieutenant's badge that hung on a lanyard around his neck. He dropped the badge into the contributions receptacle outside of the Parts Department, chuckling to himself. "There you go!" he said to no one in particular. "Let's see you make something new out of that!"

It seemed inordinately funny to him, and he laughed out loud, making his mouth hurt. He pulled the sweatshirt back over his arms and chest. There was blood on his shirt; he could not remember why.

Sometime later, Manny realized that he was sitting on the ground. Someone was singing. He struggled to his feet, brushing off his clothes, nearly losing his balance. The ground was swaying and tilting in an alarming manner, and he felt like he needed to vomit.

Manny wanted to go home, but was afraid of his family's disapproval. *But it's my own damn house,* he grumbled resentfully to himself. *I should be able to do whatever I want in my house.*

*What must they think of me now?* he thought dejectedly. *Julio probably won't ever speak to me again. I shouldn't have hit him so hard. And Luis! He looked at me like we were strangers.* Something thick and sticky was dripping down the front of his sweatshirt; he brushed at it with his fingers, but it was too disgusting. He left it.

~ ~ ~ ~ ~ ~

There was a light shining in his eyes. He groaned and turned his head away. Cool fingers gently gripped his chin, turning it this way, then that way. He tried to open his eyes, although they seemed to be stuck shut. His mouth hurt, especially the upper lip.

"Manny, can you hear me?" asked a female voice.

"Naz," he groaned with heartfelt relief, "*Naztazya!*" He reached for her, but she resisted. Her voice said, "Manny, it's Dr. Patel. Monica Patel. Can you open your eyes?"

*Dr. Patel. Not Naz. Naz is dead. What is Dr. Patel doing here?*

He focused, forcing his eyes to open, turning his head to look at her. His head pounded painfully, and he fought back the urge to vomit. "Where am I?" he asked.

"I'm not sure," she replied. "You asked me to meet you here."

145

"I did?" he asked, moving his head carefully to look around. He was lying on his back in bed. It took a moment to realize that he was upstairs in his old bedroom in the house on 14th Street, where he and Julio had lived when they were boys.

"How did I get here?" he asked.

"You tell me, Manny," she said, sitting down in a chair next to the bed. "All I know is that you turned on Beacon, then texted me the link so I could find you. You left the front door unlocked for me. I found you here, upstairs in this bedroom."

"I did that?" he asked, wonderingly. Beacon was the emergency app used only by police and health care workers, to locate someone's padlet in an urgent rescue situation. He had no memory of using it, or texting her the link.

"Manny, you were out cold. You've been unconscious for hours," she said seriously. "How much did you have to drink?"

"I'm not sure," he replied, his head aching. "I drank a full bottle of brandy, then I had a flask with me, too."

"I've stitched up your lip," she said. Manny reached up to run his fingers carefully over his stiff, sore upper lip. "You've got bruises on your hands and face, and a pair of black eyes, too. As far as I can see, nothing else needs medical attention, but you're going to be pretty sore for a few days."

She looked at him steadily. "Have you ever blacked out before?" she asked.

"No," he said. "I blacked out?"

"What's the last thing you remember from yesterday?" she asked.

Manny thought about the day before, the argument at dinner and the fistfight with Julio, his flight from the house - and then, nothing.

"I hit my brother," he said, shamefacedly. "We had an argument at dinner, and I was drunk. I hit him." Manny tried to sit up.

Dr. Patel put her cool, steady hand firmly on his shoulder. Manny was startled to feel her fingers on his bare skin; had he lost his shirt?

"Don't try to sit up just yet," she said. "You're going to have to wait a bit, before you get up. Here, have a glass of water." She handed him a glass.

"Where's my shirt?" he asked.

"I put it in the sink downstairs," she replied. "I needed to make sure you weren't injured, and anyway … the shirt needs washing."

Dr. Patel regarded him for a moment. "You know that you could be dead right now from alcohol poisoning?" she said seriously. "Laid out stiff and cold on a table in the morgue? Your brother could be planning your memorial service, instead of sitting downstairs in the kitchen."

"Julio is here?" Manny asked. "He's downstairs?"

"Yes, he's been waiting here for hours," she replied. "I told him that you are my patient, entitled to your privacy. I wouldn't allow him upstairs until I could ask you if you want to see him. Do you?"

"Yes," he replied. "Thank you for all that you've done for me, Dr. Patel. Monica. I appreciate it very much."

She gathered up her things and turned to leave. "Stay in touch, Manny," she said, as she made her way down the stairs.

He could hear voices murmuring in the kitchen, and then the old, familiar sound of Julio's footsteps climbing the metal staircase.

Julio appeared in the doorway. He was not smiling. Julio had six stitches in his cheek, and a considerable black eye. Walking over to the bed, he stared down at Manny.

"First. Before anything else," Julio said, drawing a deep breath. "Are you OK?"

"Yeah, I guess so," Manny replied. "And you?"

"Yeah," Julio replied tersely. He glared at Manny, rocking back and forth on his heels, hands on his hips. "So," he said, looking surprisingly like Luis when he was angry, "what do you have to say for yourself?"

"I'm glad you're alright, for starters," said Manny. "Honestly, I don't remember much of what happened.

Apparently, I drank the entire bottle of brandy and blacked out." He chuckled ruefully.

"You think this is *funny*?" asked Julio furiously. "You left me unconscious on the floor, blood everywhere, my mother in tears and the children ... they saw it all, Manny. Just because you don't remember what you did doesn't mean that you are not responsible for your actions."

Manny cringed. How many times had he thought exactly that, after his father had beaten him while he was drunk?

Manny sighed. "Julio, I'm so ashamed of myself. I could not be more sorry. It's just that ... everything at work turned to shit this week, and I just ... snapped or something," he finished lamely. Julio glared at him for a long moment, and then sat down next to him on the bed.

"Let me tell you what happened after you left," he said. "After I regained consciousness, I mean."

Manny listened as Julio recounted how Lucinda had wiped up bright red blood from the white marble floor, while Anna had taken the children over to Lucinda and Luis's house across the street to spend the night there. Luis had wanted to go after Manny, but Julio had said no, Luis was too angry and there would just be another fistfight. Against everyone's advice, Julio, battered and still bleeding, had gone out to look for his brother.

"How did you know I'd be here?" marveled Manny.

"Where else would you be?" countered Julio. "It wasn't hard to figure out."

"You have stitches," Manny said, looking at Julio's cheek.

"Yeah, Dr. Patel stitched me up while I was waiting to see you," replied Julio. "You can't imagine how surprised I was when I opened the door and she was sitting there at the kitchen table. She looked at me and we both said, 'Who are *you*?' at the same time." He chuckled, then turned serious again. "How did she know you were here?"

"Apparently, I was cognizant enough to text her that I needed help, and to use my Beacon app so she could find me. Then I guess I passed out, or something," said Manny.

"You know you can die from alcohol poisoning, right?" said Julio sternly. "You're out of your mind to drink that much. Besides, geez, you stink like an old wino." Wrinkling up his nose, he relaxed for the first time since coming upstairs.

"Maybe I'll take a shower before we go home," Manny said. "Do you have an old shirt or something I could borrow? My sweatshirt is ..."

"Yeah, I saw it downstairs. It's stinking up the kitchen. Don't worry, I have some clothes here. I'll find you a shirt," said Julio. "And after that, we are going home," he added, "and you are going to apologize to everyone, Anna, Julie, Zach, Dad, but most especially, Manny, you are going to apologize to Mama. You made her cry."

Manny, shame-faced, looked down at his hands to avoid his brother's eyes. "I'll make it right, Julio. I'll talk to them. Maybe we can get them all into the kitchen, so I can apologize to everybody at once." Embarrassment reddened his bruised and battered face.

"However you do it, man, just do it," Julio replied. "Here, I'll get you a clean sweatshirt." Julio disappeared down the stairs.

"Thanks, bro," said Manny. He slowly and carefully stood up, head banging mercilessly.

Manny gathered up his padlet, jacket and shoes. He looked around the tiny room. His badge, what had he done with it? Manny looked all around, then returned again to the bed, searching behind the pillows and beneath the blankets. Dropping to the floor, he looked beneath the bed.

*Oh, no,* he thought, *it's gotta be here!* Perspiration beaded his forehead as he searched beneath the bed.

"Julio," he called downstairs, "have you seen my detective's badge?"

# Chapter 23.

**Y**OUR DETECTIVE'S BADGE?" answered Julio, surprised. "No, I haven't seen it. Are you sure you had it with you?"

"Yeah, I'm sure. I took it with me last night when I left the house," replied Manny. He dropped painfully to his knees to look behind the Vertical. "I can't lose it. There's a fine and a two-week suspension for losing a badge."

"Then I hope you find it," said Julio in a serves-you-right tone of voice, handing Manny the clean sweatshirt. "I'll be downstairs when you're done with your shower."

Showered and changed, Manny came downstairs. He and Julio looked around the living room and kitchen of the little house, on the tables, counter and floor, but the badge was nowhere to be found.

"I can just imagine how the conversation is going to go, when I tell the Chief that I've lost it," lamented Manny. "It's bad enough that I am a walking poster child for how not to behave."

"Maybe you dropped it outside somewhere," suggested Julio. Manny had the strangest little sliver of a memory, something about pulling the lanyard over his head and laughing, dropping it into ... something.

"Oh, no," he said, his heart sinking through his stomach. "I think I may have taken it off outside."

"Maybe it's been turned in to the lost and found at the station," suggested Julio.

"Then everybody at work will know," lamented Manny. "I'll be a laughingstock forever, if someone brought my badge in to the station."

The two walked home side by side in silence, drawing curious stares from passersby, Julio with his black eye and battered cheek bristling with stitches, Manny with his two black eyes, sewn upper lip and bruised face. Manny's back hurt, not surprisingly, but he was too ashamed to mention it to Julio.

Luis was watching for them through the windows in the study. "They're here," he announced to Lucinda and Anna.

"Let's all sit down in here. Give him time, now, before we say anything. Let's let him explain himself to us."

Manny saw them sitting in chairs in the study, all waiting silently for him to speak, and suddenly his mouth went dry. Anna's accusing eyes glared at him from across the room. Luis looked angry, although it was plain that he was holding back, waiting to hear what Manny had to say. Lucinda's red-rimmed eyes were sad and hurt. Manny recalled that Julio had said he left her crying, when he came to search for Manny.

He stood in the doorway, his heart sinking. *Do I really have to do this?* he thought with dismay. *Couldn't we all just pick up from here and move on?*

"I want to apologize," he began, searching for the right words. *Be contrite, be humble, be convincing,* he thought. *Give them what they want. Let's get this over with.*

"I behaved badly last night," he said. "I hurt each one of you, and I am sorry."

"Luis," he said, "I apologize. You and Lucinda have been so good to me, and I'm sincerely sorry for what I said and did last night." He bowed formally to his foster father.

He resolutely turned to Anna. "I apologize, Anna, I was obnoxious and rude, and had no right to speak the way I did, not to you and not to Julie, either." He bowed formally to both of them. Julie squirmed in her seat and turned away from her uncle.

"Julio," he said, looking at his brother, "I'm sorry I hit you. I wish I could take it all back." He bowed formally to his brother, right hand on his left shoulder, a proper bow of respect and contrition. One side of Julio's face bristled with stitches. *Look what I did to him,* marveled Manny, *and still he came to find me, make sure I was OK.* A sudden twinge of remorse surprised him, twisting uncomfortably inside his chest.

But it was when he turned to address Lucinda that his conscience roared to life. He found that he could barely look at her. "I let you down," he said in a shaking voice. "I'm so ashamed of myself. I hope you can forgive me." He bowed low to her, deeply respectful, holding the bow a heartbeat longer than necessary to avoid looking in her eyes.

He glanced around the room, anywhere but at Lucinda. "Where is Zach?" he asked.

Lucinda pointed to the closet. "He's in there, Manny. He's hiding."

Manny reeled as though he had been kicked in the chest. The closet in the study had been his favorite childhood hiding place, whenever his father had gotten drunk and started fighting with his mother. He had been a scared little boy, terrified of his father and his brutal, clenched fists. Patrick often chased Lila Rose through the house, grabbing her and hitting her, over and over again. Manny remembered how he had felt, sliding into his hiding place and closing the door, feeling safe, certain that Patrick could not find him there.

"Well, Manny?" Luis said angrily. "Your son is afraid of you. What do you think about that?"

Manny looked away, as the consequences of his drunken rage became clear. It was a few moments before he could find his voice.

"I simply could not be more ashamed," he said sincerely. Eyes filled with tears, he turned to go upstairs. He desperately needed to be alone, to get away from their accusing faces.

Luis held up a hand to stop him. "Not so fast, Manny," he said. "We want to know what your plan is."

"W-what? My plan?" asked Manny, his face going blank.

"Yes. Your plan. Are you going to give up drinking, or not?" Luis demanded. "You did some serious damage, you know. You gave Julio a concussion as well as a broken cheekbone, and it could have been a lot worse. Look at the two of you! We raised you better than this."

Manny looked at his brother in surprise; he had not mentioned anything about a concussion. Julio shrugged. "It's nothing, I'm fine," he insisted.

"Yes, but that's only because you were lucky," said Lucinda. She turned to Manny, her hands resolutely clasped together in her lap.

"You are both my sons," she said, "and I love you both. But I will not stand by while you try to injure each other. This must never happen again."

She looked steadily at Manny, who could not look away. "Manny, *if* you are truly sorry and you are willing to stop drinking, then we welcome you back with open arms. Everyone deserves a second chance."

Lucinda. How he loved her! She had been nothing but kind to him since the day Julio had rescued him from four bullies and brought him home after school, when he was eleven years old. She had been more than kind; she had been a mother to him, loving him unconditionally, when he desperately needed exactly that. He could not risk losing her.

"I was afraid of you last night, Manny, we all were," said Lucinda, her voice trembling. "You're a powerful man. Alcohol makes you aggressive and mean. After what you did last night to Julio, I have to agree with Luis. You two are grown men now, with families. You're not boys anymore. This wasn't just a little dust-up. You could have seriously injured Julio, Manny. You're just lucky that he's up and walking around today."

"Hey, I can take care of myself!" protested Julio. Anna cut him off with an angry, sharp gesture.

"How about it?" Luis repeated. "Can you promise us that you will stop drinking?"

Faced with a room full of disapproval, Manny swallowed the last shred of his pride. Somehow, he was going to have to make this work. "I promise you all, I won't drink any more. This will never happen again," he said.

Lucinda burst into tears of relief, holding out her hands to Manny. He gratefully crossed the room and sat down on the floor next to her. One by one, everyone left the room until finally, it was just the two of them. He held her hand, the two of them sitting in silence for a few moments.

"Lucinda," he began, "I am so sorry." Alone with her, Manny did not try to stop the tears rolling down his face. "I wasn't thinking straight. I wasn't trying to hurt him, I just - ".

"Shhh, it's OK, now, Manny," she said, touching the palm of her hand to his bruised face. "All is forgiven."

Slowly, the door to the closet began to inch open. Manny and Lucinda did not move, as Zach carefully peeked out. When he saw Manny, he froze, then backed away, but Lucinda said, "Zach, look who's here! Come on out, Zach, we're just about ready to read your favorite story."

Lucinda opened up her padlet, and began to read, carefully not looking at Zach. Taking his cue from Lucinda, Manny also turned his eyes towards the padlet and away from Zach, hoping he would leave his hiding place to listen to his favorite story, BillyBob the BumbleBee.

"I'm BillyBob the BumbleBee," read Lucinda, "I fly so fast, you'll never catch me!"

Zach edged out of his hiding place, eyes on his abuela's padlet.

"I like to sing my bumblebee song, buzz buzz buzz as I fly along," read Lucinda, her voice soothing and gentle, as only a grandmother can be.

Zach somehow managed to reach Lucinda and climb into her lap without turning his back on Manny. Manny carefully did not move, the pain in his chest a tangible thing as he saw that his son was afraid of him.

Lucinda put her arms around her grandson, kissing the top of his head. Zach, safely encircled by his abuela's arms, looked solemnly at Manny with wary, unblinking eyes.

"Daddy wants to tell you something, Zach," she said.

"Zach, I'm sorry. I behaved badly, and I'm sorry," Manny said lamely. Zach did not react.

After a moment, Zach said, "Read more BillyBob, Abuela."

"In a moment, Zach, I just have to go get something from the kitchen," she said, standing up. She nodded slightly to Manny as she left the room, leaving Manny and Zach alone.

Afraid to make any sudden movements, Manny sat quietly. Zach looked at him steadily without speaking, eyes round and watchful. *I wonder what he's thinking,* Manny said to himself.

There was something strange, something not quite right, about his son's flat, unblinking gaze.

"Is this your favorite story?" he asked softly, for something to say.

In response, Zach slid down from the chair and, without taking his eyes off Manny, sidled back into the safety of his closet, pulling the door shut behind him.

~ ~ ~ ~ ~ ~

"Manny, wake up!" Julio grasped him by the arm, shaking him awake. "You're dreaming, man, you're dreaming."

Manny moaned, opening his eyes. How long had he been asleep?

After his humiliating apology to his family, Manny had resolutely gone upstairs to his room, closed the door, and lay down on the bed, staring at the walls and ceiling. His had promised not to drink, and he was determined to keep his word. But it was easier said than done.

The night faded sleeplessly into morning, then afternoon, then evening, the hours grinding slowly past. His head pounded, his skin felt clammy and sweaty, and he needed a bath. At times, he seemed to be talking to someone. Little pink lights skittered sideways across the ceiling, speaking angrily to him in high-pitched voices, the words pointy and sharp. The room swam in and out of focus. Finally, on the second morning, he had fallen asleep.

"Here, drink some water, you'll feel better," Julio said. "What were you dreaming about?"

*The dream. Naz was there, lying naked next to him, warm and yielding in his arms, but then everything changed. They were on a boat which was rocking perilously, watching huge glassy waves come towards them, whitecaps whipped by the wind. Suddenly, Naztazya kissed him once and then slipped over the side, vanishing beneath the icy waves. He leaned over the edge of the rocking boat, looking down into the swirling*

155

*gray water, screaming her name into the howling wind, searching everywhere for her.*

"It was about Naz," he mumbled, embarrassed. He took the glass of water and drank. "Thanks, man. You don't have to take care of me, you know, I can get through this by myself."

Julio looked at him with real concern. "I'm not so sure about that," he said. "Why don't you get dressed, come downstairs and have something to eat?"

"No, I don't really want anyone to see me like this," he replied. The thought of food made his stomach lurch. He really needed some white willow bark tea, a good treatment for headache, but was too ashamed to ask Julio to make it for him.

"I'll make some white willow bark tea," offered Julio, moving towards the door. "When it's ready, I'll bring it up."

"Julio," Manny said, and then stopped, shame constricting his throat.

"I know, man, it's alright," Julio said, closing the door behind him.

# Chapter 24.

**M**ANNY BRACED HIMSELF as he walked into the office on Monday morning. He was going to have to tell the Chief that he had lost his detective's badge. He knew that he would likely be put on suspension for two weeks, which would go on his permanent record, and probably would have to pay a fine.

Agnes brought his morning cup of tea, minus the brandy. He had resolutely told her to leave out the brandy from now on. Manny had clawed his way through an entire weekend without liquor, one endless hour at a time. He felt light-headed and nauseated, but was determined to keep his promise.

*Maybe I'll wait until just before lunch before I tell him,* he thought, *and then I can go out to eat, get out of the office for a while.*

The detectives in his unit had been startled by the sight of their Lieutenant's battered face and black eyes, but no one had asked him about it. He was quite sure that they were discussing it among themselves, though; he could see them gathering in little groups in the break room, eyebrows raised, voices hushed. He wished his friend Dave were around to talk to.

The door to his office opened and the Chief walked in. *Did he knock?* thought Manny distractedly. The Chief clicked the door shut, then strode forward and came to a stop, palms flat on Manny's desk, leaning forward, looming over Manny. Instantly, the hair on the back of Manny's neck stood up.

"Do you have something to tell me, Lieutenant?" demanded the Chief. "Good heavens, what happened to you?"

"It's a long story, Sir," Manny replied. "And yes, I do have something to tell you."

"Well? Let's hear it, then," snapped the Chief.

"I've lost my detective's badge," said Manny, "and I apologize, Sir."

"Stand up when I'm talking to you, Lieutenant!" demanded the Chief. Manny stood at attention, fixing his gaze on the opposite wall, formally correct.

"How exactly did this happen?" demanded Chief O'Reilly.

"I got drunk, I got into a fight, and then I walked around outside. The next morning, I realized I'd lost the badge," said Manny, hoping that this brief narrative would be enough.

It was not.

"The other person involved in this fight, did he take your badge?" asked the Chief.

"No, Sir, that was my brother, he wouldn't have taken it," answered Manny.

"Your brother! You got into a fight with Julio?" asked the Chief. "When did this happen?"

"On Friday night, after work. At my house," replied Manny.

"I see," said the Chief. He seemed to be considering something. Manny waited.

Finally, the Chief reached into his jacket pocket and pulled out a small object, which he placed on Manny's desk. Manny looked at it, stunned. It was his badge.

"Thank you, Sir!" Manny said, relieved. "How did you find it?"

"I didn't," replied the Chief. "Let's just say I have a few friends at the Parts Department. One of them brought the badge to my home on Saturday."

Manny exhaled. If the badge had gone directly from the Parts Department to the Chief's house, then a minimal number of people had seen it. It was the best he could have hoped for.

"Let's sit down, Lieutenant," the Chief said, in a more friendly tone of voice. "I want to tell you something."

Manny sat down behind his desk.

"When I was a young man, just coming up, your father was the Chief of Police. I made a ... let's just say I made a blunder. And your father, he gave me a second chance. I'm Chief of Police today because of that second chance. I've never forgotten it. I'm paying it forward today to you, Manny. I think your father would have liked that."

The Chief blinked hard, looking away, and Manny was reminded yet again of what a trio they had been, the Chief, his father and the Commissioner, not just colleagues, but friends.

For once, Manny was actually grateful to his father.

"You're confined to your desk for two weeks, Lieutenant. That's it," said the Chief.

"Thank you, Sir!" said Manny gratefully. Since he rarely left the office during the day, most likely no one would notice the change.

"You're welcome," replied the Chief. "Manny, I know you're disappointed about the Task Force. I hope you can put that behind you now. You know, if you put your mind to it, you could be the best damn lieutenant this unit has ever had. There will be other job openings in the future, other promotions, and you want yours to be the first name that comes to mind when an opening becomes available. Always be thinking of your next step, Manny; steer the boat, don't just ride along in it!"

The Chief pulled out his pocket flask, taking a swallow. He offered it to Manny, who held up a hand.

"Come on, now, I think you deserve a little nip," said the Chief encouragingly, sliding the flask across the desk towards Manny. "Let me guess, they've made you promise at home that you won't drink any more, right?"

Manny looked up in surprise. "Yeah, that's exactly what they did," he said.

"Well, we've all been there!" said the Chief, not unkindly. "And what they don't know won't hurt them. Besides, it's early. You'll be stone cold sober by the time you go home for dinner."

His boss had been lenient, more generous than Manny could have hoped for. And now he was offering a drink from his own personal flask. Manny dared not risk offending him by refusing.

Manny picked up the flask, its curved metal surface cool against the palm of his hand, the contents gently rolling back and forth inside. His nostrils flared as he inhaled the fragrance of the alcohol wafting delicately from the opening. One sip, then, just to be polite.

He took a sip. It was smooth and mellow on his tongue, burning fire in his throat and stomach before transforming itself into aaahhh. He took a larger swallow, more substantial this time, before handing the flask back to his boss. His eyes followed the flask hungrily as the Chief took another swallow before capping it and putting it away in his pocket.

The Chief stood. "How's Julio, is he OK?" he asked.

"He's got a few bruises, but he'll live," Manny said dryly.

The Chief laughed. "Boys will be boys, you know," he said. "A good fight now and then clears the air."

After the Chief left, Manny hesitated only a moment before he closed his office door and poured himself a double shot of brandy, downing it quickly, sitting for a moment in appreciative silence as the brandy sang through his veins.

"Agnes!" he said through his intercom. "How about another cup of tea?"

In the days that followed, Manny fell into a pattern of putting brandy in his tea first thing in the morning, and then again after lunch. *But no alcohol after lunchtime,* he admonished himself sternly. *And no drinking at home, not ever. These are the rules.*

~ ~ ~ ~ ~ ~

"Where's Abuela?" Zach said, as Manny came into his bedroom later that night, padlet in hand.

"It's late, Zach, she's gone home," he replied. "I'll read your bedtime story to you. What would you like to hear?"

When Zach did not reply, Manny selected the first story that came to mind, Josiah and the Dragon, and started to read.

"Once upon a time, there was a tiny little firefly named Zach," he read.

"That's not how it goes!" exclaimed Zach. "The firefly is named Josiah!"

"Josiah!?" asked Manny. "That's not a good name for a firefly! Let's call him Zach."

Manny continued to read, sitting awkwardly on the bed next to Zach, not too close to him. *At least he isn't shying away from me,* he thought.

"Because unlike fireflies, dragons live forever. The End," he read.

"What's 'forever' mean?" asked Zach.

"Well," Manny said, "it means there is no end."

"So then it's never over?" he asked.

"That's right, Zach," explained Manny. "When something lasts forever, it's never over."

"The dragon gets to live forever," he said.

"Dragons are made up, Zach," explained Manny. "They aren't real. It's just a story."

"Is Mommy's going to be dead forever?" he asked, his eyes filling with tears.

"Yes," Manny said, "that's right." He reached over and put his arm protectively around his son's shoulders. He was so slender, so small and sad. "It's just how things are."

Zach leaned back against the pillows. "Read it again, Daddy," he said.

When Manny had finished reading the story a second time, he gently pulled the quilt up to Zach's chin, and kissed him on the top of his bright red curls. "Go to sleep now, Bud. Good night."

"Are we going to live with Abuela?" Zach asked sleepily, his little face starkly white against the pillow.

"What?" asked Manny. "Why would we go live with Abuela?"

"Auntie Anna said we should all go live with Abuela," he replied. "She was mad."

"She was, was she?" asked Manny. "What was she mad about, Zach, do you know?"

"I don't know. Uncle Julio told her to stop saying that. But Auntie Anna said a bad word. Then she told him to shut up," he said.

"Well. Don't worry about that, Zach, it's nothing," he said reassuringly. "Nobody's going anywhere. Go to sleep now." He kissed him again, turning out the light and closing the door behind him.

# Chapter 25.

**W**HAT'S THAT, JULIE?" asked Manny. He had stopped by the kitchen intending to grab a piece of toast on his way out the door. Instead, he was standing in front of the kitchen table, admiring what looked like a miniature 3-D civic planning model, made out of colored sugar cubes.

"It's my school project," Julianna said proudly. "Look, here's the playground, the school, and the park. And here's where the fountain goes, in the middle of the park."

School had started a few weeks earlier. Nearly nine years old, she seemed intrigued by the assignment, happily stacking sugar cubes in place. Manny watched with curiosity as Julie hesitated, her fingers hovering over the project, and then built a perfectly round fountain out of square sugar cubes, stacking them three-deep in an overlapping, colorful pattern.

One eyebrow raised, he glanced up at Anna, who was watching him from across the room. Anna, while not exactly hostile, had been quite cool towards him since the night of the fight. He opened his mouth to speak, then thought better of it. Picking up a piece of toast, he said simply, "See you all later," and left for work.

A few hours later, the doorbell rang at the Stewart mansion. Two locksmiths stood waiting patiently.

"Yes?" asked Anna, stopping work to answer the door. "We didn't call any locksmiths - are you sure you have the right house?"

"Yeah, we have it right here," said one of the workmen. He showed Anna the work order, signed by Lieutenant Stewart.

"OK, then, come in," Anna replied reluctantly, trailing behind them as they came into the foyer. Like most people, they stopped short and looked straight up at the impossibly high ceiling, and then at the long, curved wooden staircase in the middle of the house. Trained professionals, neither lock-smith commented on the opulence of their surroundings.

After a moment, one of the locksmiths asked politely, "It says here 'the master bedroom door.' Which one would that be?"

"Here, I'll show you," Anna said, leading them up the stairs to the master bedroom. The locksmiths, used to clambering up the traditional spiral staircases with their triangular-shaped metal steps, clomped clumsily straight up the wooden staircase.

"What work are you doing in the master bedroom?" she asked curiously.

"It says here that we are to install a token lock on the master bedroom door," read one of them. Anna's eyebrows shot up, but she said nothing.

"I'll leave you to it, then," she said. Going downstairs, she yanked out her padlet and hologrammed Julio.

Anna: *Your brother has locksmiths here to install a token lock on his bedroom door.*

Julio: *What??*

Anna: *Do you know anything about this?*

Julio: *No, he didn't say anything to me.*

Anna: *It's to keep Julie out, why else does he need a lock?*

Julio: *Can we talk about this tonight? I'm kind of busy right now.*

Anna: *So you want me to just let them do it?!*

Julio: *It's his house, Anna, so yeah, let them do it. I'm sure there's an explanation.*

Anna: *There's an explanation, alright, it's to keep our daughter out of his bedroom. And maybe there's another explanation, too, Julio. What's he hiding in his bedroom that he doesn't want anyone to see?*

Julio: *Can we please talk about this later? I have to go now.*

Anna put down her padlet. Furious, she paced back and forth in the kitchen, breathing deeply to calm herself.

When the locksmiths were finished, one of them handed her three metal tokens, small tab-shaped rectangles fitted with a series of tongue-and-groove ridges, on a small key-chain. "Could you please give these to the Lieutenant, Miss?" one of them said politely.

After they left, she slammed the tokens down onto the table in the foyer, and went back to work, fuming.

When Manny returned home from the office around 7:00 pm that night, Julio was waiting for him outside, by the front door.

"What are you doing out here in the yard?" asked Manny, coming up the short walk to the door.

"I'm waiting for you," Julio replied. "Anna's on the warpath. I wanted to give you a heads-up."

"What on earth for?" asked Manny.

"Did you order a couple of locksmiths to come here and put a token lock on your bedroom door?" asked Julio carefully.

"So they were here?" asked Manny, his hand on the doorknob.

"Why would you do that?" asked Julio bluntly, his hand against the door to keep Manny from opening it.

"What's wrong with putting a lock on my door?" countered Manny.

Julio lowered his voice. "She thinks maybe you don't trust Julie to stay out. And ... she thinks you want to hide liquor in your bedroom."

"Is that what you think, too?" asked Manny, his face impassive.

"I wanted to hear from you, before I think anything," he said.

"Then let's go inside and I'll explain," said Manny. He walked in, with Julio trailing behind him.

"Anna!" Manny called loudly. When she appeared, he said, "I understand the locksmiths were here."

"Yes, they were here this morning," she said, picking up the three tokens from the table and handing them to Manny. "Do you want to tell us why you feel the need to keep your bedroom door locked?" Despite herself, her voice betrayed her anger.

"Where are the children?" asked Manny, lowering his voice.

164

"They are upstairs in Zach's room, playing," she said.

"Let's all go in here," he said, walking into the library. He closed the door behind them.

"This morning as I was leaving for work," began Manny, "I was watching Julie build a model of a new community. For a child, she solved the problem of how to build a round fountain out of square sugar cubes pretty quickly. She's a smart little girl, gifted when it comes to how things work."

He turned to Anna, lowering his voice. "There's a gun in my bedroom, Anna. Actually, there are three guns and several rounds of ammunition, on the closet shelf. I don't keep them loaded, but smart as she is, it would take Julie all of three seconds to figure out how to load them.

"Two of the guns are locked in a safe box, but the other one isn't, as I wear it all day when I'm at work, so I just leave it in the holster overnight. Even if I kept it locked in the safe box, I am guessing that she could figure out the combination to the box.

"Kids get into all sorts of things," he explained. He glanced at Julio, whose mouth quirked up at the corners. They both remembered how Julio had spent hours patiently teaching Manny how to break into a home by practicing on their bedroom window.

Manny continued, "As Julie gets older, she's going to be more curious about how things work. Zach, too, he won't always be five years old. I don't want to take any chances on either one of them getting into the guns."

Silence filled the room. "And what about the tokens?" asked Anna, a little uncertainly. "Suppose you're not home and we need to get into your room. Where will you keep them?"

"I specifically asked for three tokens," Manny explained. "One of them is mine. One of them is for you and Julio," he said, handing it to her, "and the other one is for Lucinda and Luis. I want all of you to know that you should unlock the door and take a good look around my bedroom whenever you want, so you can be satisfied that I am not hiding anything. I'm at work all day, and you have my permission to go ahead, so ... I don't know how to make my intentions any clearer than that."

Julio cleared his throat, looking pointedly at his wife.

"Manny," she began, clearly reluctant. Her face was a roadmap of emotions, hostility and suspicion at odds with guilt and shame. "I'm sorry. I jumped to conclusions. I misjudged you, and I apologize."

"Don't worry about it," he said graciously. "You don't trust me, I know that, I have to earn that back. And I will."

A moment passed, as Manny looked down at his hands, deciding whether or not to speak. "As long as we are all here, I want to ask you both something." He paused, drawing a deep breath.

"Are you planning on moving in with Lucinda and Luis?" he asked.

"What?! No!" said Julio.

At the same time, Anna said, "No, of course not!"

"What gave you that idea?" asked Julio, his eyes suddenly wary.

"Zach told me. He overheard you talking about it," Manny replied.

Anna's eyes flicked nervously towards Julio, who exhaled sharply before turning to his brother. "Manny, it was something that came up, but we didn't mean it seriously. It was right after the fight. Anna was upset."

"Julio is right. I was so angry," Anna said. "I thought that maybe the children might be better off if ... it was just a thought, Manny. I spoke out of anger. It was only meant for Julio to hear. I'm sorry Zach overheard it."

"He wanted to know if we were moving," Manny replied. "I told him no, nobody's moving anywhere." He turned to Anna. "Were you really thinking that you could take Zach away from me?"

"Manny, nobody was trying to take Zach away from you!" she cried. "Please don't misunderstand! He's your son, he belongs with you!" Her fingers laced together tightly in her lap.

"That's good to hear," Manny replied, and decided to drop it. If it came down to it, she couldn't take his son away from him, not on the basis of one little fistfight, especially one which had not involved his son. No court would agree to do that.

Manny was fairly sure that she just had been angry and speaking a bit too freely, blowing off steam after the fight. He knew this. But he didn't want Anna to know that he knew it.

Afterwards, alone upstairs in his room, Manny pulled out the flask that he now carried at all times in his jacket pocket. Taking a long drink, he finished its contents, relaxing as he savored the brandy's aroma, the flavor, the slow burn down his throat, the steady burgeoning warmth in his stomach.

It had gone well, he thought, even better than he had planned. Anna seemed quite ashamed of herself, both for her suspicions regarding the new lock on his bedroom door, and for saying that everyone, except for Manny, should move in with her in-laws. *And now,* he thought with satisfaction as the brandy worked its magic, *Anna will think twice before she accuses me of anything.*

# Chapter 26.

**M**ANNY WAS SEATED at his desk one morning when he received a text:

*Please join the Commissioner and Chief O'Reilly for lunch today to discuss the latest Council meetings. The Commissioner will stop by your office at noon.*

It was signed "N. Peterson, Aide to the Commissioner."

Manny read the message twice, once for context and then again because the text was not signed by Raimone. *I wonder if that means the little bastard is gone,* he thought hopefully.

The restaurant was a tiny Vietnamese place within walking distance from the office. Like most restaurants in the Colony, it mostly filled take-out orders, but had a small number of tables and chairs for eat-in customers.

The server bot, a lumpish cube-shaped robot on wheels with two functional arms for carrying heavy plates on a tray, rolled up to the table with glasses of water. Manny picked up the restaurant's ordering tablet from the center of the table, scrolling through the various menu choices, reading the descriptions beneath the colorful, glossy photos. Manny had never had Vietnamese food, so when it was his turn to order, he ordered what the Commissioner ordered, a tofu bahn mi sandwich on freshly baked French bread and iced petunia tea.

"Manny," said the Commissioner, clearing his throat, "before we get started, I just want to say that I am grateful to you for dropping the, uh, the thing with Raimone. I know that his actions cost you a promotion, which wasn't fair to you. Your decision not to pursue him is much appreciated. I won't forget it, Manny."

"You're welcome, Sir," Manny said, surprised. "I've decided to put it behind me. Besides, I believe that we make our own fairness."

The Commissioner and the Chief exchanged glances. "Your old man used to say the same thing," said the Commissioner, with a nostalgic smile.

He took a sip of his iced tea. "Raimone has been shipped off to the Bronx for a bit, to cool his heels. I can't fire him, you know," he continued. "I promised my wife. But the Bronx is pretty far from where he lives, and he won't like the commute at all. Maybe he'll quit." He paused to savor the mental image of Raimone trudging to and from the Bronx each day.

"So why don't you tell us about the Council meetings," the Commissioner said, changing the subject. "Anything interesting come up?" He took a huge bite of his sandwich, relishing the tofu pate on the freshly baked bread. The unfamiliar aroma of the topping, pickled carrots and daikon radish, was making Manny feel slightly ill.

"There is one thing that came up," Manny replied. "I had a conversation after the meeting with Sarah Blumberg. She said that the number of cremated remains in our memorial park is growing, and soon there'll be no room for all the ashes. And there's a shortage of fill for foundations used to build new homes. I gather that these two items often come up at the same time, but no one draws the obvious connection between the two problems."

"Interesting," said the Commissioner. "Did she offer a solution?"

"No, she didn't. She said that no one dares to be the first to suggest that cremated remains could be used as fill for the foundations in new buildings," Manny said.

"And what would you do, Manny? If you were asked to offer a solution?" asked the Commissioner, strategically eyeing his sandwich before taking another gigantic bite.

"Suppose the ashes were stored for seventy-five years, that ought to be enough," Manny said. "Almost nobody lives to be seventy-five years old." It was true; the average lifespan in the Colony was sixty-two.

"After seventy-five years, no one will be left alive to mourn the deceased," Manny continued. "After that, the ashes could be added, with dignity, to the materials used to form the foundations of our buildings. We could do a public relations campaign about how in a closed environment, we recycle absolutely everything. Standing on the shoulders of our ancestors, you know, that sort of thing."

The Commissioner wiped his mouth on his napkin and said, "I like it. It's the first sensible suggestion we've had on the subject. What do you think, Joe?"

"Well, we can't continue on as we are," said the Chief, chewing thoughtfully. "Manny may be on to something here."

The Chief and the Commissioner went on to discuss other things which did not involve Manny. He struggled determinedly with his bahn mi sandwich. *This really is ghastly,* he thought, choking down another small bite.

The Commissioner took out his flask, poured a generous amount of liquor into his iced tea, and passed the flask to the Chief, who did the same. The Chief passed the flask to Manny, who poured a modest amount into his glass.

"Manny, that's not enough for a mouse!" said the Commissioner. He reached over and added more to Manny's glass. "Try it, my wife makes this! It's an old family recipe called Vodka-Aquakavit. She uses potatoes, barley and goodness knows what else. The kitchen smells like a brewery for a week after she's finished. It's good, though."

Manny took a tentative taste of his iced tea, spluttering a little as he swallowed. The Commissioner laughed. "It's a little rough. It's homemade," he said. "We love this stuff at home. It's great around the holidays."

Later that afternoon, back in the office, Manny decided to skip the usual after-lunch cup of tea and brandy. Feeling virtuous and in control, he was settling into an afternoon of work, when his padlet beeped.

Manny could see the padlet's rim lighting up, pulsing cobalt blue for a personal text. It was from the school, from Zach's teacher, Ms. Parker. School had started several weeks ago; Manny had yet to meet Ms. Parker.

Ms. Parker: *Lieutenant, there has been an incident at the school. Zach is fine. Please meet me in the principal's office as soon as you can get here.*

Manny: *What happened?? I'm not able to leave my office at present. I'll send you a secure link so we can talk virtually.*

Ms. Parker: *No, this must be in person. It is school policy. Zach is in the principal's office now. I will meet you there.*

*Well. That doesn't sound good*, thought Manny. He thought of Naz, how she had always handled everything having to do with Zach. *How's a person supposed to work?* he thought resentfully.

Stopping by the Chief's office, he said, "Sir, I need to go out. My son got himself into some sort of trouble at the school. He's in the principal's office, waiting for me to come."

The Chief grunted without looking up from his padlet. "Go ahead, but hurry back, OK?" he said.

"Yes, Sir," he said, as he headed towards the exit.

At the school, he identified himself at the front door and was quickly buzzed inside. The principal's office was not hard to find.

"Principal Troshenko," Manny said, bowing politely to the Principal. "I'm Lieutenant Stewart, Zach's father."

"Thank you for coming in, Lieutenant," the Principal said. "Do you know Zach's teacher, Ms. Parker?" Principal Troshenko gestured towards a neatly dressed blond woman who was standing by the window. She turned to greet him.

Manny looked at her face and suddenly he could not breathe. Everything around him seemed to slow down. All sounds faded away except for the beating of his heart; he felt as if he were spinning, as if he were choking on thick black smoke. White-faced, he took a deep breath, then another.

"- feeling alright?" Principal Troshenko was saying. "You look like you've seen a ghost."

Manny turned towards the woman, who was staring at him in shocked disbelief. "Zach is your son?" she asked. "Stewart is a common last name; I didn't make the connection."

"Yes, Zach is my boy," replied Manny, recovering his composure.

"You saved my son's life, Detective, and my life, too." She moved closer to him, placing her right hand on her left shoulder, bowing formally to him, a long, low and respectful bow denoting deep gratitude.

Principal Troshenko looked from one to the other, puzzled. "Is this the officer who dragged you out of the fire?" he asked her. When she nodded, he said, "Thank you for your service, Detective," pulling a chair closer for Manny to sit.

There was a brief silence. Ms. Parker took a seat, and together they turned their attention back to Zach.

"Why don't you tell us what happened?" Principal Troshenko said to her.

"Zach and another little boy got into an argument at playtime. There was some pushing and shoving, and then Zach knocked the little boy to the ground and punched him in the face. Pretty hard, actually. He's OK, we took him to the nurse, and she said nothing's broken, just a bloody nose. But he's going to have quite a bit of bruising, I'm afraid."

Manny turned to Zach. "What do you have to say for yourself, young man?" he said angrily. "You can't just go around hitting people, you know." Zach scowled, turning his face away.

"Has anything happened to upset Zach?" asked Ms. Parker. "This kind of aggressive behavior is so unusual at this age. I actually had to lift him off the other child; he was sitting on him, wouldn't let him get up, hitting him over and over in the face."

"No, I can't think of anything," said Manny, with an unfamiliar twinge of something that felt like guilt. "I'll talk to him, though."

"Lieutenant, Zach is suspended for one day from school," said Principal Troshenko. "We hope you will use that time to talk to him, find out if he is troubled about anything. If we can help in any way, please let us know." He stood, signifying that the meeting was over. 172

Manny bowed formally to the Principal and to Ms. Parker. He turned to Zach, saying, "You behave yourself, now. We'll talk later, when I get home from work tonight."

"No, Lieutenant, you don't understand," the Principal said. "Zach is suspended now. You have to take him with you. He is not allowed back in the classroom until the day after tomorrow."

"Oh. I see," Manny said, nonplussed. Turning to Zach, he said, "OK, then, let's go." He reached for Zach's hand. Zach, red-faced, pulled his hand away, but Manny grasped his arms, lifting him off the chair. Zach would not look at him.

"Goodbye, Lieutenant," said Ms. Parker, her eyes worried as she looked at them. "Zach, I'll see you soon."

Manny and Zach left, walking through the school yard towards home.

"Tell me what happened, Zach," Manny began mildly.

"No," replied Zach, scowling.

"I said, tell me what happened!" Manny insisted.

"No!" Zach said again, trying to pull his hand out of his father's grip. When Manny steadfastly refused to let go, Zach suddenly whirled around in front of his father and kicked him hard in the shins.

"Hey!" Manny said, surprised, letting go of Zach's hand. Finally free of his father's grip, Zach took off at a run.

"Zach! Come back here this instant!" he shouted, to the amusement of several passers-by. Manny, who ran regularly, easily overtook his son. He picked him up, tossed him over his shoulder in a traditional fireman's carry and began to walk home, ignoring Zach's outraged shrieks and the steady tattoo of little fists beating against his shoulders.

"What on earth?!" exclaimed Anna, as Manny and Zach walked into the house. "What happened?"

"Zach is suspended from school, that's what happened," said Manny, bending down to put Zach on the floor. "It seems that he got into a fight and beat the crap out of another little boy."

"Crap," said Zach, "crap, crap, crap."

173

"Zach, I've told you, don't say 'crap'! Now go upstairs to your room!" Manny said angrily. "You've caused enough disruption for one day."

Zach ran from the foyer up the stairs to his bedroom, slamming the door. Manny had an eerie sense of deja vu, watching his son run up the stairs and slam his bedroom door; how often had done the exact same thing as a child? He shook his head to clear it; there was no time now for those thoughts.

"I've got to get back to the office," Manny said, looking at Anna. "Can you handle this?"

"What, you're just dumping this on me and taking off?" she demanded. "Honestly, Manny, you're his father! Can't you do better than that?"

Manny looked at her, surprised. *I can't be in two places at once*, he thought angrily.

"I can't, Anna, I have things to do," Manny said, backing out of the foyer towards the door. "I'll ask Lucinda and Luis to come over and help."

"I was just on my way over there to see my Dad. I'll ask them to come over," said Julio, coming into the foyer. "Anna, can you hold down the fort until I get back?"

Anna nodded, clearly unhappy. "OK, but - Manny. What time will you be home tonight? You should talk to Zach today, if it's going to have any impact. You know how children are."

Manny clearly did not know what she meant by "how children are," but he replied, "Don't worry, I'll be home early. I just have some things at the office that need to be finished tonight, and then I'll come right home."

Julio said, "Here, walk with me." He and Manny left the house together. Manny glanced sideways at his brother's face, still discolored from the broken cheekbone.

"What happened?" asked Julio, curious.

"I don't know all of the details. His teacher said he got into an argument during recess with another boy, sat on him and punched him repeatedly. She had to lift him off the kid. The little boy had a bloody nose, but nothing broken, thank goodness," Manny said. "Kids," he added, shaking his head.

"Where do they come up with these things? I have to talk to him."

"Maybe my Mom can be there with you, you know, to help with the conversation," suggested Julio. "It could be hard to explain to him why hitting is wrong. You know, after he saw you and me going at it."

"That's got nothing to do with it," Manny replied with a shrug. "He's just a kid. Everybody knows kids fight."

Julio's eyebrows shot up. He and Manny walked the rest of the short distance to Lucinda and Luis's house in silence.

Manny explained to his foster parents that Zach had been suspended from school and was now at home, and asked them if they could help.

"Sure, we can do that," replied Lucinda. "We'll stay for dinner." She took Manny's arm as he stood by the door. "Maybe you and I can have a little talk, before you sit down with Zach?"

"I'd be grateful for that, Lucinda, thanks," Manny said, relieved. "Honestly, I don't know what to say to him. I'll text you when I'm on my way, and we can talk privately."

It was late afternoon by the time Manny returned to his office. He opened the door and stopped, surprised. Was that musk cologne that he smelled, lingering in the air in his office? He shook his head in disbelief; surely Raimone would not have dared to enter his office when he wasn't there. Besides, he was gone, shipped off to the Bronx. Deciding that he must be mistaken, Manny dismissed it from his mind. There was plenty else to think about.

"Everything OK?" asked the Chief, as Manny was hanging up his jacket.

"Yeah, just a little fistfight between Zach and some other kid. Apparently, they got into a fight and Zach really let him have it. The kid has some bruises, nothing broken, no serious injuries. Zach's suspended for a day."

"Well, don't be too hard on the boy," advised the Chief. "Kids get into fights, they need to be able to blow off some steam now and then." He laughed, adding, "You know, it's not a bad thing to learn how to handle yourself in a fight, might come in handy someday."

# *Chapter 27.*

**L**UCINDA WAS WAITING for Manny when he got home. The two of them went quickly into the study, closing the door.

"What are you going to say to Zach?" asked Lucinda, settling herself into one of the leather club chairs. Manny sat down opposite her.

"First, I want to hear from him exactly what happened, why he hit the little boy. After that ... I'm not sure," Manny replied.

"You need to let Zach know in no uncertain terms that he can't get into fights with other children. He's testing you, Manny, acting out to get your attention," Lucinda said.

"Testing me?" asked Manny. He thought longingly of Naztazya, wishing heartily that she was having this conversation with Lucinda, instead of him. *Why'd you have to die, Naz?* he thought with a surprising flicker of resentment.

"Children are not little grown-ups," Lucinda explained. "If they don't have the words to ask something, they'll use their actions instead. His behavior is a question for you, Manny. He is asking you if fighting is OK."

"And," she added, looking at him meaningfully, "your fight with Julio needs to be part of the conversation."

"That didn't have anything to do with it," Manny responded automatically. With a pang, he remembered that Julio had said much the same thing.

"Manny, the children were there," Lucinda reminded him. "They saw everything, the two of you hitting each other, Luis trying to pull you apart, the shouting, the blood smeared across the floor. You need to accept that your actions have had a bad effect on your son."

Manny looked at her, dismayed. With her words, suddenly he saw the whole scene as Zach must have seen it. His son had seen him drunk and murderously angry, fists swinging, Luis trying to make him stop, Julio defending himself honorably and with restraint, while Manny was so obviously out of control. Sharp remorse made him shift uneasily in his chair.

"How are you going to explain to Zach that he is wrong to get into a fight," Lucinda asked, "if you don't also explain that you made a mistake when you hit his uncle?"

Manny, sighing, rubbed his eyes with his hands. "Would you come with me, please?" he asked Lucinda.

"Of course," she said with a gentle smile. Together, Lucinda and Manny went upstairs to Zach's room, where he was sitting on the bed with his padlet open, watching a video.

"We want to talk to you about the fight at school," Manny began, sitting down on the bed. "Can you tell us what happened? What made you so mad that you hit the little boy?"

"He said that I took his ball and hid it," explained Zach, looking at the floor. "I told him I didn't have his stupid ball, but he kept saying it, then he started pushing me."

"Did you take his ball?" Manny asked, his voice gentle. He took Zach's hand, glancing at Lucinda, who nodded very slightly. "You can tell me, Bud," he added encouragingly.

"No, you'll get mad," said Zach, his eyes filling with tears.

"I promise, I won't get mad. Did you take his ball?" asked Manny, very softly. "It's always OK to tell the truth, Zach. You'll feel better if you do."

Zach looked up tearfully, his eyes going from his father to his grandmother. "I didn't take it!" he cried. "It was just lying there, so I gave it a little push and it just … it landed underneath the bushes." Zach took a long, shuddering breath.

"And did you tell the little boy where the ball was, when he asked if you had taken it?" Manny prompted.

"Nah, I was on the seesaw," Zach replied. "I told him it's his ball, he should go look for it himself."

"And what happened then?" asked Manny, continuing with his interrogation.

"He started yelling about his stupid ball, so I pushed him so he'd shut up. And he pushed me back. Then he fell down. So I sat on him. Then Ms. Parker came."

Manny glanced at Lucinda, who was looking on calmly. So far so good.

"Zach," he said, "do you remember when I hit Uncle Julio?"

"Yeah, I remember," Zach whispered, carefully not looking at his father.

"I was wrong to do that," Manny explained. "It was a bad mistake. I had to apologize to Uncle Julio for hurting him."

"But you kept hitting Uncle Julio," Zach pointed out, his eyes suddenly shifting to Manny's face. "Even when Abuelo tried to make you stop."

Manny paused, taken aback by the clarity of this observation.

"I'm ashamed of what I did, Zach," he said simply. Zach's eyes widened. "I wish I could take it back. But it doesn't work that way. So the best I could do was to tell Uncle Julio that I'm so sorry I hurt him, and I won't ever do it again. Lucky for me, Uncle Julio forgave me."

Zach looked at Lucinda. This was new, hearing his father admit that he had done something bad and was sorry afterwards. He was not quite sure what to make of it.

Manny continued, "Here's what we're going to do, Zach. You're going to apologize to this little boy. You need to tell him that you are sorry you hurt him, and that you will never do it again."

"Wh-what?" replied Zach. "But what if he calls me a baby and pushes me?"

"He won't," replied Manny firmly. "I'll be there with you." Zach looked up gratefully, leaning ever so slightly closer to Manny. Manny put his arm around his little boy's shoulders, resting his chin lightly on the top of Zach's head so he would not see his father's tears. Lucinda got up quietly and left the room.

~ ~ ~ ~ ~ ~

Later that night, alone in his bedroom, flask standing ready nearby, Manny texted Ms. Parker.

Manny: *Zach wants to apologize to the little boy, make sure he is OK. Could you please help us contact his family?*

Ms. Parker:  *Yes, I can look up the contact info first thing at school tomorrow, and let you know.*

Manny paused for a moment, fingers poised above the padlet. He took a fortifying swig of brandy before replying:

Manny:  *Are you free for lunch tomorrow? We could meet someplace near the school. You could give me the info then.*

There was a long pause. Manny stared at the padlet, willing it to respond. Maybe she was not going to reply. It was late; he should have waited, and not bothered her at home. Or maybe teachers didn't have lunch with their students' parents. It could show favoritism. Probably, he had broken all sorts of unspoken rules.

What had he been thinking? What must she think of him?? *Maybe she thinks I'm asking her out on a date. Which I am not. It's not a date. What if she thinks it's a date?* The palms of his hands began to perspire. He was just about to give up and close his padlet when her response came.

Ms. Parker: *Yes, that sounds fine. There's a taco place near the school, Empellon Taqueria. Do you like tacos?*
Manny: *Yes. Sounds good. I'll meet you there. Time?*
Ms. Parker: *How's 12:30 pm?*
Manny: *See you then.*

Manny folded up his padlet, wiping his sweaty palms on his pants. He had not thought about women in a long, long time. Not that he was thinking about women now. No, it was not a date, just lunch, a convenient way to exchange information.

And yet, somehow, a drone from one of the news networks' society pages was out and about at the same time Manny was entering the Taqueria with the enchanting Ms. Parker, and managed to take several candid photos of the two of them eating inside the restaurant.

The result was that within a couple of hours, the society pages had photos of Lieutenant Manny Stewart, Council Member, one of the Colony's richest and most prominent citizens, having lunch with Odesa Parker, his son's teacher. The evening news program *Worth Noting* ran a short segment on Malcolm "Manny" Stewart, detective, decorated hero whose pregnant wife had died so tragically, without mentioning his recent career setback. There were several photos and a brief biography of Ms. Parker.

~ ~ ~ ~ ~ ~

"You went out on a *date*?" demanded an outraged Anna, her voice filling the kitchen.

"What? No! What are you talking about?" replied Manny, taking off his jacket and putting down his briefcase by the door. Anna was making dinner, with the evening news projected on the wall by her padlet.

"This!!" spluttered Anna, replaying the segment for him. Indignant, she could barely wait for the segment to end before she accused, "You went out with *Zach's teacher*? With Naz *not even gone a year.*" Her voice broke and she stopped, tears in her eyes. "Manny, how could you?"

"How could I *what*?" Manny replied defensively. "I didn't do anything wrong! I needed to get the name and address of the boy Zach beat up at school, and she gave it to me. We met at lunchtime so I could get it from her."

Anna's eyes narrowed as she regarded him suspiciously. "Is your padlet not working?" she asked sarcastically. "No holograms? No texts? No phone calls?"

"I could have done it that way, I guess," he said lamely. "But it was lunchtime. We had lunch."

Anna looked like she wanted to throw something at him.

"Look, Anna, nobody misses Naz more than I do," he protested.

"I seriously doubt that, from your behavior, Manny," she snapped.

"That's unfair, Anna!" he replied, exasperated. "You know how the press can spin anything into a story. This was nothing. Just lunch."

Anna, deflated, sat down abruptly in one of the kitchen chairs. Manny sat down next to her. "So are we OK now?" he asked hopefully.

"I guess," she replied. She looked smaller somehow, as though the wind had been taken out of her sails.

"I miss her, too, Anna, every single day," he said softly, moved by the tears in Naztazya's sister's eyes. "I always will, for the rest of my life."

~ ~ ~ ~ ~ ~

Upstairs in his bedroom after dinner, Manny sat on the velvet chair next to his bed, flask in hand. Despite his sincere apologies to his family, he had never stopped drinking. He drank every day at the office, as did most of his colleagues. He was very careful not to drink in front of anyone at home. There had been no more incidents, no more ugly aggressive behavior, no belligerent outbursts. He was confident now that he was managing it well.

Besides, everyone knew that brandy was practically harmless. He picked up the flask, shaking it a little to see what remained in it. He tipped his head back and brought the flask all the way up, letting the last little drop land on his tongue. He thought he'd topped off the flask before he left the office. *I must have forgotten,* he thought.

Opening his briefcase, Manny reached underneath several thick files and withdrew a new bottle of brandy. He admired it for a moment, the cool smooth glass bottle, the lovely weight of it. *And now,* he said to the bottle, *where should I put you?*

It was simple to hide the small flask in his uniform pocket, but hiding a bottle was different. Looking around the bedroom, he considered and rejected the dresser drawer, the closet shelf, the night table drawer, all too obvious.

Years ago, when Manny and Julio had been kids upstairs in the little bedroom on 14th Street, Julio had had a hiding place for his stolen items beneath one of the wooden floor boards. Maybe there was a way to make a similar hiding place in his bedroom now. But where?

He looked around carefully. It had to be completely hidden, so beneath the furniture would be good. But it also had to be accessible, so he needed a light piece of furniture that could be moved easily, and soundlessly.

The velvet chair, the one his mother had loved – that was light and could be moved back into place in a hurry, if necessary. He stood up, pushing the velvet chair out of the way, and looked at the carpet beneath it. Surprisingly, there was a section where the carpet was not nailed to the floor. It pulled back easily.

One of the floorboards was loose. He removed it carefully with the help of a metal nail file. The opening was shallow, about three inches deep, but was about twelve inches long and four inches wide.

Manny turned on his padlet's Lamp app, examining the hole. The light reflected back; was there something already in there? Reaching into the hiding place, he let out a strangled cry of dismay as he found an unopened bottle of bourbon, undoubtedly left there years ago by Patrick. Unwittingly, he had discovered his father's hiding place.

Manny sat back on his heels, his father's bourbon in his hands, his mind reeling. *Like father, like son,* he thought bitterly, the realization making his head spin.

Someone was knocking on his bedroom door. Manny looked wildly around the room, the bottle in his hands.

"Manny, are you OK?" called Anna. "We heard a sound," she persisted, knocking again.

He heard her begin to turn the doorknob, followed by Julio's voice murmuring something too low to hear. In another instant, they would be inside the room.

Quickly putting the bourbon back in its hiding place, he replaced the loose floorboard, and hastily pulled the chair back over the area. But the brandy! He shoved the bottle of brandy beneath the pillow on the closest side of the bed, the side which had been Naztazya's.

Quick as lightning, he grabbed the apple off the night table – the one he kept there for just such an occasion – and took a huge bite out of it, to mask the smell of brandy on his breath.

Julio's voice came through the door, "Manny. We're coming in, OK?" The door swung open.

Julio and Anna walked into the room to find Manny sitting on the velvet chair, dressed in his pajamas, holding an apple in his hand.

"Hey," he said nonchalantly. "What's up?" He took another bite of the apple. It was a trick he had learned as a child; if you are chewing, you get a little extra time to think before answering.

"Everything OK in here?" asked Julio. "We thought maybe we heard you call out."

"Just stubbed my toe on the chair, that's all," said Manny. "I'm fine."

There was a moment of silence. Manny, the picture of innocence, continued calmly eating his apple, as his brother and sister-in-law exchanged glances.

Finally, Julio sat down on the end of the bed, looking meaningfully at Anna. She sat down next to him.

"Manny," she began, "I want to apologize for what I said earlier. I was wrong to be so angry. I know that eventually, you'll want to have a woman in your life. It's only natural. And of course, we want you to be happy. I just didn't expect it this afternoon. You know, so soon."

"Anna, I'm not even thinking about dating. She's Zach's teacher, that's all. Honest. It was just lunch." Manny put on his most sincere, believable facial expression, the one he had used on his father when he was lying through his teeth.

Anna's hand was resting on the bed next to her sister's pillow; the back of her hand was mindlessly caressing the edge of the pillow as they spoke. If she or Julio had happened to look, they easily could have seen the large lump which was an unopened bottle of brandy, stuffed underneath the pillow.

"And it's OK if it's more than just lunch," Julio was saying. "It's your life, bro."

Manny nodded, wishing wholeheartedly that they would leave his bedroom before they discovered that he had been drinking, or that there was a bottle of brandy practically in plain sight.

"Thanks, man," he replied to Julio. He yawned luxuriously. "It's getting late, time for bed."

Anna looked sadly at the pillow where her sister had laid her head every night for years. She gently smoothed the surface of the pillow, remembering the many times she and Naz had sat in this room, talking and laughing together. Suddenly, her hand stopped moving.

"Manny," she began, her brows drawing together into a frown.

The hairs on the back of Manny's neck stood straight up, a sure sign that the mood in the room was about to change.

"Well," said Julio, getting up from the end of the bed, "you're right, it is getting late. We'll see you in the morning." He held out his hand to Anna. Reluctantly, she rose and together, they left Manny alone in his room.

The next morning, he took the bottle of brandy to his office and put it safely in his desk drawer.

# Chapter 28.

**H**OW DID YOUR meeting with the parents go?" asked Odesa Parker. They were on a first-name basis now; it was only right, Manny thought. Odesa took a delicate nibble from the end of her taco. Manny was fascinated by her skill in eating a taco. When he bit into a taco, it invariably fell apart.

"It was fine. We kept it very brief," Manny replied. "Zach apologized, said he was glad the kid wasn't hurt, said he'd never do it again. It was over very quickly."

"Well, I'm glad that's behind you now," said Odesa, taking another bunny-bite of her taco. "How are you and Zach doing? Everything OK at home?"

"Yeah, everything's fine," Manny said off-handedly. He wondered if she had deliberately chosen her dress today because of their lunch date. It was the exact same shade of blue as her eyes, cornflower blue. Her dress had a deep square neckline, dipping down right in the middle so that

"*Manny!* Are you listening to me?" she asked, amused.

"Of course I'm listening!" he protested. "What did you say?"

"I said that I hope you can come to Father-Son Night at the school on Monday evening. We encourage the fathers to come in and speak to the children for a few minutes about their careers. And we'll be displaying all of the artwork that the children have been drawing," she continued. "As a matter of fact, Manny, that's why I asked you to meet me here today."

Manny took a careful bite of his roasted Portobello and avocado taco, heaped with a generous amount of salsa. The taco immediately disintegrated into bits, part of it landing on his lap. He reached for the basket of silver maple leaves to wipe his salsa-fingers. Tree leaves were ubiquitous, used everywhere as napkins.

"You wanted to show me Zach's drawings? Has he been drawing anything noteworthy?" he asked.

"Yes, actually, he has," she replied seriously. "There are several, Manny, but I brought two of them to show you."

"Wait just a moment," he said, pulling out his padlet. He opened the police QuietSpaces app, which immediately covered their table in a round translucent dome made up of sparkling, spinning particles.

Inside the dome, they could now speak freely; outside of the dome, all that could be heard was a gentle humming sound. This was much more sophisticated than the civilian version, and could only be ended by the officer who initiated it.

Surprised, Odesa looked up at the translucent dome whirling around them. Then she nodded. "Good idea," she said.

Pulling out the two drawings, she spread them on the table. "These two in particular gave me pause," she said.

The two drawings were both scrawled with black and red crayon, large, forceful, sweeping strokes of color. One of them showed a house on fire, with orange flames shooting out of the roof, with a single stick figure waving from the upstairs window.

The other showed all of Zach's family (with Naz notably missing), little stick figures outlined against a red, orange and black sky. Zach and Julianna were standing together, holding hands, next to a shorter, wider stick figure wearing a black dress: Lucinda. The other stick figures were in the background, looking down at something lying on the ground.

"What do you make of these?" asked Manny, pushing the drawings back across the table.

"I am not a trained child psychologist," she replied carefully, "but I think there are some problems here." She spoke hesitantly. "Perhaps some counseling could help?"

"He doesn't need counseling," Manny said flatly. "He's adjusting to his mother's death. It was not even a year ago. He's fine."

"Manny," she said gently, "he isn't fine. Taking him to a psychologist can't hurt him. If he's OK, if he's adjusting normally, then the psychologist will tell you that."

"Mmm, maybe," Manny said noncommittally, picking up some of the pieces of his taco from the plate. "I'll think about it."

He pulled out his padlet and opened the scheduler. "Tell me again," he said, "when is Father-Son Night?"

~ ~ ~ ~ ~ ~

Manny sat at his desk in the study, mulling over what he had heard in the Council meeting earlier that evening. He had been surprised by one of the items on the agenda, although no one else had seemed to think it noteworthy.

They had been going down the list of items to be discussed, and Manny was listening diligently to various complaints from private citizens about recycling, shared-border disputes, excessive noise on a weeknight evening, etc. Manny was half-listening, his rumbling stomach reminding him that he had not yet had dinner, when the last item on the agenda came up.

"And Aviva Johnson has complained once again that there is a leak in the wall in one of her bedrooms," read the Council Member. A muted ripple of laughter spread through the room.

"What, again?" asked another Council Member. "Didn't she complain about that last month?" More laughter, less muted this time.

Manny rose. "Why hasn't she gotten it fixed?" he asked mildly. Every face turned towards him. "I mean, if it's a minor problem, why is she telling us?"

A Council Member rose to face Manny. "Aviva Johnson complains about this every few months or so," he explained with a dismissive shrug. "It's nothing. She could plug this little leak with a cork."

Council Members began to rise and gather up their things, signaling the end of the meeting.

And yet, thought Manny later that evening, she hadn't tried to fix her "little leak." *Or had she tried, and was not able to fix it?* he thought. And what if it truly was a leak, not just a little whisper of water seeping through? Did anyone know exactly where the water was coming from?

The following morning at work, Manny sent a text to the Commissioner's aide, N. Peterson, asking to speak to the

Commissioner. He was just finishing his morning cup of tea, when he looked up to see the Chief and the Commissioner standing in his doorway.

"We got your text," said the Chief. *We?* thought Manny, who had sent the text only to the Commissioner. *I'll have to keep that in mind in the future.*

"We're on our way to a meeting," the Chief explained, "but thought we'd stop by." They settled themselves unhurriedly into chairs, looking expectantly at Manny.

He told them about the leak in Aviva Johnson's house, and the dismissive response to her requests for help.

"Why do they just laugh at her, and then move on to other things?" he asked. "Why don't they take her complaints seriously?"

"Take it seriously? But Manny, she needs a plumber, not the City Council," said the Chief.

"But she comes back, time after time, complaining of the same leak," Manny said. "I don't like it. If it was a simple thing, it would have been fixed by now."

The Commissioner said casually, "What do you think we should do?"

Manny took a deep breath. He didn't want them to think he was overreacting. "I think we should have a couple of engineers go over there to her house, take a look and see what is causing the leak."

"Engineers! Manny, you'll panic people, if you do that," said the Chief.

"OK then, they can be dressed as plumbers, and no one has to know that they are really engineers," Manny countered. "If you're right, and it's nothing, then that's what they'll tell us. But if there is a real leak, then we could be looking at a serious problem."

"Problem?" asked the Commissioner. "What kind of problem? For instance."

"We live in tunnels," said Manny bluntly. "We've been underground so long that nobody even stops to think about it anymore. But tunnels are not built to last forever. They erode, they crumble, they flood like they did in past decades, down at the southern end of the island. It's why we have fire doors that are also waterproof, every 200 yards in our residential areas. We should look into this. If there's a problem, wouldn't we want to know about it?"

"OK," said the Commissioner, "let's look into it. But keep it quiet, Manny, make sure that nobody finds out that they're engineers. As far as anyone knows, Ms. Johnson is going to have a visit from a couple of plumbers, to fix her little leak."

The Chief turned to Manny, his expression serious. "What exactly would you propose to do about it, if the leak turns out to be something structural? You know, that forewarns a bigger problem?"

Manny took a moment to consider his answer. "We're not there yet," he said. "Let's hope it's nothing. But at some point, we're going to need a plan to safely evacuate our citizens, in case of a true emergency. Call it Plan B."

The Commissioner gave Manny a long, unabashed look of appraisal. "Evacuate our citizens? It would take a major push to convince the public that it's safe to go outside for more than a few hours, let alone a few days. You may not ever be able to convince everyone that it's safe." He shook his head. "You'll start a general panic, if you start talking about evacuating above ground."

The Chief chuckled softly. "Now you know why the Council just laughs at Ms. Johnson and moves on." He rose, ready to leave. The Commissioner gestured with his hand, and the Chief sat back down.

"Manny," the Commissioner began, "there's something else on my mind." Manny's eyes went wary, his expression carefully blank.

"You're a skilled detective, and your leadership skills are good and getting even better. But what I like best about you, Lieutenant, is your ability to think beyond the present day. We're going to need someone like you, someone with foresight, in our government. You know, a visionary, a person who can lead us in planning for the future." He paused, looking at the Chief, who nodded almost imperceptibly.

The Commissioner continued. "The Deputy Commissioner is ill, terminally ill. He's an old man, 52 this year, barely able to work. He'll be retiring soon. Manny, you understand that this is confidential information?" Manny nodded.

"The Deputy Commissioner needs to mentor his replacement, and time is growing short. How would you like to be his shadow, for the next month or so? You can follow him through his day and learn his job directly from him. Then when he retires, you'll become Deputy Commissioner."

Manny could not believe his ears. *Deputy Commissioner?!* "Sir! I don't know how to thank you!"

The Commissioner continued. "The day-to-day duties of the Deputy Commissioner are pretty light. Basically, it's his job to be able to step in seamlessly and do *my* job, should the need arise. He'll introduce you to the people in the Mayor's office, help you learn what I do on a daily basis. After that, once you get to know your way around, I think you might actually have some time on your hands. You might want to take a look in on the Task Force, now and again. You know, supervise the new lieutenant there, maybe take a stab at one or two of the cold cases."

The Task Force! The new lieutenant there, of course, was Dave. "I'd love it, thank you, Sir!" he said enthusiastically. "But doesn't the Task Force already have a supervisor?"

"No, that position is temporary. We borrowed him from another unit; we'll just ship him back to where he came from," the Commissioner replied airily. "For now, your title will be Special Aide to the Deputy Commissioner. You'll be a Captain; no one below the rank of captain works in my office. Let's say this will begin on Monday, shall we? I'll have an announcement sent out."

The three men rose. "Thank you again, Commissioner, Chief," Manny said, bowing formally to them both. "I won't let you down."

"We know that, Captain. We're counting on you," said the Commissioner.

# Chapter 29.

"I'VE GOT GREAT news," Manny announced as the family gathered in the kitchen before dinner. A freshly baked loaf of Italian bread was on the table; a black rice and lillibud casserole was in the oven; and Lucinda was putting the finishing touches on her eggplant sliders.

"I've been promoted to Captain, and will be the new Aide to the Deputy Commissioner!" announced Manny with a wide smile.

"Wow! That's wonderful!" Luis said, clapping Manny on the shoulder. "I'm proud of you, son!"

"That's James O'Brian, right?" asked Julio. "He's pretty old, isn't he?"

"Yeah, he's getting close to retirement, and wants to train a replacement before he leaves. It'll be like I'm his intern, shadowing him through his day so I can learn what he does," Manny explained.

"That's wonderful news!" said Lucinda. "When do you start?"

"First thing on Monday morning," replied Manny. "The best part is that once I get up to speed, I'll also be supervising the Commissioner's Task Force for cold cases. I'll be working with Dave again! I may have time to actually do some detective work."

"That's great, Manny," said Anna with a genuine smile.

"Does this mean you will be Commissioner someday?" asked Lucinda.

"Maybe someday. The Commissioner is a long way from retiring, though," replied Manny.

"I think this is such good news, Manny," said Lucinda. "Congratulations!"

She motioned to the kitchen table. "Everyone, come sit down. Dinner is ready." She turned to the doorway and called out, "Kids, dinner! Come along downstairs!"

"How was school today, Zach?" asked Manny, seated next to Zach.

"OK," he said. "Ms. Parker says stars shine every night, even though there's nobody to see. Why do they do that?"

"Did you ask Ms. Parker?" asked Lucinda.

"She said they just shine, it's what stars do," he answered. Zach ate industriously, eyeing the coveted dessert on the counter across the kitchen, a plate of double-chocolate mocha cloud cookies.

"Julie, how about you? How was school?" asked Lucinda.

"Good," she replied. "Our homework is to name one extinct animal for each letter of the alphabet."

"That should be easy," said Anna.

The family ate in silence for a few moments.

"Zach, would you like more lilibuds?" asked Manny.

"No, I'm fed up," replied Zach.

"You're what?" asked Manny, laughing. "I think what you mean is that you're full, right?"

From the corner of his eye, Manny saw Anna stiffen suddenly in her chair, glancing over at Julio and then back down at her plate, her cheeks reddening.

"Yeah, I'm full. I don't want any more," replied Zach.

Upstairs later, when Manny was getting Zach ready for bed, he said casually, "Did you hear someone say they were fed up, Zach?"

"Auntie Anna, she said it to Uncle Julio. Then he closed the door so Julie and I couldn't hear," replied Zach.

"Did Auntie Anna say why she was fed up?" asked Manny, pulling the covers down so Zach could climb into bed. "Maybe she had a hard day at work?"

"I dunno, I couldn't hear her. I could only hear Uncle Julio. He's really loud when he's mad," said Zach, yawning.

"And what did Uncle Julio say to Auntie Anna when he yelled at her?" asked Manny, hoping to keep his youngster on track until he finished the tale.

Zach replied, "Uncle Julio said 'he's my brother.' Daddy, are we getting a new baby?"

"What?" asked Manny, surprised. "No, not that I know of! Why, what makes you ask?"

194

"Auntie Anna said she thinks we might be getting a baby," replied Zach, with heavy-lidded sleepy eyes.

Manny laughed softly, his hand on his little boy's shoulder. "Did she, now?" he mused. He kissed the top of his head. "Goodnight, Buddy."

"Mommy used to do that," he murmured sleepily, eyes closed.

Alone in his room, Manny mulled over the conversation with Zach. Anna, Julio and the children were often home when Manny was not. Apparently, there had been at least one conversation in which Anna had said that she was "fed up," and Julio had protested "he's my brother."

*It's not hard to imagine what the rest of that conversation sounded like,* thought Manny, taking a fortifying swig from his pocket flask. He knew that Anna had been suspicious that he was hiding something under the pillow, the night that she and Julio surprised him with a visit to his bedroom.

He'd have to tread lightly, try to win her over. He took another generous pull and then placed the flask back in his uniform pocket, so he didn't forget to take it with him when he left for work.

~ ~ ~ ~ ~ ~

Very early on Monday morning, Manny arrived at the office filled with excitement for his new job. The announcement of his promotion had not yet gone out, but that didn't worry Manny; in fact, he thought he might have a little fun with it.

Going past his office – his *old* office, he thought – Manny went upstairs to the area where the Commissioner's special Task Force was located. A few of the detectives were already there, just beginning to settle into their day. He looked into Dave's office, which was empty. Going in, he sat down in the visitor's chair and waited for his friend to arrive.

"Hey, Manny! How are you?" Dave exclaimed when he came in a few minutes later. "You'd better not let the Captain catch you in here socializing," he warned, laughing. "He's a real stickler for proper work ethic."

"He is, you're right," said Manny with a Cheshire-cat smile, leaning back and casually crossing his legs on the edge of Dave's desk.

"What's going on?" asked Dave, puzzled.

"I'm your new Captain!" Manny announced with a grin.

"You are?! Congratulations!" replied Dave.

"My official title is Special Aide to the Deputy Commissioner," explained Manny. "I've been promoted to captain. For the next few weeks, I'll be shadowing the Deputy Commissioner, learning his job. Once I've finished with that, then I'll have time to supervise the Task Force."

Dave leaned back in his chair, a smile spreading over his face. "Well, well, well," he said. "We'll be glad to have you around here. Wait until I tell Naomi! Congratulations, Captain!"

Manny's padlet beeped; a second later, Dave's padlet beeped. A moment later, beeping could be heard all over the office. The official announcement of Captain Stewart's promotion had been sent out.

A knock at the door interrupted the two friends as they admired the announcement on their padlets. The Commissioner walked in, not waiting to be invited. "Manny, there are you! Good morning, Lieutenant Wu," he said. "Manny, come with me, there's someone I want you to meet."

The Commissioner and Manny walked together to the end of the hallway, where the Commissioner knocked on the door of one of the two largest offices. "Manny, I'd like to introduce you to the Deputy Commissioner, James Angus O'Brian. James, this is Captain Manny Stewart."

Manny bowed respectfully to the Deputy Commissioner. "Health and prosperity to you, Sir. It's a pleasure to meet you."

"Please, call me James," replied the Deputy Commissioner. "Welcome! We've been talking about you for days now. It's a pleasure to finally meet you." He looked hard at Manny, searching his face. "You're Pat Stewart's boy, aren't you?" he asked.

Manny swallowed. "Yes, Sir! James," he said.

"I hear you stopped a riot dead in its tracks when the power went out last spring, is that true?" James continued.

"Something like that," said Manny.

"And he did it with Paddy's old bullhorn!" said the Commissioner. "I'm just sorry I wasn't there to see it!" The two older men laughed, enjoying their joke, remembering their colleague and friend. Manny stood silently, smile firmly in place.

"Well, why don't I let the two of you get to know each other," said the Commissioner, turning to leave.

"Thank you, Sir!" said Manny to the Commissioner as he turned away.

"You can call me Dan now, Manny," he replied. "You're one of us now."

By the end of the first morning in his new position, Manny had been introduced to everyone and had been assigned to one of the smaller offices in the back. Pikchurz, the app which projected photos onto the wall to give the illusion of a window, had an interesting collection of choices, much better quality than he had had downstairs.

There was an ancient, creaky armchair for visitors, and a completely empty, dented black metal bookshelf. There was no window. The desk, while it was regulation-size, barely fit into the little room, touching the wall on one side, leaving a small space so narrow on the other side that Manny had to turn sideways to slide past it, in order to get to his desk chair. When opened, the office door banged into the back of the well-battered visitor's chair.

"It's not glamorous, but it's all yours," said James, gingerly settling himself into the visitor's chair as Manny sat down behind his new desk. "And of course, it's temporary. You will move into my office, after I retire."

Manny wanted to ask when that would be, but did not want to appear overly eager on his first day at the job, so instead, he coughed and then changed the subject. "Do you also supervise the Task Force?"

"No, I've been winding down my duties, rather than picking up new ones. When Dan created the Task Force, we both knew that my replacement would eventually take over that responsibility," replied James.

Manny could see the Deputy Commissioner clearly in his brightly lit office. James's skin was a sickly grayish-white; he had a noticeable tremor in his right hand and arm, which had been obvious as he was pointing out the different personnel and their respective offices on their floor. James moved very slowly, shuffling forward with a limp. He seemed unsteady and fragile.

They chatted amiably about the department and the people in it, while Manny wondered what exactly James would be doing on a normal Monday morning, if he didn't have Manny to mentor. Then James stood up, stretched and said, "I'm going to go lie down for a bit. See you later, Manny."

And with that, he was gone, leaving Manny alone in his new office at 10:00 am to begin wading through the stack of reports, letters and other official communications which were sitting in his new inbox.

Manny dearly needed a cup of tea, the kind that Agnes usually made for him every morning. *First things first*, he thought, getting up to visit the tiny kitchen area. He was surprised to see Agnes there, showing his new secretary how to prepare his tea with a generous tot of brandy.

"Captain! Congratulations on your promotion," she said, bowing to him.

"Thanks, Agnes, I appreciate that," he said. "And who is this?"

"This is your new secretary; she works for everyone in the Commissioner's office. Her name is Edith."

Edith, an older woman who looked like she brooked no nonsense, bowed respectfully to him. "Health and prosperity to you, Sir. It's a pleasure to meet you."

"Edith has been with the Commissioner's office for over twenty years," added Agnes. "She knows everything, all the little ins and outs." In truth, she did look like an experienced veteran, a bit of a battle-axe, but it would take more than administrative skills to hold a position at this level, Manny knew.

"Thank you both! I feel like I am in good hands," joked Manny cordially.

The day passed slowly. Manny didn't have much else to do, after he finished his tea and read through the items in his inbox. He didn't want to take any action on those papers until he spoke to James about them, and James was snoring audibly down the hall in his office, stretched out on a sofa which had been patched so many times that it was hard to tell what it had once looked like. The Commissioner was not in his office; *he's probably downstairs talking to the Chief,* thought Manny, feeling a bit of nostalgia for the Chief.

Manny ate lunch at his desk, then wandered down the hall to see if Dave was busy.

"Hey, Manny, how's it going?" he said as Manny walked into his office. "Are they keeping you busy?"

"Not yet, not really," Manny replied. "The Deputy Commissioner is ... he's resting, and the Commissioner is out." He settled himself into the visitor's chair. "What do you know about the Deputy Commissioner, Dave?"

"You mean, how long has he been ill?" asked Dave. "For months, really. He's pretty weak, as far as I can see. There's an office pool, to see who can guess when he will retire."

"I didn't hear that," responded Manny with a grin, remembering that he was now Dave's boss.

"Are you free later?" asked Dave. "A few of us are going out for a couple of drinks after work, to Sean's. You don't have to drink, if you don't want to." Sean's Bar and Kitchen was a landmark of New York City, a favorite of the police officers in midtown, as it had been since it first opened its doors in the year 2016, well before New York had moved underground in 2085.

199

"Sure," replied Manny, "I'd like that. I'll see you later."

Manny returned to his office, where he discovered James sitting in his visitor's chair, feet up on his desk. "Let's go over some of this," he said to Manny amiably, holding a folder in his hand. "Time to get you up to speed."

They spent a couple of hours working their way through the folders in Manny's inbox. By the end of the afternoon, Manny's head was reeling with new names and procedures.

"That's enough for one day," said James. "We can pick up here, tomorrow morning. And I want to take you over to the Mayor's office in the afternoon, to introduce you all around."

The Commissioner knocked politely on the door to Manny's office. "James, can I see you before you leave?" he asked, and the two of them went into James's office, leaving Manny alone at his desk.

At exactly 5:00 pm, Manny went down the hall to find Dave, who was just finishing up work. "Ready?" he asked, and together the two friends went downstairs, past the floor where Manny used to work, outside to street level. The bar was not far from the office.

Dave looked questioningly at Manny as they ordered; Manny did not hesitate. *After all,* he reasoned, *there is nothing wrong with a drink after work with my colleagues. If the folks at home can't understand that, that was their problem.*

"Slainte!" cried Dave, as they picked up their first round of drinks, trendy little single servings of granita, an iced drink made from semi-frozen vodka. The granita was served in a miniature "bullet," a little cup scooped out of melon or some other type of fruit. Bullets were very popular. Jokes abounded about the virtues of eating fresh fruit.

Manny ordered a bowl of spinach dip, a basket of freshly baked pretzellas, and a second round of bullets. "Tell me all about the Task Force," he said to Dave. "I want to know everything. What do you think of the detectives?"

Manny and Dave talked their way through several rounds of bullets, before Manny rose to go. "So soon?" asked Dave, disappointed.

"'Sponsibility. Haf t' have dinner with my son." He grimaced. "Gotta do it," he said. Manny thought enviously of Dave's wife Jenny, at home with their kids. *Sure, you can sit here and drink,* he thought bitterly. *Your wife's not dead.*

"OK, do what you gotta do, man. I'll see you tomorrow," said Dave.

Manny reached for his jacket and headed toward the door. As he was leaving, he was surprised to see the Commissioner and Deputy Commissioner, along with another man, on their way into the bar. "Manny!" cried the Commissioner.

"Dan, James," said Manny, nodding to them both. *Should I salute?* he wondered. *Should I not use their first names in public?* His head felt fuzzy, and he needed something to lean on.

"Come right on over here, son," said Dan, motioning with his hand, waving Manny back into the bar. "Your first day on the job calls for a drink!"

# Chapter 30.

**W**ITHIN MOMENTS, MANNY found himself back in the bar, seated in a booth. A gloriously beautiful full bottle of brandy appeared magically in front of him. Two other bottles, tequila and Scotch, were also produced, as well as a platter of fried squeegies, a new aquatic hybrid fish-like creature that was remarkably good when rolled in cornmeal and fried.

"A toast to our new Aide!" called Dan, and Manny dutifully downed a healthy amount of brandy.

"And a toast to my replacement," said James, and again, everyone drank.

"I'm Nigel, by the way," said the gentleman sitting next to Dan. "I'm the Commissioner's Aide."

"You must be N. Peterson!" said Manny. "Glad to meet you."

Time passed. Drinks were consumed. There was laughter in the bar and singing, sad old Irish songs that Manny vaguely remembered hearing in his childhood. Several other officers, off duty for the day, stopped by the table to meet Manny and congratulate him on his promotion. Manny smiled and bowed, smiled and bowed. And drank.

"Whose padlet is that?" asked James, referring to the insistent beeping sounds coming from somewhere.

"Huh?" Manny listened. "Whoa, it's mine!" he said in surprise. He pulled out his padlet. Along the rim of the padlet, a tiny orange ball was bopping up and down, a reminder from his scheduler app. *That's not a good sign,* he thought, opening up the app.

"Oh, *shit!*" he said suddenly, standing up. "Sorry, I haf t' go. I'm late. Father-Son Night at my kid's school." Bowing quickly to each of James and Dan, Manny ran for the door.

Nigel called out to him, "Manny, wait up! I'll walk with you."

The evening was cool and quiet, after the noise of the crowded bar. The two men turned towards the 50th Street Station, where Manny lived. The streets in this part of the Colony were wide enough for Manny and Nigel to walk side by side. As they walked, each Danish street light came on to light their way, blinking off when they walked past it.

"How long haf you been with th' Commissioner?" asked Manny, for something to say. He was concentrating carefully on walking, making conversation difficult.

"Not that long. Since Raimone left to go to the Bronx," he replied. "It's only temporary, you know. I'll be back with my old unit when Raimone returns."

Manny's heart sank. "I thought th' lil' bastard was gone for good," he said. Manny stumbled, nearly crashing into Nigel. "Sorry," he mumbled. "So Raimone's coming back? Do y' know when?"

"I don't know, soon, I think," replied Nigel. "Why, don't you like him?" He smirked appreciatively.

Manny laughed. "No, I can't stand him. I hear he's been bounced all around th' department, but nobody wants him."

"Yeah, he never stays long with any one assignment. He's utterly unqualified, if you ask me, besides being an obnoxious boor," replied Nigel.

"It's too bad Dan's wife's related to him. Otherwise, somebody would haf fired him long ago," said Manny.

Nigel looked sideways at Manny, then quickly looked straight ahead. "Well, no, Raimone's not actually related to her. I doubt that Dan's wife even knows him. But I'll let Dan tell you all about it."

The two Special Aides said goodnight and parted, as Nigel turned down the street leading to his home.

At the Stewart house, Manny walked up the path to the front door and leaned against it, fumbling with the Scentinel sensor pad. Before he could open it, the door swung open and Luis stood in the doorway, arms crossed, eyes flashing angrily.

"You're late!" he said, moving aside to let Manny in. As Manny slid past him into the foyer, Luis's nose wrinkled up; then the expression on his face changed.

"Manny! Have you been drinking?" he demanded.
"Yesss. Yesss, I haf been drinking," Manny replied defiantly. "I went out for a lil' drink with Dave after work,

celebrate my first day on th' new job. Then the Commissioner and Deputy Commissioner came in, so I had drinks with them, too."

Lucinda had come into the foyer and was listening, an expression of dismay on her face. "Manny's drunk?" she asked.

"No. Not drunk," he replied. "I jus' had few drinks to cel'brate the promotion, tha's all."

"But you promised!" she protested. "You promised us all that you wouldn't drink anymore."

"Lucinda, you gotta understand, they all drink. Everyone I work for. I was on my way outta the bar when my boss and the Commissioner came in. They invited me to haf drink with them, too. Was I s'pposed to say no to that?!"

Exasperated, Manny wiped his mouth with the back of his hand. "C' we talk about this later? It's Father-Son Night at the school. I came home t' take Zach," Manny said, looking around for Zach, who was standing next to Anna and Julio. Both Zach and Julio had their jackets on.

"Zach, come here," Manny said, one hand holding firmly to the banister and the other outstretched to his son. Zach cringed, moving behind his uncle.

"Manny, you can't be serious," said Luis. "You can't take him to Father-Son Night like this."

"Like what, Luis?" said Manny belligerently. "Y' think I'm drunk, iss that it?" He turned to face Luis, but in doing so, he moved too quickly and nearly lost his balance.

"If you take Zach to school like this, you'll embarrass him. And yourself, too. In front of that nice Ms. Parker," said Luis pointedly.

"Nobody's gonna know that I've been drinking," retorted Manny. "I'll be fine." He looked at Zach. "Zach, come here. We're leaving."

Luis moved closer to Manny. "Don't do this, Manny," he said in an undertone. "Let Julio take him. He'll be a good substitute for you. No one will think twice about it."

"No," Manny declared indignantly. "He's *my* son, not Julio's! *I'm* taking him. Now, get outta my way." Manny let go of the banister and started unsteadily towards his son.

Luis stepped determinedly between Manny and Zach. "I can't let you do this, Manny," he said, his voice rising. "You stink like a gin factory. Everyone will notice. Look at yourself! You'll be all over the news tomorrow, the society pages. 'Newly promoted Captain Stewart shows up drunk at his son's elementary school.' Not only that - what will happen to Zach, if you fall or pass out on your way there?" he continued. "No. Let Julio take him."

Julio moved closer to Zach, holding out his hand. "Come on, Zach, you can come with me," he said reassuringly. Zach's eyes were round with fright.

Manny protested, "I'm not drunk!!" Even to his own ears, his voice sounded much too loud. "Had a few drinks, iss all. So if you'll all jus' get the hell outta my way - "

Lucinda moved closer to Manny and placed her hand on his arm. "Manny. Don't do this," she implored. "I'm begging you."

"What, you too?" he snarled scornfully. "Lucinda. Please. I'm fine." He roughly pushed her hand away. Lucinda did not back away, her eyes beseeching him.

The room was sliding slowly to the right, and the floor was making it hard to walk. He stumbled, lost his balance and reached out to steady himself by grabbing hold of Lucinda's shoulder. The two of them went down with a crash onto the hard marble floor, Lucinda on her side, Manny on top of her. Lucinda screamed, her left arm twisted beneath her. For a moment, stunned, no one moved.

"Lucinda!! Manny, get off her! Lucinda! Are you alright?" Luis exclaimed, rushing to help. "Julio, help me get him off her!"

Together Luis and Julio shoved Manny roughly to the side, where he lay on his back looking up at the astonishingly high ceiling, watching it as it slowly rotated. Lucinda was moaning, saying something about her wrist. Anna was on her padlet, calling Manny's doctor, Dr. Monica Patel.

"She's on her way, Lucinda," Anna said reassuringly. "Can you sit up?"

Lucinda sat up, cradling her arm against her chest. "I don't think it's broken," she said, wiggling her fingers, trying to assess the damage.

Luis said, "Anna. Go upstairs. Pack some things for Julie and Zach. Then take Julie across the street to our house. Julio. You stay here with your mother while the doctor sees her. I will take Zach to Father-Son Night."

"What about Manny?" asked Julio.

"What about him?" countered Luis, eyes narrowing as he looked at Manny lying on the floor, barely conscious.

"At least help me get him upstairs before you go, OK?" asked Julio.

Together, Julio and Luis half-dragged, half-carried Manny up the stairs and put him on his bed, where they left him, still protesting that he was fine.

"We'll have more to say about this tomorrow," Luis said darkly. "But for now, I need to make sure that your son gets to the school on time."

Downstairs, Lucinda was still sitting on the floor at the bottom of the steps, her arm against her chest. "Zach? Zachie, sweetheart, where are you?" she called.

Julio and Luis came down the stairs, heading into the study.

"Zach, can you hear me?" Luis called. "It's time to go. Come on, I'll take you. Zach, where are you?" he said, pretending that he did not know where Zach was. If Zach so desperately needed a safe place to hide, then his grandfather would not violate his hiding place.

Julio tried, too. "Where is Zach? He'll be the only one not there, if you don't leave soon. Doesn't he want to show off his artwork, and see all the other kids' fathers?"

The closet door slowly cracked open, Zach peeking out, looking around. "Your Dad fell asleep," said Julio. "He's tired from work, so he's gone to bed. Abuelo is going to take you to Father-Son Night."

Luis held out his hand. Zach slowly came out of the closet, looking around like a frightened mouse. Luis picked him up and hugged him. "Let's go say goodbye to Abuela and Auntie Anna, and we'll be on our way."

Manny heard Luis and Zach leave, heard Anna and Julie saying goodbye to Lucinda and Julio before they left. He heard Dr. Patel arrive and together with Julio, help Lucinda to her feet, taking her into the front parlor to examine her arm. He heard all of this and yet, it didn't seem to have anything to do with him. Something bad had happened, something to ... was it Lucinda? Yes, Lucinda. She fell, or something. Her arm. He closed his eyes and fell deeply asleep.

*Naztazya was there, gliding down the long staircase in a beautiful lavender dress trimmed with lace, the gossamer fabric seeming to float in the air behind her. Her waist-length curly red hair hung loose behind her, rippling like spun silk in the light from the chandelier. A tiny wisp of smoke rose from a spot at the top of her head. Reaching to pat it gently with his hand, he drew back with a cry, his hand burned and blistered. Alarmed, he grasped her arms and pulled her closer to him, but she was on fire, her hair suddenly flaring full up into a blazing torch, her arms turning to ashes in his hands. Naz, no, please! I'm so sorry, Naz, please don't leave me!*

# Chapter 31.

**M**ANNY SCREAMED IN his nightmare, waking himself. He sat up, wiping a trembling hand across his perspiring forehead. Shaking his head to clear it from the nightmare images, he listened to see if he had awakened anyone with his scream, but the house was still and quiet.

Sitting up so quickly had ... oh, no. Manny kicked back the blanket in one swift motion, ignoring the pounding of his head, and rushed to the bathroom, just in time. He vomited again and again, finally sitting down and leaning his throbbing head against the sweet coolness of the bathtub. He fell asleep sitting up.

When his alarm went off at 6:00 am, Manny woke, surprised to find himself sitting on the bathroom floor. He could not quite remember falling asleep in the bathroom, although he certainly could guess how it had happened.

He washed, dressed, tied back his hair, and went downstairs to kiss Zach goodbye before he left for work.

The house seemed unusually quiet. There was no one in the kitchen. No one had made breakfast. "Anna?" he called tentatively. Maybe she was in her home office, off the kitchen. Manny looked; her office was empty.

With a sinking feeling in his stomach, Manny went back upstairs. Looking in Zach's bedroom, he could see that the bed had not been slept in. Julie's room looked the same, as did Julio and Anna's bedroom. Where was everyone?

*They must be at Luis and Lucinda's house, of course,* he reassured himself. *Probably trying to teach me a lesson or something.* He wondered briefly if Zach had made it to Father-Son Night. He was not worried about Zach getting to school; Anna always made sure that Julie and Zach had a good breakfast and left the house on time. *I'll have to deal with this later,* he thought.

Fortunately for Manny, it was not a difficult day at the office. James stopped by to chat for a few minutes and then went back to his office to rest. Manny re-read the papers and reports that he had read the day before, sipping his tea. For lunch, he had a sandwich at his desk, as he was used to doing, although there was nothing keeping him from going out for lunch.

In the afternoon, Hasan Blumberg, Sarah's husband, stopped by his office to talk to him about the leak in Aviva Johnson's wall. Manny had asked Hasan to send two of his best engineers, carrying toolboxes and posing as plumbers, to inspect the leak and report back to him.

"When they got there, they could hear the water dripping from the ceiling," Hasan said to Manny. "Ms. Johnson's got a bucket underneath it, which she empties every couple of hours. But they were not able to identify the source of the leak. They did rule out condensation or a broken pipe; there was nothing broken that they could see."

"How big of a leak are we talking about?" asked Manny.

"A small but steady stream, I'd say about a quart every few hours," replied Hasan. "Any further investigation would require tearing open Ms. Johnson's walls."

"Do you have any ideas about the source of the water?" asked Manny.

"No, I wish I did. These two guys are my best men, Manny. If they don't know, then nobody does." Hasan smiled at Manny. "You know, the last time I talked to you, you were a kid. You had just broken into my house. You've certainly changed paths since then."

Manny laughed. "I never meant any harm, you know. I was just trying to avoid my father. Your neighbor tipped him off that I was waiting for Sarah outside your house." Manny, 15 years old, secretly had gone to see Sarah, his teacher, after school one day, waiting for her outside of her house. He panicked when he saw his father approaching from down the street. Adept at breaking and entering, he easily picked the lock and broke into the Blumberg house to hide from his father. That's where the Blumbergs had discovered him, sitting in their living room, when they came home.

"It was nice to see you, Manny," said Hasan.

Manny rose, and the two men bowed to each other. "Please give my regards to Sarah," Manny said.

Later that afternoon, James and Manny went to the Mayor's office, where James introduced him to the people who worked there. "These are our contacts, the people we interact with when issues come up," explained James. "The Mayor and the Commissioner usually meet once a week, to stay in touch."

After they returned to the office, Manny had questions about one of the contacts at the Mayor's office. Unfortunately, James was gone for the day; Edith, the department secretary, said that he had gone home right after they returned from the Mayor's office, not feeling well.

With nothing left to do, Manny left the office at exactly 5:00 pm. *It feels like the middle of the afternoon,* he mused, passing Dave and his unit on the way to the exit. They were all still immersed in their work, padlets out, examining a giant image projected against one of the walls. No one looked up as he passed by.

*At least I'll be home in time for dinner,* thought Manny. Thinking of the previous evening, he braced himself for whatever might be waiting for him at home. They were probably going to have lots to say about it. He wondered if Lucinda's arm was OK, realizing belatedly that he should have hologrammed her earlier in the day.

Letting himself into the house, he called out, "Zach! I'm home." There was no response. He walked into the kitchen, which was empty and dark. He looked in the library, the front parlor, the study, everywhere upstairs. No one was there. Pulling out his padlet, he texted Julio.

Manny: *Hey, where is everybody? Is dinner at Lucinda's tonight?*

Several minutes went by before Julio responded. Finally, he answered:

Julio: *Come and see Zach before he goes to bed.*

Manny sat down in an armchair in the study. They were all at Lucinda and Luis's house across the street, together. They were having dinner without him, in the house which he had gifted to them, excluding him. The message could not have been more clear.

It was quiet in the study, too quiet. He sat down at the desk, thinking maybe he would pay some bills. A moment later, too agitated to sit still, he went upstairs to his bedroom, changing into sweatpants and a teeshirt.

Flask in hand, he went back downstairs. If they didn't want to include him, fine. At least there was no one around to give him a hard time about his drinking.

Manny set the pocket flask down on the kitchen table. He poured himself a generous glassful of brandy, placing it next to the flask, admiring the brandy in its beautiful antique crystal snifter, its color, its aroma.

*Not yet. First things first*, he admonished himself. Getting up, Manny rummaged through the cabinets and bio-polymer gel coldbox, filling a plate with leftover cooked vegetables and two air-fried speckled briney-babies. Then, satisfied by his virtuous show of self-control, he sat down at the table and drank down every drop of the beautiful brandy, all at once. *Just one drink,* he cautioned himself. *A drink before dinner, very civilized.*

It was 7:00 pm, too soon to go to Lucinda's house. He would arrive at exactly 8:00 pm, Zach's bedtime. He would pick up Zach and bring him home, then read him a story and put him to bed, as he always did.

He finished his cold plate of leftovers in just a few minutes, pushing the plate away from him. With no one to talk to, dinner was over very quickly. The long kitchen table stretched out in front of him, the empty chairs mocking him. It was so quiet. It had been quiet like this when Manny was a child, home alone in the long afternoons and evenings while his father worked late at the office.

At exactly 8:00 pm, Manny walked across the street to Lucinda's house. He hesitated at the door; should he ring the bell like a guest, or should he unlock it and walk in as he always did? He decided to unlock it. Anna was waiting for him in the foyer. Zach, dressed in his pajamas, stood next to her, holding Anna's hand.

"Manny," she said. "We saw you coming. Zach is ready for a bedtime story." She turned and walked away, into the kitchen.

"Hey, Bud, how was Father-Son Night? Did you have a good time?" Manny asked. Zach did not answer; he looked away, his face reddening. *Maybe I should have waited a bit before bringing that up,* Manny thought.

"Well. I see that you have your pajamas on. Did Auntie Anna give you a bath?" Manny said.

"No, Uncle Julio," replied Zach softly, looking down at his feet.

"I see," said Manny, squelching down the tiniest spark of jealousy. He searched for something to say.

Luis came into the foyer. Manny could tell immediately by his body language that Luis was angry. "Manny," he said shortly, by way of greeting.

"Hi, Luis," he replied. "I got home and no one was there! What's going on?"

Luis's eyes narrowed. He opened his mouth to reply, but just then Lucinda walked into the foyer, her arm in a sling. She turned to Zach. "Zach, go upstairs and play with Julie, would you please? We want to talk to Daddy."

When Zach was safely out of hearing, she turned to him. Her eyes were sad and wounded. "Manny, please come inside," she said. "We need to talk."

"Lucinda, are you OK? How is your wrist?" Manny asked, eyeing the sling. Little bits and pieces of the accident came back to him. He remembered Luis and Julio roughly moving him off Lucinda, after he had fallen with all of his weight on top of her.

"It's sprained, Manny, thank you for asking," Lucinda replied with a touch of coolness. Why had he not thought to text her during the day? He could have had Edith send her flowers. Remorse twisted uncomfortably inside his chest.

"I'm sorry. It was an accident," he blurted out. "Honestly, I don't even remember much of what happened last night. I remember coming home to take Zach to Father-Son Night, I remember Luis and Julio dragging me up the stairs ... I do remember falling on top of you. I wish that had not happened, Lucinda. I can't apologize enough."

"You're right, you can't apologize enough," snapped Luis. "You *hurt her!"* Lucinda turned to her husband, frowning disapproval. Her unblinking gaze held his eyes, telling him that the time for anger was over.

"I know that, Manny. I know it was an accident." She faced him. "Still, you are responsible for your actions, even if you black out and don't remember what happened."

She took a deep breath. "Manny, when you're drunk, you're not in control of yourself. You say things, do things ... you get hostile and aggressive, you won't listen to reason. It's hard to be around you. I don't want to be around you, when you're drunk. None of us do." Her soft words sliced through him like a knife.

"Manny, there are going to be some changes," Luis announced, his voice ringing with disapproval. "Julio, Julie and Anna will be living here for the time being," he said, unable to keep a vindictive note of triumph out of his voice.

"What?" said Manny, taken aback. "They're not coming home?" He looked at Julio, who was standing next to his mother, his arm around her shoulders.

Julio shook his head. "I'm sorry, man. This isn't good for anyone," he said.

"We can't make you stop drinking, we see that now. Only you can do that," said Lucinda sadly. "The only remaining question is what to do about Zach."

Manny tried to wrap his head around the idea that they were not coming home. Julio and his family had moved out.

"Zach is my son. He lives with me, of course," said Manny. "He needs to be at home. I can read to him and put him to bed every night."

"Will you make him breakfast before school, and make sure he gets to school on time? Will you be there for him when he gets home from school?" countered Lucinda. "What about dinner, will you make dinner for him? What if he gets sick and has to stay home from school? What about school vacations?"

Manny's heart sank. He had not thought of any of that. Honestly, how could a person reasonably be expected to care for a child and hold down a full-time job? *And not just any job, either,* he thought indignantly, *but soon-to-be Deputy Commissioner.* He would hire someone to care for Zach, full-time help; that's what he would do. He had offered that to Naz, but she hadn't wanted servants raising her child. But things had changed.

"What you need to do, Manny, is put aside your own feelings for now, and think about what is best for Zach," Lucinda said earnestly. "Is it in Zach's best interest for you to take him home to live with you, or to leave him here with us? With his cousin Julie, his aunt, uncle and grandparents? We love him. We can take good care of him."

Manny was stunned. Zach was *his*. They were being so unreasonable!

"Why?" exploded Manny. "Why aren't you coming back to the house?" he demanded, looking at Julio. "Where is Anna," he asked suddenly, "why isn't she here?"

"Anna is upstairs, lying down. She didn't want to be here for this conversation," said Julio. "She and I agree on this."

Julio exchanged glances with his parents, and then turned back to Manny.

"Anna is pregnant, Manny. It's early days, and she needs quiet, and calm. She can't be angry and upset all the time. You know how it goes," Julio said. They all knew, everyone in the Colony knew about the high incident of miscarriages in their women.

214

"Congratulations, Julio!" Manny said heartily, but no one else smiled. Manny sat down awkwardly in one of the chairs, dismayed by the united facade of their disapproval. No one else sat down.

"Of course, you can come and see Zach any time you want, stay as long as you want," said Lucinda, gesturing with both palms facing outwards. "No one is trying to take your son away from you, Manny. We just want what is best for Zach. We know that you do, too," she added in a conciliatory tone.

Part of Manny was outraged. They had no right to ... but a tiny part of him said wait, maybe this might be better. He would be able to concentrate on his work, free from the kaleidoscope of responsibilities that come with parenting. He could come and go as he pleased, just see Zach before bedtime, like he used to before Naz died.

"OK," he said finally, "it might work. But not permanently, right?"

"Let's just see how this goes," said Julio smoothly. "We can make whatever changes we want, later. Why don't you plan on visiting with Zach every night after dinner? Come over and read to him, play with him, put him to bed. To Zach, it won't be that different, he'll just be here, not at your house."

Manny hesitated. Julio had made a point of saying that Manny should come "after dinner." But then he nodded. Everyone breathed a sigh of relief.

# Chapter 32.

**T**HE FAMILY SOON fell into a familiar pattern. Manny would come home from work around 7:00 pm every evening, picking up dinner on his way home. Then he would change his clothes, eat and go across the street to Lucinda's house to see Zach. He made sure that he arrived after the family had eaten, knowing that he was not welcome to join them. In the beginning, conversation was stilted and uncomfortable, but after a few days, things settled down.

The family was not only intertwined because of childcare issues; they were also in business together. Julio and Luis were Manny's partners. There were many things to discuss, and Manny found himself staying later and later at Lucinda's house in the evenings.

Still, coming home afterwards to an empty house was not easy. Manny sat in his library late at night with a glass of brandy in his hand, trying not to notice the deep silence. Sometimes he walked from room to empty room, echoes of conversations he had had with Naztazya ringing in his ears; she seemed to be behind every closed door, ever elusive.

~ ~ ~ ~ ~ ~

One morning the Commissioner came into his office and sat down as Manny was drinking his morning cup of tea. He pulled out his flask and offered it to Manny, who shook his head. This morning Edith had put more brandy than tea into his cup; he'd have to remember to tell her to use less. Dan took a swallow, and put the flask down between them on the desk.

"Did you have a chance to look over the final report on the blackout?" he asked, without preamble.

"Yeah, I read it last night," replied Manny. "It's hard to imagine a single person doing that deliberately."

After a thorough investigation, it turned out that the blackout had been caused by a single individual, a disgruntled employee who had deliberately turned off the primary group of servers, causing the blackout at night, when there was only a skeleton staff on duty. He had wanted to be a hero, single-handedly transitioning smoothly to the recovery servers, which contain the exact same code as the primary servers. However, as it turned out, the recovery servers did not contain a complete copy of the code. Much of the information had corrupted over time.

As unit supervisor, Anna was in charge. She and her colleagues had worked diligently through the night of the blackout, using the lone emergency backup server, which contained a copy of all of the Colony's code. The emergency server was old and outdated, clumsy to work with, but by dawn, they had managed to restore power to the Colony.

Rather than be arrested and imprisoned for tampering with the safety of the Colony, the disgruntled employee, a young man in his early twenties who had wanted to be famous, instead took his own life. He was found a few days after the blackout, hanging from his bedroom ceiling fan, a cord wrapped around his neck.

"Needless to say, we are not going public with that," said Dan. "When it happened, we explained that it had been a one-time event, a simple glitch that occurred during routine maintenance of the servers. I think we'll just leave it at that."

"I agree," said Manny, "no need to encourage any copycats out there." This was just the kind of crime to capture the attention of young hackers, out to make a name for themselves, or outright criminals, hoping to hold the Colony hostage for money.

Dan took another swig from his flask.

"I've been thinking about the blackout," said Manny hesitantly.

"What's on your mind?" Dan settled himself more comfortably into his chair.

"Suppose the power had stayed off for a few days. We'd have been in total darkness, the ventilation systems would have been down, no way to recharge our batteries. There would have been a general panic, and a stampede to the nearest exits. And then, people would just be milling around out there, nowhere to go, no food, no shelter. We are completely unprepared."

Dan nodded; Manny noticed that he did not seem surprised.

"We need an emergency plan to shelter and feed our citizens above ground for several days, in the event of a true emergency. And in order to prepare for that, we need to educate people about the outside world," Manny continued. "After all, we've been taught as children that the environment is dangerous for humans. Is it even still like that?"

"It's going to take more than a few public service announcements to change public opinion on this, Manny," warned Dan.

"I have an idea," said Manny. "You've seen the Suarez & Sons Trade Center?"

The Trade Center had been built half-way between the Colony and Philadelphia, next to the train tracks. Not long afterwards, a new Council provision had been passed which allowed people to leave the Colony for up to six hours, with a conditional work permit. Originally intended for workers who needed to make repairs to stairs or outer doors, these work permits could now be issued to anyone who applied for one, under the newly-expanded wording. For the first time, Manny, Julio and Luis could legally leave the grounds of the Colony, something they had been doing for many years as part of their black market business.

Seizing on the opportunity, Manny had leased their train to a startup company which shuttled people back and forth on weekend evenings as far as Lucinda's, the Trade Center's restaurant. Those few brave souls who had ventured out had been pleasantly surprised.

"Yes, I've seen it. My wife and I ate at Lucinda's when it opened," replied Dan.

"The Trade Center has an entire upstairs floor that is empty. It was originally designed with rooms for overnight guests, but hardly anyone's used it. We could get a team of scientists to set up a lab there, to study the environment."

"You mean they'd go out each day to take readings?" asked Dan.

"No, they could live there for a few weeks, recording notes about the weather and all," replied Manny. "If people see that a team of scientists can live safely outside, then they will see that there's no reason to be afraid. Maybe they could live-stream it, do some interviews for the talk shows."

Dan made a thoughtful noise, which could have been either polite interest or stifled amusement.

"You have good ideas, son," said the Commissioner, getting up from his chair. "We need more of that around here." He turned to leave, then stopped. "Have you seen James this morning?" he asked.

"No, I haven't seen him since last Friday," Manny replied. "I'm afraid he's not been feeling well."

Dan shook his head sadly. "He won't be working here much longer, I think," he said.

~ ~ ~ ~ ~ ~

With James out of the office, and Dan busy with other work, Manny once again had little to do. He read through his emails, made a few notes, and then checked his padlet. It was 11:15 am. *Maybe I'll make some lunch plans,* Manny thought. *I wonder what Dave is doing.*

Manny texted Dave, but he was busy with an ongoing investigation and planned on eating lunch at his desk. Disappointed, Manny pondered for a moment and then thought of Odesa. A moment later, he texted her:

Manny: *Want to have lunch today? Tacos?*

The answer came back almost immediately: *Yes! Great idea. Was just wondering what to do for lunch.*

Manny: *Noon?*

Odesa: *See you then.*

She was right on time, already seated, smiling and waving to him as he entered the restaurant. He slid into the chair, glad to see her.

"What a nice idea, to meet for lunch," she said.

"I thought it would be a nice break," he said. "I almost never leave the office at lunchtime, but since the promotion, I actually have more free time than I used to."

"How's that work, that a captain has more free time than a lieutenant?" she asked, taking a delicate nibble of her taco. *Does she eat this way when she's alone?* Manny wondered.

"It's temporary, I'm sure," he said, "but for now, my job is to shadow the Deputy Commissioner, and he's not in again today."

"He's been ill, hasn't he?" she asked, frowning.

"Yeah, he looks awful. He's supposed to be training me, but there's been precious little training," replied Manny. "He'll be retiring soon."

"And then you'll be Deputy Commissioner, when he retires?" she asked.

"That's the plan," he said, taking a tiny bite of his taco, which immediately fell apart all over his plate. He laughed. She laughed, too.

*She's beautiful,* he thought, watching her as she talked. She wore her hair pinned up in a prim little bun, not in the silly broomstick style that was so popular. Her dress was a plain calico cotton dress, but somehow on her, it seemed elegant.

"... a little quiet, but he's been doing his homework, paying attention in class; it's nothing I can put my finger on, but ... Manny, are you listening to me?" she asked.

"Yes, of course," Manny replied. She might be beautiful, but she was Zach's teacher and just a friend, after all. "What did you say?"

"I said that Zach has been a little quiet lately. Is everything OK at home?" she replied.

"Everything's fine," he replied smoothly.

"I noticed that your father-in-law came to Father-Son Night with him. You were not able to come?" she asked.

"Not my father-in-law; he's my foster father, Luis Suarez, Zach's grandfather. It's a long story," Manny said.

"I've got lots of time," she said encouragingly, her kind blue eyes looking steadily at him.

*I bet I could confide in her. But not here,* Manny thought. "It's not something I can go into now," he said evasively.

"Well. Maybe some other time, then," she said. "Manny, you know I don't gossip. If you need someone to talk to, I mean."

"Thanks, Odesa," he replied. He thought of his empty, quiet house, his solitary evenings. On impulse he added, "Come over tonight after dinner, why don't you? We can have a drink, sit and talk, with no one to disturb us. Are you free?"

"Yes," she replied, "as a matter of fact, I am. Robbie is spending the night at his grandparents' house."

Manny spent the rest of the afternoon fidgeting. Odesa was coming to his house! What would they talk about? Should he offer her food? He decided to stop on the way home and pick up dessert. Should he serve coffee and then brandy? Or offer her a glass of wine? What should he wear, his uniform? No, that was too formal. Sweats? No, that was too sloppy. *I have forgotten how to do this,* he thought.

By 4:00 pm, Manny was beginning to regret inviting Odesa to the house. *I should have waited,* he thought, *it's too soon for this.*

Manny left the office at 5:00 pm, picked up dessert, ate a quick sandwich at the kitchen counter, then went across the street to see Zach. He was early, but fortunately, the family had just finished eating.

He kept the visit brief, saying only that he had work to do. He read Zach a story, tucked him into bed and then left quickly to go home.

Manny was upstairs changing his clothes for the third time (the hooded denim shirt seemed OK, but it clashed with the jeans, he thought), when the doorbell rang. He flew down the stairs.

# Chapter 33.

"COME IN, COME in," Manny said with a self-conscious smile. Odesa walked in and, like every other person who came to the Stewart mansion for the first time, looked up in astonishment at the high ceiling.

"My goodness," she said softly. "It's beautiful, isn't it?"

"Yes, it is," he agreed politely. "Would you like something to drink, coffee, tea, maybe a glass of wine? Or something stronger? I stopped at the bakery on the way home; would you like some cookies?" *I'm babbling,* he thought. *She's going to think I'm an idiot.* He wiped his sweating palms against his sleeves, hoping she would not notice.

"Don't go to any trouble, Manny," she said. "A glass of wine would be nice." They went into the kitchen.

"It's so neat. And quiet," she observed. "Where is everybody?"

"It's a long story," Manny answered. "Why don't we go into the library, where we can sit and talk?"

Odessa stopped in the doorway, her eyes taking in the rows of antique books snug behind glass on floor-to-ceiling shelves, the wood paneled walls, the oil paintings between the windows.

"Manny," she breathed, "it's like a fairy tale!" She walked around the room, admiring the hand-carved artifacts on the end tables on either side of an antique sofa.

They settled into the comfortable armchairs, Odesa with a glass of razzleberry wine, Manny with a moderate-sized crystal snifter of brandy, and a plate of cookies on the table between them. *I wonder if she takes little bunny bites of cookies, too,* he thought, and watched, fascinated, as she did.

"Is your family out for the evening?" she asked. It was a reasonable question. Society had strict social norms for dating and sexual behavior, mostly to protect young women from older men until they were old enough to make decisions on their own. A young woman was absolutely expected to be a virgin on her wedding day.

With older folk, though, especially those widowed or divorced, there were fewer rules. Affairs abounded, but as long as they were discreet, they were tolerated. Still, Odesa's presence at Manny's house alone in the evening might lead to gossip if they were seen, and as a teacher, her reputation was a concern.

"Everybody's across the street," he replied. "My foster parents have a townhouse there, and the children have sleepovers sometimes."

She nodded encouragingly. Her ash blond hair was loose, flowing straight over her shoulders nearly to her waist, a waterfall of palest wheat reflected in the spill of the Tiffany lamp. Her dress was the exact same color as her hair, casually tied at the neckline with a brown velvet ribbon.

"They don't like it when I drink," he confided sheepishly. She didn't say anything, but he noticed that she stiffened slightly. "There was something of an unfortunate incident on Father-Son Night."

She waited. He explained about the culture of drinking in the police community, how he had gone out for a drink with his colleague, and then run into his new boss as he was leaving the bar. While the story was true, it downplayed his drunkenness.

"I completely forgot that it was Father-Son Night, and that's on me," Manny said. "They were adamant, though, that I couldn't be the one to take Zach to the school."

Teachers are used to hearing one side of a story, usually presented by a misbehaving child. Manny, studying the micro-expressions on her face, could see that she was considering what might have happened.

"Just a sleepover?" she asked. "Or are they trying to send you a message?"

"Oh, no, nothing like that," Manny replied confidently. "They totally over-reacted."

Odesa frowned. "My father was an alcoholic," she said. "It's insidious, the way it sneaks up on a person. There are all kinds of alcoholics, you know. Some people can't drink even one drink without losing control. Others are fine most of the time with a drink or two."

She paused, but Manny steadfastly did not rise to the bait. Instead, the picture of innocence, he munched on a cookie. The two sat in silence.

"Another cookie?" asked Manny politely. She shook her head.

Odesa sighed. "I'll tell you honestly, Manny," she said, "I don't want an alcoholic in my life, even as a friend. Most alcoholics become such good liars, very clever about hiding their drinking. That is not what I want for myself and Robbie."

Manny nodded. "I don't blame you," he said easily. "I'm definitely not like that."

Manny and Odesa talked well into the night, unmindful of the time, as it got dark outside. Finally, Odesa rose and stretched, then took out her padlet. "My goodness, look at the time!" she said. "It's nearly midnight! I have to be at work in the morning!"

Manny stood, too. How he longed to put his arms around her, run his fingers through her beautiful blond hair, untie the velvet ribbon dangling so invitingly at her neckline.

"Stay here tonight," he said softly. Her eyes widened. He reached out a tentative hand, hovering a few inches from her bare arm, not quite touching her. "You can get up early tomorrow and go home."

"That's a big step, Manny, one that I don't take lightly," she replied, shaking her head. "No, it's too soon."

He dropped his hand to his side. "I understand," he said. "I hope you're not offended."

"No, I'm not offended," she replied. Her feet hadn't moved, but somehow her body was leaning closer to him, her blue eyes dark with desire. The air between them crackled. He wanted badly to kiss her, but more than that, he wanted to show her that he respected her.

"Well. It's too late for you to walk home alone," he said. "If I walk you home, the two of us together in the middle of the night, we are sure to be seen by someone, and we'll be all over the society pages by morning. Let me see what I can do."

He took out his padlet and hologrammed the precinct. "Desk Sargeant, please," he said to the A.I. software.

"This is Yoshi Martinson," answered the Desk Sargeant, his tiny hologram figure appearing on the tabletop next to the plate of cookies.

"Sargeant, this is Lieutenant Stewart," Manny said smoothly. "I need a favor. Could you have a couple of officers stop by my house?"

"Everything OK there, Lieutenant?" asked Sargeant Martinson.

"Fine, fine, I just need an escort for my guest, who is ready to leave. It's late for her to be walking home alone," responded Manny.

"Sure thing, Lieutenant. Ten minutes," said the Desk Sargeant.

"Thanks very much. I owe you one, Sarge," said Manny. Turning to Odesa, he said, "They'll make sure you get home safely."

"That's very kind of you, Manny," she said. "My own escort!" She laughed, and he laughed with her.

How nice it was to have her here in his house! He'd grown tired of waking up alone, coming home after work to an empty, quiet house, going to bed alone. Odesa. Even her name made him smile.

After she left, Manny went back into the library and poured himself a substantial nightcap. Swirling the liquor around in the glass, he reflected on his evening. Odesa was not just beautiful, she was a teacher, a well-respected member of society.

*Suppose we see each other for a while, and we decide to get married,* Manny mused. *I could have a fresh start, just me, Odesa, and her little boy Robbie.* Manny took another substantial swallow of his brandy, savoring the warmth as it spread through his stomach, soothing his doubts, bolstering his confidence.

*Maybe Julio and Anna did me a favor, moving out when they did. They probably wouldn't want to live here with Odesa, Robbie and me.* Manny poured another glassful of brandy, holding the bottle carefully with both hands. *I don't remember why I wanted to live with them anyway,* he thought with a touch of resentment. *They're always judging me, pointing out my faults, getting in my way. Maybe we'd all be better off apart.*

~ ~ ~ ~ ~ ~

Manny was in his office later that week when the Commissioner came in and sat down.

"What's going on with Ms. Johnson?" he asked.

"I sent two engineers to her house, disguised as plumbers, to analyze the leak. They were not able to find the source of the leak, so the water is still running down her wall," Manny replied.

"What do you propose we should do?" asked the Commissioner.

"The next step would be to relocate Ms. Johnson temporarily, and tear down the wall to see where the water is coming from," Manny replied.

"Do it," replied the Commissioner. "You're in charge of this, OK, Manny? You're more than capable. James, he's not doing well. I went to his house yesterday to discuss some things with him. He's white as a ghost, very weak. He'll probably retire at the end of this week." Dan sighed, thinking of his friend and colleague.

"I'm sorry to hear that," said Manny. "Don't worry about the leak; I'll take care of it."

The day dragged on. Manny worried about James. *Suppose he never comes back to the office?* he thought. *How will I ever learn to do my new job?* Manny pushed some papers around on his desk, made a chain out of paperclips.

*Worrying doesn't help,* he decided finally. *There's plenty of other things to do. Maybe it's time to get to know the Task Force members.* He opened up his padlet.

As their supervisor, Manny could read through their cases, get to know the detectives, maybe pick a case or two for his own involvement. It would be good to work a case again. He started reading.

Later that night, Manny returned home to eat a cold sandwich while standing by the kitchen sink, then dutifully went across the street and visited with Zach. After the visit, he continued reading through some of the case files of the Task Force, sitting until well past midnight at his father's old desk in the study. It was late when he finally went to bed.

Manny was awakened at 3:00 am by his padlet beeping urgently. The rim was pulsing neon gold, an urgent text message regarding work. Rubbing sleep from his eyes, he opened the padlet.

# Chapter 34.

**T**HE TEXT MESSAGE was from the Commissioner's Aide, Nigel:

Nigel: *Come to infirmary at once, urgent. Confirm.*
Manny: *On my way.*

As he quickly pulled on clothes, Manny thought sadly of James. *He must be dying,* he thought. He liked James, and wished that they had had more time together. Dressed, he flew down the stairs, grabbing his jacket, and took off at a run.

There was no one else on the streets, no one at all. It felt surreal, running in the middle of the night, running to see James, running to bear witness to the passing of his colleague, one of the Colony's leaders.

Manny arrived at the infirmary, pausing to catch his breath. A crowd of police officers had formed, milling around the infirmary. Some were in uniform, others, like Manny, in civilian clothes.

"Manny! There you are," said a voice. Manny turned around and was stunned to see James, leaning on a cane, with a younger officer hovering nearby, ready to assist.

"James! I ... I didn't think you'd be here," he said, attempting to hide his surprise.

"So sad! Have you heard? Dan had a heart attack after dinner," James said, shaking his head. "No warning at all, just out of nowhere!"

Manny said, "How is he?"

"Hanging by a thread, I'm afraid," James replied with tears in his eyes. "They wouldn't have called us in the middle of the night if there was any hope, you know."

The Mayor arrived, looking through the crowd for James, who waved to her. The crowd of police officers parted to make way for her.

"Any news?" she asked. James shook his head.

The door to the infirmary opened, a white-coated doctor appearing in the doorway. The Mayor and James moved quickly to the front of the crowd, with Manny following close behind.

"I'm sorry," said the doctor. "We did everything we could." He shook his head gravely, then bowed formally to the Mayor and James. "Health and prosperity to you, Madame Mayor and Commissioner O'Brian," he said simply. Then he went back inside the infirmary.

The Mayor said, "James, we will swear you in as Commissioner right away." She turned to Manny. "And Manny, I need to swear you in as Deputy Commissioner."

James nodded. They all knew the protocol; the Office of the Commissioner must always be filled. Despite the raw emotions of this terrible moment, there could be no gap in leadership.

Manny shook his head to clear it. *Deputy Commissioner?* he thought. *Now??* And then, a moment later, his stomach flipped over as he had another thought: *For how long? How long before James is also gone? And then what?*

An Aide to the Mayor appeared, holding two Bibles, the Old Bible, and the Bible of the Goddess, written two hundred years earlier. And right there, outside of the infirmary in the dead of night, the Mayor administered the oath of office to James, and then to Manny. Every padlet was out snapping photos as the two men stood unsmiling, side by side with the Mayor.

"We'll have a formal inauguration later, with the press in attendance and your relatives and friends invited," said the Mayor. Manny nodded; he was too overwhelmed to speak.

No order was given, but the crowd of police officers spontaneously formed into two long lines, standing at attention with their hands held up in salute, as the Mayor, the new Commissioner, and his new Deputy Commissioner, walked past them.

"Manny," said James, gesturing for Manny to step up alongside him. Now that the urgency of the moment had passed, James was walking very slowly, bent with sorrow for his colleague and friend.

"I'm sorry it's turned out this way," he said simply. "I'll do my best to spend as much time with you as I can."

Manny cleared his throat. "Thank you, James," said Manny, his voice thick with emotion. They both knew that James's time was dwindling, that soon there would be another death.

James smiled sadly, exhausted. "I'll be in the office later. Don't worry. I'll be there."

Manny went home. There was no point in trying to sleep; he changed his clothes and ate breakfast. When he showed up at the office at 6:00 am, James was already there, waiting in Manny's office.

"Commissioner!" said Manny. "I'm glad to see you here. How are you doing?"

"Not bad, Manny, not bad," said James. His face was grayish with an unhealthy sheen of perspiration across his forehead, but his eyes were clear and alert. "I think it's important for me to be here this morning, and every day until I retire. It'll show continuity. Give people confidence and all."

"Maybe for part of each day, if you want," suggested Manny gently. "Why don't I come to your house after lunch each day, and we can continue our conversations there? Would you be more comfortable?"

"Let's see how it goes," said James. "But first, here's a list of things I think we should go over. The most important items are at the top." He handed Manny a list of tasks which had been on Dan's calendar before his death.

They spent the morning discussing the most pressing items. Manny could see that James was fading, utterly worn out, his voice growing more and more faint.

"Why don't you have a rest now, and we can pick this up in a couple of hours," Manny suggested tactfully. James nodded gratefully, going back to his office to lie down.

Edith knocked on Manny's door. "Would you like me to have your things packed and moved into your new office, Sir?" she asked. "Now that the Deputy Commissioner will be moving into the Commissioner's office," she added.

"Maybe check with James first," Manny said. "No point packing up my office if James isn't moving, too." She nodded, turning away, but not before Manny saw the tears in her eyes. Edith had worked for Dan and James for years.

"He was a great man, Edith," Manny said. "We're all going to miss him." Edith pressed a handkerchief to her face and fled out into the hall.

The morning dragged on. Unable to concentrate on work, Manny picked up his jacket, heading towards the stairs, looking forward to an early lunch. In the hallway, he ran into the Chief.

"Deputy Commissioner Stewart!" said the Chief, bowing respectfully to him. "Health and prosperity to you!"

"Chief! How are you?" replied Manny, glad to see him.

"How's everything going up there?" the Chief asked.

"It's such a sudden change! So unexpected, you know?" responded Manny. "And James, he was supposed to be my mentor until he retired. He's not going to be working much longer." Manny tactfully avoided mentioning James's health, although surely the Chief must know about it.

"That's unfortunate, Manny," replied the Chief. "If there's anything I can do to help with this transition, you know you can always call on me. We can have lunch, talk things over."

Manny nodded gratefully. "Thank you, Sir. I appreciate it."

James dutifully continued to come into the office every morning. By lunchtime, though, he was worn out and on his way home. Manny would have lunch, taking his time reading through emails and reports, and then go over to James's house, spending the rest of the afternoon there in discussion with James.

On the Friday following Dan's death, Manny went over to James's house after lunch, as usual. He was surprised to see one of the Colony's lawyers there, when he arrived.

"Manny, you know Jole?" asked James. "Jole, this is Manny Stewart, the new Deputy Commissioner."

The two men bowed to each other, murmuring a polite greeting. "Manny, as you know," began Jole, "it is the privilege of the Commissioner to appoint his successor. Dan appointed

James. James has now appointed you to be his successor, when he retires."

Manny turned to James, bowing low. "I am honored, Sir," he said simply. "I'll do my very best."

James, reclining on the sofa, looked up at him with clear eyes. "I think you'll do well, Manny," he said, as Jole handed Manny an official signed copy of the designation. "We vetted several candidates, you know, when we were looking for a new Deputy Commissioner. There was only one reservation that Dan and I had about you. You're young, about ten years too young. If things had gone according to plan, you'd have had several years as Deputy Commissioner to learn the Commissioner's job, before he retired. You're twenty-six, right?" he asked.

"Twenty-seven," Manny replied. In a time when people retired in their mid-fifties, thirty was considered the beginning of middle age.

"Well, there are going to be many older officers who will resent your promotion. They'll be jealous; just ignore them." James coughed. "Remember, never show weakness. You're the boss now, Manny." He coughed again, harder this time.

"Do you have a close friend in the department, someone you can trust? Someone you can talk to freely, without worrying about gossip or leaks?" James continued.

"Yes," replied Manny.

"Good. That's your Deputy Commissioner. The two of you can brainstorm solutions to the everyday stuff, and keep the wheels turning in the department. It's Lieutenant Wu you're thinking of?" asked James.

"Yes, I was thinking of Dave," replied Manny. "And I know that could be problematic, because of his Chinese heritage."

"That's a whole different ball of wax, Manny," said James. "If you're willing to take that on, then Dave would be a good choice. He's an excellent detective, very precise, one of our best. But think about it for a bit, Manny. There's going to be resistance, you can be sure of that."

232

They were silent, as Manny thought about Dave and what it would mean to promote him. James gathered his strength before continuing.

"You're a planner, Manny, you can see ten steps ahead of yourself, while most of these others are just ..." He coughed again, harder this time, wiping his mouth on a handkerchief. Manny tried not to look at the bright blood splattered against the white cloth.

James drew a deep, shuddering breath, lying back against the cushions. "You'll do just fine, son," he said, nodding encouragingly.

Two days later, James was dead.

# Chapter 35.

**W**ALKING INTO THE office the following Monday morning was like nothing that Manny could have imagined. According to tradition, every person in the department rose as one when Manny walked in, saluting to the new Commissioner as he passed by.

"Good morning, Commissioner," said Edith, bowing respectfully as she stood in the doorway of his old office. "Over the weekend, I've had your things moved into your new office." She was smiling bravely, but Manny could see the emotion on her face.

"Thank you, Edith," he said. "Is Nigel here?"

"Here, Sir," said Nigel, coming up behind him.

"Come with me," said Manny, motioning with his hand as he led the way into his new office. Hanging up his jacket on the hook behind the door, Manny made his way to the large antique leather armchair behind his voluminous one-person wooden desk. He motioned Nigel to sit.

"First things first," Manny began, as he had rehearsed in front of his bedroom mirror earlier in the day. "Would you like to stay on here permanently, as my Aide?"

"But Sir, what about Raimone?" asked Nigel. "Won't he be coming back here?"

"Let's not worry about Raimone for now," replied Manny. "I have other, more urgent matters to deal with than that snake."

"Then yes, I would like to work for you permanently as your Aide," said Nigel. He seemed pleased, relaxed and smiling.

"Good. Then I think the first order of business should be choosing a Deputy Commissioner. When we are finished here, could you please ask Lieutenant Wu to come in?" Nigel nodded, making notes on his padlet. "We'll need an Aide for him, too."

"If I may speak freely, Sir," said Nigel.

"Nigel, you don't have to stand on ceremony here, when it's just the two of us in my office. Just spit it out," replied Manny.

"Thank you, Sir," replied Nigel. He lowered his voice. "If you were to appoint Lieutenant Wu as Deputy Commissioner on your first day in office, there would be an uproar. Because of his heritage, you know. How about appointing an Acting Deputy Commissioner for a few months? With Lieutenant Wu as his Aide? And then, after the hubbub has died down and people have gotten used to the idea, you can move Lieutenant Wu up to the position of Deputy Commissioner."

"I like that, Nigel. It's a great idea," said Manny.

The two men spent the morning together. Manny asked Nigel to clear his calendar of all events for the week except for a ribbon-cutting ceremony at a new park.

Nigel motioned to the schedule and asked, "When would you like the public swearing-in ceremony to be, Sir? How about Friday afternoon?"

"That's fine, before the week off," Manny said. The Colony's annual spring break was beginning on Friday night, with schools and municipal offices closed the following week. Manny rose, stretching, and Nigel dutifully rose, too.

"I think that's enough for now, Nigel, thank you. Could you ask Edith to come in, please?"

Nigel nodded and left. Alone in his new office for the first time, Manny sat in his armchair, which both swiveled and squeaked, and looked around at his very large new office. It was simply massive, at least 12 feet square, with two visitors' chairs, and a round table that could seat six people for impromptu meetings. Bookcases lined the walls.

There was a convenient closet, narrow and as tall as the ceiling, fitted with pegs for hanging jackets and bags; stored inside was Mister Grabby, a common long-handled mechanism with a "grabber" at the end for retrieving items. A framed photograph of Dan and his family was hung on the inside of the closet door; Manny took it down.

"You wanted to see me, Sir?" Edith said, coming into the office.

"Yes, here, can you take this?" he asked, handing her the picture.

"Yes, Sir," Edith said, carefully holding the precious photograph.

"And I just want to let you know – from now on, I'll be putting the brandy myself into my morning cup of tea," said Manny.

"Was it not satisfactory?" she asked, raising her red-rimmed, puffy eyes to his.

"No, it was fine, I've just decided to do it myself," Manny replied. "It will give me a better sense of how much I'm drinking."

He removed a new bottle of brandy from his desk drawer, placing it on the desk next to the set of vintage cut-crystal glasses that Dan had used. "I guess these are mine now," he said softly, touching the glasses.

Edith stiffened, still holding the photograph close. She was one of several people in the office who had worked with both Dan and James for years. They were understandably saddened by the sudden passing of both men. Manny had not worked with either Dan or James for very long before they died, which made him something of an outsider. There was an awkward pause. He was trying to think of something suitable to say when Dave arrived.

"Dave! Come in, come in," he said, as Edith left.

Dave sat down, looking all around. "Nice place you have here, boss," he said.

"Thank you," said Manny, lacing his hands together behind his head as he leaned back in his spacious, squeaky chair. "I need to ask you something."

Dave waited while Manny cleared his throat. "What would you say to becoming Deputy Commissioner?"

Dave's face went blank for a moment, an expression which turned to surprise, then sheer joy.

"It would be an honor, Sir!" he exclaimed. "Are you sure? There's never been a Chinese-American in the Colony's police department above the rank of lieutenant. There's going to be super blowback!"

"Yes, I'm quite sure," Manny said decisively. "I need someone I can count on, someone who'll be willing to argue with me, tell me when I'm wrong, someone I can trust when it comes to confidential conversations. I can't think of anyone better for this job than you, Dave."

"Wow, wait until I tell Jenny!" Dave said excitedly. "And my parents!" His eyes filled with tears at the thought of his parents. As the eldest son, the responsibility of caring for his aging parents would soon fall solely on his shoulders. This promotion would make them very proud.

"Here's how I'd like to do this," said Manny, talking so that Dave could have a moment to compose himself. "To begin, you'll be promoted to Special Aide to the Acting Deputy Commissioner. Then in a few months, when people have had a chance to get used to the idea, you'll be promoted to Deputy Commissioner."

"Who's the Acting Deputy Commissioner going to be?" asked Dave.

"I'm not sure yet," said Manny, who had been pondering the same question. "I'll be naming someone soon. But for now, your job will be to get the Task Force in order so it can function if you're not there. The job of Deputy Commissioner is mostly ceremonial, so once you learn the ropes, you should be able to continue with the Task Force pretty much as you do now."

Manny made a mental note to send out an official announcement of Dave's promotion. Then he made another mental note to hold off on that, until he had named a Deputy Commissioner, so he could do both announcements at once. It would be more professional that way. People would be watching him closely for the first few weeks, he knew, and some of them would be quick to criticize him.

At lunchtime, Manny ate a sandwich at his desk, and then went downstairs to see Chief O'Reilly. Out of habit, he stopped in the doorway, knocking on the Chief's door.

"Come in, come in," said the Chief, respectfully standing up from behind his desk. "The Commissioner doesn't need to knock!" He gestured to his visitor's chair. "Please sit down."

"Thank you, Sir," said Manny. "I have an idea that I'd like to run by you."

"I'm all ears," said the Chief.

"How would you like to be Acting Deputy Commissioner for a few months?" he said.

The Chief smiled broadly. "Let me guess. You are moving Lieutenant Wu up to Special Aide to the Acting Deputy Commissioner?" the Chief said, eyeing Manny shrewdly. "And when the uproar dies down, then you're going to quietly promote Dave to be Deputy Commissioner?"

"That's my plan," said Manny. "What do you think? It could be good to have an experienced officer like yourself around to offer advice. And it will give Dave time to learn the ropes before he's promoted."

"That's fine, Manny. Of course, I go where the Department needs me, and it will be my pleasure to be your Acting Deputy Commissioner," replied the Chief.

"Thank you, Sir," said Manny. "If you could start tomorrow, that would be great." The Chief nodded. He was silent a moment, thinking of the arrangements he would need to make to cover his unit.

"There's just one thing," he said to Manny.

"What's that?" asked Manny.

"You need to start calling me Joe."

~ ~ ~ ~ ~ ~

By the middle of the week, Manny was feeling upbeat and excited about his new job. Vacant positions had been filled; Nigel would stay on permanently; the memo had gone out announcing the Chief's and Dave's promotions. He breathed a sigh of relief. It was an added bonus, having the Chief right next door, ready to offer advice. Employees were already moving back and forth, carrying boxes of Dave's and the Chief's belongings into their new offices.

Manny chuckled to himself as he recalled Dave's reaction when he first saw the tiny little office of the Aide to the Deputy Commissioner, the office which had been Manny's so recently. Dave had swung open the door, which promptly banged into the back of the old, well-battered visitor's chair; then he had to turn sideways to slide between the wall and the side of the desk in order to get behind it to sit down. The expression on his face had been comical. "Just so long as it's temporary," he said.

The week went by quickly. All in all, it had been hard, but looking back on it, Manny felt a sense of satisfaction, even pride. The ribbon-cutting ceremony on Thursday at the new park had almost been fun. Lots of reporters were there, taking dozens of photos of the new Commissioner as he officially opened the new park. He'd been all over the news.

The public swearing-in ceremony on Friday afternoon truly had been a high point in his professional career. The Chief had been there, sworn in as Acting Deputy Commissioner. Dave and Nigel, the two Aides, had been right there in the front row, seated next to Luis and Lucinda, Julio and Anna.

Afterwards, Lucinda had hugged him, saying softly in his ear, "I'm so proud of you, Manny! Congratulations!" Luis had bowed formally to him and then impulsively gave him a huge bear-hug. Julio and Anna also congratulated him, their smiles warm and genuine.

Manny was hoping that maybe they might invite him back to their house for a celebration. However, he got caught up in conversation with the Mayor for a moment, and when he looked up, they were headed out the door. Lucinda waved to him as they left.

Dave, who was next to Manny on the podium, saw them leaving and asked, "Aren't you celebrating with your family?"

"Oh, I'll catch up to them afterwards," replied Manny off-handedly. He was embarrassed that they had left so quickly. He thought briefly of inviting Dave and Jenny over to celebrate, but by then, Dave was surrounded by a large group of emotional relatives, all of them bowing low to him.

Friday night began the Colony's traditional week-long spring break. The holiday was meant to serve as a combination of Easter, Passover and Ramadan, which were still celebrated by many families. Police stations never really closed, even on holidays, but for the first time, Manny would not need to be in the office during spring break. He could easily manage his work from home.

# Chapter 36.

**M**ANNY WAVED HIS hand over the Scentinel sensor pad and unlocked the heavy double oak doors to his house. Once inside, the house seemed unnaturally silent and still, after the bustling excitement of the afternoon. He felt again the humiliation of watching his family leave the ceremony without him. Jenny Wu had waited for him by the door to ask if he wanted to come home with Dave and herself. It was very kind of them, but he didn't want anybody's pity. On the day of the greatest achievement in his career, he had walked home alone.

He wished that Naz was there to celebrate with him. He missed her gentle companionship, their easy conversations. She always seemed to understand how he felt.

Manny checked his padlet to see what time it was: 5:35 pm, too early to go see Zach. He didn't want to appear needy by arriving too early.

Manny opened up the coldbox, looking for anything that he could eat, but it was nearly empty. He closed it with a pang, firmly squelching down disquieting childhood memories of coming home from school to an empty house with nothing to eat in the kitchen.

*I need a housekeeper,* thought Manny, *to take care of the house and do a little cooking, leaving food in the kitchen for me.* An unbidden wave of nostalgia swept over him for the Suarez house on 14th Street, as it had been when he and Julio were children.

Back then, Julio's house had been a haven to him, filled with kind, loving people who, without making a big deal out of it, simply took him in as Julio's friend, and later, as part of the family. He remembered the aromas in Lucinda's kitchen, the lemon cookies and chocolate desserts, the smell of food cooking on the stove, how he and Lucinda would stand together at the kitchen counter preparing dinner, talking about the events of the day.

Rousing himself, Manny decided that he would order something to eat later from DroneDash. He reached into one of the cabinets for a new bottle of brandy. *The new Commissioner deserves a drink before dinner,* he thought with a little chuckle. He poured a reasonably-sized glassful of brandy.

Sitting down in the library with his glass, Manny pulled out his padlet and began wading through the dozens of messages he had received during the afternoon. Everyone wanted to congratulate the new Commissioner, already jockeying for position to gain his favor. Most of the messages could wait, but there was a text from Odesa. He texted back to her.

Odesa: *Congratulations, Commissioner! I was there, seated in the back, and saw the whole ceremony. Very impressive.*

Manny: *Thanks! I'm glad you were there.*

Odesa: *Is your family still with you? I don't want to interrupt.*

Manny: *No, I'm alone. I'm working, there's so much to do!*

Odesa: *Have you eaten?*

Manny: *No, not hungry. I'll eat later. I'm just going to read case file studies for a few hours and then go to bed.*

Odesa: *Ok, well, I just wanted to say congrats.*

Manny: *Let's get together in a few days, once I get a handle on the emails and other stuff.*

Odesa: *Sounds good!*

Manny closed up his padlet, leaned back in his brown leather armchair and took a deep swallow of brandy. He wanted to see her, talk to her, wanted her here in his house next to him. He wondered what it would feel like to kiss her, to hold her naked in his arms. It had been too long since there was a woman in his life.

But it had been a big day, and he was so tired. He leaned back and closed his eyes, his mind drifting. Before he knew it, he was asleep.

*He was climbing a hill, very steep, covered with loose dirt and small rocks. His feet kept slipping out from under him. Reduced to crawling on his hands and knees, Manny struggled upward, inch by inch, until he could see the top of the hill. There were several people milling around at the top, Patrick Stewart among them.*

*"Dad! Give me a hand, will you?" he called, stretching out one hand so his father could pull him up.*

*"Help you? You want me to help you??" cried Patrick incredulously. He snorted derisively. "Malcolm, you know you don't belong up here, right?"*

*Manny was stung by his father's rebuff. A shower of dirt and small pebbles rained down on him, covering his face, making it hard to see. He stopped to wipe his eyes with the back of one hand. Patrick was calling to him, taunting him, laughing at him as he slipped and stumbled, but he couldn't quite make out the words.*

*Manny could see his father's feet hanging over the edge of the hill above him, deliberately kicking stones and dirt down on him, into his mouth, his eyes.*

*"Get out of here, Malcolm," his father said harshly, "before everyone discovers what a fraud you are."*

Manny woke up with a start, the sudden movement knocking his empty glass onto the floor. He breathed deeply several times, rubbing his face hard with one hand. Stress, that's what had caused the nightmare, just the stress of the day, plain and simple. That's all. Nothing more.

Manny stood up, stretching slowly and deliberately, willing the remnants of the nightmare to subside. He picked up the empty glass from the floor, and headed back into the kitchen for another glass of brandy.

*Not too much, now,* he thought. *I need to visit Zach before he goes to bed.* Manny poured brandy into his glass until it was full, then drank down half of it at once. *Ahhh, that is so much better,* he thought with relief, as the dream receded.

How many days had it been since he'd seen Zach? He couldn't quite remember. When the family had first moved out, he'd diligently visited Zach every night before bedtime, but then with the changes at work and the passage of time, he'd seen less and less of him. His visits had become awkward again; Luis and Lucinda were cordial, but distant. And Zach seemed to be afraid of him. Even reading a bedtime story to Zach had become uncomfortable for both of them.

Manny sat down at the kitchen table, glass in hand. It was never easy seeing Zach, but tonight was going to be especially awkward, after Luis and Lucinda had made a point of leaving the ceremony without him. He was not looking forward to this visit. He swirled the brandy around a little, watching the amber liquid coat the inside of the glass. He drank it down and poured another glassful.

An hour later, the empty bottle on its side next to him, Manny laid his head down on the kitchen table and slept.

And then, somehow, it was morning.

*I don't remember coming upstairs to bed*, he realized, looking around. He was fully dressed beneath the covers, except for his shoes. His head ached abominably; he drank a few sips of water from the glass near his bedside and immediately regretted it, lurching into the bathroom.

Manny showered, then dressed in sweatpants and a short sleeve teeshirt. He pulled his dark shoulder-length hair back into a ponytail, tying it with a broad black ribbon.

But something wasn't right. There was an uneasiness in his memory, tender and sore like a bruise, yet he kept returning to it. It was there, just beyond his recollection ...

It was way too bright in the room. His head felt like a drum that had been stretched too tightly around the edges. *What is it that relieves headaches?* he thought. *Oh, that's right - white willow bark tea.* Manny was gingerly heading down the stairs towards the kitchen when his eyes fell upon an object at the bottom of the stairs that did not belong. He skidded to a halt.

He moved closer, looking it over. It was a shopping bag filled with Chinese take-out containers, the food congealed and gloppy. Something had splashed onto the white marble floor and then hardened into a yellowish mess, as if someone had set it down in a hurry, not very carefully.

*You're drunk, Manny.*

Suddenly, Manny's knees felt weak. He sat down on the bottom step of the staircase. He remembered a voice yelling, loud, angry. He'd fallen deeply asleep at the kitchen table after finishing the bottle of brandy, and the doorbell had awakened him around 9:00 pm. Staggering to the front door, he'd opened it, holding onto the doorknob with both hands to keep his balance.

Odesa was standing on the front steps, holding a bag filled with food. "Surprise, Commissioner!" she'd said, smiling at him. She was beautiful in a black velvet mini-dress, low-cut in front, just for him.

He remembered her eyes, blue as could be, her hair invitingly unbound and loose down her back. He had grabbed for her with one hand while holding onto the doorknob with the other, but she'd drawn back out of reach, affronted.

*I texted you to say that I had a surprise for you,* she said accusingly. *Now I see why you haven't answered.* Her beautiful blue eyes were blazing, as if Manny had stolen something precious from her.

Then she'd dropped the bag of food onto the floor just inside the door, ignoring the soup as it spread into a puddle across the cold marble. *And tomorrow,* she shouted at him, *when you wake up all sorry and want to apologize, don't bother texting me. I told you before Manny, I won't get involved with a drunk!!*

Then she left, slamming the door behind her.

Manny had considered running after her, but in his condition, that might not end well. There were often media drones flying about; the press would love nothing better than a photo or two of the Colony's new Commissioner, flat on his face on the ground.

Sitting at the bottom of the stairs in the morning light, looking at the bag of congealed food by the front door, Manny hung his head. He had hoped to get his drinking under control before she discovered just how bad it was. Too late for that now, though.

Manny went into the kitchen, where he brewed himself a cup of white willow bark tea with honey. Out of habit, he reached into the cabinet to check for a fresh bottle of brandy, but the cabinet was empty. He made toast, taking his breakfast into the front parlor.

Manny sipped his tea, his pounding headache slowly easing. *Well,* he thought, *it's 10:00 am. What shall I do today?* He thought again of the empty kitchen cabinet. He could go out and buy a bottle of brandy, bringing it home with him. Or better yet, he could call one of his company's distributors and have them deliver a case to his house.

*And then what? Start drinking a little early today?* With a full holiday week stretching out endlessly ahead of him, Manny's courage failed him. A terrible sense of isolation settled over him. There was no one he could call, no one he could talk to. Everyone was gone, his family, his son, even his best friend and foster brother Julio. Now Odesa was gone, too; she'd probably never speak to him again.

For the first time, it occurred to him that his drinking came with a terrible price. What had been casual and easy in the beginning now had an iron grip on him; he was no longer in control. It was as if he had carelessly invited a monster into his home, without realizing that it would not ever want to leave.

There are moments in a person's life when he or she sees clearly the kind of person he has become, not the person he wishes to be, or is trying to be, but the way other people perceive him. Clearly, Odesa thought he was a drunk. Luis thought he was a drunk. Maybe he was.

It was warm in the house, but Manny shivered. In his mind's eye, he saw himself, friendless and estranged from his family, growing older and older in his job as Commissioner, coming home every night to an empty house, drinking every night until he passed out. He remembered all too well his father, Patrick Stewart, alone at the end of the long kitchen table, passed out drunk, empty bottle lying where it had rolled to a stop. Manny had been disgusted by his father's drinking. He had once poured all of Patrick's bourbon down the kitchen sink.

He sat for a long time, his face covered by his hands. He could not continue on this path. Somehow, he was going to have to turn things around.

# Chapter 37.

**I** WAS GLAD to hear from you today," said Julio, his concerned eyes scanning Manny's face. "What's going on with you? You look like shit this morning."

The two of them were dressed for running, but were sitting on a park bench near a little group of potted moonflowers. A tiny Zolar-powered water fountain gurgled nearby. When Manny and Julio had been in the habit of running together regularly, this was their half-way spot, where they turned and headed home. This morning, though, Manny had not been able to run any further, so they had stopped to rest.

"I'm OK," Manny said self-consciously. "It's just that I've given up drinking, so I'm not feeling so good this morning."

"That's great, Manny," Julio replied, after too long a pause. "How long's it been?"

"Today is the first day," Manny mumbled, embarrassed. He stared at the ground between his feet.

"What made you decide to stop?" asked Julio curiously.

Manny took a deep breath. How could he explain his utter despair to his brother? "I'm so sick of being alone," he said. "I've alienated my family, I don't have any friends outside of work, even Odesa wants nothing to do with me anymore," he explained, hanging his head. "And my son is afraid of me. I've ruined everything. It's just that – I dunno, Julio, I can't take it anymore."

His voice trembling, Manny struggled for control. "I want you guys to come back, to move back into the house. And I do understand that means I have to stop drinking."

There was a long, long silence. Manny was aware of people walking past them in groups of twos and threes, families together, enjoying the morning, talking, laughing.

"I don't know about that," Julio said hesitantly. "I mean, the drinking is a huge problem. Anna and I don't want to raise Julie in a house with an alcoholic."

Manny winced. "I understand," he said. "And with Anna being pregnant and all ..."

248

"She miscarried," Julio said bluntly. "A few weeks ago. It's her job, the stress was just too much for her. Or maybe she would have miscarried anyway, who knows?"

"I didn't know. Jeez, I'm sorry, Julio," Manny said. He'd seen Anna at the swearing-in ceremony, but it hadn't occurred to him to ask how she was doing. "How's Anna, is she OK?"

"She's fine," he said brusquely. The silence grew, awkward and uncomfortable, as Manny pondered why no one had told him.

Then Julio said accusingly, "Where've you been, man? You've missed out on a lot of stuff, family things. My Dad, he insisted we leave you alone, that you'd come around eventually. But no one thought it would take this long. We're starting to think maybe you like living alone."

"No, I really don't," Manny said. "I never wanted you to move out."

"Well, we can't stay indefinitely at my Dad's, it's just too crowded," Julio mused. "We're thinking of getting a place of our own. Maybe we would move back into the house on 14th Street. Or we could buy a house, close by my Dad's," Julio said. "We're talking it over."

"But Julio!" Manny protested, surprised and dismayed that his brother's plans did not include him. "We've got a perfectly good house, there's lots of space!"

"Are you really finished drinking?" Julio countered, his voice stern and hard. "Tell me the truth, Manny. I have a family to think about." Manny glanced at his brother's cheek, where the broken cheekbone had healed, leaving a scar on his handsome face.

"Yeah, I'm done," he said miserably. "Look at me, Julio. My hands are shaking, I'm clammy and disgusting. I feel like an old man. The worst thing is, I did this to myself. Nobody made me drink, I just embraced it. And it's like I fell into this big, deep hole." He casually brushed the back of his hand against his face, hoping that Julio had not seen the tear rolling down his cheek. The silence grew, as Manny pondered what life would be like without Julio and his family.

"Well, you do sound like you mean it," Julio said. He frowned, thinking. Then he stood up. "Come on then!" he said. "Let's go tell the others!"

"Now?" protested Manny. "Wait! I don't know what to say. I need to think."

"No, you don't. You need to be genuine and sincere, not well-rehearsed," replied Julio firmly. "Now, Manny."

When Julio pushed open the door to Lucinda and Luis's house, the children were playing dress-up in the living room. Julie was dressed as a magician, while Zach was dressed as a sort of rabbit, with a fluffy white tail made from an old dishcloth. Julie was chasing Zach around and around the room, both of them screaming with laughter.

"Manny!" exclaimed Lucinda. "Sit down, sit down. What brings you here?"

She motioned to the sofa, looking more closely at him. "Are you OK? Would you like something to ... would you like some water, Manny? Julio, can you get Manny some water?"

Luis and Anna came into the room, curious. Anna nodded to him, but Luis stood in the doorway, arms folded across his chest, a wary expression on his face. Julio handed Manny a glass of water, sitting down close to him on the sofa.

"So. What brings you here?" asked Luis brusquely.

"I've come to tell you that I've stopped drinking," Manny said.

"Haven't we heard that before?" countered Luis suspiciously, eyes narrowing.

"Has something happened, Manny?" asked Lucinda, more gently. "Did something change?"

Manny's mind sifted through the things he wanted to tell them, all of them crowding into his throat at once. All that came out was an inarticulate croak.

"Maybe the children could go play upstairs while we talk," Anna suggested, waving Julie and Zach towards the stairs.

Once they were out of the room, Manny tried again. "Well, yes, something did change," he began. Then his fragile composure dissolved, and he blurted out, "I can't do this anymore!" To his utter embarrassment, he started to cry. No one moved.

"I don't want to live alone. I miss you all! And Zach – I don't even know where to start," Manny said miserably, his eyes on the floor.

"It's like living in hell," he said. "I black out sometimes and can't remember what happened the night before. Odesa – you know, Ms. Parker, Zach's teacher – that's over, after she saw me drunk last night."

He looked up. "I'm done. I've hit rock bottom. I've alienated the most important people in my life, pushed everyone away. I don't ever want to feel like this again. I promise, I'm finished. No more excuses, no more lies. Period."

"Manny," said Anna kindly, "it's not easy, admitting you have a problem. This is an important first step."

Manny managed a weak smile. "Thank you, Anna."

"You look like shit," said Luis, and Julio laughed. "That's exactly what I said to him," Julio said to his father.

Luis was still standing in the doorway, mistrust showing plainly on his face. "How long's it been since you've had a drink?" he asked, testing to see if Manny would answer him honestly.

"Since late last night, before I blacked out," Manny said, looking Luis squarely in the eyes. "I finished a bottle of brandy and fell asleep in the kitchen, then woke up in my bed, fully dressed."

Luis nodded once, his mouth set in a grim line. Then he moved into the living room and sat down. "OK, then," he said briskly. "How can we help?"

"I just need to know that you're there," Manny said. "I'll work through this myself, weaning myself off the alcohol. Nobody can do that for me anyway. But what I really need is for things to go back to the way they were. I don't want to live alone. It's just depressing, coming home to an empty house."

Lucinda opened her mouth to reply, but Luis cut her off with a motion of his hand. "Not yet, Manny, not yet," he said. "Promises are good, but actions are better. If you really want to be part of this family, then let's see you stop drinking. But know this, son," he warned, "if you start drinking again, that's it. We're through. Do you understand? And agree?"

"Yes," said Manny. "Yes, I hear you, and I agree." He lifted the glass of water with both hands to his mouth, but his hands were shaking, the water spilling out over the top. Ashamed, he put the glass back down on the table.

"Manny," said Lucinda softly, glancing towards Luis, "why don't you come over later this afternoon and help me make dinner? I'm going to fry some of the new Zazulies, you know, the mushrooms with the little spiny things? I could use your help."

"I'd like that," he replied gratefully, tears in his eyes.

~ ~ ~ ~ ~ ~

Manny walked slowly back to his house, lost in thought. His family seemed supportive; even Luis had come around by the end of the conversation. And Lucinda had invited him to dinner! He had so missed his conversations with Lucinda, as the two of them prepared dinner together. He could sit next to Zach during dinner, just as he used to do. Now if he could just make it through the rest of the afternoon ...

Turning into his yard, he came to an abrupt halt. The hairs on the back of Manny's neck stood up. There was a faint but unmistakable smell hanging in the air, the musk of a man's cologne. Manny knew only one person who wore that scent, Raimone, the former aide to his predecessor.

Turning to the side of the house, he quickly looked behind the bushes where he kept the recycling bins. The windows were properly locked, and nothing seemed out of place. Hurrying back around the house, he inspected the other side, too, but there was nothing unusual to be seen. The scent was gone by the time he finished.

*Am I imagining things?* he thought. For the first time, he wished that he had updated the surveillance system on his property.

*Maybe it's like a hallucination - just part of the alcohol withdrawal,* he thought. *Why would Raimone want to come here, to my house? He can just walk into my office any time he wants.*

Still, that uneasy feeling lingered.

# Chapter 38.

*T*HE WORST PART *about giving up drinking,* thought Manny, *is that you can't drink. The second worst part is that you can't sleep.* It was 3:00 am, and Manny was sitting up on the edge of his bed, wide awake. It had been three days and almost three nights of sobriety. While his mind had slowly cleared, his body still felt ill.

*What do you do, if you can't sleep?* he wondered restlessly. He didn't feel like reading, or watching the news. Despite his firm resolution, his mind kept returning to the bottle of bourbon secreted in its hiding place underneath the velvet chair. It was still there. He decided to retrieve it, and empty it out in the kitchen sink.

He knelt in front of the chair, pushing it to the side. There beneath the carpet and the floorboards was the full, unopened bottle of bourbon left by Manny's father.

Reaching into the hiding place, he grasped the bottle and was about to remove it, when he felt something brush against his hand. Intrigued, he used the LampLight app on his padlet, shining the light into the opening. There was a tiny dark brown leather pouch and a sheet of paper folded into a small square, underneath the bottle.

Manny took the bottle, the pouch and the sheet of paper and closed up the hiding place. He went downstairs, where he resolutely opened the bourbon and poured it down the kitchen sink. *Good riddance,* he thought with relief.

He made himself a glass of BoBo's tea, a marijuana-infused white tea flavored with dark red pokemeberries, grateful again for Anna's suggestion that it might make the alcohol withdrawal easier. Then he took the leather pouch and the folded sheet of paper into the library, sitting down in one of the armchairs.

The pouch was small, a couple of inches wide, closed by a simple drawstring. It opened easily. Manny turned it upside down into the palm of his hand, drawing in his breath sharply as the contents spilled into his palm.

The rings! These were the two antique diamond rings that Manny had stolen from the old lady's house when he was sixteen years old, the burglary that had been on surveillance at the company where Raimone was working. Patrick had taken the rings after his arrest, telling him that they would be returned to the owner, who had agreed not to press charges since she was getting her property back.

But apparently, they had never been returned to her. Manny had no idea how his father had appeased the old lady without returning the rings. Probably he had bribed or blackmailed her, his father's two favorite methods of dealing with people.

*Now what am I going to do with you,* he mused, turning the rings over and over in his hand. They were lovely, white gold with many glittering little round diamonds. The engagement ring had a large oval diamond in the center which shone like a star.

His first thought was to show them to Julio, and ask what he thought Manny should do with them. But he couldn't involve his brother, couldn't create a situation where if Julio were questioned, he would have to lie to protect Manny. No, he couldn't tell anyone that he had found the rings. It was the safest way.

*But maybe I should tell Tyler Watkins,* he thought; Tyler was his lawyer, and had also been his father's lawyer. Most likely, Tyler would tell him that he couldn't advise him as to how to handle stolen property. No, Manny was on his own. Maybe it was better that way. He'd always insisted that he didn't know what his father had done with the rings, that he had assumed they had been returned to the owner.

But what was he going to do with them?

And then, unbidden, he recalled the smell of cologne in his yard a few days earlier. What if it really had been Raimone? What if he knew people in the department and was able to get a search warrant for Manny's house? It would take a good detective all of two minutes to find the hiding place in his bedroom. He certainly couldn't put the rings back there.

Manny had been promoted to Commissioner very fast, and there were others in the department, men who were more senior than he, who felt that it had been a mistake to promote him so quickly. He'd heard the comments, the whispers, seen the sideways glances as he walked by. Was Raimone involved in some kind of plot to discredit him and remove him from office?

*Maybe it's just the alcohol withdrawal making me paranoid,* he said to himself, trying to laugh.

Putting the rings aside for the moment, he turned to the sheet of paper, unfolding it carefully, smoothing it open on his knee. It was a handwritten letter, rare in these days, written in a graceful feminine hand:

*Patrick,*

*I am sorry, I cannot marry you. We've had some good times together, you and I. But now that has to come to an end.*

*My husband and I have decided to reconcile, and I will be moving back in with him. Please don't try and change my mind. And yes, he knows about us. I told him last night.*

*I will always have a soft spot in my heart for you, Patrick. With kindness and my warmest regards,*
*MerryBeth*

MerryBeth! That old battle-axe, she had been Patrick's secretary for as long as Manny could remember. All of those nights when Patrick had been "working late," the nights when he had forgotten to leave dinner in the coldbox for his young son, nights when Manny had done his homework and then gone to bed without ever seeing his father ... Manny could feel his hands clenching at his sides, his anger rising like a volcano in his gut.

Suddenly, he stood up and hurled his glass at the wall, watching with grim satisfaction as the glass shattered and its dark red contents dripped down the wall. *You bastard,* he thought, *it's a good thing you're dead, or I'd kill you myself.*

256

~ ~ ~ ~ ~ ~

Manny took the handwritten letter and the rings back upstairs, mulling over what to do with them. As a detective, he knew all of the usual hiding places: the closet shelf, a pocket in a garment hanging in the closet, under the mattress, inside a canister in the kitchen, etc. No, he needed to find a place for the rings where no one would ever look.

Going downstairs to the kitchen, he opened up the coldbox and retrieved a container of tofu. Carefully, he cut the tofu into nine equal cubes. Then he picked up one of the cubes, delicately making a tiny slit in the middle. Taking one of the rings, he slid it carefully into the opening, relieved when it seamlessly disappeared from sight. He repeated the process for the second ring. Then he pushed the nine cubes of tofu together and poured a bottle of marinade over the whole thing, covering it and placing it back in the coldbox.

*That should do it,* he thought. *Even I can't tell which ones contain the rings.*

Manny was having breakfast in the kitchen at 8:30 am, standing by the sink preparing a fresh cup of BoBo's tea, when someone rang the doorbell. Opening the front door, he was surprised to see a tiny old lady with electric-blue hair, leaning with both hands on a cane and looking up at him.

"Commissioner?" she asked.

"Yes, that would be me," he replied. "Can I help you?"

"I certainly hope so, young man. My name is Aviva Johnson." She pushed past him uninvited and stood in the foyer, looking up at the ceiling, momentarily speechless. But only momentarily.

# Chapter 39.

**M**S. JOHNSON, YOU have my word that I'll take care of this right away. Let me make a few calls, and I'll have someone over to your house today," he said as reassuringly as possible, while gently but firmly ushering the tiny woman towards the door. She certainly liked to talk, and had a tendency to repeat herself. Sometimes, she did not stop talking even when Manny tried to answer her. *No wonder they laugh when her name comes up in Council meetings,* he thought wryly. Still, the leak was no laughing matter.

Once he had closed the door firmly behind her, he texted Hasan Blumberg, who had previously sent two of his best men to Ms. Johnson's home to inspect the leak.

Manny: *Hasan, we need to meet. Sorry to bother you during this holiday week, but the matter is urgent and confidential. Can you come to my home later today, say 4:00 pm?*

Hasan: *Sure thing, 4:00. See you later.*

But first, before the meeting with Hasan, Manny had plans to join Lucinda, Anna and the children on a trip to the greenhouse, to see a new exhibit. It was an exciting excursion for the children, and a good way for Manny to ease back into the children's lives.

"Daddy!" exclaimed Zach, opening the door.

"Hey, Bud," he said, self-consciously rumpling his son's bright red curls. "How are you today?"

"Good," Zach replied shyly. He moved sideways to hide behind his Auntie Marya, standing next to him.

"Marya, hi," Manny said. Marya was Anna and Naztazya's sister, the middle of the five girls. She had been helping care for the children since Anna's family had moved in with Lucinda and Luis. At twenty years old, she was quite a bit younger than Anna and Julio, who were twenty-eight. Manny knew her, of course, but not well.

"Hi, Manny," she replied, trying to extricate Zach from the folds of her skirt, where he seemed to be trying to disappear.

"Do I hear Manny?" Lucinda said, coming in from the kitchen, wiping her hands on her apron. "How are you today?" she asked, scanning his face. "Have you had lunch?"

"No, not really," he replied. "I'm doing OK, I just wish I could get some sleep."

"Here, come into the kitchen," she replied. "The insomnia will work itself out, you just have to be patient." He grimaced.

"Have you tried Valerian root?" she asked. "It's supposed to be a good sedative. Maybe try some before bedtime."

Lucinda waved him into a seat at the kitchen table, placing a pan-fried Portobello sandwich and a glass of iced cantadew juice in front of him.

Luis walked into the kitchen, holding his padlet in his hand. "Do I hear Manny?" he asked. "Hello! You look like you're doing a little better today."

"Thanks," Manny replied gratefully. "I think the worst of it has passed."

"You think you'll be OK to go back to the office on Monday?" Luis asked.

"I hope so," Manny replied. "What I really need is some sleep, but other than that, yeah, I'm ready."

Luis said, "It's not going to be easy, you know. There will be times when it will be right there in front of you, other people drinking in their offices, offering it to you. Are you ready for that?"

"I'm as ready as I'm ever going to be, put it that way," Manny replied. "Besides, the tone is set from the top. If I refuse a couple of times, people will get the idea, and it will become OK to say no."

Manny took a bite out of his sandwich, distracted as Marya walked through the kitchen on her way to the laundry room, arms full of laundry. *When had Marya grown up?* he wondered, surprised by her swaying shapeliness.

"Marya's been a real help to us," Lucinda said, following his eyes. "She's got one year left of school before she gets her engineering degree. She couldn't find a part-time job, so we hired her as an au pair."

At the greenhouse, there was a long line waiting to get into the children's exhibit. Manny, standing in line with Zach, Julie, Lucinda and Marya, stifled his impatience as he thought of the work waiting for him at home, and his meeting later with Hasan. If he wanted to be a good father, then he was going to have to spend time with Zach.

"You're awfully quiet," Lucinda said. "What's on your mind?"

"Just work stuff," he replied.

"How are you doing, Manny? Was it hard, giving up drinking?" she asked softly.

"It was horrible, Lucinda, the first few days were a nightmare," he replied honestly, speaking softly so only Lucinda could hear him. "I wondered if I was going to be able to do it. But it's just a question of perseverance, really, plowing through one hour after another until enough hours pass that you start to feel better."

She nodded, her hand on his shoulder. "I never doubted you could do it, Manny."

"And I'm never going to do it again," he said firmly. "I've given it up for good."

"That's great to hear," she said.

The exhibit, all about the greenhouse and how it worked, was interesting for children and adults, too. Everyone had a good time, even Manny.

On the way home, Marya glanced at Lucinda and then said shyly to Manny, "You'll be coming for dinner tonight?"

"I'll be there," he replied. "I wouldn't miss Lucinda's brown rice casserole! I just have a meeting at 4:00 pm at the house, and then I'll be over for dinner."

~ ~ ~ ~ ~ ~

Hasan was right on time, ringing the doorbell at 4:00 pm sharp.

"Ms. Johnson came here in person this morning, to try and convince me that she should be taken seriously," Manny said, as he led Hasan into the study. "Honestly, she's a bit of a character, but that leak is no joke. She says it's gotten worse, that she has to get up at night to empty the buckets or they will overflow. Have a seat. Can I offer you something cold to drink, maybe some iced tea?"

Hasan looked around at the room, with its tall glass windows lining the wall overlooking the little front yard, the thick carpet on the floor, the antique desk at one end of the room and the deep, comfortable leather chairs. He reached out a hand to touch the seat of one of the chairs before gingerly sitting down. "Is this real cow leather?" he asked, leaning back carefully so as to not sink down too far.

"So I've been told," Manny replied, sitting down. "They're very old."

"This is a beautiful room," Hasan said, gazing with wonder at the artwork hanging on the walls. Manny smiled politely, then turned the subject back to Ms. Johnson and her leak.

"I'd like you to open up the wall in Ms. Johnson's house and look behind it. I know your men have already done that, but look again. Drill into the back wall, if you have to. The water is coming from somewhere, and I'm afraid that it's only going to get worse," Manny said.

"OK, but we'll have to get Ms. Johnson to vacate the house before we can do that. It'll be extensive work, and she'd just be in the way," replied Hasan.

"I'll see what I can do about that. Maybe she has family that she could move in with for a week or so," Manny said. "Do you think that would be long enough?"

"Depends on what we find, but yeah, that sounds reasonable," Hasan replied.

"Good. I'll have my Aide relocate Ms. Johnson, either with family or maybe I could put her up myself in one of our properties, until she can return home," Manny said. "We need to keep her calm, so she doesn't run around telling people that the sky is falling." The two men laughed at the arcane expression.

Manny ran his fingers through his hair. "Hasan, I have a bad feeling about this leak. The sooner you find out the cause, the better. Can you get on it right away? Of course, you will bill us triple time for emergency work on a holiday."

Hasan nodded. "Sure, I can do that. I'll have a couple of engineers over there tomorrow."

"There's something else I want to talk to you about, as long as you're here," Manny said. "Could your company put in a security system here at the house?"

"You mean a surveillance system?" asked Hasan, surprised. "The house doesn't have one?" Manny shook his head.

"I can set you up with a surveillance unit in each of the rooms. Here, take a look at this," Hasan said, reaching into his jacket pocket.

"This is new," Hasan said, "it's called 'Guardian Plus.' I just happen to have a sample on me." He handed Manny a small, translucent sphere the size of a large blueberry. "It's smaller than the typical surveillance drone, and nearly invisible once it's in place. It doesn't move unless it detects motion, and then it slides closer to the source of the movement.

"You want monitoring 24/7, right?" Hasan continued. "And the option for the monitors to turn on voice recording, if the situation seems dangerous or threatening?"

"Yeah, and I want to be able to see if anyone is poking around outside of the house," Manny said.

"OK, we can put units around the outside of the house, too. Have you had any trouble with someone trying to break in?" asked Hasan.

"No, nothing like that," replied Manny, shifting uneasily as he remembered the scent of musk permeating the air in his yard. "It's just that with the kids here and all, I want to make sure my family is safe, even if I'm not home."

"Here, let me show you how it works," Hasan said. "It's really kind of genius, much better than anything else on the market." He turned on the app which controlled the tiny drone.

Manny could feel the smooth sphere turn slightly warm in the palm of his hand before it shivered all over, and then ascended slowly up towards the ceiling, where it nestled into the corner of the room, at the intersection where two walls met. Once in place, it was nearly invisible, and did not make a sound.

"This drone will transmit a steady stream of information back to your padlet and the surveillance company," Hasan explained. "We'll put one in every room. It will monitor your home and the yard 24/7, and alert the police at once if there's a problem. Is there anyone special you would you like them to contact, in addition to the police?"

"I'd like to use Dave Wu as my emergency contact," Manny said.

"Fine. I can have this up and running for you right away. Shall I have the installation set for this week?" Hasan said.

"Sounds good," replied Manny. "Make sure you bill the Colony for the work. Just call it general maintenance."

Once Hasan left, Manny settled down to work until dinner time. He texted Nigel, asking him to take care of relocating Ms. Johnson so the engineers could work on her leak.

He yawned hugely, shaking his head to clear it. The alcohol withdrawal had left him feeling exhausted. He changed his mind about working and moved over to one of the armchairs, settling down for a little catnap before dinner, carefully setting his alarm.

He woke with a start when his alarm went off at 6:00 pm. *At least I got some sleep,* he thought, rubbing his face with his hands.

Standing at the front door of Lucinda and Luis's house, Manny pulled out his padlet and unlocked the door. "Daddy's here!" shouted Zach, running into the foyer.

"Hey, Bud," Manny said. He rumpled his son's hair, glad to see that he did not shy away from him.

"Manny," called Lucinda, "why don't you and Zach come into the kitchen. I could use your help making dinner."

# *Chapter 40.*

**D**INNER WAS A simple weeknight meal, but to Manny, it was wonderful. He sat quietly, listening to the conversation swirling around him, soaking it in like a plant turning its face towards the sun.

"Manny, you look like you are thinking about something profound," Marya said to him. She was seated near him, on the other side of Zach.

"Oh, just glad to be here," he replied lightly, looking at her and then at Lucinda, who was watching approvingly.

"We're glad you're here, too, Manny," Lucinda said, passing him the bread basket.

Luis cleared his throat. "I thought maybe on Monday, we could start moving some of the children's things back over to the house," he said gruffly.

"Monday is good," Manny replied. "I won't be home until late, but you don't need to wait for me. Let's get a couple of our guys to come over and carry everything. Oh, and I'm having a security system installed at the house, so there might be workmen there."

"A security system? What made you think of that?" asked Anna.

"I don't know, it just seems like a good idea," Manny replied. "Especially with so many of us coming and going," he said, glancing at Marya. "It can't hurt."

Luis regarded him for a moment, head tilted to one side. "Did something happen to bring this up?" he asked.

"Nothing special," Manny replied blandly. "The Commissioner's house should be secure at all times." Luis looked as though he was wondering if there was more to it than that, but he didn't pursue it.

Marya reached for another piece of bread, spreading whipped tofu and honey on it and handing it to Zach. "This is delicious, Manny," she said. "Where did you get it?"

"I stopped at Ferrara Bakery on my way here," he said, referring to a famous New York City bakery that had been around at one location or another for hundreds of years.

"Marya would like to move to the house with us, too," Anna said casually. "She's been such a help to us, and the children love her."

Marya and Anna glanced at each other. It lasted less than a second, but Manny saw once again the unspoken understanding passing between two sisters, a question asked and answered. For a moment, a wave of nostalgia swept over him. Naz and Anna so often had done just that.

"Of course Marya can come," he said. "We'll open up one of the guest suites."

Marya turned to him and said, "Thank you, Manny." She smiled invitingly, showing all of her even white teeth. Then she tossed her unbound, wavy dark red hair over her shoulder, and turned back to her food.

Manny did not miss any of this, spoken or unspoken. The smile, the hair toss – was she flirting with him? He looked up questioningly at Anna, who looked back at him with wide-eyed innocence. Yes, something was definitely going on.

Marya, seven years younger than Manny, was attractive, intelligent, and single. It was not at all uncommon for a widower to marry his wife's sister, especially if he had young children. In an era when families stayed close, as much from custom as from lack of space, it was common to see two or three generations living together, pooling their resources and sharing their responsibilities. If a woman died in childbirth, family members would step up to help out. If there were un-married sisters or female cousins available, so much the better.

After dinner, Manny and Lucinda cleared the table and brought the dishes into the kitchen.

"Did you and Zach have a good time today?" Lucinda asked, as they washed and dried the dinner dishes.

"Yeah, it was OK. He's so grown up now! He doesn't want me to read to him anymore," Manny said. "He wants to read to me."

"Yes, he's growing up. It's good that you are part of his life, Manny," Lucinda said placidly, handing him another dish to dry.

"I'm a terrible father," Manny admitted softly. "When Naz and I decided to have a family, I didn't realize how hard it would be. It's a huge responsibility. I want to do better, be a better father to him than my father was to me."

"That's a good goal," she replied. "You've been doing some serious thinking, I see."

"Yeah, it's about all I've been doing, the past few days," Manny said heavily.

Lucinda nodded, giving him time.

"It's too easy to be like my Dad," Manny said. "He was the worst possible role model."

"Then Manny, be the father you wish you'd had," Lucinda urged. "You just may find that a loving relationship with Zach goes a long way to undoing the harm your father caused you."

The two worked together in silence for a few moments, until they were nearly finished.

"What was that going on with Marya? Did you notice?" Manny asked in a conspiratorial undertone as the two of them hung up the dish towels to dry.

Lucinda laughed. "You know, Manny, you're a good-looking young man with a little boy. And he's going to need a mother. I know, you're not thinking about that yet, but you could do worse than Marya. She's sensitive and intelligent, smart as anything, and the children love her. She seems to like you, too."

She turned to face him. "You're quite a catch, Manny. You've grown up to be a wealthy, powerful man. Women will be throwing themselves at you. It'll be hard to sort out the ones who are only interested in your money. But with Marya, you know she's sincere. And she already knows about the drinking."

Manny shook his head. "I'm not ready to have this conversation," he replied. "I'm not saying that I don't find her attractive, only that it's too soon." He chose his words carefully, as he was quite sure that they would be repeated to Marya and

Anna as soon as he left. "So much has happened this past year. I just need to breathe for a bit."

Luis came into the kitchen carrying a box filled with files, folders and knick-knacks. A blue stuffed frog, a teddy bear and several crayon drawings stood up from the top.

"Since you're going back to the house," he said, putting the box down on the kitchen table, "do you think you could take this with you, and put it in my office?"

~ ~ ~ ~ ~ ~

Manny returned to the house, putting Luis's box of cherished possessions on the desk in Luis's "office," a small room off one of the guest bedrooms which had been designed as a walk-in closet. After Manny had bought the house across the street for Lucinda and Luis, Luis had continued to use the little room occasionally, mostly as a place to display his grandchildren's artwork.

Manny settled down in the study, intending to work. He would have a full day at the office on Monday, now that the holiday week was ending. Monday afternoon, there would be a Council meeting, the first one since he had become Commissioner. He wanted to address the leak in Ms. Johnson's house, but before he could prepare his remarks, he needed to hear from Hasan, to see what his workers had found.

Manny yawned. He was tired, but it was too early to go to bed, if he wanted to sleep through the night. He opened up his padlet, then put it aside, going back into the kitchen for some BoBo's tea. A few minutes later, he was back in the study, sprawled in the desk chair, tea untouched, snoring soundly.

It was the smell that woke him, the cloying scent of musk. The room had darkened while he was asleep, the tall study windows letting in the fading twilight from outside. Manny could barely see him at first, standing too close him, dressed completely in black: pants, shirt, shoes, even a black knitted cap. Only his face showed, pale as a pearl in the gathering dusk.

"How did you get in here?" Manny asked.

267

# Chapter 41.

"THAT'S NOT REALLY the question, now, is it?" said Raimone mockingly. "Maybe you should ask what I want."

"Here's what *I* want, Raimone," replied Manny. "I want you to leave. Now."

"Or what?" retorted Raimone, gesturing to Manny's feet. Manny, looking down, saw to his dismay that his feet had been zip-tied to his desk chair.

"What the hell?" said Manny angrily. A prickle of fear stirred in his chest. The two of them were quite alone; it was unlikely that anyone would come to the house.

"There's something you should know about me," said Raimone, dragging one of the armchairs closer to Manny, settling himself back with a smug smile. "I'm IAD," he said, meaning that he was with the Internal Affairs Department of the police. "That's why I never stay too long in any one assignment. Very few people know, not even the Chief. I go undercover to different precincts, wherever the department needs me."

Raimone crossed his legs, taking his time, relishing the moment. "I've been watching you on and off for years, ever since you broke into that old lady's house when you were a kid."

"I was a juvenile then, Raimone. It was a long time ago!" Manny said indignantly. "You've got no business going through sealed court records!"

"Oh, did that seem *unfair* to you?" asked Raimone. "What's really unfair is *you*, you little prig, getting off scot-free after that burglary. You were sixteen, you could've gone to jail. Your old man shoulda knocked the crap outta you, not let you go home with a slap on the wrist."

Raimone reached down to his knapsack on the floor next to his chair, removing a bottle of bourbon.

"You're going to go on a little bender tonight," said Raimone. "I've got two guys on their way here now, to help me.

We're going to turn this place upside down, and I want you out of the way by the time they get here."

"Two guys?" said Manny, playing for time. "The same two people who detained Loosey? I know they weren't real police officers."

"Maybe they were, maybe they weren't," replied Raimone. "But a judge is signing a search warrant right now."

"A judge would authorize a search of the Commissioner's home?" asked Manny, surprised. "For what?"

"Stolen property, that's what!" Raimone laughed humorlessly. "Those two rings didn't just get up and walk away, you know. They were never returned to the old lady. They're not anywhere at the office, so I'm guessing they must be here in your house."

"Why are you doing this?" asked Manny, his heart pounding inside his chest. He steadfastly did not look in the direction of the kitchen. It was common for a thief to give himself away by glancing furtively at the spot where something was hidden, as every police officer knew.

"*Why?* Because *I hate you*, you little bastard," Raimone sneered, his voice low and menacing. "You've had it so easy, everything handed to you on a silver platter. You and your half-brother, what's his name, Julius, living in your fancy houses with your wives and children, so damned lucky, so *entitled*. Well, that's all about to change.

"You've got enemies," he continued. "There's a whole group of police who think you're the wrong man to be Commissioner. You're nothing but a two-bit detective. If it wasn't for your father, nobody would've looked twice at you!" He glared at Manny, his face contorted. "You need to be removed, by any means necessary. And I'm here to make sure that happens."

Raimone reached into the knapsack once again. When he removed his hand, he was pointing a handgun at Manny. "Drink," he said. "Now."

Manny looked at the bottle, and the gun. "I stopped drinking a week ago," he responded. "That much bourbon could kill me."

269

"This is not a debate," Raimone replied. "Get started."

Manny didn't move. Raimone pulled back the safety on the gun, the distinctive click loud in the quiet room.

"You're not going to shoot me," Manny said. "Because if you do, then it's over for you. But, Raimone, if you leave right now, who's to say that you were even here."

"I know what you're trying to do!" exclaimed Raimone. "And it's not going to work!" He gestured towards the bottle. "I mean it. Bottoms up."

"No," replied Manny.

The gun went off with a bang in the quiet room. Manny screamed, the bullet grazing his thigh, searing a long wound into the flesh. A bright little streamlet of blood appeared, running down his leg, pooling onto the floor.

Raimone reached into his jacket pocket. He removed a dozen bullets, carefully lining them up in two neat little rows along the arm of his chair, relishing the sudden sharp smell of fear in the room.

He pointed to the bullets. "Start drinking, or I swear, the next two are going in your kneecaps."

Manny opened the bottle and took a small swallow. The smell of it made him gag. He struggled to control his lurching stomach. Light-headed, he tried not to look at the blood soaking into the rug.

"More," Raimone said impatiently. "Take a good belt, come on, Stewart, you know how to drink."

His eyes on Raimone, Manny picked up the bottle and took a more substantial swallow. He could feel the warmth of it as it hit his stomach. Despite his desperate determination to stay strong, his body reacted like a sponge, greedily absorbing the bourbon. It didn't just feel good; it felt marvelous, like cool water flowing over dry, parched soil. He lifted the bottle again, this time unprompted. The sharpness of the gunshot wound eased as the bourbon soothed and blurred its edges.

*I'll soon be too drunk to defend myself,* he thought, a desperate plan taking shape. Manny held the bottle of bourbon to his mouth with both hands, drinking deeply. His gorge rising in protest, he flung the empty bottle across the room. Raimone, distracted, turned his head for a second to follow the sound of breaking glass. Manny stood up, feet still tied to the chair, and took a single forceful, hobbled step towards him. Then he leaned forward and vomited, hugely and forcefully, all over his tormentor.

Stunned, Raimone's attention shifted to the noxious mess dripping down his head and chest, the gun sliding unnoticed to the floor. Manny swayed in front of him, then despite himself, he slowly crumpled to the floor, pulling the desk chair down on top of him, the room careening dizzily around him. He stretched out his hand to reach for the gun, but could not reach it.

Manny heard the sound of his front door opening, then closing, very quietly. *Here come his guys,* Manny thought with despair. *It's all over now.*

Several pairs of feet were in the foyer; Manny could hear whispering and a female voice. *That's a lot of people,* Manny thought groggily. *Didn't Raimone say there were two guys coming?*

"Gun!" he shouted desperately, one arm waving in the air. "Gun!" He tried to say more, but could not.

"A lot of good that's going to do you," Raimone said, laughing heartily. "Those will be my guys with the search warrant."

David Wu strode into the room, followed by half a dozen police officers, all of them with weapons drawn. "Put your hands in the air," he ordered, kicking the gun away, out of reach. "Stand up and turn around."

Raimone stood, covered with vomit. "Wu, this is none of your business," he said. "You'd best leave, now."

Dave laughed. "The Commissioner's been shot. We all heard you threaten him, forcing him at gunpoint to drink an entire bottle of bourbon. Let's see, attempted murder, assault with a deadly weapon, kidnapping, resisting arrest; yeah, you're going away for a long time, pal. Either put your hands behind your back, or I'll have these officers here restrain you properly."

A few minutes later, Raimone was in handcuffs, escorted out the door by several officers. There was a brief scuffle outside when Raimone's two "detectives" arrived with the search warrant; they were detained in short order and bustled off to the station along with Raimone. Only Dave stayed behind.

"Manny, hey, it's me, Dave," he said, using his pocket knife to cut through the restraints. "It's OK, he's gone now. You're bleeding." Gently, he put his hand on his friend's shoulder. "Wake up, Manny! Can you tell me where you're hurt?"

Manny mumbled something, eyes opening to tiniest slits. The room was spinning precariously, so he closed them again. Someone was kneeling next to him on the floor, saying words.

*Floor is good,* Manny thought fuzzily, *you can't fall, if you're already on the floor.* His hand moved back and forth across the carpet. His head hurt, his mouth tasted like compost. Then he remembered that he'd been shot, and opened his eyes to look down at his leg.

"Dave?" he asked blearily. "How??"

"Your surveillance company, they called me to say there was a break-in," Dave said. "I'm your contact person."

"Oh, right," he replied.

"Your leg is bleeding," Dave said. "Are you hurt anywhere else? Shall I call your doctor?" Manny mumbled something in reply and then began to snore. Dave pulled out his padlet and activated Beacon, the police and EMT emergency app, calling for Dr. Stubbs to meet him at the mansion immediately.

Dr. Stubbs arrived six minutes later, dressed in an evening gown. "I was at a wedding," she explained. "Where's the patient?"

After examining Manny, who was out cold on the floor, she determined that aside from the wound on his leg, he was unharmed. A dozen stitches closed the wound.

"Help me get him upstairs, would you please? We'll put him to bed and let him sleep it off," she said to Dave. The two of them carefully carried Manny up the stairs and laid him in his bed, removing his shoes and covering him with the quilt. Then they left, a little after 9:00 pm, closing the front door behind them.

Silence descended upon the house once again, unchanged except for the puddle of sick on the floor and a bullet hole in the wall in the study.

Unfortunately, the peace and quiet didn't last very long.

# Chapter 42.

**I** CAN'T SLEEP," Zach complained, climbing onto his grand-father's lap. "I need Froggie."

"Zach, I've told you, Froggie is over at the house," explained Luis for the third time. "I sent a box of things back to the house with your Dad, when he went home after dinner."

"But Abuelo," Zach whined. "I need Froggie!" Zach was quite attached to his blue stuffed frog, a birthday gift from Naz when he was three.

"I think maybe you're worried about Froggie because he's not here," explained Luis. "But Froggie is safe and sound, asleep in your bedroom at the house."

"Can you go and get Froggie, Abuelo?" asked Zach. "Please?"

Luis smiled indulgently at his grandson. "OK, Zach, I'll go get Froggie, if you'll go upstairs and get into bed. Do we have a deal?"

Zach nodded solemnly, wrapping his slender arms around Luis's neck to hug him. Luis briefly explained where he was going to an amused Lucinda, then left for the quick walk to the mansion.

Luis waved his hand over the Scentinel sensor pad to unlock the front door, but the door wasn't locked. *That's odd,* he thought, pushing the door open.

"Manny?" he called. "It's Luis. Where are you?"

He looked in the kitchen, then moved back to the foyer. There was a distinctly sour smell coming from somewhere. He followed his nose into the study and stopped in the doorway.

There was a puddle of unspeakable glop on the floor, soaked into the carpet. An empty bottle of bourbon lay on the floor. "Son of a bitch!" he exploded. He walked quickly back into the foyer.

"MANNY!" he shouted angrily. "WHERE ARE YOU?" Enraged, he moved quickly up the stairs, following the sound of snoring to Manny's bedroom. Manny was sound asleep in his bed. When Luis shook him by the arm to try to wake him, he did not respond. The funk of bourbon lay around him like a fog, sour and rank.

"You bastard!" Luis fumed at his sleeping foster son. "I believed you, I *trusted* you! And you *lied* to me!" Furious, he left Manny's bedroom. He searched through the kitchen cabinets, the closets and the cabinet in the study, but did not find any other bottles. He went outside, checking the recycling bin. About to return home, Luis remembered Froggie, going back inside to retrieve the stuffed toy. After consideration, he picked up the entire box and carried it out of the house.

~ ~ ~ ~ ~ ~

"Lucinda! Lucinda, come quick!" he called as he walked into their house. "*Lucinda!*" He told her everything he had seen, including the mess on the floor in the study.

"But I just talked to him!" she said, her eyes wide with surprise. "He was so sincere. He wants to work on his relationship with Zach, he seemed so relieved that Julio's family is moving back into the house. He loves us, Luis."

"Maybe. Maybe he does. But even if that's true, Lucinda," Luis said, "we can't trust him, not ever again."

~ ~ ~ ~ ~ ~

Manny returned to the office the next morning. Aside from a banging headache and a bit of a limp from his injured leg, he felt pretty good, and was relieved that he didn't have an overwhelming craving to drink.

"Nigel," he told his aide, "I've given up drinking over the past week. Please make sure that no one comes into my office with alcohol. I don't want to see it, I don't want to be anywhere near it."

"Sure thing, Manny," said Nigel. He liked that about his aide; Nigel didn't ask him a lot of questions, he just followed instructions.

A few minutes later, there was a knock on his door.

"Good morning, Hasan," he said, waving him into the visitor's chair.

"Commissioner," Hasan responded with a smile. "How are you feeling today?"

"Well, there's been some excitement," Manny responded. "I was going to text you later. How did the surveillance company know there was a break-in at my house? You haven't installed the system yet!"

"Actually, it wasn't the surveillance company," replied Hasan. "Remember when we were talking in the study, and I showed you how Guardian Plus works? It floated up to the ceiling."

"Yeah, I remember," Manny said.

"Well, when I got back to my house, I couldn't find the sample anywhere, so I used the app to locate it. When I opened up the app, I could see and hear what was going on in your study," Hasan explained. "The first thing I saw was that man, holding a gun pointed at you. At first I couldn't believe what I was seeing, but I notified the police right away, and contacted Da – uh, the Assistant Deputy Commissioner."

"So actually, it wasn't the surveillance company who sent the police, it was you," Manny said. "Hasan, I think you may have saved my life."

"That guy, was he the reason you wanted a security system?" asked Hasan.

Manny nodded. "I had a feeling he'd turn up eventually, and he did."

"I'm glad you're OK, Commissioner," Hasan said.

Manny stood up, walked around the side of his desk and with his right hand on his left shoulder, bowed deeply to him, a sign of respect. "Thank you, Hasan," he said simply.

A moment passed as the two men reflected on how things had unfolded.

"That's not the only reason I came by," Hasan said. "I want to update you on the leak at Ms. Johnson's house."

~ ~ ~ ~ ~ ~

Manny worked diligently through the morning. With Hasan's report finally in hand, Manny at last was able to prepare his remarks for the Council meeting about Ms. Johnson and her leak.

At lunchtime, Manny ordered a tofu gorilla burger from SilverBax, a nearby vegetarian restaurant, to be delivered by DroneDash; then he leaned back in his chair to relax for a moment. His leg ached steadily, but he ignored it.

Manny stared at his padlet, wondering if he should text Julio to see if they had started moving back into the house, but decided against it. When he got home later, after the Council meeting, they would be there. He was looking forward to it.

At the Council meeting, Manny told them first that Ms. Johnson had come to see him at his home, desperate to be taken seriously. As he had expected, they laughed.

"It wasn't just a little leak," Manny admonished. "There was a steady stream of water flowing from a crack in the rear wall of her home. At my direction, Hasan Blumberg's construction company ripped out the wall, sealing the leak once and for all. But we're not sure where the water was coming from, and that's a problem.

"I want you to consider this carefully," Manny continued. "We were lucky this time. Eventually, though, there's going to be a true system-wide emergency, whether it's a broken water main, a blackout, or something else. Remember, we live in tunnels, built by human hands. And nothing built by humans lasts forever.

"We need to create a plan so we can safely evacuate all of our citizens. It is our responsibility. We need to be able to shelter and feed everyone outside, for at least a few days, in the event of a system-wide emergency. Call it Plan B. Otherwise, lives are going to be lost." Manny sat down, watching their reactions carefully.

There was a stunned silence. No one was sure what to make of this wild new idea. Council Elder Alixander Jha, a retired lawyer, stood up, ponderous and slow.

"Commissioner, if I may?" he said. Manny nodded. "How are you going to *evacuate*," he said, deliberately pronouncing the word as if it were a lump of coal in his mouth, "thousands of people?"

Manny replied, "Obviously, we are several steps away from that. To begin, we need to verify that it's safe for humans to live above ground, something that hasn't been evaluated in decades. I'd like to send a team of scientists to study the environment for several weeks, and see exactly what it's like out there."

"But to evacuate thousands of people," persisted Mr. Jha, "that's just not practical. For instance, where are you going to put them?" Hands on his hips, he looked at Manny the way an exasperated parent looks at a dim-witted child. "How are you going to feed them? Keep them safe from the deadly night air?"

"Thank you for your comments, Mr. Jha," said Manny crisply. "This isn't something we're going to debate today. For now, I am simply presenting to the Council my thoughts on the subject, so our members can understand the direction in which my administration is headed."

Manny had been prepared to be challenged. He knew that Mr. Jha was the informal leader of a group of Council members who had opposed his appointment. After watching the reactions to his comments today, Manny had a better idea of who the others might be.

Manny made a mental note to have Nigel arrange for a deep-dive tax audit for Mr. Jha, just a little something to teach him some manners.

~ ~ ~ ~ ~ ~

After the Council meeting ended, Manny walked home, eagerly looking forward to seeing his family. He walked quickly up the path to the front door and unlocked it.

There was no one there. The house was still and silent. He walked into the kitchen, which was dark and cold.

Pulling out his padlet, he hologrammed Julio.

Manny: *Where is everyone?? I thought you guys would be here, all moved in.*

There was no response. Manny waited, then put away his padlet and rummaged through the coldbox to see what was available for dinner. He found a half-eaten tofu pie, a purple dotted potato pancake and a leftover salad, limp and soggy.

After he ate, he thought of holograming Lucinda, but decided against it. *I'm sure there's a good explanation,* he told himself. *Maybe Julio and Anna got busy packing and decided to put off actually moving until tomorrow.* He worked on some reports for a couple of hours. Exhausted, he went to bed.

The following morning, Manny rose, made a solitary breakfast and left for work. He had just settled into his office, opening up his padlet, when Nigel appeared in the doorway.

"Your father is here to see you, Sir," he said respectfully. He stepped aside just in time, as Luis strode past him into Manny's office.

"You!" he exclaimed angrily, pointing a finger at Manny. Nigel tactfully closed the office door, leaving the two men alone.

"Luis! Hey, what's going on? Where's everybody been?" Manny asked. "I thought Julio and Anna were moving back to the house. Is everything OK?"

"No one is moving back to the house, Manny!" said Luis, his voice shaking with rage. "You *lied* to us! Again!"

"What are you talking about, Luis?" asked Manny, genuinely puzzled.

"I *saw* you! I went over to the house looking for Froggie, you know, Zach's toy. I saw the mess on the floor in the study, and the empty bottle of bourbon! And I saw *you*, passed out drunk in your bed! What do you have to say for yourself?!" he demanded.

Manny was speechless. Suddenly, he saw how it must have looked to Luis, coming into the house after Raimone had been arrested, after Dave and Dr. Patel had left.

279

"Remember Raimone?" Manny said. "He broke into the house. He said if I didn't drink an entire bottle of bourbon, he was going to shoot me! He wanted me passed out drunk, so he and his men could search the house."

Luis's eyes narrowed. "Wait a minute. You're telling me that someone broke into the house and forced you to drink?" he asked, his voice dripping with sarcasm. "What did he do, hold a gun to your head?"

"Yes, that's exactly what he did!" Manny exclaimed. "I can show you, Luis, if you'll just give me a - "

"What the hell kind of game are you trying to play?!" Luis retorted angrily. "You think you can just make up lie after lie, and I'll believe you?! Well, you're not lying your way out of this one!"

"But, it's true, Luis!" Manny insisted. "I've stopped drinking, you know I have! I don't even like bourbon!"

"Oh, really? Then why did I find an empty bottle of bourbon in the recycling, around the side of the house?" Luis demanded triumphantly, fists clenched at his sides.

"Oh, that," Manny said, surprised. "I found it in an old hiding place of my Dad's, underneath the floorboards in my bedroom one night when I couldn't sleep. I poured it out and put the empty bottle in the recycling bin."

"You've got an answer for everything, don't you?" Luis sneered. "I can't believe anything you say! You're a drunk, Manny, and a liar. I'm finished with you! Frankly, I'm sorry we ever agreed to take you in."

"Agreed to *take me in*?" repeated Manny, stunned. "You didn't *take me in*. Lucinda asked my Dad if I could come and live with you, and he agreed."

Luis snorted with disgust. "Your father's secretary called us, what's her name, MerryBetty or something. She asked if we would come and get you from the infirmary. Remember, after the accident?" he said, referring to an incident when Manny was fifteen, when his father had dislocated Manny's shoulder, causing Manny to fall headfirst down the stairs.

"But Lucinda said … she said he'd agreed to it," Manny said, feeling ill.

"Oh, he agreed to it alright. It was *his idea!!*" Luis replied angrily. "He had his secretary call us and arrange for monthly payments for your keep. He said you could stay as long as we wanted you around. I never should have given in to her! I told her, look who his father is, nothing good is going to come of this. But you know Lucinda, she's so soft-hearted."

There was a stunned silence, the words clattering to the floor.

Manny stood up from behind his desk. He walked to the door and opened it. "I think you had better go, Luis," he said with dignity, averting his gaze.

After Luis left, Manny sat motionless behind his desk for a long, long time. His father had given him away, plain and simple, paying Lucinda and Luis to keep him. *Funny how much that hurts, even now,* he thought.

And Luis … he had been more than just angry. Manny knew that he could show Luis a copy of the surveillance tape from Raimone's arrest; that would prove that Manny had been telling the truth. But Manny was badly shaken not just by what Luis had said, but by his hostility and unwillingness to listen to him. Even showing him the surveillance tape would not fix that.

*Sufficient unto the day is the evil thereof,* thought Manny, wondering distractedly if anyone even knew what that meant.

Emotionally exhausted, he looked bleakly at the stack of reports and messages on his desk. *It's enough to drive a person to drink,* he thought with a sad little chuckle. He definitely didn't feel like working.

Besides, there was someone he had to see.

# Chapter 43.

**T**HANKS SO MUCH for coming here," said Manny, sitting across the table from Lucinda. He had hologrammed her with an urgent request to meet him, hoping that Luis would not keep her away. The two of them were in a tiny sandwich shop called Bellini Panini, not far from Manny's office.

Lucinda's eyes were red-rimmed and puffy. "First, I need to ask you, Manny. Did you go home and get drunk, after you left our house? After we talked?" Her voice was reserved, decidedly cool, but calm. *At least she is willing to listen,* thought Manny.

"There is something I want you to see," Manny replied in response, pulling out his padlet. He opened a restricted folder of official police evidence, then found the video he was looking for.

"Here," he said, passing the padlet to her. He waited in silence as Lucinda watched the entire break-in, as captured by the surveillance drone.

"Oh, Manny, how horrible," she breathed, when the video ended. She looked up, her eyes wide. "He shot you! Are you OK? Is this why you wanted to have a security system installed? You knew this man was coming?"

"My leg is OK," he replied briefly. "His name is Raimone. I had a suspicion that he had been sniffing around the outside of the house, so yeah, I was hoping to have the system installed before he came back."

"Why didn't you show this to Luis?" she asked, gesturing towards the video.

"I was going to," he said, "but before I had a chance, Luis said some things. Did he tell you?"

"Yes, he did," she replied. "I wish he hadn't done that, Manny."

"Is it true? Did my father just give me away?" Manny asked, his voice cracking with emotion. He paused, inhaling slowly. "I thought you asked him if I could come and live with you, with Julio. You know, after the dislocated shoulder?"

"I'm sorry, Manny, it's true," she said softly, her eyes on his. "Your father's secretary called and asked if I would come get you from the infirmary and bring you home to live with us, indefinitely. Manny, we couldn't leave you there, to go back to that house where your father was so cruel to you."

"You didn't have to do that, you and Luis," Manny said. "I'll always be grateful to you. But Luis, he doesn't want to have anything to do with me now. The things he said! He really hates me."

The two sat in silence, sipping their iced tea. "You'll show this to Luis, won't you?" Lucinda said, motioning to the video on the padlet. "He needs to see it."

"Why don't you show it to him?" Manny asked. "Here, I'll send a copy to you. I'm not ready to see him just yet."

"I'll make sure he watches it," she said, a determined look on her face. She rose to leave, then impulsively came around the little table and hugged him. "We'll see you soon, Manny," she said.

~ ~ ~ ~ ~ ~

Luis came to the house to see Manny later that day, after work. The two of them went into the front parlor.

"Manny, I saw the video," he began, sitting down. "Why didn't you tell me?"

"I tried to tell you," Manny protested, "but you wouldn't listen. Apparently, you've had some things on your mind that you've wanted to say to me for some time."

"About that," Luis said, shamefaced. "I'm so sorry. I was really angry. I said things that I should not have said."

"But is it true? Are you sorry that you took me in when I was a kid?" asked Manny coldly.

"No, of course not!" said Luis. "You know me better than that. It's just that I thought you were lying to me. I'm ashamed of myself for what I said to you."

There was an uncomfortable silence, and then Manny sighed. "OK. Apology accepted. I've certainly made mistakes in my life, too, some big ones. Everybody deserves a second chance."

Luis stood up awkwardly and bowed to Manny, his right hand on his left shoulder. "Thank you, son," he said, sounding both humbled and relieved. Manny stood up and bowed back, and then the two of them sat back down. A short silence ensued in which both men seemed intensely interested in studying their hands.

"Well. Shall we go over to the house?" asked Luis. "Lucinda is holding dinner for us."

When Manny and Luis walked into Lucinda's kitchen, they could hear the video playing in the kitchen.

"Play it again! Play the part where he barfs all over the guy!" said Julio, eyes riveted to the video projected against the wall in the kitchen. Anna, Julio and Marya were gathered around the big table while Lucinda prepared dinner at the stove. Manny glanced at the video, grimacing.

"That was sheer genius, man," Julio said to Manny. "How did you think to do that?"

"It was the only plan I could come up with," explained Manny. "I didn't have a weapon, my feet were tied to the chair, and I knew that in a few more minutes, I was going to be passed out cold. I was running out of time, and had to think fast."

"Good job," said Anna, laughing. "The look on the guy's face is priceless!"

"Let's turn this off now," said Lucinda sternly. "Remember, Manny was shot in the leg and could have been badly injured. It was no laughing matter to him."

They sat down to eat, everyone talking at once. Zach, seated to one side of Manny, asked, "Can I have more buttons, please?" The "buttons," small round beige and ivory spotted mushrooms, were sautéed in avocado oil and sprinkled with black and white sesame seeds. Manny reached for the dish at the same time as Marya, who was seated on the other side of Zach, their hands brushing against each other.

"Sorry," murmured Manny, releasing the dish so that Marya could take it. *Was that an accident?* he wondered. He glanced at her. She looked up at him from beneath her long eyelashes, then quickly looked away, cheeks pink. Manny glanced sideways at Anna, who was watching them both with interest. *No, definitely not an accident,* he thought. He smiled inwardly.

"Tell us about your Council meeting," suggested Lucinda. "How did it go?"

Manny told them about Ms. Johnson and the leak in her wall, how the wall was torn open to close the leak, sealing it for good. He noticed that Marya, an engineering student, was listening closely.

Manny went on to explain how he had presented his concerns about a potential emergency evacuation of the Colony. "It was not well received," he said dryly. "We have no Plan B, you know, but nobody wants to hear that."

"You can't blame them, Manny," said Anna. "It's going to be pretty hard to convince people that it's safe to evacuate to the surface, even temporarily."

"We have to start somewhere," he replied. "I'd like to put a team of scientists into the upstairs of the Trade Center, if that's OK with you guys," Manny said, looking to his two partners. "They could live in the building for a few weeks, study the weather and compile a report for the Council."

"That sounds like a good first step," said Luis. Julio nodded.

"Are we moving back into the house?" asked Julie, looking from her mother to her father.

Julio nodded. "Yes. As a matter of fact, we'll be moving tomorrow," he said. "I have a crew coming over in the afternoon to pick up everything and take it over, so let's be ready in the morning."

The move back into the house was easily accomplished. The workmen hoisted boxes and bags to their shoulders, walked across the street to deposit them at the mansion's front door, and were finished within an hour. By the end of the day, everything was unpacked and back in its place, Julie was upstairs doing her homework and Zach was in the front parlor playing with his blocks.

A few days went by, as life eased back into a familiar pattern. One evening, when Manny had gone up to his bedroom, there were footsteps in the hall, followed by a knock on the door.

"Marya, come in," said Manny guardedly. It was late, and he had been about to go to bed. It was highly improper for a young woman to come to a man's bedroom, especially late at night.

"No, thank you, Manny. I just wanted to give you this," she said, handing him a fragile leather-bound book entitled, "IPCC AR5 Synthesis Report: Climate Change (2014)."

"I found it downstairs in the library. Even though it's really old, it might be interesting. Maybe it can offer some insight into why people felt no urgency about global warming, right up until they were driven underground by it. Anyway, I thought it might be helpful."

"Thank you, Marya," replied Manny. "That's very thoughtful of you."

"Well, goodnight, then," she said, and turned to leave.

"Goodnight," he replied. He started to close the door when he noticed that she had dropped a handkerchief on the floor. It must have been underneath the book. He was about to call out to her, when he thought better of it.

*She could have given this book to me tomorrow,* thought Manny, *but she didn't. She came to my bedroom late at night and 'accidentally' dropped something, knowing that I will return it to her. Should I go down the hall and knock on her bedroom door? Or should I wait until tomorrow morning to return it to her?*

The more Manny thought about it, the more it seemed like each option had its pluses and minuses. And while that seemed intriguing, he didn't want to act first and think later. He thoughtfully laid the handkerchief on top of his night table and got into bed.

Manny felt drawn to Marya. Zach adored her, he could see that. She was smart, funny, easy-going, and she fit right in with

Julio and Anna. But she was his sister-in-law. What would Naz have thought about all of this?

Manny turned out the lights, but could not sleep. He was closing in on middle age in this era when people had a lifespan of about 60 years, but he was still strong and good-looking, a wealthy, eligible bachelor. He didn't want to spend the rest of his life as a single man.

*Zach deserves a mother*, he decided, *that much I know for sure.* He thought briefly of Odesa; she would have made a fine wife, but her parting words still made him cringe. *That ship has sailed,* he thought regretfully. *But I still need a woman, someone to talk to, someone to reach for in the night.*

Manny quailed at the thought of dating strangers, vetting one candidate after another on *MatchMakers* or some other app, always wondering if they were sincerely interested in him, or just interested in his wealth and position.

By morning, his mind was made up.

# Chapter 44.

**M**ANNY ROSE EARLY, dressed in his uniform and went downstairs to have breakfast. Marya, still in her pajamas, was sitting sleepy-eyed at the table with a cup of coffee in front of her, watching as Zach and Julie ate their breakfast before school.

"Good morning," he said to her, glad to find her alone except for the children. "I want to return this to you," he said quietly, handing her the handkerchief. "You dropped it when you handed me the book last night."

"Oh, thank you," she replied, her eyes carefully on the handkerchief.

"Are you busy tonight, Marya? Do you want to have dinner, just the two of us?" he asked shyly. "Afterwards, we could go for a walk and I could show you the Johnson house, where the wall is being rebuilt."

She blushed to the tips of her ears. "I'd like that, Manny," she replied. "Shall I meet you at the office, or here?"

"Why don't you come to the office around 6:30 or so, if that's OK. We can walk to the restaurant from there. It's on the way to Ms. Johnson's house," he replied.

Anna came into the kitchen, yawning. "Good morning, everybody," she said. She seemed to sense that she had interrupted something. She glanced once at Marya, one eyebrow arched delicately as she turned away to fill her coffee cup. There it was again, that non-verbal communication thing. He suspected that Marya and Anna had been talking about him. It made him feel warm inside, to be the topic of such speculation.

"Well. I'll see you all later then," Manny said, kissing Zach on the top of the head as he left for the office.

The day dragged along. Manny found himself looking at the clock far more often than he usually did, thinking about his plans for the evening. At 11:30 am, he walked down to Dave's office and asked him if he wanted to have lunch.

"It's a little early, don't you think?" asked Dave, laughing. "I just finished breakfast."

"No, I need to talk to you," Manny answered. "Besides, your boss won't mind if you take a long lunch."

They went to the local veggie gyro restaurant, ordering pita-stuffed sandwiches slathered with tzatziki, a delicious tangy yogurt sauce made with chopped orange cucumbers and fresh, fragrant purple dill.

"OK," Dave said as he swallowed a hearty mouthful, "what's on your mind?"

"I have a date tonight," Manny said. "The thing is, it's with my sister-in-law."

"Oh, man," groaned Dave. He put down his sandwich. "You need to tread very lightly with this, my friend. One way or another, she's still going to be your sister-in-law for the rest of your life. You're going to see her at family gatherings, on holidays. I'm just saying, you know, you can't mess this up, like date her for a while and then decide you don't want her. It would be awkward forever."

"I know, I've thought of that," Manny said. "I'll be casual, non-committal. I just want to get to know her better. She's always been this little kid, so much younger than me. But now she's twenty, and she lives in my house. She's a big help with the kids."

"Send her flowers, women like that," suggested Dave. "But don't make it too romantic, you know, keep it casual."

Manny did send Marya flowers, later that afternoon. He had Nigel pick out a beautiful arrangement to be sent to the house. Manny worked hard on the note, drafting several versions before finally settling on something which seemed to be appropriate, friendly but not romantic.

The note read, "Thank you for helping us take care of Zach and Julie!"

When Marya received the flowers, she opened the note and read it out loud to Anna. "Seriously?" she said. "He sent me flowers to thank me for being *a servant??*"

"Maybe he's afraid of scaring you by sounding too romantic on your first date," Anna replied. "I've known Manny since we were kids, and he never was a ladies' man, not like my Julio."

"Maybe," said Marya doubtfully, re-reading the card. "Now I don't know what to think."

At exactly 6:30 pm, Marya was shown into the Commissioner's office by Nigel. She was dressed nicely, but not in a suggestive or revealing way. As she had described it to Anna, she was dressed "as the family's au pair."

Manny took in her beige linen dress at a glance, the shirt front buttoned all the way up to her chin, the long, full skirt, her russet hair braided into a tightly twisted bun behind her head. He adjusted his expectations accordingly.

"Thank you for inviting me," said Marya, eyes wide as she looked around his office. It truly was a wonder, the biggest office she'd ever seen.

"You're going to like this restaurant," he said smoothly, picking up his jacket and opening the door for her. "It's not far from here. I've had lunch there many times, but never dinner." He respectfully stood far back as she passed through the door. She noticed that he seemed to want to keep his distance. Like Manny, she adjusted her expectations accordingly.

At the restaurant, they ordered by using the touchscreen on the table, and then sat back to wait for their beverages to arrive. There was a brief silence.

"I got the flowers," Marya said. "They are beautiful! Such a lovely arrangement. Thank you, Manny. It's so nice to be appreciated."

"I'm glad you like them," he said. "You know, it wasn't only -" he began, breaking off as the serverbot came closer with a tray containing two tall frosty glasses, one containing Marya's sweetened peashoot nectar and the other containing his beet and lime juice. The bot's arms were dipping alarmingly as it rolled alongside the table.

Manny reached over and quickly took both glasses off the tray, handing Marya her glass.

"Delicious!" she exclaimed. "I wasn't sure what to expect from peashoot nectar, but this is good." She sipped appreciatively.

Manny sipped his drink, too. Conversation came to a halt. Quickly, he reviewed the mental list of topics he had so carefully rehearsed earlier.

"So, Marya," he said, "how do you like being an engineering student?" *No, no! I sound like I'm talking to a child,* he groaned inwardly.

"It's wonderful. I love engineering, and I'm looking forward to getting my degree," she replied calmly. "It's a great career for a woman."

"That's great," he said. "Did you always want to be an engineer?" *Geez, can't you do better than that?* he admonished himself. He reminded himself that he needed to listen to her answers. Beneath the table, he wiped his damp hands against his pants.

" – and that's why I decided to go into engineering," she finished. He nodded, scrambling to think of another topic for conversation. He reached for his glass, perspiration making the glass slide treacherously as he picked it up.

"Did you always know you wanted to be a cop?" she asked, surprising him. She seemed sincerely interested. Manny explained briefly about his father, who had been the Chief of Police for years, and how Manny had chosen to go to the Academy after his last year of high school.

He stopped, taking another sip of his beet juice. *Don't monopolize the conversation,* he thought. *Ask her another question.*

"And then what, Manny? How did you go from recent graduate to Lieutenant to being the Commissioner?" she asked. He noted that she seemed quite relaxed, much more poised and mature than he had expected. She was looking directly at him, calmly waiting for him to explain. Manny began to relate the timeline of his career, forgetting his self-consciousness as he explained how he had become Commissioner in such a short amount of time.

The main dishes arrived, fish sautéed with leeks and fakon (bacon made from tofu, "fake bacon"). "This is real fish, Manny? Actual, you know, with fins and tails?" Marya asked.

"That's right, from the new fish farm," Manny replied. The newest facility had opened only recently, and so far was making a larger profit from curious people taking tours of the facility than from actual customers buying fish.

They both regarded their plates with curiosity. "Looks good," he said. She nodded, taking a cautious nibble.

"It's delicious!" she said, taking a bigger mouthful.

"What else do you like to do besides engineering?" asked Manny. *Idiot,* he savaged himself, *it's not a job interview!* He swallowed hard.

"Well, there's the computer," she replied. "I've always been interested in computer programming, things like that."

"Right, I remember how you helped with the choreography at the wedding." Manny broke off, flustered. It was a mistake to bring up the wedding. It was true that Marya had helped Naztazya and Anna work on the choreography for the two high-functioning androids who had danced at their wedding reception, much to the enjoyment of their guests. But Manny had promised himself he would not talk about Naztazya.

"I can't believe she's gone, that she died a year ago," Marya said. "You must miss her terribly."

"I do," Manny acknowledged stiffly. "You have no idea." And then suddenly he was talking, pouring out his heart to his dead wife's sister, who had stopped eating and was listening to him as if no one else in the world existed. "It was like half of me died with her," he finished.

At some point while he was talking, Marya had extended her hand part-way across the table, reaching towards him. In this age when touching was forbidden between two people who were not related, it was the equivalent of placing her hand on his arm as a kind gesture of support.

Manny looked at her hand for a moment, then up at her face. Her eyes, bright with unshed tears, were very beautiful, almond-shaped and olive green, flecked with tiny bits of gold.

"You miss her too, I know," he said. He placed his hand next to hers on the table, not quite touching her. He could feel the warmth of her fingers, so close to his. Neither of them moved.

"Marya," he said, his voice sounding strange to his own ears, "are you seeing anyone?"

"No, Manny," she replied, "I was dating someone last winter, but that didn't work out."

"No?" he asked. "What happened, if you don't mind my asking?"

"He was very immature," she replied, "a year younger than me, and besides, he doesn't want children. Two good reasons to end it."

"And do you?" Manny asked lightly. "Want children, I mean?"

"Yes," she replied, reddening slightly, but holding his gaze. "I'd like at least three." He laughed. "Or maybe four or five," she teased, seeing his reaction. "After all, I'm one of five."

She regarded him with a level gaze. "And what about you? Are you and Ms. Parker no longer seeing each other?"

"No, she ran away when she saw I had a drinking problem," he said. "That's done, I'm finished drinking." Marya nodded; as part of the family, she knew all about the drinking.

When dinner was over, they left the restaurant and began to walk over to Aviva Johnson's house. "I think you'll find this interesting," Manny said. "There was a leak here for months. The engineers had to rip open the back wall."

Manny unlocked the door using Hasan's temporary passcode, walking into the empty, modest row-house. Construction debris still covered the floor, and tools left by the workmen were scattered everywhere. "They'll be finishing up in a day or two. Here, this is where the water was coming from."

Manny showed her around. In one large area, the wall was still open right down to the foundation. She walked around the perimeter of the modest room, examining the walls. "It looks nice and dry, Manny," she said. "I don't see any wet spots anywhere."

He waited until her back was turned, then quickly reached around behind his neck to loosen the black ribbon holding his ponytail in place.

The two of them lingered, chatting, until finally, Manny joked, "It's late. We'd better get started on our way home, or someone is likely to call the police."

As they left through the front door, Manny ran his hands through his hair. "Oh, I lost my hair ribbon," he said. "Wait here a moment, will you? I think I know where I dropped it."

Before she could respond, he went back into the house, making sure the door clicked shut behind him. Walking over to the spot where the wall was still open, he paused.

Reaching inside his jacket pocket, he retrieved the two diamond rings which he had rescued earlier from their tofu hiding place. He held them in his hand for a moment, knowing that if found, they could derail his career. Then he dropped them down into the rubble at the bottom of the opening. Reaching over the edge, he pushed them out of sight, covering them with crushed concrete and other debris. The next day, the workmen would be filling in the rest of the space, and the rings would be gone forever.

Manny breathed a sigh of relief. *No one ever needs to know that I found them,* he thought.

Picking up the hair ribbon from the floor, he hurried back to where Marya was waiting. "Found it!" he said, holding up the ribbon.

It was late, and the streets were mostly empty. A few lights were on here and there in the houses as they passed by, but overall, it was quiet and peaceful. A drone appeared at the end of the street, searching this way and that, then flying directly towards them.

"And here they come," Manny said softly. Marya looked up curiously. The drone was owned by one of the news outlets; it had a distinctive color code on the underside which enabled it to be identified from beneath. Manny waved, and the drone dipped one wing.

"We'll be all over the gossip columns tomorrow," he said ruefully. "Do you mind?"

"No, Manny, I don't think I do," she replied, reaching over and linking her arm through his. She smiled, looking up at him with eyes filled with promise, and he felt his heart expand.

# Chapter 45.

**D** ID YOU HAVE a good time?" asked Anna, closing the bedroom door behind her. Marya stood in the middle of the room, head back and arms outstretched as she twirled in a circle, her full skirt swirling around her legs.

"Oh, yes," she cried, "it was wonderful! We talked and talked ... he's really nice, Anna!"

"Marya, I have to tell you. You and Manny were all over the news tonight. Not just on *Enquiring Minds*, either," Anna said. "You were on other shows, too."

"I know that, Anna, we saw the drone," Marya replied. "It was waiting for us."

"And still you walked arm-in-arm with him?" Anna said, eyebrows raised. "Whatever were you thinking, Marya, out in public behaving like that?"

"I don't care what people think, Anna, you know that," Marya responded.

"Well, you'd better start caring!" Anna scolded, sounding very much like the married elder sister. "Think of what you're doing, Marya! People will talk, and soon no one else will ask you out, thinking that you and Manny are romantically involved."

"And what's wrong with that?" countered Marya defiantly. "Maybe we are romantically involved! Or maybe we will be."

"Think carefully, young lady," Anna admonished. "Your future depends on it."

"You are so old-fashioned, Anna!" scoffed Marya. "You sound like Mom! We are related, you know, he's my brother-in-law. Technically, it's not wrong for me to lean on his arm."

"Yes, but any idiot could see that you didn't require assistance; you were so obviously out walking together," Anna responded. "If you won't listen to me, then maybe you'll listen to Mom."

"Mom? She hologrammed you?" Marya said, the smile fading from her face.

"Yes, twice. She saw the coverage too, along with everyone else. She's beside herself!" Anna said grimly. "I told her I'd have you hologram her as soon as you came in."

Downstairs in the front parlor, Julio and Manny were having a similar conversation.

"So, did you two have a good time?" asked Julio cautiously.

"Very nice," said Manny, with a smile. "She's a nice girl."

"You know that you're all over the news tonight, right?" continued Julio.

"Yeah, I figured that would happen," replied Manny easily. "You know how the gossip columns love to follow me."

"But, Manny," continued Julio, "everybody can see the two of you, out together. You know, walking together." He struggled to find the right words. Anna had been adamant; she insisted that he talk to Manny about this.

Julio tried again. "Marya is twenty years old. If people think -" He stopped, at a loss for words, then blurted out, "Anna is afraid that no one else will ask her out."

"I hear you, bro," Manny replied. "This is complicated. But I really like her."

~ ~ ~ ~ ~ ~

"Morning, Manny," said Marya, looking up from her coffee as Manny walked into the kitchen. She smiled at him, handing him a plate of frybread decorated generously with sprinkles.

"What's this?" he asked, looking down at the plate.

"Frybread. Zach and I made it this morning." She yawned. "The kids were up early today."

He took a bite; it was greasy, heavy and too sweet. "Mmm, delicious!" he said, reaching over to tousle Zach's hair. "Thank you, both of you."

"Want to go for a run later, Marya? After work?" Manny asked.

"Are you sure you're up for it?" she asked teasingly. "I just might beat you, you know."

"Hah, you can try," Manny replied. "I've been running for years."

"We'll see about that," she replied, a glint in her eye.

Manny came home from work early that night, after a tedious day of meetings at the Mayor's office. As he opened the front door, he was surprised to see Marya standing on a footstool in the kitchen, dressed in heels and a formal evening gown.

"If you're planning on running in that, then I'll definitely beat you," Manny said, unabashedly looking her up and down.

"I didn't think you'd be home so early," Marya said. "I've got a wedding to go to next week, and I'm trying on different shoes with my dress to make sure it's not too long."

"Here, try it again," said Anna, who had been kneeling on the floor behind Marya. She let go of the dress and stood up. "Take a few steps and see if your shoes catch in the hem."

Marya obligingly walked into the foyer. Manny stood watching her, mesmerized. She was wearing a floor-length blue chiffon dress, in the style which was so popular that year, called Guinevere. The floor-length skirt was full, with many overlapping layers of different shades of blue, and was shaped into a short train at the back, designed to lie on the floor. The rest of the design was slender with a modest scoop neckline and little cap sleeves. When she turned and walked back into the kitchen, Manny was startled to see that the back of the dress was completely bare from the shoulders to an inch or so below her waist.

Manny suddenly realized that he was grinning, and carefully rearranged his face into a more respectful expression.

"What do you think, Manny?" Marya asked, over her shoulder.

"It looks fine," he said, his face reddening. "You look fine." *For goodness sake! That's the best I can do?* "Very nice. I'm going to go upstairs now and change for our run. Let me know whenever you're ready to go."

As he left the room, Anna looked questioningly at her younger sister, one eyebrow delicately arching upwards. "Excellent timing," she said. Marya laughed.

As it turned out, Marya was a good running partner. She and Manny kept up a steady pace, running side by side, talking from time to time. Manny took her on his favorite route, planning to turn around at the half-way point, where he would ask her if she wanted to stop and rest.

As they approached the spot, Marya turned to him and asked, "Are you warmed up yet? Can we pick up the pace a bit?" And she was off, running like the wind, looking for him over her shoulder.

Manny sprinted towards her, but was not able to catch her. The past year had not been kind to Manny, and he was out of shape. Winded, he stopped, hands on his knees, bent over, breathing hard. Marya circled back.

"OK, Manny?" she asked, concerned. He nodded, breathing too hard to speak. "Shall we stop to rest?" she asked. He tried to laugh, but was too winded, so he just shook his head. A minute later, they were off again, this time running more slowly, side by side.

He liked that she was competitive; it made him run faster. But there was no question that she was fast, maybe even faster than he was when he was in his best shape. As they came closer to home, she said, "I'll race you to the door, Manny!" and she was off, running like the wind, dark red ponytail swinging from side to side, the pink soles of her running shoes pounding out a steady staccato in the gathering twilight. He plodded heavily up the front walk, grateful to be home.

Soon they were running regularly before dinner, a few times each week. Manny made it a point to leave the office at 5:30 pm. It gave him more time with Zach, too, to be home at dinnertime.

One evening about a month after their first date, Manny was in his study, working on some reports, when he heard the doorbell ring. Anna answered it. A man's voice inquired politely, "Is Ms. Owrzinskaya at home?"

"Marya! You have a visitor!" Anna called up the stairs. A moment later Marya, dressed in a tightly-fitted, very short pink mini dress and scarlet high heels, came into the foyer.

"Come in," she said to her visitor, "have a seat in the front parlor. I'll just be a minute."

Curious, Manny left his desk in the study and casually strolled into the kitchen for a glass of water, looking into the front parlor as he did so. There was a young man sitting bolt upright on the edge of the sofa, looking quite nervous. He seemed to be about 18 or 19 years of age, and was surreptitiously wiping the corners of his mouth on his hand as Manny walked by.

As soon as he saw Manny, the young man sprang to attention. "Sir!" he exclaimed. Manny automatically responded with a nod and a murmured, "At ease." *So,* he thought to himself, *he's a police officer. No, probably a cadet.*

"What brings you here today?" asked Manny in a neutral voice, and the young man's face turned white. "Is there something I can help you with?"

"I'm here to see Ms. Owrzinskaya," he replied, his Adam's apple bobbing up and down. He looked very young to Manny, younger with each passing minute.

Manny looked at him quizzically, but said nothing. He knew that most people find silence unsettling, and will feel a need to talk. He waited.

"We're going to the park, and then out for dinner," the young man blurted almost apologetically. "She said it would be OK."

"Of course it's OK!" exclaimed Marya brightly, coming into the front parlor. "Why wouldn't it be?" She smiled at the young man, showing all of her even white teeth. "Come on, Daniel, let's go," she said, nodding briefly to Manny. Then they were gone, Daniel following too close behind her.

"Who's that?" Manny asked Julio, who had come into the foyer.

"That's the guy she used to go out with last year," he replied. "They broke up a while ago."

"So what's he doing here now?" asked Manny. "She's dating him again?"

"I don't know, man, maybe you should ask Anna," Julio said uneasily. "She usually knows what Marya's up to."

Manny sauntered casually into the kitchen. "Anna, why was Daniel here?" he asked. Lucinda was at the stove bent over the Dutch oven, putting the finishing touches on their meal, while Anna set the table.

"I'm not sure, Manny. Maybe you should ask Marya," Anna responded. She looked at him pointedly. "It's not like the two of you are engaged, you know. She can go out with whomever she pleases."

"But, Anna. We've been getting along so well! I thought we had an understanding," Manny said helplessly.

"For two people to have an understanding, they need to discuss things. Out loud," said Lucinda, stirring the pot. "Not just assume that they are in agreement."

Manny sat down at the table, looking down at his plate. Where had they gone, that boy and Marya in her tight little mini dress? What were they doing? Were they talking, laughing, having a good time? He didn't like it, not at all.

"Manny," Lucinda said softly. She put down her wooden spoon, turning to face him. "What's stopping you from asking her to marry you?" she asked bluntly.

"Really, there's just this one thing," he said hesitantly. Both women came to sit down at the table with him. "I can't bring myself to gather up all of Naztazya's belongings and get rid of them. Her clothes are still in her closet and in her dresser." He sighed. "It seems like maybe I should be able to do that, before I ask her to be my wife."

Lucinda and Anna exchange a long look. "Why not let us take care of that for you, Manny?" Lucinda asked kindly. "We can gather up all of Naz's clothes and donate them to charity. You know that Naz would not have wanted this to stand in your way."

"OK," he agreed, relieved. He looked up, his eyes bright. "Thank you both."

# Chapter 46.

**T**RUE TO THEIR word, when Manny came home from work the following evening, Lucinda and Anna had cleaned out Naztazya's closet and dresser. A collection of bulging linen bags and covered baskets were lined up in the foyer, discreetly pushed to one side, waiting for pickup the following morning by Redux the Tux, a company specializing in high-quality second-hand clothing.

After dinner, Manny went outside to where Julio was playing catch with Zach and Julie on the front lawn.

"Julio!" Manny called to him. "Can I interrupt? I need to talk to you about something."

The two men went into the upstairs sitting room, a small room shared by the two children's bedrooms, closing the door behind them. "What's up?" asked Julio.

"I've decided I want to marry Marya," Manny said, perspiring as he said the words out loud.

Julio broke into a huge grin. "Congratulations, man!" he said heartily. "We knew you'd eventually come around!"

"You'll be my best man, right?" Manny asked.

"Of course I will," said Julio. The two brothers paused for a moment, both of them remembering the night so many years ago, when Manny had asked Julio to be his best man for his first wedding. "I'm glad you're moving forward. Naz would have approved, I'm sure."

Manny opened up his jacket pocket and pulled out a small brown leather pouch which had Marya's initials embossed on the front. "See what you think," he said, handing it to Julio.

Julio opened the pouch and shook the contents into his palm. A beautiful engagement ring winked back at him, a heavy gold band set with four little diamonds on each side of a simply enormous ruby. "Wow!" he said. "That's gorgeous! She'll love it, Manny. Have you actually proposed yet?"

"Not yet, no," said Manny. "I've got to find the right time. I want to do a bridenapping, you know, to make the day more special for her."

"Well, if you're going to do a proper bridenapping, you should get engaged first. It's better that way," advised his brother.

Because a second marriage was traditionally a small, quiet affair, the bride would not have the opportunity to walk down the aisle in a beautiful long wedding gown, to the admiration of her friends and relatives. For second marriages, bridenappings were a fun way to make the occasion more special and festive for the bride. It had become a thriving niche industry.

The idea for bridenapping came from the widespread European custom centuries earlier, in which the bride was simply kidnapped. Usually, the bride was willing, although her family was not; she likely would have known that she was about to be abducted. But in these modern times, the couple was almost always engaged before the bridenapping occurred.

A group of the couples' friends would arrive unannounced at the young woman's home to "abduct" her, whisking her away to City Hall or a wedding chapel. Bystanders often called out best wishes as the bride and her "captors" passed by on their way, lending a jovial holiday atmosphere to the procession.

"Are you going to use one of the bridenapping companies?" asked Julio. BrideDuctions Ltd. and BrideNappers, LLC were the two most popular companies in the Colony, although there were plenty of smaller start-ups, too.

"No, I've got some ideas of my own," replied Manny. "I've been giving this some serious thought."

The following morning, Manny had Nigel send flowers to Marya with a card which read, "Dinner tonight?"

At lunchtime, he received a text from Marya that said simply, "Sorry, can't make it. Another time! The flowers are lovely, thank you."

Manny got up and paced around his office, breathing deeply to calm himself. Why couldn't she make it? What if she was seeing that boy again, what was his name?

Suddenly inspired, Manny returned to his desk and opened up his padlet, searching the Police Academy website, looking for photos of current cadets.

It took him less than twenty minutes to find young Daniel, and even less time to process the order that would award him an internship at a precinct in the Bronx. The internship was an excellent opportunity for career advancement after graduation. However, it began immediately, and Daniel would have to relocate to the north end of the Bronx, so far from midtown Manhattan where Marya lived. Manny chuckled to himself. *I have a feeling my old man would have approved,* he thought. Patrick Stewart had never been shy about wielding his influence.

Manny got home even earlier than usual that night, but Marya had already gone out. He waited for her to come home, but she was still out at midnight, when he finally gave up and went to bed.

The following evening, after dinner had been eaten and the dishes had been cleared, Marya rose to help Lucinda with the dishes. "I've got this, Lucinda," Manny said, "Marya and I can clean up. Why don't you go sit down?"

"Thank you, Manny," Lucinda said, giving him an encouraging smile as she left them alone in the kitchen.

"Marya," he began, "I've been meaning to talk to you about something." His hand went to his jacket pocket, where the ring was waiting.

"Manny, did you arrange to have Daniel transferred?" she asked bluntly, turning to face him.

"He wasn't exactly transferred, Marya," Manny explained. "I arranged to have him placed in an internship at a precinct in the Bronx. It's an excellent opportunity, one that is awarded only to the most qualified cadets."

"You arranged for him to be a coffee boy at a precinct as far from midtown as possible," she said, eyes flashing angrily.

"Marya, do you care for him?" he asked simply.

His sincerity caught her off guard. She exhaled in a rush, her eyes searching his face. "No, not really. Not in the way you mean, Manny."

"Then marry me," he blurted out.

She froze quite still, standing near the kitchen sink. "Marry you?" she echoed, as if she had not heard him correctly.

"Marya, the thought of that boy with his hands ... not that I thought he did," he added hastily, seeing her face. "It's just that it made me realize how much I want you. I mean, care for you. Marya, the thought of losing you," he spluttered, as his carefully rehearsed speech dissolved into thin air.

"Manny," she breathed, "he means nothing to me!" Her smile warmed his heart. "I would be happy to be your wife!"

Manny reached out and took her hand, very gently. "There's one more thing," he said, taking out the little brown leather pouch. "This is for you. I hope you like it." He took the ring out of the pouch, and slid it onto her finger.

"It's so beautiful!" she exclaimed, admiring her hand from every possible angle. She twined her fingers through his. "Thank you, Manny! Let's go tell the others!"

Manny and Marya walked into the front parlor, where Luis, Lucinda and the children were playing a game. Lucinda was the first to notice them, standing shyly in the doorway, hands clasped. She stood up, a huge smile on her face, and hugged them both.

Julio came into the room, grinning. He clapped Manny on the shoulder. "Congratulations!" he said. Luis gave Manny a huge hug.

"And now, young lady," said Lucinda, pretending to be stern, "you are coming home to our house tonight!"

"What? Why?" asked Marya, puzzled.

"I've already promised your mother," explained Lucinda. "Now that the two of you are officially a couple, you can't sleep under Manny's roof until you are married. No arguments, please!"

Julio looked at Manny, who laughed. "Maybe a short engagement is in order," he said.

~ ~ ~ ~ ~ ~

One morning a few weeks later, Anna was home alone in her office working; Marya was out shopping. Anna heard the front door open, and was surprised to hear voices in her foyer. "Who's there?" she called out.

"Are you Ms. Owrzinskaya?" asked Naomi, one of the detectives who worked with Manny and Dave Wu.

"Who are you?" demanded Anna, eyeing the police officer in formal dress uniform standing in her foyer. "How did you get in here?!"

"I need you to come with us, ma'am," replied Naomi. Several other officers had also come into the foyer, all of them in dress uniform. "Put your hands behind your back, please." She pulled a pair of handcuffs from her belt.

"What is this about, Officer?" asked Anna warily. "I'm not going anywhere with you until I know why!" She backed away from Naomi, who with practiced ease was suddenly behind her, firmly grasping her arms.

"Stop this at once! I need to speak to my brother-in-law, the Commissioner!" exclaimed Anna loudly, struggling to get free.

The door opened in the foyer, and Marya, dressed in shorts and a teeshirt, came into the house.

"What's going on?" Marya asked Anna. She dropped her packages onto the floor.

"Call Manny! I'm being arrested!" exclaimed Anna, struggling to get out of the handcuffs.

Naomi turned Anna around to face her. "No one's being arrested," she said gently. "Today is your wedding day. The Commissioner wants especially for you not to be afraid. Here, let us take you to him."

Anna sat down abruptly on the bottom step of the stairs. "No, no, it's not me you want, it's my sister!" she laughed, recovering her composure. She pointed her chin towards Marya. "I'm Anna, Julio's wife. Marya's engaged to the Commissioner, not me."

Naomi gasped, looking from one woman to the other. She quickly removed the handcuffs from Anna's hands. "I apologize for my error," she said, bowing formally. Then she turned towards Marya, who was watching her with utter astonishment.

"It's OK, Marya," said Anna. She stood up and put her arm around Marya's shoulders. "You're being bridenapped! How exciting! Today is your wedding day!"

"I can't get married like this!" she cried, aghast. "My hair! What will I wear?"

"Don't worry," Naomi answered reassuringly. "Everything is there waiting for you, Miss, makeup artist, hair stylist. You have three dresses to choose from. Better bring shoes, though, a pair with heels."

"Three dresses?" repeated Marya, baffled. "But how?"

"They're from Kleinfeld Brooklyn Bridal. The Commissioner took care of everything," said Naomi. "When we get there, you can choose the one you'd like to wear."

"No handcuffs," Marya said firmly to Naomi.

"As you wish, Miss," Naomi replied.

Outside the house, the police officers quickly arranged themselves in phalanx formation around Marya and Anna. A small crowd of onlookers had formed in front of the mansion, curious to see what the police were doing there. A drone was hovering overhead; someone had already alerted the media.

One of the officers handed a large bouquet of flowers to Marya. "Look, Anna, they're bluebells," exclaimed Marya, sniffing them appreciatively. "My favorite color!"

A ripple of excitement went through the crowd, which continued to grow. Bits and pieces of conversation among onlookers were audible as the group began to walk towards City Hall.

"Bridenapping!" said a stout, gray-haired matron who lived across the street, clasping her hands in front of her chest as she remembered her own bridenapping, so many years ago.

"Isn't that the Commissioner's fiancé?" said another.

"Yes, and that's her sister, the one married to the Commissioner's brother," replied another neighbor.

Someone began to sing the traditional bridenapping song, and others soon joined in, clapping and cheering as they followed along behind the procession:

Happy, happy wedding day, happy, happy day!
Run and tell the bridegroom, his bride is on her way!
Pave her way with flowers, line the streets to say,
May you always be as happy as you are today!

There were other verses, made up on the spot, some of them remarkably bawdy. By the time the procession arrived at City Hall, no less than three drones were live-streaming the event on social media. A large crowd was trailing behind the bridenappers, singing and cheering, clapping in time to the song, all jockeying for position to get a better look at the Commissioner's bride on her wedding day.

On the steps of City Hall, the concierge came down the steps to greet them. "Ladies, if you will come with me, please," he said, taking them to the rooms that had been set aside for the bride.

An hour later, Marya emerged from the dressing room with her russet hair elaborately braided, secured by an antique diamond hairclip, a wedding gift from Manny. She was wearing a fitted pastel blue crepe-de-chine silk gown with a modest neckline and sheer lace long sleeves, and with a billowing full skirt that was dramatically longer in back. Manny was resplendent in full dress uniform, with white gloves and hat.

The wedding ceremony itself was brief, a civil ceremony with the Mayor officiating. Manny stood next to Julio; Marya stood next to Anna. There was no sermon and few guests, but as Manny described it later, "It was just perfect." Marya agreed.

Soon they were back at the house. When Marya opened the door, she exclaimed, "Who are all of these people?"

There were at least six caterers dressed in white uniforms in the kitchen, all bustling about as they prepared the wedding breakfast for the family. The florist had filled the house with bluebells. Upstairs, there were strange sounds of hammers banging and furniture being moved, and the voices of many workmen.

"They're HERE!" exclaimed a voice from upstairs, and all of the noise abruptly stopped. No less than ten burly workmen came rushing down the stairs, bustling out the door. In the kitchen, the caterers quickly finished setting the table. One woman sang out, "Congratulations, Madam!" to Marya as she left the house.

Manny closed the door. A hushed silence filled the house. "Welcome home, Mrs. Stewart," he said softly, putting his arms around his wife.

"Mrs. Stewart," she repeated softly. "I think I like the sound of that."

"Let's go upstairs. There's something I want to show you," Manny said. Holding hands, the two of them went up to the master bedroom.

# Chapter 47.

**W**HAT ON EARTH??" asked Marya, looking around the master bedroom. The velvet chair and the bed had been moved across the room to a new spot in front of the window; the Vertical dresser had been moved closer to the closet; and the carpet had been removed. She noted with secret relief that her walk-in closet was completely empty.

"I wanted to make this room ours, only ours," explained Manny. "I had the furniture moved around, and I bought us a new mattress. If you want, you can pick out new carpet and wallpaper, whatever you want. New furniture, too, if you'd like. I want you to love it."

"Oh, Manny, it's wonderful," she breathed. "Thank you! That was very considerate of you." She looked around again. "You know, I think I'd like to redecorate. It would be fun."

Manny reached for his bride, pulling her close. She rested her head against his shoulder for a moment. "Here we are all alone," she mused with a mischievous chuckle. "How about that."

He laughed. "Everyone will be here soon for the wedding breakfast, though, no telling when they might walk in. But we could change our clothes, if you want. I mean, if you'd be more comfortable for the rest of the day."

"This dress is so beautiful, I don't want to take it off," she sighed. "The dresses you chose were all so lovely! How did you do it?"

"I borrowed one of your dresses. Then I took photos with me when I met with the stylist; she helped me pick them out," he replied. "You can wear the dress again to the party, if you want."

"Party? We're having a party?" she asked. A large party was often held the day after a second wedding, for framily who did not attend the wedding.

"Oh, yes," said Manny, chuckling. "I've invited about a hundred of our closest friends here, tomorrow night."

There was a pause. The silence in the room folded itself around them, filled with intriguing possibilities.

"Well, I'm going to change," said Manny, unbuttoning his uniform jacket. "I think the bride and groom should get to wear whatever they want to their wedding breakfast."

Marya kicked off her shoes and reached around to unbutton the back of her silk dress. "Oh, these old-fashioned little buttons!" she exclaimed. "I don't think I can unbutton them by myself."

"How did you button them?" asked Manny, mesmerized, watching his new bride hop around from one foot to the other as she tried unsuccessfully to unbutton the back of her dress.

"Anna helped me," she explained. "She had this little hook-thing called a button hook."

"Here, let me see if I can do it," offered Manny, standing behind her. He carefully grasped the tiny top button.

"There aren't any buttonholes," he said, puzzled. "Each button has a little loop around it. They're really stuck in there! I think you may have to wear this dress for the rest of your life, Marya."

She looked at him, bemused. "I can wait for Anna to help me, Manny," she said thoughtfully, "but we're never going to hear the end of it, how the two of us were all alone here, and I couldn't figure out how to get out of my wedding dress."

"How about pulling it up over your head?" suggested Manny. She reached down and pulled the skirt upwards, slowly wiggling out of it as Manny watched, trying hard not to laugh.

"It's really tight," said Marya's muffled voice. She bent over, pulling carefully as the dress slowly inched upwards over her waist. "Oh no, Manny – I'm stuck!"

"Stuck?!" he exclaimed. He put his arms around her, looking down, enjoying the view of her bare legs. The two of them collapsed onto the bed amidst gales of laughter.

"Hold on a second," he said, "I have an idea."

A moment later, Manny had retrieved a pair of scissors from his dresser. He carefully snipped the top button loop, which popped open. He continued carefully cutting one button loop

311

after another, until Marya could inhale deeply. "That's so much better!" she exclaimed, laughing. "But what about my beautiful dress?"

"We'll send it back to be repaired," Manny replied. "Can you manage now, or should I cut the rest of them?"

Marya wriggled and pulled, and the dress came off with a whoosh, up over her head in a waterfall of blue silk. Manny, kneeling next to the bed, took the dress from her hands and unceremoniously dropped it to the floor, never taking his eyes from his bride.

"You are so beautiful," he murmured, kissing her bare shoulder. Her perfume was lovely and subtle, and her hair smelled of hibiscus shampoo. She put her arms around his neck, pulling him closer.

Downstairs, the front door opened, then banged shut. "Manny?" called Julio from downstairs. He cleared his throat noisily. "Manny? Marya?" He went into the kitchen, ostensibly to look for them, walking into a chair, turning on the water in the sink, making as much noise as possible.

Manny gently kissed his bride on the lips. "Sounds like they're here," he murmured to her, getting up and straightening his clothes. "I'll go downstairs. You take your time and get dressed." He smiled at her. Her answering smile lit up the room.

The family looked up expectantly as Manny came into the kitchen.

"Marya will be right down," he said, tousling Zach's hair as he walked past him. He slid into his seat at the head of the table. "The food looks wonderful," he exclaimed, helping himself to a heart-shaped chocolate croissant.

All eyes turned towards the entrance to the room as Marya, dressed in her usual jogging pants and teeshirt, walked into the kitchen. Like a jack-in-the-box, Anna popped up from the table and grabbed Marya's arm, steering her back out into the foyer. Manny could see Marya, leaning close to her sister and whispering something in her ear. Suddenly Anna gasped, her hand flying to her mouth; then the two women burst into gales of laughter. Julio, eyebrows raised, looked at Manny, who shrugged.

"You'll hear all about it later, I'm sure," he commented drily. Lucinda looked at her two sons, smiling placidly to herself.

Anna and Marya took their seats, faces flushed from laughing. Luis looked quizzically at Lucinda, who winked at him and then turned to face the others.

"Have some of these rolls, Julie," said Lucinda, passing the bread to the other end of the table.

"So, Manny," began Luis, filling his plate with smoked fish, a new delicacy from the fish farm. "How are things going at work? Anything new with the Council?"

"Luis, maybe Manny would like to enjoy his wedding breakfast and not talk about work," Lucinda suggested.

"Am I supposed to call you Mommy?" asked Zach, looking across the table at Marya. Conversation ceased.

"If you'd like to, Zach," she replied, glancing at Manny. "Or, you can call me Auntie Marya. Maybe try calling me Mommy, and see how you like it."

"OK," said Zach, suddenly shy. Everyone was looking at him. He looked down at his plate.

"It's OK, Zach," said Julie, sitting next to him. "Here, have some of these. They explode."

"They *what*?" he asked, his attention diverted to the plate filled with round golden berries with tiny green and blue striped leaves.

"It's true," Anna said, laughing. "They are exploding kwartinaberries, so everyone please keep your mouths closed when you chew!"

~ ~ ~ ~ ~ ~

Manny closed the bedroom door behind him and paused, his back to the door. Although it was not yet 5:00 pm, Marya had drawn the curtains and the room was in semi-darkness.

She stood near the bed wearing a pearl gray silk negligee with a matching robe. She had taken down her dark red hair,

313

which was rippling over her shoulders and down her back. In the darkness, her green eyes gleamed like emeralds. He crossed the room and took her in his arms.

"Mrs. Stewart," he said, kissing her on the forehead. "I love you, Marya."

He tilted her chin up with one finger and kissed her gently on the lips. Then he kissed her more hungrily, drawing her close to him, hands on her shoulders.

"Manny," she said, pulling back a bit, "there's something I want to talk to you about."

Uneasy thoughts blossomed unbidden. He could think of few issues that a bride might need to discuss on her wedding night, none of them good. Did it have to do with that boy, Daniel, the one she had dated?

"I'm listening," he replied warily.

"Anna talked to me, you know, about tonight," she began, struggling to control a slight quaver in her voice. "She told me what to expect. But she said something that I didn't understand. And when I asked her to explain it, she said to ask you."

Breathing a secret sigh of relief, Manny replied, "What was it that you didn't understand?"

"Promise me that you won't laugh at me," she said, twisting the fabric of her robe around her fingers.

"Sweetheart, I promise, I won't laugh," he said solemnly.

Marya took a deep breath. "Is it true that people ... that there's more than one way to do it?" she asked. "Or was Anna just playing a joke on me, because I'm a virgin?"

Manny struggled not to laugh. "Actually, Anna's right," he replied straight-faced. "I can confirm that there are different ways. We'll start off with the easiest. That will be best for the first time."

Her eyes widened. "But Manny," she said, looking closely at him to see if he was teasing her, "how do you know which way to do it?"

Manny smiled reassuringly at his bride. She looked so young and vulnerable, although Manny had been even younger on his first wedding night. He sat down on the bed, patting the spot next to him. "Why don't you come over here and sit down," he said, "and we can talk about this."

~ ~ ~ ~ ~ ~

The house was filled with the sound of music, from the group of violinists seated in the library. The butler was stationed at the front door; maids in uniform were passing trays of hors d'oeuvres among the guests, who were arriving in a steady stream. Most of those invited were Manny's colleagues from the police department, as well as the Colony's most prominent politicians. The Mayor had arrived and was seated as a guest of honor in the front parlor. Friends of the bride and various relatives were clustered in small groups around the house.

The staircase was decorated with so many blue flowers that the long curved wooden railing was all but invisible. To honor the bride, vases all over the house were filled with bluebells.

"It was a nice touch, having the party here at the house," said Julio to Manny, as the two of them stood in the foyer greeting guests.

"I thought so, too. If I need to take a break, I know where to find an empty room," explained Manny with a grin.

"Are you OK with people drinking champagne around you?" asked Julio with concern.

"It's OK," said Manny. "I don't really like being around liquor any more, but it's a special occasion and I want to do it right. Besides, it's Marya's party, too."

The two men glanced up at the top of the staircase. Anna and Marya had yet to emerge from Anna's bedroom, where they had been closeted for some time, getting dressed and arranging each other's hair.

The door opened, and the butler intoned, "Mr. and Mrs. Suarez, Senior." Julio's eyebrows rose at the unaccustomed formality, as he moved to greet his parents.

"Manny, the place looks wonderful," said Lucinda approvingly, eyeing the flowers on the stairs. "Where are Marya and Anna?"

A stir in the crowd of guests around them caused everyone to stop and turn their eyes towards the staircase, as Marya and Anna came slowly down the stairs, arm in arm. The sisters were dressed in beautiful evening gowns, their hair swept up and pinned into elaborately plaited buns, decorated with tiny blue flowers. Marya's diamond hair clip twinkled in her russet hair. As they moved down the staircase, the guests burst into spontaneous applause.

Manny put his arm around his bride's shoulder and kissed her, to the great approval of the guests. Someone proposed a toast, the maids scrambling to make sure everyone had a glass of champagne. Manny's glass was filled with delicious passion fruit punch, a nice touch by the caterer. By now, everyone knew that the new Commissioner did not drink, and frowned upon over-indulgence in alcohol.

"Manny, let's go into the study," suggested Luis after the toast. "There is something I want to discuss with you."

The noise from the party faded as the two settled into the brown leather chairs. "What's on your mind?" asked Manny, putting his feet up on the ottoman.

"Now that you're Commissioner, can you push the Council to allow trade with Philadelphia?" asked Luis.

"Luis, I can't force them to do anything; they're elected officials. No, it's too soon to bring it up," Manny said, shaking his head. "I have enemies who are just waiting for me to make a mistake. How would it look if in the first year of my administration, I propose a major change in our laws that will benefit me personally?"

Luis paused. Legal trade with Philadelphia had been his dream since Manny had inherited the business, making Luis and Julio his partners. But Manny was not just his partner now; he was the Commissioner. That did complicate things. He looked appraisingly at Manny, who seemed more clear-headed and focused than he had in months.

What Luis didn't know was that Manny, who was now responsible in large part for the safety of the citizens in the Colony, was having second thoughts about legalizing trade with Philadelphia. The two colonies had been separate for hundreds of years. There were legitimate worries about contagion. Whenever he or Julio went to Philadelphia, they always stayed outside. There was never more than a brief interaction between the two sides, with few people involved. Who knew what might happen if large numbers of people from the two colonies began to mingle.

The front doorbell rang. Manny heard the butler open the door, and a man's voice said, "Delivery for Mrs. Stewart." Manny looked at Luis, smiling in anticipation.

Marya unwrapped the package. "The dresses!" she exclaimed. "From the wedding, the ones I didn't wear!" She rushed into the study, holding one on each arm. "Thank you," she said. "I loved them all so much, it was hard to choose! This was very thoughtful of you."

"Anna told me you couldn't make up your mind," Manny said, "so I had them sent here for you."

She kissed him lightly on the lips, and was surprised when he flinched. "Manny, what is it?" she asked, frowning. "Is it the champagne?"

"It's fine, Marya, I'm fine," he replied.

"But you can smell it on my breath, right? I'll go eat something." She left quickly, leaving Manny and Luis alone again.

Luis looked at him questioningly.

"It's just one night," Manny said. "I'm hoping to stay here in the study until it's over."

Dave Wu, his wife Jenny and the Chief came into the study. "There you are!" said Dave jovially. "The Mayor wants to leave, and we weren't sure where you were. Come and say goodbye to her."

With a wry smile for Luis, Manny returned to the party. He found the Mayor and walked her to the door, thanking her again for so graciously agreeing to officiate at the wedding.

317

When Manny turned around, he saw the maids scurrying among the guests, picking up champagne flutes and carrying them into the kitchen. He turned to the butler with a quizzical look.

The butler responded to Manny's unspoken question. "Mrs. Stewart said that the toasts have been made, and the champagne should be put away."

Manny nodded to the butler and went back to the study, surprised and touched by his wife's thoughtfulness.

# Chapter 48.

**F**OUR MONTHS FLEW by. Marya took her place in the household with barely a ripple, seamlessly sharing childcare responsibilities with Anna, taking care of Julie and Zach. Manny had returned to focusing on his work, although he made sure to be home each night in time for dinner.

Alone in his office, Manny sat staring at his padlet, reading through what he had written. It was his first Executive Order as Commissioner, and he wanted to be sure that he had it right. Once he clicked "send," a team of scientists would be authorized to live in the Trade Center to study the environment "until their studies shall be completed."

*Mr. Jha is going to have a fit,* he thought, grinning. The elderly lawyer had voted against Manny's Plan B agenda at four consecutive meetings. Mr. Jha was becoming more and more bombastic in his rhetoric. At the last meeting, he had said, "Suppose we evacuate everyone, and a storm destroys the shelters, or the night air poisons the children. What will you say then?" Mr. Jha pointed his finger at Manny in his best courtroom manner and thundered, "Take care, Commissioner! In trying to avoid a catastrophe, you may well be the cause of one!"

Manny, Dave and the Chief had spent hours talking it through. Yes, there were risks. In an evacuation, someone could be injured, or even die. But a catastrophic emergency inside the Colony could be even more dangerous.

*And what happens,* mused Manny, *if we find out that the weather out there is not as volatile as it used to be? If we have evacuation drills, and people decide that they like being outside? Are they going to be content living underground, once they've seen the sun again?*

Manny, whose black market business had often taken him outside of the Colony, thought for a moment of the beauty of a natural sunrise, which he first had seen with Julio when they were boys. He remembered the feeling of the wind blowing through his hair, the sun warming his bare arms and face. He felt a wave of nostalgia as he remembered what evening felt like, the gentle darkening of sunset as the sun slipped away, the air cooled and the stars came out.

*What was it Zach had said? Why do the stars shine when there's no one there to see them?* Manny thought. *Maybe they are waiting for us to return.*

Fingers poised above the keyboard, Manny read through the Executive Order one last time, and then clicked "send." He exhaled hugely, knowing that he was setting in motion a series of events that could change their lives forever. If the environment was stable, how long would it be before people would want to live permanently above ground? Would that improve their lives? Or had he simply succeeded in opening up Pandora's box?

His head aching from the many possibilities, Manny put on his jacket and hat, and headed for home. He ignored his padlet, which was already lighting up with texts and holograms from outraged Council members.

# EPILOGUE

**I**N THE MIDDLE of the night, Manny was suddenly wide awake. His bed was trembling, ever so slightly.

Marya stirred, then suddenly woke up. "Manny!" she whispered fearfully, "what is that?"

"I'm not sure," he replied. His hand reached for hers.

The two of them lay quite still. A glass of water on the bedside table trembled and sloshed, then stopped. A second later, a book slid off the table and landed on the floor. Then all was still.

"Well, whatever it was, it seems to be over," Manny said soothingly to his wife. "Everything's fine." He kissed the top of her head. "Go back to sleep."

Manny waited until Marya had fallen asleep, then rose and went downstairs. He went into the kitchen, turned on the lights and then stopped, surprised. The kitchen wall behind the sink had a long black crack in it. He looked around the kitchen, walking from one end of the room to the other. Two of the four walls had cracks, although not as large as the one behind the sink.

*What the hell?* he thought. He shook his head, incredulous. His house had been damaged; had others experienced damage, too?

Manny opened the front door and took a few steps outside. It all seemed normal, silent and deserted as it should be at 4:00 am. Relieved, he returned to the kitchen to make coffee.

*It's too early to call Hasan,* Manny thought. *I'll wait until it's nearly time to leave for work. He can send someone over to see if there was any structural damage.* He made a mental note to check with the Housing Authority to see if anyone else had reported damage.

Yawning, Manny sat down with his steaming cup of coffee. Just as he was raising the cup to his lips, his padlet beeped, showing a text pulsing scarlet, denoting an urgent personal message, coming in from the Geological Institute. Before he could open it, a hologram came in from Nigel, his aide. The rim was pulsing neon gold, denoting the most urgent of work messages.

"Commissioner!" Nigel exclaimed, not bothering with a greeting. "I'm at the Mayor's office. You'd better get down here now!"

The End.

# *About the Author*

**Susan Greenberg Feltman** went to Windham College in Putney, Vermont, graduating with a BA in History. She worked in New York City as a legal secretary for several years, and then left the work force to raise her infant daughter. After starting an online business in 1998, Custom Design Sweater Studio, she spent many happy years designing and knitting unique one-of-a-kind sweaters for actors, musicians and collectors. Now that she has retired from the design business, she has time at last to devote to her writing.

Susan lives in Leonia, New Jersey with her husband of 38 years.

*Starlight, Shadows and Tears* is the sequel to *Never See the Sun Again,* Ms. Feltman's debut novel. She is looking forward to beginning work on the third and final book in this series.

www.ingramcontent.com/pod-product-compliance
Lightning Source LLC
Chambersburg PA
CBHW060514180626
46817CB00002B/361